SHAPING

TAMING DESTINY

BOOK THREE: SHAPING

S. L . Winter

Podium

To Anya:
Maybe one day you'll read this and enjoy it
as much as you enjoy your books now.

Cover design by Tommypocket Illustrator

ISBN: 978-1-0394-8243-2

Published in 2025 by Podium Publishing
www.podiumentertainment.com

Podium

SHAPING

CHAPTER ONE

Masochist

How does it feel?" I ask as I watch River rotate his newly regrown arm, an awed look still in his eyes and playing across his spikes in flashes of blue, green, and an oddly metallic golden color.

Like my arm, he murmurs, his tone full of a soul-deep relief. He turns his head slowly towards me, and his eyes are the last to move, like he is concerned that if he stops looking at his arm, it will disappear like a dream in the dawn's light. But he does look at me, and the depth of gratitude in his bronze orbs makes me so uncomfortable that I can barely hold his gaze.

Master, thank you. He breathes the words as if speaking at an altar of prayer. My sense of profound discomfort deepens. I won't deny that regrowing his arm has been hard. Heck, there were times in the last few hours when I wasn't sure if I would be able to push through the block that was in my way—magic, knowledge, or will failing me. But ultimately, all I was doing was righting a wrong. Destruction is always so much easier than construction, but if I had done what I should have, River wouldn't have lost his arm to begin with. It's right that I fix what my actions have broken.

And it's not like I haven't benefited from it. The sheer number of hours I've just spent reconstructing his arm have improved my understanding of my new Skill to no end. I've now got a far more solid idea of its similarities and differences in comparison to Lay-on-Hands.

With that in mind, I really don't deserve any sort of adulation—and that's the only way I can describe the feeling coming across the Bond from River.

I clear my throat uncomfortably.

"I'm glad it feels right to you. Why don't you test it out? Try doing some things with it?"

River looks thoughtful. I'm glad that it wipes away the awe and amazement, though I can still feel an uncomfortably large amount of gratitude directed towards me through our Bond. It's not that I dislike gratitude—if anything, I usually feel that people aren't grateful *enough.* It's just that I feel uncomfortable with *undeserved* gratitude.

As River distracts himself with testing out his arm, I busy myself with checking my notifications. I felt the nagging sense of something waiting for me during the night, but I didn't want to be distracted from my task—part of me feared that if I stopped pushing, I would break the sense of inspiration that had seized me.

The first notification that comes up is unsurprising. It would have been far more surprising if as much Flesh-Shaping as I did last night *didn't* result in a rank-up.

Congratulations!

You have advanced a Skill past Beginner. Flesh-Shaping is now Novice 1. You have improved your ability to use your mana to shape different aspects of flesh. You have gained a greater understanding of how different forms of flesh work together to create a whole that is greater than the sum of its parts. Healing applications of Flesh-Shaping have become easier and more instinctual for you, as your extensive practice enables you to concentrate less to accomplish basic Flesh-Shaping changes according to the body's natural patterns. You have also learned to become more efficient in your healing: Flesh-Shaping according to the body's natural patterns now uses less mana. This efficiency depends on your level of familiarity with the task and the anatomy you are affecting.

The rank-up message makes sense, especially when I consider how much easier things like replicating the cells and growing the different aspects of River's arm became. I wouldn't say they were ever *easy*, exactly, but I certainly noticed a fluidity and ease developing over time. I hadn't thought much of it while working—anything that is practiced becomes easier, after all. Now I see the notification, though, I realize that the System was giving me a little helping hand.

The only thing I'm concerned about is how it's very clear that it's only "healing applications" or Flesh-Shaping "according to the body's natural patterns" that are easier and more efficient. I theorized before that this Skill might be capable of doing more than just healing. Though, the fact that I just was able to build River a new arm with it when I was unable to do so with Lay-on-Hands means that I'm already ahead there. But that doesn't mean I want to potentially miss out on all the non-healing applications of Flesh-Shaping just because I usually use it for healing.

I don't know exactly what the non-healing applications could be. I'm hoping that it could be useful in combat, and perhaps it could be useful for improving body parts beyond the body's "natural patterns." And maybe there are other ways of using it too. The point is that I don't want to be pigeonholed into becoming a knockoff healer just because I've used it a lot for healing. I make a mental note to explore different things I can use Flesh-Shaping for, if only to influence my next rank-up bonuses.

Still, the fact that it's more efficient helps too—I stopped counting the number of times I emptied my mana pool last night to the point where I felt nauseous and had a head-splitting migraine. Each time, it took several minutes of sitting in Meditation to regenerate it enough to overcome the urge to vomit, then even longer to regenerate it completely.

At some point, I noticed that it started taking longer to fully regenerate my pool, which made me fear at the time that I would have to stop even if the physical side effects from emptying my pool didn't appear to be getting worse. But then it turned out that the pool actually lasted for longer, so I'm not sure what was going on there. Perhaps the next notification will tell me.

> Achievement awarded: Masochist
> The ill effects that happen when the mana inside one's Core runs low are generally heeded as indications that the Core should not be emptied so thoroughly. You, however, have shown a disturbing tendency to continually ignore your body's warnings. Fortunately for you, your Core has been strengthened by the stress you have put it under rather than damaged. As a result, it has become proportionately more able to hold mana. You can hold an additional 5 units of mana per point in Intelligence.

A burgeoning smile at the appearance of an achievement is checked by the rather snarky message that follows. Then, as I actually see what benefits the achievement has awarded me, my smile grows to stretch across my face. A half-again increase in mana points? Yes please! That makes all the nausea and pain worth it.

Still, I'm rather glad that I didn't realize the risks of emptying my mana pool so many times in a row. At least, I'm glad now that it turned out fine—I wouldn't be too pleased if I fractured my Core again, though at least now I know what to do about it. *I haven't fractured my Core again, have I?* I think worriedly to myself.

I pull up my status screen just to check.

Name: Markus Wolfe		Race: Human	Class: Tamer
Level: 12	Energy to next level: 100%	Energy absorption rate: 26u/hr	Energy towards debt: 78%
Intelligence	36	Mana: 450/540	
Wisdom	36	Mana regeneration rate: 900u/hr	
Willpower	42+8 (+20%)	Health regeneration rate: 40u/hr (-20%)	
Constitution	19	Health: 190/190	
Strength	16	Stamina: 90/90	
Dexterity	15	Stamina regeneration rate: 150u/hr	
Class Skills: Dominate – Novice 4 Tame – Beginner 6 Fade – Initiate 1		Non-Class Skills: Flesh-Shaping – Novice 9 Stealth – Novice 1 Animal Empathy – Novice 6 Meditation – Initiate 3 Energy Manipulation – Initiate 3 Sensation Management – Beginner 6	

I breathe a sigh of relief when I realize that the only reduction is the one to my

Willpower, which I still haven't figured out how to fix. I haven't done more damage to myself accidentally, even if the Masochist achievement indicates that it was possible. Though, it does set me to wondering why it stresses my Core to be emptied so many times in a row and also why strengthening my Core has had the result of giving me more mana units to work with. Not to mention whether I can repeat the effects or do something similar for my health and stamina points, considering just how valuable this achievement has been. But considering the risks that I seem to have happily avoided, maybe that's not such a smart idea.

Thirty-six points in Intelligence counting for fifteen units each means that instead of 360 units of mana, I now have a cool 540 units available. No wonder it was enabling me to extend my healing sessions longer, especially with the increased efficiency and ease granted by my rank in Flesh-Shaping.

I note that the Skill in question, despite only ranking up to Novice last night, is already at Novice *nine*. Which means it's on the cusp of Initiate. If I want to avoid specializing as a healer, I need to do some experimenting with it—and soon.

But not right now. Frankly, even if it's been long enough since I finished healing River's arm for me to get most of my mana pool back, I'm hungry and tired. I could do with a nap, never mind the fact that the sun is climbing into the sky.

Dismissing my status screen, I look at River. He's currently testing different strokes of his wood-bladed knife, chopping leaves from the bushes around into different sized pieces. Fine motor control testing, I presume.

"Is everything moving correctly?" I ask with a hint of concern—I can't help but fear that I've healed things wrongly.

It's perfect, Master, River assures me immediately before wincing. *Markus. I apologize.*

I wave the apology away even if discomfort does go through me at the address. Just something else I'll probably need to speak to him about later.

"Good to know. Make sure you tell me if there's anything that doesn't feel right. *Anything.* You hear me?" I ask firmly, looking him full in the eyes. There's no way I want him to be happy with "good enough" if I've made a mistake somewhere and limited his motion or weakened something.

As you command, River agrees submissively, tilting his chin up to the sky. *I promise. It feels a little weak and stiff, but merely in a way that a limb does if not used for a while.*

"All right," I reply, mollified that at least he's told me that there's something not perfect about it. "Tell me if the weakness and stiffness remain after you've used it for a while. I'm going to eat and go to bed. Would you like to join me?"

River hesitates, eyeing me cautiously as if not sure what my reaction will be. I sigh, too tired to deal with this—the tension and exhaustion from the night is all coming to a head now that I've been able to relax for a bit and the high of realizing that I've succeeded has worn away.

"Just say what you would prefer. I don't mind either way," I tell him tiredly.

Then, if it pleases you, I would prefer to stay out here and continue strengthening my arm, River says hesitatingly.

"All right, fine," I say then hesitate myself for a moment. He hasn't said whether he's hungry or not, but I know that healing takes a lot out of a body, and it's been a while since he ate. I pull out a carcass from my Inventory instead of trying to get a straight answer out of him—I figure it's quicker. And if he's not hungry now, he might be later. Or one of my other Bound, who seem to be emerging from the cave now, will be happy to eat it for him.

I head towards the cave, greet Bastet, the cubs, and Fenrir as they come out, and exchange a few words with Kalanthia as I walk past her to get to the alcove. Honestly, I don't remember what I said to her even a moment afterwards, so tired am I. The moment my head hits the pillow, I'm out like a light.

CHAPTER TWO

Martial Student of Life

By the time I wake from my sleep of the dead and emerge from my cave, the sun is well on its way to its zenith. But I can't be sad about the loss of time, not when I spent the night doing something that even modern medicine back on Earth isn't capable of.

Now merely tired rather than exhausted, I find my emotions are a little more stable—I'm never at my best when I'm fatigued. I come out of my cave to find River moving through a number of stances with a spear. The rest of my Bound and Kalanthia are nowhere to be seen.

"Where is everyone?" I ask River with a frown.

The Great Predator has taken her cub out on a hunt. Bastet left not too long after that with her three cubs. Fenrir and Sirocco followed. I don't know what they're doing.

"All right, thanks," I say, then close my eyes and reach out to touch their Bonds. Unable to talk to them, I'm at least able to get a sense that all three of my absent Bound are fine—Bastet is very intent on whatever she's doing, Fenrir is content, and Sirocco is vaguely bored. Perhaps Bastet was inspired by Kalanthia and took the cubs out to hunt?

Opening my eyes, I see that my sole remaining companion is moving slowly with his spear. My spear, technically, but I've basically given it to him at this point.

"What are you doing?" I ask River curiously. It kind of looks like kata for a martial art—my impression drawn from the single sample lesson I did of karate when I was a teenager, which never turned into anything. If I had known that one day I'd have to fight for my life, I might have been more interested in doing some sort of martial art or weapons lessons.

It is something I saw the Warriors do at times when I was not busy helping my mas—Pathwalker Herbalist. They did these sorts of movements with different weapons and then practiced fighting together. I tried copying when I had a moment and found that the practice helped me become stronger and more fluid.

"Practice makes perfect," I agree, watching him thoughtfully. "And how is your arm responding? Are you still feeling that it's stiff and weak, or is it improving?"

It is improving, Mas—Markus. Thank you for your concern. It almost feels like my arm before.

"Good, good," I comment, then hesitate for a moment. "Would you . . . How do you feel about sparring? You and I?"

Sparring? Practicing fighting? River checks. I nod.

The fact is that the idea of sparring should have occurred to me before now. I remember how badly my first attempt to hunt with my bow went because I hadn't practiced shooting before I went out. The loss of Spike was definitely preventable, and the fact that I shot my arrows everywhere except the target was part of that.

Although my archery has gotten a lot better, as has my fighting in general, I'm sure it would be better if I took some time to focus on it. Besides, River might even be able to teach me something—he's been fighting in the forest for years, I guess. Certainly for longer than I have.

I am happy to aid you where I can, Ma—Markus, River answers solemnly, that same light from earlier entering his eyes and making me shift uncomfortably. Perhaps reading my body language, he continues more briskly, *Would you like to . . . spar now?*

"All right," I agree, then pull my wooden spear out of my Inventory. The sight reminds me that I need to fix my broken flint-headed one. I don't want to take the one I gave to River, but a flint-headed spear is a lot better than just a wooden spear. I'm rather low on arrows too. Something else to do later.

"Ready?" I ask. Then, when River tilts his chin up briefly in assent, I thrust my spear forwards, focusing on the movement. As I do, I frown. Now that I'm thinking about it, the movement feels . . . wrong. "Hold on a moment," I ask River as I realize that I've taken my attention away from the fight. In fact, I'm surprised that he didn't hit me while I was distracted. Maybe he realized I was and chose not to attack. Kind of him.

What is wrong, Mas—Markus? River inquires with concern.

"Just give me a moment," I tell him absently as I draw on the memories I absorbed to try to figure out why it feels that everything I'm doing, from how I'm holding the spear to how I'm standing, is wrong. The memories from the hunting knowledge stone aren't as clear as they would have been if I'd done this immediately after absorbing it, but the stones must have some mechanism to ensure that the information contained within them is somehow protected. If they didn't, I'd have forgotten a *lot* more information that I actually have—I think, anyway. It's impossible for me to know what I've forgotten.

I sigh in frustration. I know that I'm doing things *wrong*, but I don't really know what to do *right*. "I'm no expert Warrior, that's for sure," I mutter with a humorless laugh.

You are far more of a Pathwalker, M-Markus, and would therefore not be expected to be an expert in physical fighting, River interjects in as much of a chiding tone as he can perhaps bring himself to use. *Your use of healing magic is beyond anything I have heard my people capable of in anything but the oldest of legends. Any village would be grateful to have you for that alone, and the Unevolved and Warriors within it would protect you with their lives.*

His words remind me of just how little I know about the lizard folk's culture. I know that they have three main classes: Pathwalkers, who are capable of magic and seem to be smaller than most; Warriors, who are capable of physical feats and tend to be bigger; and Unevolved, who are neither but have the potential to become either. I suppose with my use of Flesh-Shaping it makes sense that I might be considered a Pathwalker, though with a lack of other options, I fight with a mace, spear, or bow. Or knife, rock, fist, or whatever else I have at hand in a pinch.

Anyway, I'm human, so none of those designations would truly work for me. Though, if I'm going to take over the village, which Kalanthia requires me to do if I don't want her to massacre them as a preventative measure against them hurting Lathani in the future, I'm going to have to figure out how I'll fit in. Or maybe I don't need to—maybe I can just be the nominal head to make sure they don't overstep with Lathani and not need to be involved in everyday interactions.

But that's something I can consider later. For now, I focus back on River, giving him a slightly strained smile.

"Well, using weapons has kept me alive so far, but if I can use them better, I might reduce the risk of dying in my next fight. Any suggestions you have from your own experiences or observations would be appreciated."

Of course, I'm happy to share that with you, River answers immediately, and I move forwards to stand near him, holding my spear firmly.

We stand facing each other, and River settles into a stance. I try to copy him and then lower myself further when my absorbed memories prompt me to do so. It's a deeper stance than I'm used to, and my muscles soon start complaining about it. I do have to admit that I feel more stable in it, though.

Try to keep the tip of your spear level with your eyes, he advises, his tone slightly uncertain. *It helps protect your eyes better and makes it easier for you to strike at your opponent's eyes as well. If your target is shorter, of course, the tip of the spear needs to lower accordingly.* His tone gains more confidence as he speaks. He demonstrates what he means.

I follow his instructions—I'd thought that keeping my spear level with my waist was the best position so I would be able to put my weight behind my thrusts, but his words about protecting one's eyes make sense. Perhaps I've had too much experience fighting with killer chickens and monkiles, neither of which go far above my waist.

While practicing, I realize that I have a problem with my grip on the spear and do my best to correct it. When I'm mostly there already, the memories give me the nudge I need to show me how to do it properly. It feels a bit awkward at first but also like it will offer me more flexibility of movement. I have a tendency to keep my hands too far apart on the spear, treating it more like a quarterstaff than a spear, and it's limiting my thrusts.

We continue like that with River demonstrating various techniques for me to practice. I find the experience both interesting and engaging in a way that I've never found sports activities—I went to the gym because I wanted to be healthy and lower my stress levels, not because I liked it.

After some practice, we engage in some slow sparring, more to drill the techniques I was just learning than to actually fight. I'm glad when it turns out that I can help River too—although the Warriors apparently spar, River never has. It means that practicing *with* someone is something new to him, and I'm able to spot a couple of small flaws in his own movements, which he immediately works on correcting.

Though easy at first, repeating the actions with increasing speed does take its toll on me, and eventually my stamina pool runs out. At that point, we stop, and I run mana through both of our bodies, healing the damage caused by exertion. It's a little challenging to make sure that I heal the damage in a way that builds the muscles up from where they were damaged rather than returning them to their original state pre-exercise.

That wasn't something I needed to worry about with Lay-on-Hands. With that Skill, there seemed to be an automatic function that recognized when damage was caused by exertion rather than injury in a fight. Which was fortunate because otherwise any healing I'd done would have undone any beneficial effects of exercise. Flesh-Shaping is far more flexible, but that means I have to give it more detailed instructions, and healing muscles so they become stronger isn't something I've used Flesh-Shaping for before.

Still, it's not too hard to do. After reconstructing the muscle tissue of River's arm from nothing, working out how to repair the micro-tears so that my muscles are stronger than before is simple. Though, due to the exercise working different muscles in the body, the task does challenge me to actually *find* those micro-tears. It's not at all the same as my task last night, since that was working in a logical way from a single starting point. And although I was working on a cellular level there, *finding* such small injuries takes more focus than I was expecting. It's certainly good practice for me.

Curiously, healing my body doesn't seem to have much impact on my stamina regeneration. I would have thought that removing the cause of the stamina reduction would replace the stamina itself, but apparently not. My stamina replenishes, yes, but at the same rate as normal when I take a rest.

After healing our muscles and regenerating a good portion of our stamina pools, we start practicing again. When I've had enough of practicing with the spear, I continue with the mace. River is happy to continue sparring with me—though he doesn't know much about how to use a mace, he is keen to practice fighting against different weapons. Now that I think about it, maybe getting the others involved would be a good idea—that way, my companions who rely on tooth and claw can practice fighting against weapons and vice versa.

By the time River and I decide to call an end to our practice for today, mostly because we're both famished and it's *way* past lunch, I've had enough practice healing sore muscles that it's now affected by the almost automatic aspect of my recent Flesh-Shaping rank-up.

I take a moment to pull some meat out of my Inventory to chew on even as River makes a beeline for the carcass I gave him this morning, now tucked in the shade so it doesn't go off too quickly. Making a face at the too-familiar taste, I decide that I *really* need to extend my diet somehow. I'm starting to seriously crave more food than just meat and potatoes. If nothing else, I need to gather some more pondweed, but honestly, if I can find some other edible vegetation in the area, that would be even better.

After I've eaten, I find a nice spot in the sun and sit to check my notifications—I sense that there are a few of them.

Congratulations!
You have advanced a Skill past Novice. Flesh-Shaping is now Initiate 1. You have experimented significantly with this Skill and are now more cognizant of the differences between it and your previous Skill. You have learned to heal a number of injuries both major and minor in yourself and others. You have learned to scan another's body to discover injuries. Due to your focus on healing up to this point, your Skill has grown to be able to heal even more efficiently and effectively even without your full focus, especially when working with consenting targets. You have a much higher chance of discovering even very small or minor physical abnormalities in your target's body.

This first notification makes me grimace a little. I should have realized that using Flesh-Shaping to heal our muscle aches would cause the Skill to increase by a level—and thereby to rank up. And once again, the benefits are all linked to healing. Worse, in a way, they seem to be increasingly linked to "consenting" targets. Not that having more efficient and effective healing is a *bad* thing, but as I was thinking only hours ago, I have the opportunity to move beyond just healing.

I've missed the opportunity to use my final level in Novice to experiment a bit outside healing; I promise myself that I won't let the levels of Initiate pass me by like that.

I should try using Flesh-Shaping on the hides I've got in my Inventory, I think to myself. If Flesh-Shaping can work even on parts of dead creatures, then that opens up several possibilities for crafting. Not to mention that it would give me the opportunity to test various non-healing options out without the moral issues of testing them out on live enemies or the practical concerns with testing them out on myself or my Bound.

It's also worth testing out exactly what is defined as "flesh." After all, Kalanthia has made it clear that she can control almost anything that lies beneath her feet. I don't think that she can control roots, but she can certainly control both rock and soil. And soil includes organic matter, not just fragments of rock.

I know that bones, muscles, tendons—basically, it seems, any body cells—are included within Flesh-Shaping. And it clearly isn't just *my* body cells, since I was able to heal River. But does Flesh-Shaping only apply to animals, or could it affect all *living* creatures? Fish? Insects? *Plants?* They might have a very different type of cell than humans, but they still have cells and even a rudimentary blood vessel network. If I could shape plants as well as animals, that would be insane—and insanely useful.

More things for later. At this rate, I need to find a way of writing a to-do list that preferably doesn't require ripping out pages from my poor books.

Moving onto the next message, I'm surprised to see that it's an achievement. After receiving the Masochist one during the night, I wasn't expecting to see another one so soon.

Achievement awarded: Martial Student of Life

You have had no formal training, yet you have succeeded in improving your technique in at least three martial disciplines. You have learned from live battles, observation, and focused practice with another non-expert. As a result, you have earned the ability to access weapon Skills provided you practice sufficiently with them. Be aware that being self-taught can only take you so far.

The achievement is rather curious. It's not like any of the others I've received—there are no stat bonuses to it, for one thing. Instead, it seems to be . . . opening up access to new Skills? Suspecting I know what the other notifications are about, I look at them.

Sure enough, I've earned a new Skill. Immediately, I look at its description.

Spearmanship

You have taken the first step along the path to spear mastery. You have displayed an understanding that wielding a spear means more than simply jabbing a stick at a target. Continue practicing techniques designed for the more efficient and effective use of a spear in order to advance this Skill. Gain 1% to the effects of Strength and 1% to the effects of Dexterity per level in this Skill when using a spear.

I think that's the first Skill I've had that has so directly affected my stats, I decide, remembering the various descriptions of my other Skills. Some of my Skills leverage my stats—like Fade and Dominate—and others seem to link indirectly to them—like Energy Manipulation. None so far, however, have given me *more* stat points. Though, neither does this, if I'm reading it correctly.

I'm not completely certain of my interpretation, but I think it means that if I have a base status of twenty points in Strength and I reach Novice in Spearmanship, then when I use a spear, I'll be able to act like I have twenty-two points.

Perhaps that doesn't seem like much, but what about forty points acting like forty-four? Or if Novice also adds another one percent per level and makes it twenty-four points by the time I get to Journeyman, assuming I don't add any more to Strength or Dexterity when I get to twenty points in them. Or what if instead of Novice adding one percent to each of those stats, it adds two percent? Then I could be gaining a thirty percent increase to my stats by the time I hit Journeyman.

I quickly glance through the rest of my notifications, and a frown grows on my face as it appears that that's my only new Skill. I return to the description for the achievement. Sure enough, it mentions *three* martial disciplines. I would have thought that those would be related to the spear, mace, and bow. Yet I only have a Skill for the spear. Is it that I need to continue practicing to gain the mace and bow Skills?

I didn't properly read the last line of the achievement—I do now, and it makes me frown a little more. Being self-taught only takes me "so far." What is that meant to mean? Will I be limited in how far I can rank up? Or does it offer less per rank-up than for someone who had learned the Skill from someone else actively teaching them?

It's disappointing, but I suppose it makes sense: there's a reason why libraries and teachers are important and why language and writing became so consequential to the development of civilization. Without it, everyone has to start from scratch. And ultimately, I don't know what I don't know.

Neither River nor I are experts with any type of weapon—River hasn't had any formal training either. His experience is just as much born of fighting for his life as mine is. The difference is that he was able to watch the Warriors, arguably the local experts, train. But we're both fumbling around in the dark here.

I'll have to make time to practice with my bow and mace and maybe do some sparring with them in hopes that that will give me new Skills. Even if they *are* limited in some way, there are clear benefits to having them.

I look at the last two notifications in more detail. Though they're not new Skills, I'm still glad to see them.

Congratulations!
You have worked hard on your Dexterity and have earned a point. This has been applied to your status.

Congratulations!
You have worked hard on your Dexterity and have earned a point. Would you like to apply this to your status?

Apply point / Refuse point

Of course, I choose to apply it. The point to Dexterity that I had to "pay" for takes me down to ninety-six percent towards my next level. Not that I mind too much—I'm not intending on leveling up right now anyway. Though I've healed my

Core and my internal matrix, I'm not sure what would happen if I leveled up with the continued reduction to my Willpower stat. Besides, it gives me the time to shore up my weakest stats. Ideally, I'd like to get both Strength and Dexterity to twenty points before I commit any more points to my mental stats.

With Dexterity now sitting at seventeen points and Strength at sixteen, I still have a bit of a way to go until then.

The thought about healing my internal matrix reminds me of something. *Didn't I get Skill points when I leveled up all those times after touching the Pure Energy?* I remember that, at the time, I was unable to choose my Skills because my internal matrix was compromised. However, with that fixed, there shouldn't be any problems there now. I was rather more concerned about getting Flesh-Shaping at the time, but now I can focus on the other Skills available to me.

Here goes.

CHAPTER THREE

New Skills

S*ee Skill list,* I think at the screen, crossing my fingers. I grin when no error
message appears. Eight Skills spool in front of me, filling the space. I suppose
that makes sense: three Skills offered per level threshold plus the two I passed over
before. I've also got six points available: two for level five, four for level ten. I wonder if the number of points will keep doubling—that would be both awesome and
worrying. I guess I'll find out.

Stun (1)
Release your remaining mana in a single directed blast from your hands to render
your opponent unmoving for between one and ten seconds. Note: the effects of
the blast depend on both the amount of mana remaining and distance from the
epicenter of the discharge. The disparity between your Willpower and that of your
opponent will also partially determine the length of time the target is stunned.
Maximum effect can be achieved at full mana and when touching the target.

Track (1)
Notice and be able to follow marks that show the passage of your target. This
Skill scales with Intelligence.

Inspect Fauna (2)
Use a pulse of mana to retrieve information about an animal. The more mana used,
the more information may be retrieved. Warning: Tier-two beasts and up have a
chance of detecting this pulse and may be enraged by it. The chance of detection
increases with the level of the beast. Wisdom determines how much information is
collected, and Intelligence determines how much information is processed.

Inspect Flora (2)
Use a pulse of mana to retrieve information about a plant. The more mana used,
the more information may be retrieved. Warning: Tier-two plants and up have a
chance of detecting this pulse and may be enraged by it. The chance of detection
increases with the level of the plant. Wisdom determines how much information
is collected, and Intelligence determines how much information is processed.

Inspect Environment (2)

Use a pulse of mana to retrieve information about an area and the potential resources held within. This Skill may also indicate the presence of traps. At higher levels, this Skill can be used to detect the lingering presence of beings that have passed through an area. The more mana used, the more information may be retrieved. Warning: Tier-two beasts and up as well as tier-two plants and up have a chance of detecting this pulse and may be enraged by it. The chance of detection increases with the level of the beast or plant. Wisdom determines how much information is collected, and Intelligence determines how much information is processed.

Bond Eyes (4)
See through the visual senses of one of your Bound at any time. At lower levels, this sight replaces your own; at higher levels, and with practice, it is possible to view through both sets of visual senses. This Skill becomes easier the greater the positive disparity between your Willpower and that of your Bound. It may also be easier or harder depending on the Bond you have. It is easier to view through a tightly controlled Bond or a Bond with a deep sense of trust. The distance limits of this Skill are determined by Wisdom, Willpower, and the strength of the Bond.

Bond Ears (4)
Hear through the auditory senses of one of your Bound at any time. At lower levels, this hearing replaces your own; at higher levels, and with practice, it is possible to hear through both sets of auditory senses. This Skill becomes easier the greater the positive disparity between your Willpower and that of your Bound. It may also be easier or harder depending on the Bond you have. It is easier to hear through a tightly controlled Bond or a Bond with a deep sense of trust. The distance limits of this Skill are determined by Wisdom, Willpower, and the strength of the Bond.

Bond Puppet (4)
Send your consciousness into the body of one of your Bound and control their limbs as you would your own. Any damage sustained to their physical form will not affect your own body. Mental or soul attacks, however, may still damage your true mind or soul. This Skill becomes easier the greater the positive disparity between your Willpower and that of your Bound. It may also be easier or harder depending on the Bond you have. It is easier to puppet a Bound through a tightly controlled Bond or a Bond with a deep sense of trust. The distance limits of this Skill are determined by Wisdom, Willpower, and the strength of the Bond.

You have 6 Skill points available. Either choose a Skill to use your Skill points now or choose "Bank" to store the points for later and close the Skill selection menu.

Well, that's a bit of a doozy, I think as I finish reading the Skill descriptions. First, it's interesting to note that regardless of how much my Skill points increase per level, it's possible to purchase either one of the newest Skills, two of the previous threshold's Skills, or all of the previous threshold's offerings. That relieves me as much as it disappoints me—I guess that the Skills gain in power as levels increase, so the thought that someone at level forty, for example, could have several high-powered Skills is a little worrying if the number of Skill points offered doubles but the cost of the Skills only increases linearly.

I mean, I suppose the potential is still there for them to have several high-powered Skills—look at what that fire mage did with his level-one Firebolt Skill, after all. The difference is that they'll have had to put in the effort to turn the lower-level Skills into something powerful. Or choose to miss out on lower-level Skills in order to purchase higher-level ones later.

Of course, I could be completely wrong about higher levels giving more powerful skills, though it seems logical. Additionally, Skills seem to be fairly situational—the right Skill at the right time can have a lot more impact than the wrong Skill, even if the other Skill is arguably more powerful—Fade is arguably more powerful than Stealth, but if I'm around a beast that's able to sense my use of magic, Stealth would probably be better suited to going undetected.

The other thing I note is that each of the thresholds seems to have something of a theme. My level-one Skills seemed to be about survival: Fade allows me to avoid danger; Stun would have allowed me to escape it if I got too close; and Track would have enabled me to determine what danger I was likely to walk into, and thereby to avoid it if I wanted.

The level-five Skills are all about gaining information from what's around me: the animals, the plants, and the environment itself. Any one of these Skills would be a godsend—I just wish there were a single Skill that encompassed all of them. With the Skills being split as they are, I have a harder choice to make.

The level-ten Skills are as intriguing as they are disturbing. All of them seem to be based on the same idea: using the Bond to send part or all of my consciousness into one of my Bound. The disturbing factor comes from the implications of the success conditions of the Skill. It talked about deep trust, which makes sense, but it also mentioned the alternative being a "tightly controlled Bond." When I consider how much power I sense that I have over my Bound, I shiver a little. I promise myself again that I won't go down that route.

After going over the Skills a couple of times more, my decision of what to choose firms up. Time will tell if my choice is a good one, but if I second-guess myself constantly, I will never make a choice at all.

After spending my Skill points, I quickly dip into my Core space, curious to see what happens. It's different from before when Lay-on-Hands transformed into Flesh-Shaping. Then, the changes were located only in an area that had already been transformed by the Skill. This time, the changes are all happening to areas of the weave that were previously untouched.

The weave . . . *hums*. I'm not sure how else to describe it. It's not an audible hum either, more something that I feel within. I didn't feel it before when gaining a new Skill—is it because this is a Skill that comes directly from the System rather than having been earned? Or because my stats have increased significantly since that time? Or because I'm more familiar with my internal matrix? Or even because it's more than one Skill suddenly growing? Perhaps it's a mixture of all of the above.

Either way, it's different from my experiences before. The weave hums and vibrates, light seems to flow and collect in three spots on my internal matrix. The spots are all in the same sort of area, peripherally close to what I think are my Tame and Dominate Skills, which are themselves almost close enough to intertwine, though at the same time entirely separate from each other. I quickly see that the three are forming a triangle a bit off to the side and below Tame and Dominate. If directions even mean anything in this place, that is.

Interestingly enough, as the Skills weave themselves into place, I notice similarities between them. I guess that's inevitable, considering the nature of them. As they grow, I also see tendrils reaching out to touch each other. At the moment, it's only a couple of threads, but it makes me wonder whether these three Skills could one day be woven together to create one catch-all Skill. Whether there's any additional benefit to that, I don't know. I guess I'll find out if it ever happens.

Finally, the process seems done. The light that collected into place to weave the new threads dims and flows back into the rest of the matrix. I suppose it makes sense that I wasn't able to choose my Skills with a damaged matrix if *that* was what was needed to happen in order to weave the Skills into place.

I pull out of my Core space and access my status screen.

Name: Markus Wolfe		Race: Human	Class: Tamer
Level: 12	Energy to next level: 100%	Energy absorption rate: 26u/hr	Energy towards debt: 80%
Intelligence	36	Mana: 450/540	
Wisdom	36	Mana regeneration rate: 900u/hr	
Willpower	42+8 (+20%)	Health regeneration rate: 40u/hr (-20%)	
Constitution	19	Health: 190/190	
Strength	16	Stamina: 90/90	
Dexterity	17	Stamina regeneration rate: 170u/hr	
Class Skills: Dominate – Novice 4 Tame – Beginner 6 Fade – Initiate 1 Inspect Fauna – Beginner 1 Inspect Flora – Beginner 1 Inspect Environment – Beginner 1		Non-Class Skills: Flesh-Shaping – Initiate 1 Stealth – Novice 1 Animal Empathy – Novice 6 Meditation – Initiate 3 Energy Manipulation – Initiate 3 Sensation Management – Beginner 6 Spearmanship – Beginner 1	

I nod in satisfaction at the new additions to my Skills. Perhaps it seems stupid to go all in on inspect Skills, especially when there were some other interesting options, but to me it was the logical choice.

Track was as much of an easy elimination as the last time I looked at it. Nothing has changed in my reasoning not to go for that one. Stun was still a bit of a temptation, but the fact is that as long as I don't let myself be pigeonholed into being a knockoff healer, I have close-combat potential with my Flesh-Shaping. And frankly, I think that as long as I can get a handle on it, Flesh-Shaping will be far more versatile than Stun.

If Flesh-Shaping is a scalpel, Stun seems to be like, well, a stun grenade. A burst of mana to lock my opponent in place. Great in certain circumstances or as a last-ditch escape attempt. The problem is the lack of control it offers me. It says it in the Skill description: I have to empty my whole mana pool for the effect. And the effect isn't even that great—one to ten seconds of stillness.

And what if one of my Bound is biting or attacking the being at the same time? Would they get caught in the effect, or does the stun only affect my opponent? Also, this seems good against a single more powerful enemy, but more often than not I've been facing up against weaker but more numerous enemies. Could Stun be used on multiple enemies or just the one I'm facing? Because if it's the latter, it isn't a good addition to my arsenal.

Flesh-Shaping, on the other hand, should offer me the same ability to paralyze my opponents and in a much more efficient and long-lasting way. If I could send magic into an enemy and block or damage their spinal cord, they wouldn't be able to control any limbs beyond that point. Or if facing an invertebrate, I could grow the creature's exoskeleton to stymie their movements. And I wouldn't necessarily have to empty my mana pool to do that.

Sure, Stun offers a more fast-acting Skill, but that's not enough to make me want to take it—I suspect that with enough practice and a wide enough disparity between our mental stats, I'll be able to do the same with Flesh-Shaping. So, no Stun.

As for the Skills offered at level ten, I'll admit to being tempted. Being able to hear or see through my Bound would be pretty awesome, despite my feeling of unease about the "tightly controlled Bond" mentioned in the description. Clearly, it would also work with trust, which was all I really needed to know. The reason I didn't take either of those was because . . . I can already do it. Sort of.

I remember accidentally going into Fenrir's mind when I was investigating the source of the flashes of Energy that entered my system from the outside. I was in his thoughts, smelling what he smelled, seeing what he saw, hearing what he heard.

I've also had memories passed across the Bond from my Bound, showing me things from their perspectives; though, admittedly, that's not in real time. And, as I recently noticed with Bastet, it's also not necessarily true to life or what *I* would have seen if I'd been present.

Still, it's enough for me to have a good feeling about being able to develop those Skills by myself, no Skill points necessary. I don't have any confidence about being able to develop inspection Skills by myself, though I suppose I might have been able to develop a second after getting to know the first.

If I'd only chosen one of the inspection Skills, I would have then been able to take the final Skill, which I'll admit *did* intrigue me. For all that I don't like the idea of being a puppet master to my Bound, if one of them trusted me enough to let me control their limbs, I could see some ways I could use that.

Though, I do question what the benefit of being able to puppet a Bound is if you can't actually see what you're doing. Bond Puppet has to have some sort of connection to the Bound's senses implicit in it—in which case, why have separate Skills for seeing and hearing through the Bond—or it seems pretty useless. Well, I suppose it could have been useful to be able to puppet River in the lizard folk's village if I'd needed him to do something within the area I could see. But then wouldn't it be easier to just order him with the Bond to do whatever?

After all, I can't help but think that puppeting one of my Bound would take practice. I'm not used to their bodies; would I gain an instinctual knowledge of how to move their limbs, or would I just have to work it out for myself? Because in the case of the latter, it would really be more helpful if I could just be present in their minds at a distance and then *tell* them what I wanted them to do, rather than trying to do it myself directly.

And frankly, if I succeed in repeating what I did with Fenrir, this time with my Bound's permission, I reckon that would be superior to any of the offered Skills, especially since they were all individual.

So, with no reason to save four of my points for any of the level-ten Skills, I decided to go all in with the inspection ones. Curious about how they work, I dismiss my status screen and stare at the first thing my eyes alight upon. A bush.

Inspect Flora, I invoke, paying close attention to the sensations within me. It's only because I'm being so attentive that I feel a faint movement of mana flow from my Core, through my body, and out through my feet. There, I lose track of it and only detect it a fraction of a second later when it returns to me. It reenters my body, and I feel a sudden wave of knowledge hit me even as I sense a notification waiting for me.

Common plant: Myceria Xilapse
Edible: Yes (leaves, flowers, branches, roots)
Alchemical uses: Unknown, soothing balm (flowers)
Medical uses: None
This bush flowers twice yearly and loses its leaves only when temperatures drop below 0°C. The flowers exude a scent that soothes the nerves of those who smell it.

The notification matches the information that I received upon the return of the pulse. In fact, if anything, I got *more* information from the pulse than I did from the notification. The pulse also told me that the plant is healthy, not sapient or sentient, and a long, *long* way from Evolution. Still, it's all useful stuff, especially the fact that it's edible. I might not try just stuffing the leaves in my mouth, though—they look a bit difficult to digest.

So far pleased with what I've learned about that new Skill, I try the next.

Inspect Environment turns out to be a bit different from Inspect Flora, interestingly enough. The same pulse of mana is sent out from me, but this time it doesn't just go through my feet; it seems to emerge from all parts of my body, shooting in all directions.

When it returns, there's no notification. Instead, it's like there's a filter over my sight. Certain plants are haloed in a golden light, and one or two are haloed in red. The plant I just inspected is one of those outlined in gold, so I have to guess that it's related to being edible or useful in alchemy or something.

The plants aren't the only things haloed—there is a subtle glow to the cave itself; though, when I venture closer, the light doesn't seem to be around anything in particular. Interestingly, I notice a bright golden light coming from my side—my knife. It's brighter than anything I've seen so far, and I realize that the gold must indicate that my knife is indeed as special as I thought it was. *Is this proof of its enchantment?* The gold is even brighter in a small place on the blade near the hilt. I frown as I squint to see it more clearly. *Are those shapes or just fluctuations in the glow?*

The overlay doesn't last more than about fifteen seconds before it fades from view. Good to know. I wonder if I can somehow give it more mana in order to make it last longer, like I did when turning Lay-on-Hands into its channeled version. Perhaps it's not necessary, though—I could just use the Skill again for the same benefit.

Right, time to test my last new Skill. For this, I need a target. Looking around, I see all my Bound absorbed in their activities. Still, there's one person I'm going to have to disturb in a moment anyway, so it might as well be now.

"River," I call quietly. The lizard-man jolts a little despite my low volume, opening his eyes immediately.

Ma—Markus, do you need something? He practically jumps to his feet.

"No need to panic," I half joke. "I was just hoping to try something on you, if you're okay with it?" He tilts his head, a questioning sense coming down the Bond. "I've got a new Skill to find out information about . . . creatures. I wanted to know both what information it gives me and what it feels like for the . . . for you." River just waits expectantly. "Are you okay with me using it?"

Of course, he answers. *I am at your service.*

Predictable, I say to myself privately with a subvocal sigh. It's not that I wanted him to argue—his easy acceptance is ideal for me. It's just . . . uncomfortable. I'm not going to overanalyze it now, though—I doubt that this will hurt him in any way, after all. *Inspect Fauna*, I trigger mentally, hoping that it will work like the other two did. I don't see why not.

The pulse of mana that leaves me this time is much like Inspect Flora. The only difference is that like Inspect Environment, it doesn't just leave through my feet. *So, Inspect Flora expects the plants to be rooted in some way? Makes sense, I suppose, but what if they're flying plants or something? If trap trees exist, why not flying plants?*

It doesn't move entirely like Inspect Environment either, though. That one just expanded out from me in a rolling pulse. This one expands from multiple parts of me but seems completely focused on River. Before I lose sense of the connections, I feel them spooling off directly at my Bound.

Then the pulse returns, and I feel knowledge enter my mind just as the nagging of a notification starts niggling at me. Opening it, I see something much like Inspect Flora showed me. *Does that mean that Inspect Flora and Inspect Fauna are more similar to each other than each are to Inspect Environment?*

Lizard Folk: Runs-with-the-river (River)

Tier 1 beast (Unevolved)

Special abilities: None detected

Health: 830u

Mana: 70u

Minimum Willpower recommended to Dominate without other impacting factors: 25

Bound (Dominate) of Markus Luke Wolfe. Most commonly used weapon is a spear, though this beast is capable of using claws and teeth when required. Social beast with a strong capacity to form bonds.

Nothing I hadn't already known from my Bound tab or experience with River himself, though the minimum Willpower is quite interesting to see. If I hadn't thought of asking for my Bounds' stats to be added to my status screen, I would be quite happy to have the information.

However, it does raise a question: do I only see so much information *because* I already know it? Or would I see the same thing for any creature? I guess I'll have to try it on different animals just to see.

"How did it feel?" I ask River curiously. He seems unsure for a moment.

Odd, he says finally. *Like a poke in a place I didn't realize existed.*

"Did it hurt?" I check, abruptly concerned that it had.

No . . . , he replies, though he doesn't sound completely sure about that. *It was . . . not pleasant, but it wasn't terribly* un*pleasant either. Just . . . odd.*

"Good to know," I say finally. I suppose that, in a way, it's surprising that River felt anything at all: the description talked about beasts in tier two and up having a chance to feel the inspection, and River is very clearly still in tier one. Is that why it was "a poke" in a place he "didn't realize existed"? Because for him it didn't yet? "Thanks for your help."

Of course, River says again, as if I didn't even need to ask. *I will happily help you with anything you need,* he offers. I smile awkwardly at him in return. We *really* need to have a conversation so I can find out where his head is at. Because no way should he be so willing to please after such a short time together. Is this because of the Bond? Or because of me healing his arm? Or a combination?

I try to distract myself. I've got too many other things to do to just sit around and worry over whether having a Dominate Bond with River is changing his mental state into some sort of servile creature who begs to be of use to me. I shiver. The thought of River acting like one of those house-elves in my favorite childhood series is a very uncomfortable one. Though, Dobby *was* awesome.

I shake my head and concentrate on the present even as the thought of once having any book I wanted to read at my fingertips contributes to my melancholy mood.

First on the list is repairing my spear. It's a quick fix, and a flint-tipped spear is far better than my sharpened wooden stake. This time I use a bit of pitch to help hold the sinew in place and protect it from damp—with the sinew already prepared and the pitch warm, all I need to do is knap the flint tip. That, of course, takes me a few tries, but at least I have plenty of flint nodules available to me.

Finally done, I also repair a few arrows that only need minor fixes. The ones with broken shafts I leave for now—that's going to require more dedicated effort. If it's just a question of fixing a bit of sinew that has come adrift or replacing one of the vanes, however, I quickly do it. After an hour or so of work, I've refurbished eight more arrows, taking my supply up to almost half of what I started with.

The ones that will take the longest are, of course, the arrows where the flint head is broken or lost. I'm hesitating between replacing those or waiting for my iron ore to be processed in order to replace them with metal ones, though. For now, I just sharpen the arrows themselves and harden their tips in the embers of the fire—vaguely sharp wooden arrows are better than nothing. I make a mental note that I probably need to practice with shooting them to get an idea of how they fly since the balance of each of them has changed.

My next task is one that isn't so essential for my survival but is important for my sense of decency: a needle and thread. After pulling out some of the bones I've collected, I hunt through my collection of stones to find appropriate ones for the task.

The first step is to get a decent bone shard. Using a large mostly flat stone as the anvil, I hold another stone in my hand as the hammer. Cracking the bones with my new Strength isn't exactly hard; getting the right sort of size and shape shard is more frustrating. Plus, I find when I crack open some of the bones that they're actually semi-hollow, which won't work all that well. I guess those were from the killer chickens?

Adding to my irritation is the fact that my fine-motor control seems to have got *worse,* meaning that I frequently rub too hard and crack the bones at the wrong points. I find my temper mounting, rising with a rapidity that might alarm me if I wasn't deep in the emotion.

After I've got a shard that is about ten centimeters long and reasonably thin, I use a rough stone to start rubbing away at it. It takes time and hard-won patience, but little by little I manage to get the thickness of the shard down to something more resembling a needle. Now I need to get a vaguely round shape to it.

As I'm filing away at it with my rough rock, I put a little too much pressure on the emerging needle. A snapping sound meets my ears and I freeze. Holding the shard up to my eyes, I curse, then throw it down in annoyance.

Sighing heavily to try to breathe out the impatience and irritation filling me, I forcibly unclench my fists. *It's normal,* I tell myself. *I was never going to succeed the first time.* As much as I would have liked to, this is a task that requires dexterity, focus, and practice. On the upside, hopefully my struggle now will mean I half earn another point in Dexterity soon. If not, I'm definitely complaining to the management.

Breathing in and out slowly, I feel my frustration ebb out of me. My brief flicker of humor helps it to go just a little faster. When I feel like it's lowered to at least a manageable level again, I pick up my pounding rock and start again.

CHAPTER FOUR

It Is Forbidden

I swear loudly as the fifteenth "needle" snaps under my fingers. *I was so close to finishing it!* I moan to myself. Still, I have a sense that I'm almost there. Each time I snap the needle, I do so with it closer to completion. If only I could just get another point in Dexterity, I reckon that my chances of success would improve. As it is, I'm still waiting for the nagging sensation of a message waiting to appear.

When my sixteenth attempt fails just as I'm sharpening its end, I actually stand up and throw it down on the ground, shouting expletives. I barely even notice the startled looks that my Bound throw at me or the disapproving one from Kalanthia—the whole gang returned at some point between breaking my eighth needle and my ninth. I was right—Bastet *was* trying to teach the cubs how to hunt. From what I understood of Fenrir's impressions, he decided to follow in a mixture of curiosity and wanting to help protect the young of his pack. Sirocco seems to have joined them simply because she was tired of absorbing Energy Hearts and was hungry for fresh meat and berries.

Throwing myself at the ground, I glare at the many bone shards littering the area with resentment. I don't even feel like I'm getting any better at this. Maybe I should just give up? Do more later? Maybe I should look after the cubs for a bit? By this point, Fenrir and Sirocco are both back at absorbing Energy Hearts. Bastet is trying to do so too, but she keeps getting bothered by the cubs. If I can't make my needles, I can at least help her out.

Then again, there are other things I need to do even if my needle-making is too frustrating to continue with.

I desperately need some better armor than just plates of chitin held in place by easily cut sinew. I've survived this long through luck and Lay-on-Hands, but that's not guaranteed to continue. Plus, I don't exactly *enjoy* pain. The more injuries I can avoid, the happier I'll be. But in order to get some armor, I need to do some tanning.

The problem is that it's a painfully long process. Ideally, I'll work out some way of using magic to help me, but before I can even consider doing that, I need to actually tan something for real—as I've learned, memories are not the same thing as experience. Considering how much there is to do in the process, the sooner I start, the better.

For tanning, I need hides, a tanning basin, tanning solution, and a rack to stretch the hides on after they've soaked in the tanning solution.

I have the hides, and good ones at that—not only do I have the crocodile hide from when it tried to eat me, but I also have several pieces of the salamander hide. They'll need to be flensed—the fat and remaining scraps of flesh scraped off their inner layers—but otherwise, I've got that component.

A tanning basin is more complicated. My thoughts immediately go towards making it out of wood, but problems with that spring to mind. If I make it out of planks, not only do I have to process those planks, but I also need to make sure it's sealed fully. I foresee plenty of hairpulling with that method, considering the tools I have at hand.

An alternative is to use a tree trunk and dig out a basin shape in it. That's certainly tempting since it will give me a sturdy container that I might be able to reuse for other crafts. On the other hand, again, it's a *lot* of work since I have to cut down the tree, then cut it *again* to get the chunk of trunk for the basin—and if I want a decent-sized basin, I'll need a decent-sized trunk—and that's even before digging into the wood to actually make the container.

Perhaps an easier solution would be to dig a hole in the ground and line it with clay. It's not a perfect solution, as clay *is* porous, but if I make the clay thick enough, it should be able to hold my tanning solution for a reasonable amount of time. I don't need it to be a permanent pool or reservoir; if it can hold the water long enough to saturate the hide, that's good enough. If anything, I'm more likely to have issues *emptying* it—a log basin could be tipped onto its side to drain; a pit can't. But perhaps I could break a hole in the base to let it drain, and then fix it for the next time I need it.

And even better, I already *have* a pit dug—the one I used for firing my pottery. All I need to do is collect enough clay to line it. That should be significantly less work than cutting down and hollowing out a tree trunk. I should probably process the clay a bit. From what my memories indicate, clay becomes less porous the finer it is, which means I need to take out as many of the stones as I can. So, it will still be a laborious job. But perhaps that's just what I need to reach twenty in Strength without committing any level-up points to it.

I look up at the sky. The sun is already well on its way to the horizon. It's a bit late to set out for the clay now—although it only took an hour last time to get there and I could probably do the journey in half that now, I want to have the time to dig at the clay. No, it's probably best if I put that as the first job to do tomorrow morning.

Sighing, I consider what else I need. A tanning solution is easy enough to make. I could either boil bark or use a brain solution. It might be worth testing with each technique, finding out what works best—if I have time, that is. For now, I have *lots* of brains from my most recent butchery interlude, so I'll probably start with that technique.

Which leaves only the rack to create. I'm going to need to stretch and dry the hides over a period of time so a decent rack is a must. That's something that I might be able to do now.

I open my Inventory and pull out the longest sticks I have and lay them on the ground. The longest is about a meter and a half; the shortest is a meter. I collected these sticks more for firewood than with creating a tanning rack in mind, and it shows.

Sighing, I decide that I need to go and collect some better wood. In fact, I might actually be better served by using my axe to harvest some green wood from the trees themselves. Although green wood is more flexible, it's consequently less brittle. I'm worried that some of this dry wood will just snap as soon as it's put under pressure—not ideal. I return the sticks to my Inventory in disgust.

"Hey, River, want to go down into the forest with me?" I ask before I look up and realize that he's meditating with an Energy Heart. Nonetheless, his eyelids practically spring open, and he pushes himself to his feet hurriedly.

Of course, M-Markus. Do you wish to go now? He sounds . . . eager. I eye him carefully.

"You don't have to go," I tell him, finding it ironic that after having asked if he wants to go, I'm almost dissuading him. "It's only if you want to."

I want to help you, he insists. *Will it help you if I come?*

"Well, yes," I admit—even if he only keeps guard, having him present will be useful.

Then I wish to come.

"All right," I say after a moment. Perhaps this is a good opportunity to have that discussion with him.

I check with my other Bound, but none of them seems keen on going out into the forest again. Fenrir has gotten bored of absorbing his Energy Heart and has started romping around with the cubs. They're delighted with their playmate, of course, and his intervention means that Bastet is finally getting a chance to concentrate on her own Energy Heart.

She does offer to come with me, but I sense her reluctance and so tell her to stay here. I won't be going far—River and I should easily be enough to face anything we'll find this high up the mountainside.

River and I walk down the hill in silence. My bow is to hand just in case something appears that needs shooting, and River has his spear. My own repaired spear and mace are both in my Inventory—having them out will just impede me with my archery, so I hope that I'll have the time to get them out if I need them.

As soon as we hit the forest, I use Inspect Environment, curious to see what it's like in the more cluttered environment of the forest. As it did on the plateau, a pulse of mana goes out from me, and a number of plants are haloed in either red or gold. Focusing on one of the plants haloed in red, I use Inspect Flora.

Common plant: Aasmuclanor
Edible: Poisonous (leaves, flowers, roots)
Alchemical uses: Poison (leaves, flowers, roots)

Medical uses: Unknown
This plant is a perennial that poisons most creatures that consume it. Its distinc-
tive red patterning is a warning to those who encounter it.

"Do you recognize this plant, River?" I ask, gesturing towards it. He stoops to
look at it more closely, then sniffs at it, and using a claw to tilt its leaves upwards,
he reveals small white flowers beneath.

It looks similar to one I recognize, he answered. *It's smaller though.*

"What do you use that other plant for?"

He shrugs. *It's a poison when eaten directly. It sends a numbing through the body,
stopping the heart in relatively small quantities. However, my . . . Herbalist can add it in
small quantities to other substances to create a numbing effect that does not harm. She uses
it particularly in balm for soothing sunburn, injuries, and a potion for pain in general.*

Interesting. An analgesic in the right quantities. I shoot another Inspect Flora at
the same plant, wondering if my new knowledge will make a difference to its results.

Common plant: Aasmuclanor
Edible: Poisonous (leaves, flowers, roots)
Alchemical uses: Poison (cardiotoxic) (leaves, flowers, roots)
Medical uses: Analgesic in correct quantities
This plant is a perennial that poisons most creatures that consume it. Its distinc-
tive red patterning is a warning to those who encounter it.

So my own knowledge does *matter,* I conclude. *And as I learn more, more information is added. Good to know.*

By this point, Inspect Environment has long ceased its effects, so I cast it again. I
don't really *need* to—one of the benefits of increased Intelligence appears to be a better
memory; I therefore could technically identify all the nearby plants that had previously been haloed in gold or red. However, I do need to level up the Skills as much as
possible, and each of the casts of Inspect Environment only takes ten mana, so there's
no reason not to cast again. Besides, I think the light effects look kind of cool.

This time I pick a plant that is haloed in gold. This one is a darker green than
the previous, its leaves thinner and longer. It doesn't seem to have any flowers at all,
though maybe that's just because it's not the right season.

Common plant: Sycopsis franguloides
Edible: Yes (leaves)
Alchemical uses: Unknown
Medical uses: Unknown
This plant is an evergreen that may have specific properties when exposed to
extremes of temperature.

"How about this one?" I ask, gesturing towards it. River once more stoops to inspect the small plant.

I don't recognize this one, River replies thoughtfully after a few moments. *Either it doesn't grow near us, or it's not one that Herbalist uses. Certainly, she never asked me to gather it for her.*

I nod and cast Inspect Flora again on it. Unsurprisingly, the information that I receive is the same as before.

We continue walking. Now without the distraction the desire to test my new Skills offered me, I find my thoughts turning to the upcoming discussion. The truth is that talking about emotions often makes me feel awkward. Especially with another man. Well, sort of. Though, I'm not much better with women—my ex, Lucy, would be able to tell anyone that.

But perhaps it would be easier if I look at this like a meeting with an employee who's been flagged due to some concerning statistics. I'd probably feel more confident if we were sitting in an office with a desk between us, but we're a bit short of offices and desks here. Besides, I learned before that River appreciates activity: we dealt with a previous issue standing over a giant salamander corpse.

"Will you help me collect some wood, please?" I ask River. "I need some fresh wood for tanning racks, but we might as well collect some firewood while we're at it." River makes a funny sound with a questioning feel. I smile as I realize he must be asking about tanning. "It's where I take animal hides and basically put them through a process to preserve them for use as armor or clothing." I cast a gaze over his naked form, the woven belt his only clothing. "I suppose you guys don't use clothes."

We do not hide our skin the way you do, no, he agrees, and I'm glad he seems to be getting back to "normal." *We decorate it with our woven adornments, but our scales are armor enough. A Warrior might use a shield if they face a particularly fierce foe, but we have no need of coverings.*

"Well, I do," I say as I head off into the trees, keeping my eye out for useful wood. There isn't a huge amount of firewood; I've already been through this area several times, and a few weeks isn't enough time for the forest to accumulate much dry stuff. Other kinds of wood, however . . . "Keep an eye out for attackers, would you?" I ask River, waiting for his nod before grunting in approval and starting to climb the tree. The lower branches here are too thick, but the ones a little above head-height . . .

Finding a couple of likely prospects, I wedge myself against the trunk and pull out my axe. The angle is a little awkward, but I make it work.

This is a perfect moment to talk about River's excess submissiveness, I say to myself and open my mouth. "So, can you tell me more about your people?" I chicken out. How do I even broach this topic? Why have you been weird? Why have you been looking at me like I hung the moon and stars and lit up the sun on my way out? Those are all *terrible* ways to start it. But maybe my chickening out still has a purpose—perhaps if I know more about his culture, I'll have a better idea of where he's coming from.

What do you want to know about my people? he asks, seeming a little taken aback.

"I don't know," I admit. "Just . . . what do you do every day? What's life like in the village? You've talked about your . . . master. What does that even mean? And . . . when Kalanthia was suggesting that I take over your village, you seemed to indicate that some might be . . . better off. What did you mean by that?" The questions pour out of my mouth. I hadn't even realized how many I had been keeping behind my teeth.

There's silence for a time, but I sense that it's not a refusal to speak; he's considering what to say. I give him some space to think while I work on cutting down the first branch. I've dropped that one to the forest floor and started working on the next by the time he speaks, his thoughts apparently ordered.

I've never had to describe my village before, he admits. *It is hard to know where to start. I shall begin with my master. My previous master,* he emphasizes. *You need not be concerned about split loyalties.*

"I wasn't," I assure him, though I'm not actually sure that either of us are being fully truthful. Logically, he's been with his village for as long as he's lived and with me for a few days. It doesn't actually make sense for his loyalties to have so easily switched. If they have, there are only two real explanations that I can think of, neither of which fills me with joy: either he's fickle in his affections or this is an effect of the Bond.

River doesn't seem to recognize my suddenly tumultuous emotions as he continues speaking.

Good. My previous master was, as you know, Herbalist, one of the Pathwalkers who leads our village. A sudden sense of uncertainty comes through the Bond, but River pushes on before I can ask about it. *Not all Pathwalkers take an assistant, but my mas—my previous master did because she needs so many specific resources. It is easier for her to teach a single villager how to retrieve the plants and body parts that she needs than to ask a different Unevolved each day to collect them and perhaps not do so properly.*

In return for dedicating my service to her, my master ensured that I received food tokens every day and from time to time taught me elements of her craft. I cannot use magic in the way she can, but I can create certain concoctions that don't require anything more than appropriate combinations of ingredients. I have also prepared concoctions for her to add her magic into once they were ready. I was at her service for anything she needed. Even when she attended the sick and the injured, I was there to aid her as much as I could. River feels wistful. *I appreciated being able to help my village almost as much as I valued being able to eat every day.*

"Wait." I stop him with a frown. "Are you saying that if you weren't this . . . assistant, you *wouldn't* be allowed to eat every day?"

It would depend on my success in hunting or resource gathering, but most likely not. It is hard to be successful every day, River admits. My frown deepens.

"Hang on a moment. Can you just tell me what the different groups do? Warriors, Pathwalkers, and Unevolved?" I ask, hoping that my suspicions are wrong, then realize that I've made an assumption. "If tasks are group specific, that is."

They are, River confirms. *The Warriors are responsible for the safety of the village. They primarily stand guard in the village but may patrol in the local area if there are reports of a particularly dangerous beast or group of beasts. If we are attacked, they are responsible for our defense.*

"Attacked? By what, beasts?"

River's tail sways from side to side. I suddenly realize that I've gotten so interested in his words that I've stopped my work. I quickly resume chopping at the branch.

By beasts or others of our kind. Though, that hasn't happened in my lifetime, River replies nonchalantly. He waits, perhaps to see if I want to say anything. When I don't, he continues. *The Honored Pathwalkers are responsible for using their magic to the benefit of the village. Since every Pathwalker has a different ability, that takes different forms. My master used hers to develop concoctions to treat the sick and the injured.*

I nod—that make sense, I suppose.

The Unevolved are responsible for all other tasks. We are by far the most numerous and while we aren't as strong as the Warriors, usually, or have the special abilities of the Pathwalkers, we are capable of many things. We hunt the beasts for the village and collect the other resources that our village needs. If there is to be a new construction in the village, or if the fence must be extended, it is we who take on that task.

I might not like a class system, but it does seem like the labor is divided according to capabilities—to a certain extent, anyway. It does bother me a little that the Warriors—those who, to all appearances, are the most proficient fighters—are not the ones hunting, but I can imagine that the food needs of a village would be too high to be supplied by the small group of Warriors I saw.

Although it was hard for me to tell most of them apart—except the ones with drastic size differences, of course—I only ever saw about fifteen Warriors at the same time. And I only ever saw the seven Pathwalkers who I came into contact with when first entering the village. In comparison, there were *significantly* more Unevolved. I couldn't say exactly how many—it was too many to get an accurate count—but there were at least three times as many Unevolved as Evolved; maybe more.

That said, River's words hint at an uncomfortable sense of expendability. As if the reason why the Unevolved are sent into the forest is far more to do with the fact that they are more numerous than the others, rather than them actually being best suited to it. But I'm not sure River could tell me the real reason for that—it's unlikely the average Unevolved would be informed *why* they were being sent into the forest instead of the Warriors or Pathwalkers.

"So, what were you saying earlier about food being dependent on your success in hunting or gathering?" I ask, returning to what caught my attention earlier. River's tail sways again in the lizard folk's version of a shrug.

To be allowed to eat, we must earn food tokens. A successful hunt is almost guaranteed to earn a food token from the communal carcasses unless it is a very small beast that can only feed one villager. We have to collect a much more significant number of resources to earn a food token. Fortunately, my master—previous master—supplied me with a token to the communal carcasses on a daily basis, as long as I helped her to the best of my ability.

My frown reappears on my face, and I strike with my axe hard enough that the branch finally gives way. I have to turn my attention to helping it down to the ground without risking it knocking me out of the tree. Eyeing the two branches, I decide that I need only one more, and then I need to process them a little.

Once I'm settled in the crook of another branch and beginning to work on my third, I return to the conversation.

"Do the Warriors and Pathwalkers have to do certain tasks to earn food tokens too?" I ask, suspecting I know the answer. It was very clear during my time in the village where the power lay.

No, River answers, confirming my suspicion. *It is important that our leaders and defenders are in good health,* he says earnestly, sounding as if he fully believes that. *As the only ones capable of bearing eggs for our village, the Pathwalkers would be considered the heart of our village even if they were not able to use magic. As it is, they are essential to our village's survival. Our Warriors, as the defenders of our Pathwalkers, are just as integral.*

"Yes, but from the sounds of it, the Unevolved do everything else!" I exclaim, once more using a bit more force than I probably should to strike the tree branch. It shudders but doesn't yet crack free. "It just doesn't seem fair that the Unevolved are the ones bringing in all the food, yet are the *only* ones who have to earn the right to eat it!" My final blow is almost enough. I hear a cracking within the core of the branch and just need to use a final strike to send it plummeting to the forest floor.

After following it down, I start cutting away the side shoots from the main branches—those will be useful for firewood once they've dried out a bit, so I tuck them into my Inventory. Without instruction, River starts breaking away the smaller twigs up at the top end of the branches.

I had never thought about it like that before, River admits quietly after we've been working for a little while in silence. *It was just normal to me. The best way to earn privileges was to Evolve. The second-best way was to become an assistant. I counted myself as lucky beyond all measure that my master chose me out of everyone. And I was considered a reasonable hunter. I ate more days than I did not, which not everyone can say.* He's silent for a long moment. *There are some in the village who barely eat at all. I have seen brothers waste away, their hunts becoming harder and more desperate with every day. Or those who have suffered an illness or injury and are struggling to find their balance once more. Sometimes they are lucky and manage to have a few good days of hunts or resource gathering; sometimes they aren't. All too often, they disappear one day, and we rarely find any evidence of what has happened to them. And even then, it is usually a few bones found in the detritus left by a beast.*

And then I learned a different way with you. You do not require us to perform certain tasks to eat. You even give us Energy Hearts without asking for anything more than cooperation with the others! And . . . that is why I thought that perhaps under your rule some in my village might be better off. That perhaps there is another way.

He avoids my eyes, and I sense the tension from his side of the Bond, as if he's concerned about how I might react. And having heard about what things are like in his village, I have to acknowledge that he's right to be concerned. I know that societies have to function around a certain amount of give and take, but starving your hunters doesn't seem to be a very good idea. If there isn't enough food coming into the village to feed everyone, then at least those who are hunting the food must be kept strong—if not, how can they expect that *more* food will be brought in? Leaving everything else aside, it's shortsighted.

Besides, how does it even work? They're the ones with the food! Why don't they just . . . eat it? Who would know? I voice my question to River.

He actually flinches a little in response; the reaction is enough to make me look up at him and pay full attention.

It is forbidden, he emphasizes. *To steal from the village, from the mouths of the Pathwalkers and Warriors . . . it is the worst thing someone can do.*

"I would have thought attacking one of the Pathwalkers would be worse," I remark. From the wide-eyed look River gives me and the sense of horror that comes over the Bond, I get the idea that he's never considered that as a possibility. Which he probably should have, considering that I *killed* one when we left, and he would probably be considered at least an accessory to the murder.

Perhaps River thinks of the moment as I do, as I sense him closing in on himself a little, both physically and through the Bond.

It is forbidden, he repeats, though I don't know whether he's talking about eating food without permission or hurting a Pathwalker. As he continues speaking, I realize it's the former. Perhaps he doesn't want to face what happened when we left the village, not yet. *I remember that one of my hatching committed that crime. He was beaten until he was almost dead. The whole village each contributed a blow. Even we had to do so, his hatch-mates. And then he was left outside the fence at night.* River's spikes flicker with a mixture of red and black. *I remember him begging for half the night, apologizing, pleading to be let in, promising he would never do it again . . . and then I remember hearing his cries as beasts ripped at him and he was unable to fend them off or escape them. The next morning, there was nothing but blood and scraps of flesh where he had lain.*

I stare at River with utter horror. For such a small crime, *that* was the outcome? Then again, I realize, perhaps according to the Evolved, it *wasn't* a small crime—if the Unevolved gained control over their food supply, it would be *them* in control of the village. And no autocratic leader would want that to happen.

I swallow as bile rises. For the first time, I start to believe that taking control of River's village is actually a good solution for the lizard folk as well as for Kalanthia.

CHAPTER FIVE

Just Be Yourself

R iver," I say seriously, standing upright and approaching him. He slowly stands from his crouched position to match me. "I can promise you here and now that I will *never* do something like that to you. Or to *anyone*."

Killing, I've done that. Heck, by this point I've even murdered a fully sentient and sapient being, if River is anything to judge by. Perhaps I should feel worse about that than I do, but I honestly hadn't really thought much about killing the Pathwalker—the rest of that day ended up far too frantic to react at the time. And with what I know now . . . I have to say that I'm not terribly sorry either. But this kind of brutality? Not just killing someone but *torturing* them first? And then condemning them to be *eaten alive*? No. Just . . . no.

River looks at me solemnly, then lifts his chin up to the sky for a long moment before lowering it again.

I believe you, he says quietly. *And that's why I want you to take over my village. You have done* so much *for me.*

And we're back to awkwardness. Because how can that be true? He's said it himself—even if the average Unevolved seems to have the rough end of the stick in the village, he was in a pretty cushy position as the assistant to the herbalist. So while some of his brethren might have benefited from becoming my Bound, *he* hasn't.

Ultimately, I've taken him away from everything he knows and then put him in a position where he lost his arm. To my mind, managing to heal it barely makes up for losing it in the first place.

The branches are stripped of their offshoots. I pick them up one by one and push them into my Inventory. I *love* the fact that my Inventory doesn't seem to have any size limits—and the weight limits are according to what I can lift off the ground. These branches might be about three times my length, but my Strength stat isn't just for show, even if a good portion of it is Endurance rather than Power.

The task justifies not responding for a while, but by the time we're walking back to the hill, the awkwardness is growing too much for me to bear. Just . . . the way River's looking at me. It's getting under my skin.

Master? I mean, Markus? he ventures.

"Look, *please* don't call me that," I request as a shudder goes down my spine. Now, in addition to the vague discomfort that I have with the term since it brings to mind masters and slaves, when I'm already concerned about what my Bonds do to my Bound, there's another dimension of discomfort. River called the herbalist his master—the herbalist, who at the very least is part of the ruling group that uses brutal methods like *torturing their subjects to death* in order to maintain control.

I'm sorry, M-Markus, River responds, sounding stricken.

"And why are you acting like this, anyway?" I ask, my frustration loosening my tongue in a way it didn't earlier when I was trying to broach the conversation.

Like what? the lizard-man asks. I feel even worse due to the fact that he seems to think he's done something wrong. That's not what I wanted him to feel—I really am *rubbish* at these emotional conversations!

"Being so . . . submissive. So overly affected by even the *slightest* hint of me being angry or even vaguely displeased!" I gesture at him to indicate that his current reactions are a case in point. "I mean, I'm not saying that I don't want you to cooperate with me, but surely you don't agree with me *all* the time?" River doesn't react. Even the Bond is quiescent. The silence drags out a little until I feel forced to continue. I sigh. "It's just . . . I thought that after everything we've been through, we'd managed to relax a bit with each other. Become . . . friends. But since being back here—well, not being *back* for you. Anyway, since being here, you seem to have become . . . more distant than ever, if that's possible, considering we started as enemies."

I'm sorry I displease you, Markus, he says quietly, his clicks barely audible. I look over to see that he's lowered his muzzle and eyes so they're pointing almost at the floor. His tail is down and even his spikes are flickering slowly. Somehow, his clearly submissive posture just annoys me even more.

"That, *that* is what I'm talking about," I say as I step to stand right in front of him. We've arrived at the river by now and need to cross it to get back to the hill, but right now I want to make a point. I cross my arms and stare him in the eyes. Or I would, if he was looking at me.

I stay there until his orbs roll forwards to meet my gaze. The Bond roils uncertainly. I sigh and then modulate my tone a bit, letting my arms fall to my sides so I don't look angry. "Look, I appreciate you trying to show me—I don't know—respect? But I'm just a guy. Not some sort of . . . god. And I'm not going to . . . to . . . *torture* you to death for 'displeasing' me. If you don't agree, I want to hear it. If you don't want to do something, I want to know. If you think I'm being an idiot, go ahead and tell me. Just . . . be yourself."

There's a long silence, but I let it linger, sensing that River's building up the courage to ask something. Lifting his chin slightly, he looks at me almost fearfully.

I don't understand what you want from me, River admits quietly. *If you wish me to disagree with you, to not do what you want me to do, why am I here? If you don't wish to accept my service, what do you wish of me?*

And this is always the issue when I start talking about emotions. Somehow, I always manage to garble things so that they confuse rather than illuminate. If this weren't so important, I'd give up now.

"It's not that I don't want your service," I say carefully, trying to be clearer than I evidently have been so far. "It's just . . . I don't want you sticking around only because you feel you *have* to do so. That you owe me, and that's why you're here. That you need to please me or I'm going to do something horrible to you. I'm not like that." I eye him, but the confusion still flickering across our Bond indicates that I'm not getting through yet.

I sigh. "Look. We made a deal: you help me get Lathani back to Kalanthia, and I help your village deal with their vine-strangler problem. You've fulfilled your part of the deal; I'll fulfil mine. You don't have to do a single thing more for me if you don't want to. I know the situation with Kalanthia is a bit complicated, and it would be easier to make sure she doesn't kill you if you stick around until we've earned the Cores we need to give her, but you don't have to. I offered you the opportunity to leave my service whenever you want before I healed your arm, and I'm not going back on my word. If you want out, all you have to do is say so. I'll cover for you with Kalanthia," I promise. I won't be happy about losing him, but at least then I'll know he's made his choice. And honestly, if he wants out now . . . Well, better now than later. It might sound cold, but at least right now, I'd only be out a few Energy Hearts. And a friend. If I can call River that. "Would you like me to release your Bond?"

What? His reaction isn't what I'd have thought. He's not joyful or even confused. He's *horrified*.

Please, Master, Markus, please don't. I'm almost shocked when he makes to go down on his knees in front of me like he did with Kalanthia. Not only does it make me profoundly uncomfortable to see him like that, but this is hardly the place to make himself more vulnerable than necessary. I immediately put my hands out to stop him shifting downwards.

"Stop that," I tell him a little helplessly. "It's . . . You don't need to." He stops but looks at me, the feeling of a matching helplessness coming across the Bond.

Don't send me away. Please! I shake my head, but it's in incomprehension; fortunately, River's not so conversant with human body language yet that he misinterprets it. That or the Bond translated it correctly to whatever his own body language would be.

"I'm not going to *send* you away! Where did you get *that* idea from?"

River's mouth opens and closes, but he seems as unable to cross the vast gulf between our understandings as I am. We stand there staring at each other like idiots.

Abruptly, River's eyes look beyond me and widen.

Master, there! I hear just as I look behind me.

A mouth appears out of the water and slams shut on my leg, a crushing bite piercing my skin in a second.

Before I can react with more than a hiss of pain, a powerful yank pulls me into the water, which closes over my head.

CHAPTER SIX

Drown

F or one crucial instant, I'm frozen. I've had a lot of fights, but none of them has been underwater.

It's immediately disorientating. I hadn't been expecting to be pulled under, so I didn't take a proper breath before the waters enveloped me. My sense of hearing is muffled, my sense of sight blurred by the water.

Having lost my footing, I can't immediately tell which way is up. Reaching out with my free hand, I manage to touch the bed of the river—that's down, then. Bracing my free foot against it, I push up enough to break the surface briefly. Enough time to gasp in air, but no more.

Because it's then that the creature crushing my leg makes its move. Before I know what's happening, I'm being twisted in the water, my leg forcing my body to turn or be ripped away.

It's all happening so quickly! I don't have time . . . *Time.* This seems like the worst moment to do it, but I dive into Meditation and my Core space. Fortunately, all the practice I've had with this allows me to do it even when I'm so disorientated and, yes, panicked.

In my Core space, my perception speed is much faster, giving me more time to think. I don't waste a single moment.

I've been attacked, I establish. *By what?* I think back to what happened. Neither of us saw the creature until the last moment—it must have been camouflaged or had some ability to make itself invisible. Its jaws are big enough to go around my leg. Its teeth are sharp enough to pierce my skin, but they're not that long. Its jaw pressure is immense. It's in the river. It's all very familiar.

The crocodile.

I last saw those jaws when they snapped together an inch from my nose. But that time, the crocodile was on dry land, my turf; this time I'm in its chosen environment.

I also remember something about crocodiles on Earth: the death roll. From what happened just before I entered my Core space, I suspect that that's exactly what's happening here.

That's not good.

Although my experience with River's arm indicates I could regrow my leg with Flesh-Shaping, I have no desire to actually do so. Unfortunately, being dismembered seems the most likely consequence of the death roll. Unless I can change something somehow.

Aware that time is still passing in the real world, I quickly run through a couple of strategies mentally before I pull out of my Core space. Now I'll have to play it by ear and get my Bound involved where appropriate.

Coming back to a full awareness of my body, I'm already aware of the strain being applied to my leg, of the pain that's already verging on excruciating. Willing the pain to reduce, I don't try to ignore it completely—I need to know if my limb is about to tear free, after all.

The crocodile is fully engaged in its roll by this point. The consequent force being applied to my body means that it's very difficult for me to do any more than just try to keep my limbs as close to my body as possible and keep hold of my knife with a white-knuckled grip.

River! Try to interrupt its roll with your spear! I order even as I focus my own attention on going with the movement. My aim right now is to preserve my limb if I possibly can—reducing the force trying to tear it away is the best thing I can think of doing.

My lungs are already starting to complain about the lack of fresh air, but there's nothing I can do about that either. *Come on, River,* I say silently to myself. The Bond already tells me that he's heard my order and is trying to follow it—further encouragement is more likely to panic him than help.

I'm trying to think of other options if he doesn't succeed when I feel the frantic twisting motion start slowing. *Finally.*

If it was hard for me before to know which way was up, it's even harder now that the riverbed has been thoroughly disturbed and my brain thoroughly rattled. The water is no longer clear; instead, it's thick with dirt and debris. Still, my dizzy brain is able to interpret the input of my eyes to work out that the area that is lighter is probably the surface.

Using the crocodile's own grip on my leg to give me leverage, I force my upper body upwards. Briefly breaking the surface, I breathe out explosively and then back in again with a great big gasp. Thus armed, I pull myself down to where my foot is trapped.

The crocodile isn't lying still. I don't know what River is doing, but either the massive reptile is trying to escape his stabs or it's trying to fight back without opening its mouth. Either way, I'm jerked about a lot before I manage to grab at its head with my free hand.

Its head is smooth, with no easy place to grip. I end up actually sliding my fingers between its teeth while hoping that it doesn't bite them. But then, to do that, it would have to open its jaws and let my leg out, which is exactly what I want.

I heave against the jaws, trying to force them open. An utter failure. Apparently, sixteen points in Strength isn't anywhere near a match for the bite pressure of these jaws.

Using my knife, I try to lever the jaws or cut the muscles to the sides of them. The crocodile doesn't like that and tosses and twists its head to try to deter me.

Grinning humorlessly, I just redouble my effort—is this the weak spot I need?

The crocodile starts bucking. One moment I break the surface again, and then the next, I slam into the ground. The force winds me, knocking out at least half of the precious air I had in my lungs.

Worse, it jars my elbow. I feel a sharp shooting pain go through my arm. My hand spasms and goes numb. A moment later when feeling returns, I realize that something's missing.

The bottom drops out of my stomach as I realize that I've lost my knife.

With only one possible strategy remaining, I pull myself closer to the crocodile's head, meet its bronze-colored eyes, and mentally shout at it.

Dominate!

The space we enter is familiar, but the amount of pressure against me is not. I'm almost forced back a pace from the very start.

How is it this strong? I ask myself. But there's no time for that. I don't know if there's any time dilation with a Battle of Wills, and I don't want to drown because I'm taking too long in it.

I set my face to the deluge of pressure against me and force my foot forwards a step. Pace by pace, foot by foot, inch by inch, I gain on the foreboding presence on the other side of the space.

It's more than an uphill battle. It's an uphill battle through a river rushing with meltwater in the spring, which gets stronger with every second. Only my knowledge that giving up will render me paralyzed for ten vital seconds keeps me going.

Starting this was a mistake.

I thought it would be a quick battle. I was even prepared to forgo my moral qualms and forcibly Dominate the crocodile if only to get out of its clutches. But that's not going to work; if there's no time dilation, I'm going to drown before I succeed. If I can at all.

Two thirds of the way towards the crocodile, I find I'm unable to make any more headway. The pressure has built and built and now feels like a solid wall of poured concrete in front of me.

I shout in frustration, anger, and fear, the sound echoing oddly around the space. What am I to do now?

And then, without warning, the concrete wavers. A moment later, it vanishes completely. I stagger forwards, the abrupt lack of pressure against me bewildering. Looking towards the crocodile's form, I suddenly realize that it's not there anymore.

A moment later, the space around me collapses and I come back to myself. I'm coughing violently, lying on my back. I push myself weakly onto my knees and elbows as my chest continues convulsing painfully.

Water splashes out of my mouth as I hack up the fluid in my lungs. My stomach, deciding to join the party, convulses too, and I vomit up everything I've eaten in the last few hours. As soon as my airway opens again, my coughs resume.

I dearly hope that nothing is about to attack me because I wouldn't be able to fight off a kitten at this moment.

After a few long minutes, my coughs subside. My lungs still feel irritated and uncomfortable, my breathing labored, but I *can* breathe, and I'm not being forced to cough every moment.

Carefully, I sit upright and look around me. I'm on land. That's the first thing I notice. I mean, I should have realized that before, but I was a little distracted. I'm on the bank next to the river. The crocodile that attacked me is mostly still in the river, but its head and forelegs are on the bank.

It's dead. That's clear enough. The blood at the back of its head, the glassiness in its eyes, and its sheer stillness are enough clues to tell me that.

"Your work, I presume?" I croak out, looking at River. He's standing over me, the emotions from his side of the Bond only a hair away from panic.

Yes, he answered. *I'm sorry, Master! I know you were trying to Bind the crocodile, but you were both still, and you were going blue, and I didn't think that you could breathe water and—* I cut him off with a raised hand.

"You did the right thing," I say before grimacing at the pain talking causes me. I continue speaking mentally to him. *I wasn't making headway fast enough. I would have drowned before succeeding—if I succeeded at all. Thank you for saving me.*

Of course, he replies, sounding a little calmer. *I apologize profusely for not seeing it in time. I failed in my task of guarding you while you were vulnerable. I beg you to punish me as you see fit for my lapse.* He sounds absolutely miserable. I shake my head.

I didn't see it either. And I should have known better than to pause near a river I didn't know was safe. I've encountered this type of creature before. It can camouflage itself against the riverbed. Though that suddenly makes me think about something. Could Inspect Environment have detected it? A thought for later, though. I focus back on my remorseful Bound. *You saved my life—again. That more than makes up for any "failure" to see it in the first place. I should be rewarding you, not punishing you.*

River actually recoils at that.

No, I . . . Reward? I could not accept a reward when you almost died from my negligence.

And I'm telling you, I repeat with as much sincerity as I can in my mental voice, *that I do not consider it negligence. There are many, many dangers in this forest that none of us know about, and probably a good number of them are not ones we could hope to win against.* Certainly there's one in particular that I would still not dare to face, even with as much progress as I've made personally and we've made as a group. *If you don't want a reward, fine, but I'm not punishing you for it either.*

But Mast—Markus! You could have died.

I've almost died more times than I can count since I came to this forest, I tell him bluntly. *And considering how hard that crocodile was to Bind, I probably* would *have died without you. Like I said, it's not your fault I was attacked, but it is entirely thanks to you that I'm alive. You saved my life, River. Thank you.*

The lizard-man meets my eyes and seems about to say something, but a moment later he closes his jaws and looks down.

As you say, he responds quietly, and I can all but hear the silent "Master" at the end. I sigh silently—I can tell that stopping him from calling me that is going to be an uphill battle. And perhaps it's not one I should fight. I don't like it—no—but clearly it's automatic for him due to my undeniable position of authority over him and the resources I give him. And considering how I've taken him away from everything he knows, is it fair for me to project *my* issues onto him? I have to admit that it isn't. With any luck, he'll grow out of it.

Look . . . if you want to call me "Master," fine. I'm happier being called by my name, but I accept whatever makes you most comfortable, I say to him before I can talk myself out of it and once more put my own comfort above his.

River looks at me searchingly for a long moment, then tilts his chin up in silent acquiescence.

Can I do anything for you, Master? he asks quietly.

Just keep watch. I need to heal myself. Were you hurt in the battle? I realize I've forgotten to ask.

I am well, River replies dismissively. I nod in acknowledgement and then settle more comfortably in a cross-legged position and close my eyes. Time to check out the damage.

CHAPTER SEVEN

Service

Sinking my magic into myself, I do a whole-body scan, a new technique I learned during our sparring this morning. It takes time, and we're not in the safest place, as has just been proven. Even so, I don't want to risk the damage I've sustained worsening in the time it will take to get back through the trees and up the hill to the cave. With any luck, the crocodile has scared away any potential attackers. And we're close enough to home that I can call on Bastet or Fenrir to come and join us if necessary.

Because I *have* sustained damage. The joints of my leg, of course, underwent significant strain with the death roll of the crocodile. Then there's the impact I had with the ground. The wounds created by the crocodile's teeth are actually probably the least of the injuries I've suffered, but they're there too. The worst, however, are my lungs.

The influx of river water has messed with their delicate tissue, explaining the shortness of breath and difficulty in speaking that I've been experiencing. That's where I start my healing.

It's a bit like dealing with a poison. I have to shift the water out of my lungs entirely while retaining and repairing the mucous membrane that normally covers the alveoli to protect them. I actually take a moment to pull myself out of my mental disconnection to reposition myself.

After returning to the position on my elbows and knees with my head relaxing downwards, I go back to working on my lungs. With gravity aiding me, it's a lot easier to purge my breathing apparatus of the intrusive liquid. Another pass through that area of my body to ensure that there are no foreign bodies or bacteria that could harm me and I'm pretty much done there.

I shift back to a position on my back to tackle my leg next. My consciousness streams down to where I feel a sharp ache, and I start with the open wounds. Getting rid of the bacteria from the crocodile's mouth takes longer than healing the holes its teeth made—it obviously never tried brushing its teeth. Fortunately, all my practice with Flesh-Shaping so far has made it easier to notice what belongs and what doesn't; the bacteria and fragments of rotten meat from the crocodile's teeth most certainly don't belong.

With those lacerations done, I move up to my knee joint. It's actually quite interesting to see: the initial injury caused the tendons to swell around where they were torn a little, but my own healing has clearly already kicked in—I can see indications that the damage was worse before.

I quickly finish what my natural healing has already started and then move on to my hip. The damage is more extensive here, but it's fairly similar in type to my knee. I guess this is the bit that took the most strain when I was being flung around.

Once I've finished dealing with that, I open my eyes again, feeling *much* better. River is standing with his spear ready, vigilantly guarding my vulnerable form—clearly, he's still being eaten up over his "failure."

Damn camouflaged crocodiles, I think to myself grumpily. *Who thought that was a good idea? Let's take one of nature's killers and give it chameleon-style camouflage.* There I was, having an important conversation with River, and the crocodile just had to intrude. I push myself to my feet and walk over to the crocodile itself.

I don't know if my inspect Skill will work on a creature that's already dead, but I might as well try.

I cast Inspect Fauna and am pleased when a box appears in my vision.

> Nere
> Tier 2 beast (Evolved)
> Dead
> Able to camouflage itself thoroughly against the bottom of the riverbed.

It turns out that even if Inspect Fauna works on bodies, it doesn't give me much more than I already knew.

The only new information is basically that it was tier two. That's good—as far as I've been able to conclude, tier twos tend to have Cores. If there's one in this body, it can be put against River's debt. Given the size of the creature and the fact that it's tier two, Kalanthia might even be willing to count that as two Cores as long as I bring the body back without putting it in my Inventory and stripping the Energy from it.

I next step forward to examine the creature itself thoughtfully. I didn't have Inspect Fauna when I last fought one of these crocodile creatures—both the System and Kalanthia call them nere—but I don't think that one was Evolved. Certainly, Kalanthia never mentioned finding a Core, though maybe she did but just didn't mention it, assuming that I'd intentionally given it to her.

This one looks bigger than the previous, about half again as long and much heavier. Maybe I should use this one's hide rather than the others for my armor? Or maybe I should use the first nere's hide as an experiment—if I mess up the tanning for it, it doesn't matter too much.

Getting it back is going to be a trial, though.

A glint of metal catches my eye as I turn my head to the side. Frowning, I step forwards for a closer look. Then I spot it.

My knife! I realize, and my heart skips a beat. Of course—I dropped it in the middle of the fight. My heart resumes its usual rhythm, though somewhat faster than before. If I'd lost that . . . I'm lucky that the current isn't too strong and only pulled it a little bit downstream.

Wading in, I grab it and quickly return it to my Inventory with slightly shaky hands. I'm still a *long* way away from being able to create a metal knife, let alone something of this quality. Not to forget, of course, that I suspect there are enchantments strengthening and keeping it sharp.

The same can't be said of my clothes. I look down at my torn trousers with a grimace—one leg is now nothing but rags from the knee downwards and I've lost that shoe. Trudging over to the nere's mouth, I heave it open and look inside. *There it is.* My grimace deepens as I yank the shoe out of the crocodile's throat and slip it back on my foot. Lovely—it now stinks of rotten meat.

My armor has taken a beating too. It was utterly useless in that fight, and the death roll the crocodile had me in and the water resistance has led to it hanging on by a single length of sinew. I pull it off and stick it in my Inventory—I'll have to fix it later.

Now, how to get the crocodile back?

I tap my chin a few times as I consider options. The nere is just too awkward for us to carry it together—its body is long and slippery. Perhaps we can use some rope? Tied around its front and back legs, it should allow us to at least keep it off the ground. Or perhaps tying it to a length of wood? And what do you know—I've got some decent lengths of wood newly added to my Inventory.

Decision made, I pull out one of the shorter and lighter branches I put in my Inventory earlier and crouch down to start tying the nere firmly to it.

"So," I say as my hands get busy with the processing of the bodies. "Going back to what we were talking about, what about my words indicated that I might send you away?"

If you have no use for me, no service that I can perform, why would you keep me? he answers simply. And, okay, I kind of get it. And even if I've tried to make it clear that that's not why I'm happy keeping him around, maybe I should have expected that he would have difficulty grasping it. After all, he's made it clear that in his village, the only thing he's ever known, if Unevolved aren't working, they don't eat. And even if they *are* working, if they don't do enough, they don't eat either. So, my attempts to make him comfortable by telling him that he has a choice in what to do and that I don't want to force him to do anything he doesn't want to do are probably alien enough as to be incomprehensible. And somehow were interpreted as me not wanting him around anymore.

Maybe I should just give him instructions? Tell him what I want from him? Because I certainly don't want to chase him away. He's an excellent sparring partner and the only one apart from me with opposable thumbs. He's also more sapient than any of my other Bound and capable of communicating in a way that the Bond translates into actual words. I *want* him to become part of the team. Properly.

But at the same time, I'm still concerned that the Bond is influencing him. Sure, I'm putting his behavior down to his conditioning at his village, and that might be the only thing influencing him. But on the other hand, it might not.

Perhaps I'll only know for sure when I remove the Bond—something I'm willing to do if River wants to go, but which Kalanthia probably shouldn't see him without. Not until we've accrued the Cores River needs to pay her.

I open my mouth and then close it again, unsure what to say. I think for a few moments before trying again.

"River . . . Listen, you don't *have* to provide a service to make me want to keep you around," I tell him earnestly. "Our relationship started off as contractual—you bargained with me over the price of your help. But now you've gone way above and beyond those terms. We agreed that you would help get Lathani out of the village and back to her mother. You did that and then continued to help me, to the point that you lost your *arm*. And considering that the bargain can at best be called coerced, that your actions to help me involved killing one of those Honored Pathwalkers of yours, and that you've now just *saved my life*, I'd say we are so far past the original agreement that, as far as I'm concerned, as long as you are peaceful, you're welcome to stay with us and share carcasses even if you spend most of the time lounging around and doing nothing."

I want to help you, River replies firmly. *You offered me the option between my own freedom and the good of my village, including all of those I hold most dear, sought to save my village from the Great Predator, saved me from the Great Predator by putting yourself at risk, and completely restored my arm to the extent that it feels like I never lost it. Even Pathwalker Herbalist would not have been able to do that even if she'd been willing.* River's eyes are flashing almost as brightly as his spikes as he argues with me. A moment later, he seems to take a mental step back, lifting his chin and lowering his tail. *My apologies, M-Markus.*

I actually laugh in slight relief.

"Don't apologize—if anything, I want to see *more* of that fire." Maybe then I'll be able to overcome this nagging suspicion that most of what he feels is manufactured by the Bond.

Then . . . He seems to summon up his courage to speak. *Do you have some service for me?*

And this time I think I know what he's *actually* asking. He's asking if he can be part of our group. Properly. At least, I *think* he is. But assumptions are dangerous.

"First, I need an answer to something. The first option is that you stay. That you become part of the team. That we work together according to the goals I set, and you benefit from Energy Hearts and any other resources we find. The second is that you stay but are not a full part of the group. You'll have full access to carcasses but not Energy Hearts, and you'll have no obligation to do anything other than remain peaceful. When we go down to save your village, we will break the Bond entirely and you can do whatever you like at that point. The third option is that you leave with my blessing, either now or when the Cores have been collected to pay off your debt with Kalanthia. I will give you a supply of Energy Hearts, food, and anything else reasonable that you ask for. Out of those three options, answer me honestly. Which would you prefer?" I doubt that he'll go for the third option, given everything he's said so far, but I want to make it clear that it's there nonetheless.

River is silent for a few moments, his hands still as he looks at me steadily. Although feeling on tenterhooks about his response, I show some discipline of my own and refrain from touching the Bond to read his emotions. I still get a sense of them being tumultuous, but nothing more specific than that. No indication of which way he is leaning.

Which option do you wish me to take? The question is asked with impressive neutrality considering the direct link I have to his emotions.

I hesitate before shaking my head.

"I won't answer that. This is a decision that you need to make independent of my own preferences."

There is more silence for a few long moments. Unable to bear the silent tension without moving, I return to my task of tying the crocodile to the branch. I've finished with its front legs and move onto the back legs.

I wish to stay, he says finally. I let out a quiet breath I didn't realize I was holding. *I owe you more than I can ever repay.*

"I thought it was *me* who owed *you* the debt," I point out. "You know, because you just, uh, *saved my life,* going beyond the terms of your agreement with me."

Helping Lathani return to her mother was not some self-sacrificing act, he says, acting like he feels this is some sort of confession. *I believed you when you said the Great Predator was alive, and I was clearly right to do so. Keeping the cub, letting the shaman and my . . . Herbalist continue with their plan would have sounded the death knell of our village as surely as if they did nothing and allowed the Forest of Death to engulf us. If anything, I feel like what you consider to be my side of the bargain was in fact to my own benefit anyway. And in doing so, you ran a great risk. If the Pathwalkers had been less interested in your creations, you would have ended up the next communal carcass. I owe you my life—multiple times over. And perhaps I might not have lost my arm if I had not fought in that battle, but perhaps I would have lost it in a different one. If I had lost it in a different battle, I would never have regained it. So I judge that I owe you that too.*

"Then perhaps we just agree that we owe each other and be done with it," I suggest, a reluctantly amused smile tugging at the corners of my mouth. *Arguing over who is more in debt to the other . . .*

Very well, but as long as you permit it, you are my master, whether you wish me to call you such or not, and I will willingly and happily *render you as much service as I can.*

His declaration is so earnest, it makes my insides tie themselves in knots. Can I trust it? It's what I want, but is River actually in a fit state to make a decision on this? Both as a result of the messed-up way his village works and because of the influence of the Bond.

He said it himself at the beginning of all this: the Bond imposes an external set of ideals—the protection of and obedience to the master of the Bond. Can I trust anything he says while he's still under its influence?

But ultimately, unless I want to *force* him to leave, when everything he's said indicates that he doesn't want to, there aren't any other choices. And it certainly would be easier to stop Kalanthia from eating him if he stayed Bound to me.

Perhaps it's better to wait until I've finished my quest to change the status quo. We'll have had more time together to learn more about each other. Once we've paid off his debt with Kalanthia, I could release him from the Bond, and then he could make his decision whether to stay or go free of its influence. Though, maybe it's worth waiting until I've dealt with the vine-stranglers too—that way there's no chance he'll feel obliged to stay for fear that I won't fulfil my end of the bargain if he doesn't.

"All right," I say in the end, finally answering River's declaration. "I'll accept your service until we've sorted out the threat of the vine-stranglers to your village. Then we'll reassess the situation, okay?"

As you wish, River accepts.

"But you don't have to be so . . . submissive," I say, grimacing again at the word. But who knows what that translates to in River's language. "Just . . . be like you were on our journey here. Even if you want to call me 'Master,' I'd rather you act like a . . . friend. A teammate. Not an . . . assistant to a master." Perhaps this might get through where other requests haven't. "It makes me uncomfortable when you treat me with too much formality. I can't be relaxed with you if you aren't relaxed with me." River eyes me for a moment.

Very well, he agrees hesitantly. *I will try. But will you tell me what service you wish to have from me?*

I sigh. We've come back around to the beginning of the conversation again. Though, at least now I know *why* he was acting in that way. And if I'm going to honestly accept his service, I guess I'd better actually give him tasks to fulfil.

I take a few moments to think. What *do* I want him to do? It's hard when I don't know whether he'll be staying with us past saving the village—assuming I even *can*. Should I plan for the short or long term? If I plan for the long term, all I risk losing is a few Energy Hearts; if I plan for the short term, I risk losing the time now for River to improve himself. Between the two, Energy Hearts are probably easier to find than time. In fact, they definitely are, considering I know the location of more.

"I want you to grow and improve," I say finally. "That was as true before as it is now. The sooner you can hit your Evolution, the better for everyone. At the same time, using poison on the lizogs certainly helped, and we never know when we're going to need more of that. I'll admit that I've been collecting venoms here and there, but I don't have the faintest idea of where to start with using them, apart from just smearing them directly on my weapons. Any other potions that might offer benefits to health or stamina could be useful too." I sigh. "Perhaps you should focus on using Energy Hearts to make progress towards your Evolution and then also make forays into the forest to find ingredients for your concoctions?"

So, you would prefer me not to focus on hunting? River checks with me, his mien intent.

"Not specifically, I suppose. If something attacks you, then by all means kill it and bring its body back with you, but I suspect you won't find much challenge in the area around here."

I have noticed how much easier most prey is here, he agrees. *And the air feels . . . lighter.*

"That's probably the Energy density," I note. "And Kalanthia made it clear that relying entirely on Energy Hearts isn't healthy, so I guess you'll need to go hunting a bit." I finish up tying the crocodile's tail to the branch. Not having the space to tie it lengthwise, I curl it up so it's attached to the middle part of the branch.

Very well, I understand that you wish me to practice the skills I learned with my . . . previous master, to absorb Energy Hearts, and to go hunting from time to time when necessary either for collecting ingredients or for my own development. He hesitates for a moment. *Do you wish me to come with you to help protect you when you go out into the forest?* he asks.

"That's probably a good idea," I admit. I gesture at the crocodile. "It isn't the first time I've encountered one of these, though the last time was further away from here. And there are always creatures looking for easy prey."

Your lack of claws or sharp teeth probably doesn't help you in that respect, River agrees. *They cannot see how dangerous you truly are.* My indignant feelings at his first sentence die away with his second.

"No," I agree, instead of getting annoyed. "I probably won't leave the den area too much, though—I've got lots of crafting to do. I need to go out to collect some clay tomorrow, which I could use your help with. And I'd definitely like to continue sparring."

River tilts his chin up briefly in respectful acknowledgement. I get the sense that he wants to say something even though he doesn't give any physical indication of it.

Master, Markus . . . I was wondering . . . He hesitates, eyeing me cautiously. I sigh quietly—even if we've had a good conversation, clearly it's going to take more than that to get him to relax.

"I'm not going to bite," I tell him, then decide to make a joke out of it and point at my teeth. "These wouldn't even get through your scales, anyway." A flicker of amusement comes through the Bond. "Just say what's on your mind."

When . . . you spoke of going to help my village . . . ?

"When am I planning on doing so?"

Yes, he confesses, sounding almost reluctant. I push myself to my feet as I lift one end of the branch onto my shoulder. River follows my non-verbal direction and lifts the other onto his. I give a quiet "Oof" of effort, not looking forwards to walking up the hill. But at least it's manageable, and without any wheeled contraption, I don't have many other options.

"The vine-stranglers are a difficult prospect," I admit. "They're bigger than I thought they were, and though they're vulnerable to fire, creating a fire big enough to wipe them all out is likely to cause a whole lot more collateral damage with an uncontrollable forest fire. In the short term, it might be possible to keep them off your village by burning any that get close and slowly working our way outwards from there. But I'm still considering options—there may be a better solution than that. But I've also got taking over your village to consider. And for that, I want better armor, better weapons, and, ideally, a few more fighters to help me. So, in short, I can't tell you exactly when we'll go down to help your village, but I want to ensure that when we do go there, we *can* help them."

River is silent, but I sense that he understands, even if he seems troubled about it. But as we walk up the hill, I find I can't give him any better answer.

CHAPTER EIGHT

Not So Relaxing

As we walk, my mind wanders a little. This whole situation has brought up something else that I hadn't thought of. Or rather, someone. Bastet.

The raptorcat has been with me through thick and thin. Her loyalty has been unquestionable, and she has also gone above and beyond what we originally agreed. If I've offered River the opportunity to be free from the Dominate Bond, how can I not offer it to her as well? I blame the fact that I haven't thought of it until now on the fact that she looks more like a regular animal than River and can't speak in recognizable words—yet, anyway. Her mental communication has been becoming clearer and clearer the closer her progress ticks towards Evolution.

Still, I find they are weak justifications now that I think about it. She's not incapable of making the decision; I just never thought of offering it to her. And there's no debt tying her to me, no sword of Damocles hanging above her head that would give me a good reason to argue against giving her the option.

The thought is depressing. *What would I do if she chose to leave me and take the cubs with her? She's . . . she's a rock in this new life of mine.* Yet now the thought has occurred, I know that it will keep niggling at me if I don't give her the option. She's done more than enough to deserve it.

I think River must sense my increasingly dark mood, as he doesn't try to say anything while we walk. By the time we get back, after briefly taking the time by the river to wash both ourselves and the corpse, my mood is in the abyss. I've pretty much convinced myself that Bastet leaving with the cubs without a second glance would be the best possible outcome of me breaking the Bond; I would hate to have to raise a weapon against my friend but will have to if she tries to threaten any of us.

And if she tries to threaten Kalanthia or Lathani . . . No. Even in a worst-case scenario, I doubt that would happen. Bastet knows Kalanthia's power well enough; that wouldn't change with the disappearance of the Bond.

At the top of the hill, I head straight for Kalanthia, River following with the other end of the pole. It's a good excuse to put off facing Bastet right away.

Your trip to the forest was not so relaxing, I take it, Kalanthia says in amusement. The corners of my mouth curl up in a slightly shame-faced smile as River and I put the crocodile's body down. He stays silent, and I sense the fear he still has of Kalanthia. Unsurprisingly.

"Not exactly," I respond to the massive nunda. "But it's a tier-two beast, so it hopefully has a Core. If you think that the meat would be useful to Lathani, you can have it. But please be careful not to make too many openings in the hide in that case—I'd like to keep it."

You wish the meat as well as the Core to count against the wergild your Bound owes my cub?

"Exactly."

The nunda stands up and moves over to inspect the body. *A strong beast. I suspect you were lucky to survive.*

"Pretty much," I agree with a sigh. "I didn't even see it until it bit me." I don't mention that I was having a heated conversation with River near the water like an idiot.

Common with these—their ability to hide themselves is particularly powerful. It's fortunate you were able to get free.

"Teamwork," I say with a smile that quickly fades.

Very well. The hide would do Lathani no good to eat anyway. She lifts a paw and pushes the nere over so it is lying on its back and then uses one of her swordlike claws to make a surprisingly delicate slit down from its throat to its tail. Leaning down, she takes a bite of the revealed flesh, then chews it thoughtfully. *Tasty, full of Energy, and a powerful beast. Taking that into account, and the likely size of its Core, I shall count this as two Cores towards your Bound's debt.*

"I understand. And thanks." To be fair, a two-for-one Core deal is more generous than I was expecting. Clearly the Energy content of the carcass is higher than I thought it would be.

I'm clearly dismissed when Kalanthia calls Lathani over and they both bury their muzzles in the crocodile's entrails. Stepping away, I look at Bastet with a feeling of nervous hesitance that immediately turns into annoyance at myself. Better just to rip the bandage off all at once. Looking over at River, I decide that I don't want an audience. And if Bastet *does* get violent for some reason, I don't want him accidentally killing her because of a misunderstanding.

"Why don't you absorb some Energy from an Energy Heart?" I suggest pointedly. "Do you need a new one?"

It's fine, thank you, he says politely, *I haven't yet finished absorbing the other you gave me.*

"Okay, well let me know when you need a new one," I tell him, and he takes the hint easily. Tipping his chin up briefly, he steps into the cave and returns shortly after with a partly used Energy Heart in his hands. I watch as he sits in a sunny patch and closes his eyes, going still.

No more excuses.

"Bastet," I call quietly, the lump in my throat making it hard to say anything. Nonetheless, her hearing is perfectly capable of detecting even that low sound. Plus, even if she hadn't heard the message with her ears, she'd have received it through the Bond.

The raptorcat looks at me, her head tilted to one side curiously. She's clearly picking up my tumultuous emotions, as both confusion and wariness come over from her side of our connection. "Can you come here, please?" I ask. She obeys immediately, padding closer on surprisingly quiet talons.

Is something wrong? she seems to ask, concern bleeding through even as she looks around warily.

"No, nothing wrong," I tell her, trying to smile but failing to make my lips do more than twitch a little. Ah well, she wouldn't understand the gesture anyway. Nothing's wrong—yet. "Listen, I just wanted to say . . . to tell you how much I appreciate what you've done for me. You've been a solid partner in every fight we've had, you've kept us safe with scouting, and you don't know how much you've helped me in other ways." Confusion but wary appreciation comes across from her side, like she's pleased I'm happy with her but is wondering why this would make me so sad.

"I feel like repaying the loyalty you've shown me by keeping you bound to me is unfair to you. I'm . . . I'm going to break the Bond." Shock and lack of understanding emanates from the other side of the Bond, followed quickly by hurt and upset. Since that's the opposite of what I'm aiming for, I hastily try to reassure her. "It's not because you've done anything wrong or because I don't want you, I promise!" I tell her. "In fact, the reverse is true. I just want you to *choose* to be here."

Her emotions settle a little with my reassurance, but there's still a whole lot of wariness and concern underlying everything. "Look," I say, taking a deep breath. I've started something; I need to finish it and to do it *right*. Otherwise, I could risk losing another person I care about. "I'm going to break the Bond and then immediately offer you a Taming Bond, like with Sirocco. That will offer you the chance to put whatever you want into the Bond, like she did. Or"—and here I have to swallow—"you could choose to leave. Take the cubs with you and go. If you leave peaceably, none of us will offer threat to you." I bite back the words that threaten to spill out, words that want to beg her not to go, to try to convince her to stay.

"If you stay, I want it to be because that's what *you* want," I say again. "Equally, if you leave, I want it to be because *you* want to." Feeling like there's a stone sitting in my stomach, I reach with metaphysical hands to the place where I know Bastet's Bond is.

It takes but a moment to break it—all that's required is my Will to do so. The ease with which it snaps feels incongruous with how important it is for me. I immediately feel the lack, the emptiness where her presence used to be. This is *far* worse than with Spike, for all that it was voluntary on my part, and I almost curl over myself with a groan.

Bastet hasn't moved, her eyes wide with shock. Without my connection to her, I have no way of feeling her emotions, but I know her body language well enough to recognize that she feels the lack of the Bond even worse than I do. Fearful that wasting even a moment will see her suddenly turn tail and vanish, I stare into her eyes.

"Tame," I say, my voice filled with desperate hope.

CHAPTER NINE

Companion Bond

I've barely even opened the trade window before Bastet has piled a whole lot of sensation in and shoved it in my direction. It's hard to describe, and I have to take a few moments to parse through it all. When I have, I just stare at her in disbelief.

"Really?" I ask, too dumbfounded to say anything more. Given that we no longer have a Bond, she shouldn't be able to understand me. Maybe it's that we've been together long enough that she can read my tone and body language, because she clearly does. And from how easily I interpret her exasperation, I reckon the understanding isn't only one-way.

The best way I can describe what Bastet has just done is to once more draw on the comparison to a trade window in a game. It's like I offered a trade and she offloaded her entire inventory, heck, her entire *bank* into the window. Then, without waiting for me to show any of my goods, she just accepted the trade.

Obviously, she's not giving me any *goods* exactly, but what she has given me is far more precious: trust. All the aspects of Dominate that were the reason for me doing this in the first place, all those elements of control . . . she's offering them to me again.

It's not that she's done what Sirocco did by laying out specific demands. She hasn't even laid out specific offers, separating the different aspects of the Bond. No, she basically said, "I was happy with what we had, and I want it back."

The sheer amount of trust she's offering me here is staggering. She's already accepted the Bond. It's like she's written me a blank check. I could make whatever demands I wanted of her right now, and she would be powerless to reject them.

But I'm not going to do that. Of course I'm not—it would be an utter betrayal of her, and of her trust. *And,* I think ruefully, *knowing how I'd react is probably* exactly *why she did it in the first place.*

Instead, I pour in my own promises to her. To never take her for granted. To respect her opinion, even if I ultimately choose something different. To work towards her growth as I also work towards my own progress and the improvement of the team. To protect her cubs until they are old enough to make their own choices. And then I accept the trade.

The Bond snaps back into place like it had never vanished, brighter and stronger than ever before. I feel Bastet's pleasure and satisfaction pour through from her side of things, and I can't help but let my own wave of emotions crash back across the link. If it's tinged with a good bit of relief, only Bastet and I will ever know.

"Thank you," I say to her, a little hoarsely through the sudden lump in my throat. "I don't know what I would have done without you."

Don't be silly, she seems to say, though it still comes across in emotions rather than words. *I'm not going anywhere*. With that, she pads close to rub her face against mine. I bring my arms up to give her a hug and realize that it's the first time I've done that. She's slighter than I would have expected, her pseudo-feathers serving to make her appear a little bigger. Yet below them, she doesn't feel fragile—the reverse, in fact. Her sinewy muscles feel like I'm holding a creature made of steel, even though she's clearly made of warm flesh and blood.

Bastet endures my embrace for a few moments but then pulls away. I don't fight her on it, not wanting to ruin the moment. Without a backwards glance, she pads over to where the cubs are now playing, having moved during our discussion. Lying down, she clearly relaxes again, obviously far less moved by what just happened than I am.

Maybe I should follow her example, not make such a big deal of it. But for me it *is* a big deal. Despite how our relationship started, despite all the dangerous situations I've led her—and the cubs—into, she still trusts me enough to Bond with me. More, she trusts me with all the power I held over her before.

There's the nagging sense of a notification. I'm not terribly surprised. I know I need to go and work on my internal matrix, but there's no way I'm going to be able to ignore whatever message is waiting for me. I quickly open it to check.

Skill Evolution!
You have gained a Skill Evolution to your Class Skill: Dominate. Unusually, this Skill Evolution does not affect your base Skill, but instead adds another option to it. Your new Skill is Companion Bond.

Companion Bond
You have learned that if you wish to know whether something is yours, you must let it go. If it returns, it is yours; if it does not, it never was. A derivative Skill of Dominate, Companion Bond contains almost all of the same features and limitations for both Binder and Companion and will not advance independently of the base Skill. However, Companion Bond has one difference: both Binder and Companion have the power to break the Bond at any moment. A Companion Bond once broken may not be reinstated. A different Bond may or may not be able to be created depending on the circumstances.
Limitations: In order to use Companion Bond, a bond of significant depth must already exist between the Binder and the prospective Companion. Any previous Bond must be sundered. The Companion must choose willingly and with no coercion to accept the Companion Bond.

Curious, I close my eyes and dive into my Core space and zoom away to the dense clusters of threads that, based on the fact that my Bonds seem to emerge from them, represent my Tame and Dominate Skills. Since it's a derivative Skill of Dominate, I would expect Companion Bond to have placed itself nearby.

My guess isn't quite correct: my new Skill isn't just *near* Dominate but is instead intrinsically connected to it. In a way, it looks a little like a polarized electron cloud. Most of its "body" is out to one side of Dominate, but I can see threads that weave their way around the whole of the Dominate Skill. Interestingly, there are also a few threads that touch Tame, which gives me hope that it might be possible one day to offer the same Bond to those like Sirocco. If she was willing to give up the control that it would require. Or maybe a Companion Bond converted from a Tame Bond would be different from a converted Dominate Bond?

After pulling myself out of my Core space and opening my eyes, I quickly navigate to my status screen to see the new addition.

Name: Markus Wolfe		Race: Human	Class: Tamer
Level: 12	Energy to next level: 100%	Energy absorption rate: 26u/hr	Energy towards debt: 84%
Intelligence	36	Mana: 450/540	
Wisdom	36	Mana regeneration rate: 900u/hr	
Willpower	42+8 (+20%)	Health regeneration rate: 40u/hr (-20%)	
Constitution	19	Health: 190/190	
Strength	16	Stamina: 90/90	
Dexterity	17	Stamina regeneration rate: 170u/hr	
Class Skills: Dominate – Novice 6 *Companion Bond Tame – Beginner 7 Fade – Initiate 1 Inspect Fauna – Beginner 2 Inspect Flora – Beginner 2 Inspect Environment – Beginner 2		Non-Class Skills: Flesh-Shaping – Initiate 1 Stealth – Novice 1 Animal Empathy – Novice 7 Meditation – Initiate 3 Energy Manipulation – Initiate 3 Sensation Management – Beginner 6 Spearmanship – Beginner 1	

My new Skill is immediately marked as different from the others by virtue of it being preceded by an asterisk and the lack of level indication. I guess that's because, according to the information box, Companion Bond appears to be intrinsically tied to Dominate, which has itself risen two levels in one go. I can only assume that further evolutions to Dominate will also affect Companion Bond. I don't really know how to feel about that, but then I'm not sure how to feel about any of it, really. I push my confusion to one side and try to work out what the consequences are of all this.

After a few moments of thought, I realize that this is the answer to my increasing moral concerns about essentially enslaving my Bound. It says it in the description:

they have to be free to choose to take the Bond or not, free of any other Bond, free of coercion. That means that if they *do* choose the Bond, they're doing so knowing what it entails.

Not only do they choose to *enter* the Bond, but they also have the option to *leave* it. It sounds like either of us breaking the Bond would be pretty final, though, so not a choice to be made casually. But just knowing that the option is there is a relief: I cannot feel I'm holding them against their will when they have the option to leave.

Yes, there are arguably issues with indirect coercion—Bastet might have made the decision to stay for the sake of the cubs, for example, though I don't believe that's the case. Her reaction was just too quick and sincere for me to have any doubts about that. But it does reinforce my decision to wait to release River until I've dealt with the threat to his village—even if we pay his debt to Kalanthia before that, I don't think he'll mentally feel free enough to choose until then. And possibly not even at that point, given how he was trying to convince me that he owes me far more than I owe him. Perhaps with more time I'll be able to convince him differently.

But in a way, I can't be too worried about all of that. We make decisions with all sorts of motivations, whether it's for our own good, the good of our family, or avoiding something we don't want to happen. All I can do is try to make sure that my Bound are given as much freedom as possible and that they know that if they want to leave—as long as they don't do it in the middle of a battle or then turn around and attack me—it will be no harm, no foul. Hopefully, that will be enough.

The main question I have about the new changes is actually about what it means by "a bond of significant depth." It's not exactly clear. And is it talking about a *Bond* bond, or a more casual relationship bond? Then again, I suppose that I could go by my Bond—or bond—with Bastet for guidance, since that was clearly sufficiently deep enough. But that . . . is a big ask.

The Bond I had—have, I suppose—with Bastet was—*is*—deep. I don't idly call her family. I don't think I have that kind of Bond with anyone else. I feel like I'm getting there with River, but it's more complicated—*he's* more complicated. It comes of being fully sapient, I guess.

Should I offer it to Fenrir? Sirocco? I consider the possibility for a moment before shaking my head. No. My Bond with Fenrir is far too new; we're still trying to find our place with each other. Maybe that's why a Companion Bond can only be offered to a being once they have a bond of significant depth—that way they know better what they'd be getting into by consenting . . . or losing by rejecting it.

Sirocco is an even easier decision. She's only just starting to adjust to the role of being an actual part of the team rather than just an external ally hanging around for benefits. No way is our bond even remotely deep enough for this; I doubt if she'd even want it, anyway. Actually, *could* I even offer it to her? She's Bonded to me through Tame, not Dominate.

Then again, it didn't actually specify what *kind* of bond had to be in place, just how deep it had to be. Anyway, it's not something that's feasible for now. Maybe in the future, if our relationship changes.

So, Bastet is the only one to be a Companion for now. Maybe River will be later, but not now.

I look up at the sky. There's not much daylight left, but it's enough that I don't want to just sit around. Not when I know I have so much to do. I could practice using one of my other weapons, see if that will get me an appropriate Skill, but after the incident with the crocodile, I don't feel like doing anything combat related.

Instead, perhaps it would be a good idea to test if it's even possible to use Flesh-Shaping on a dead body. I hesitate about what to do first, then I pull out the hide from the first nere I killed—the one I executed via dropping a massive boulder on its head.

I decide that it might help if I can get an idea of what I should be aiming for with traditional manual methods before using magical experimentation. Flesh-Shaping requires enough detail focus that just pouring magic in and vaguely telling it what I want to happen won't work. If I have something to compare it to, that will work better. And if it turns out that I *can't* use Flesh-Shaping on a dead body, or a fragment of a dead body, it would be good to get some practice. After all, as I've learned, having the memories of skinning a hundred different beasts doesn't necessarily mean that my hands are capable of doing the task.

Resigning myself to getting all messy and bloody, I take out the crocodile hide and lay it out flat, scales downwards. My skinning job was decent for the beginner that I still am, but there's still plenty of unwanted material attached to the hide. Fat, bits of flesh, blood . . . They will just make the hide rot if left.

After hesitating for a moment, I take off my trousers. Ridiculous embarrassment makes my cheeks flush despite knowing that there isn't a single human within a hundred miles. Heck, as far as I know, not in this whole world. And even if the most humanoid of my Bound is present, he probably doesn't care—he doesn't have visible genitals and his adornments are purely for decorative or practical purposes. Besides, I'm still wearing briefs, even if they're a bit torn up and dirty from hard use. It's just the stupidly useless sense of modesty I still have that makes me blush.

The reason I take my trousers off is because I don't want them getting dirty during my next task. Kneeling on the crocodile hide to keep it in place, I lean forwards with my knife angled. I don't want to cut the hide, after all, just scrape it. Perhaps I should have made a tool for this, but hopefully the knife will work well enough.

Holding the ever-sharp blade at an angle, I scrape off the bits of the crocodile's body that still cling to its hide. I'm very aware of my inexperience in this task, despite the number of memories I have that try to prove otherwise, and that's why I've chosen the first nere's hide rather than the salamander or the recent tier-two nere's hide. If I make a few accidental holes, it's not the end of the world.

Then again, the reason I'm even doing this is because I need armor. And let's face it: I killed this crocodile with a massive rock for a reason. I doubt I can accidentally make holes when I'm not even trying.

I work my way down the hide methodically. First, I shift my handhold sideways along the width of the skin, then I shuffle backwards to move along its length. I don't bother to try skinning the crocodile's legs manually, though I do skin the majority of its tail. The skin is therefore a vaguely rectangular shape, though with narrowing and widening in different places along its length.

The work makes my back, knees, and hands ache. My back hurts from its bent-forward position. My knees are bruised by the hard ground below the skin. My hands shake from having to maintain a specific grip. I have to take breaks every so often to stretch the aches out. Once, I even get up and walk around a bit, but I don't repeat that—returning to my knees after leaving them makes the forming bruises feel even worse.

It would be nice if I could earn a Constitution point from all this, but I doubt that such aches are sufficiently damaging to count—they're just annoying, and I don't want to be bothered with healing them right now.

When I get halfway down the crocodile's body, I stop. That's probably enough to help me get an idea of what to aim for with Flesh-Shaping. I can't stop a smile of satisfaction from making its way onto my face. Getting up, I link my hands together and stretch them above my head, luxuriating in the release of tension.

I'm a bit messy from the hide, but I don't feel like going back down to the river. The sun is already behind the clouds, which are hovering over the horizon, and for all I know there's another nere lurking around waiting for me. Instead, I just pour some water from a pot in my Inventory onto a rag and rub myself down while sighing and thinking longingly of a nice hot shower.

I'm getting hungry, so I go inside to stoke up my fire and put some meat and "potatoes" on to boil with some salt. I look sternly at the three cubs, who are currently cuddled up to Bastet's side.

"Don't you even think about messing with this or I'll skin you," I threaten. They eye me fearlessly—even if they understood my words, they'd probably be fully aware that I wouldn't carry out my threat. Still, I hope that Bastet at least will keep them away.

I suddenly have a thought that hadn't occurred to me earlier.

"Should we give some Energy Hearts to the cubs now that they're old enough to travel with the pack?"

Bastet hesitates, the feeling coming over the Bond one of consideration. After some moments of thought, she sends over a sense of negation—for now. I get the idea that the cubs are still too young. They need to get some kills under their figurative belts before they can start using Energy Hearts. Cores like we found in the bodies of those woodlice-like creatures seem to be fine for them, though.

I still don't fully understand how things work for beasts, but I'll willingly bow to Bastet's knowledge of the situation.

"All right. Just let me know when they're ready. They're part of our team too. As long as I have some left, they'll be welcome to partake." Bastet sends me a sense of pleasure, but also a hint of chiding, like it should have been able to go without saying.

With my meal on to boil, I have a bit of time before it will be ready. I decide that I might as well explore whether Flesh-Shaping will work the way I want it to on the hide.

Since it's too big to lay out inside, I go back outdoors to where it's still stretched out. Gazing at it thoughtfully, I decide that it might be better to start with something more familiar. I have no idea where to start using Flesh-Shaping on a skin, but thanks to my efforts with River, I have a reasonable idea of how to heal a being other than myself. I pull out the body of one of the last remaining monkile things in my Inventory. Time to see if it being dead is any impediment. Thankfully, it's as fresh as it was when I stored it in there; though, whether that makes any difference to my chances of success, I don't know.

Suddenly curious about whether my Inspect Fauna works on dead bodies that have been in my Inventory, I cast it.

The answer to my question seems to be "Kind of."

Paranax
Tier 1 beast (Unevolved)
Dead
Unknown

Actually, the information that *isn't* present is just as interesting as the information that is. Apparently, the Skill can identify the species and tier of the beast even with it being dead and empty of Energy. However, it doesn't give me any information about the function of the species or its strengths or weaknesses. That it doesn't indicate how much Willpower I should have to Dominate it is unsurprising: Dominate doesn't work on the dead. Or, at least, I doubt it does given everything I've discovered about it so far. I haven't actually checked, though.

Just wanting to be thorough, I turn the monkile—paranax—corpse so that I'm meeting its sightless gaze with my own. After muttering "Dominate," I'm completely unsurprised when nothing happens. But it's good to know that that's not a feature. For all I knew, Dominate could have been used as a necromancer's tool if the target was already dead.

Returning to the notification with information about the paranax, I tap at my lip in thought as I scan it again. How does the Skill know the name of the species? I get how it would know about the tier level—if the creature is in tier two, it probably has a Core. And who knows what other physical changes are made when moving from tier two to tier three? So a scan that can identify such information is somewhat expected.

The species name is something else. To me, that indicates that there must be some sort of "database" somewhere with all these names in it and the inspect Skills somehow have access to it. But then that raises the question of the language. It's not English, that's for sure. The plants I inspected had names with a Latinate sense to them, but I'm pretty sure it isn't actually Latin.

So, then, is it in the language of Nicholas's world? That would make sense in that the stones I received were from him and it's clear that I've gained the ability to speak his language. Either that or the memories downloaded into my mind have been translated automatically into English. At least, I've never had any problems understanding them, even though it's clear that they do not speak or write in a way that I'm familiar with.

The problem I have with that theory is that this is not Nicholas's world, so how would a System using a database from Nicholas's world be able to identify creatures on this one? Unless the animals are the same, of course, and the Skill is drawing from the same database as would be found on Nicholas's world. That's assuming that the Skill would even be able to use the database this far away from its source—unless, of course, it's contained within the Skill itself.

The problem with *that* is that the biodiversity of life on Earth shows just how differently creatures can develop once they are no longer interacting and interbreeding on a regular basis. I find it highly unlikely that this world and Nicholas's have the same animals on it.

So, how does it work? If it gave them the names I'd been giving them mentally, that would be one thing—pulling from my conscious mind would make sense. Heck, calling the paranaxes "monkey lizards" or something would be fine too; it would have been obviously drawing on my own subconscious. But as it is, I would never call them "paranaxes." So where did the name come from?

Or am I overthinking this? Is there just some sort of random generator built into the Skill, where if it has no information to draw on, it just makes something up? Perhaps, though that then raises the question of what would happen if there were another person with Inspect Fauna here: would they get the same names as I have?

In the end, I have to shake my head and move on. There *isn't* another person to compare results with, so I'll just have to live with my curiosity until I get to Nicholas's world. *Though*, I think, suddenly struck with inspiration, *perhaps I should talk to Kalanthia about it. After all, she has her own names for each of my Bound. I should compare them and see if they're the same.*

And *that* raises another point. When I Inspected my Bound, their species names came up as lizard folk, raptorcat, lizog, and bird. Why were *they* drawn from my mind when all these other creatures were not? Is that another way the Bond has influenced things?

I shake my head again. I have spent too much time musing on something that's largely irrelevant—what matters is if they can kill me and my Bound or not. I focus on the carcass of the paranax lying on the ground before me.

Let's see if this will work, I tell myself as I touch the body and feed mana down to my fingertips.

The first part of the process is much the same as with River. I have to push my way past the barriers of our skin and into its body properly, my mind following my mana. Immediately, I notice the differences with this experience compared to when I experimented with River.

When I first started healing River, I noticed how there was a sort of resistance to my movement in his body. It was actually more of a help than a hindrance, as it lessened the amount of energy I had to spend corralling my mana—it was happy enough to stick near me, unlike in my own body. When I needed to move in River's body, the resistance wasn't an issue.

Here, however, there is *no* resistance. If anything, the flesh I travel through seems to suck at my mana, pulling it away from me rather than pushing it together. I find that it's highly draining to move in the body, making it more of a struggle than I was expecting. There's also . . . something missing. I can't quite put my finger on what, but I feel a lack. *Hmm, worth trying to identify later,* I decide.

Scanning the body is even easier than doing it with River, but there is one drawback to the body being dead: when I encounter an organ I don't recognize, I have no idea what it could be for.

When I did this with River, I found two mysterious organs: one in his uninjured hand and one in his lower torso. The first, I managed to identify as a gland that might produce some sort of fluid based on its thin connections to his claws. The gland didn't feel fully formed, but I reproduced it carefully and in mirror form when reconstructing his lost arm. Based on the evidence and what I felt, I have to guess that it's some sort of poison gland—I don't see why it would be connected to his claws otherwise. Still, it's curious because River's claws *aren't* venomous. I can only guess that it's something vestigial or that only becomes active in certain circumstances. The other organ, though, I have very little clue about, merely that it's not fully formed. I suspect from its "feel," however, that it's to do with reproduction.

At least I was able to get more of an idea of what River's mysterious organs could be for than the one I'm finding in the monkile, or paranax. Now it's dead, there's very, very little evidence for what it could be for: digestion, reproduction, or even magic. I'd have to become an old-fashioned doctor and cut into multiple bodies and compare them to gain any sort of information.

When I'm finished with my scan, I head to one of the wounds closest to where I'm touching with my fingertips. Not that I care much about this body, but it's a good test of whether I can heal damage even after the creature is dead. It's quite possible I'll damage a desirable hide while killing the creature it belongs to, so being able to repair it after the fact would be rather useful.

Getting to it, I start directing my mana into the body.

After a bit of experimentation, I conclude that yes, I can heal the damage to a dead body. However, it takes a *lot* of mana. And considering I restored River's arm, that's saying something.

After all my practice, I've gotten pretty good at judging how much mana something takes. Healing a relatively shallow slice through the paranax's skin from Bastet's claws takes as much mana as growing River's bone by about five centimeters. Which is a *lot*. The bone was the most mana-intensive of all the aspects of his arm, even if his nerve network was the most complicated and fiddly. From what I can tell, it takes so much mana because of how much is lost to the flesh around. The way my mana keeps getting drained is a pain since it means I have to keep returning to my body to grab some more—I haven't yet worked out how to have a steady draw running from my body without returning to my Core to replenish.

After pulling my consciousness out of the body, I tap my chin thoughtfully. Either I need to seriously improve my efficiency so I can make changes to the body with as little wastage as possible . . . or I need to flood the area with my mana so that it's saturated enough not to interfere with the healing itself.

Still, I'm pleased to see that my experimentation has increased my Flesh-Shaping Skill's level by one, taking it to Initiate two. Plus, all the back-and-forth between my Core and the wound has also pushed my Energy Manipulation up a level to Initiate four. I wonder if trying to manipulate my Energy in a dead body instead of a live one might be part of the reason for the relatively quick increase. That might be why Flesh-Shaping leveled up too.

Focusing on other slashes on the paranax's body, I attempt to make the healing as efficient as possible, using Energy control to reduce the amount of mana wastage. It takes a while before I manage to have any effect at all and even longer before the effect grows enough to determine that it is helpful. Still, it's good practice: by the time I manage to improve my efficiency so that the amount of Energy I use drops by about a third, Flesh-Shaping has gone up by another level and Energy Manipulation has increased by *two*.

By this point, I think I've seen enough of how my Skills level up to conclude that repeating the same action again and again *might* make it level up in time but trying *different* actions is a far better way of leveling it up. But then, I suppose that makes sense. Sticking to a single strategy makes someone an expert in that strategy, but nothing more. Trying *different* strategies to achieve the same end makes someone far more adaptable and knowledgeable.

Which means that when I feel that I've reached a wall in terms of being able to increase the mana efficiency any more, I stop and decide to change my method.

Pulling back into myself, I suddenly become aware of a nice scent drifting out of the cave—and my rumbling stomach.

"My stew!"

Jumping up, I abandon my experimentation as I head back into the cave. My stew has definitely bubbled for long enough—the "potatoes" have practically disintegrated into the boiling mass. Oh well. At least it will be a thick and hearty dinner.

Though, I was a little bit distracted when down at the river and never harvested any pondweed, so it's rather lacking in greenery. Lucy wouldn't approve.

I eat as soon as I can, almost burning my mouth a few times at the beginning. Despite the salt, the stew is not particularly tasty, but it's hot and filling, which is good enough for now. Then, lighting a torch, I go back outside, keen on continuing my experimentation. While eating, I was thinking about ways forwards; now, I want to find out what happens if I saturate the body completely with my own mana—if that's at all possible, and the mana isn't being lost to the environment or something.

I start feeding mana into the paranax's corpse, but I realize fairly swiftly that there's a problem. Or rather, it's not exactly a *problem* but a limitation. The amount of mana the paranax's body is absorbing is simply incredible, and it absorbs it as soon as I let my control over my mana go. I'm spending more time ferrying the mana from my Core than it takes for the body to absorb it. Which means I'm wasting time and, from what I've seen so far, it's going to take a lot more mana than I've fed in so far for it to be saturated.

But this is a learning opportunity. It took me a while to learn how to have a steady stream of Energy or mana from my Core to heal my channels; it should take me less time to learn how to maintain that steady stream beyond the barrier of my skin. And it's something I *need* to learn—what if one of my companions has a serious wound that requires more mana to heal than I can carry into their body in one go? They could die in the time it takes me to fetch some more from my Core.

I think back to how helpless I felt next to Bastet as I waited for my mana to regenerate while her life dripped out of her with her blood, and I shudder. No, I need to figure this out. With my increased mana pool, hopefully that won't happen again, especially if I add some more points into Wisdom and level Meditation up a few times.

But for now, I work on channeling my mana even through my skin.

It takes me a while to figure it out, and when I do, I have an unnerving experience. As I feed mana into the corpse, it feels like a vacuum has opened up on the other side, and it begins *dragging* my mana in. While the pull is not as strong as that of the Pure Energy I once had trapped in my hand, the feeling is similar enough that I immediately flinch back and cut the flow.

I open my eyes and stare at the corpse warily. *What just happened?* I wonder.

Nothing has happened to the corpse itself. It hasn't changed color, twitched, opened its eyes, or suddenly lunged for my throat. Fortunately. *Should I continue?* I question myself uncertainly. As I breathe slowly in and out, my heart slows down from its suddenly frantic beat; the last time I had something latch onto my mana and drag at it, I almost died. I'm not surprised that the trauma of that experience hasn't completely left me.

But maybe there's an explanation for it. After all, I've already noted how much less resistance I feel when I'm in this body, how it takes so much more mana to heal, even when I've increased my efficiency significantly. Perhaps the reason for all of that is the same: there is no Energy in this body. Not only does it get lost after death, but it's been in my Inventory, which I know wipes out the Energy in carcasses. Even though I'm dealing with mana and not Energy, perhaps the lack of the latter creates something of a vacuum, which I'm only feeling now that I've established a direct link with the carcass.

If it is that, I say to myself, *then allowing it to draw on my mana until it's full should work.* Though I'm a little hesitant to reestablish contact, I decide that it's worth a try since I was able to so easily cut the connection—not like with the Pure Energy.

Putting my finger to the same spot on the paranax's body, I cautiously establish the connection. Once more there's a hungry drag on my mana, but I quickly realize that I'm in complete control of it. Not like with the Pure Energy, which pulled my resources from me like a reeling machine would a rope, but more like a fish trying to pull on a line. While I'm not trying to reel it in as I would if I was fishing, I *am* able to control the flow of my mana as well as still feel my mana in the body I'm touching.

Feeling my confidence return, I start working on being able to enter the paranax's body with my mind even while I'm channeling my mana—that's something I haven't yet been able to accomplish, but it's important that I do.

Though I'm not really able to control my mana in the other body until I work out how to get my mind in there, I'm able to feel that it's saturating the corpse, spreading out like dye in cloth.

I break the connection as soon as I hit ten mana units remaining and heave a sigh. This is going to take a while. Oh well—perhaps I'll level up in Meditation again before too long. If it gives me another set of increases to my mana regeneration, it'll be worth the time and effort spent now.

When my mana is fully replenished, I start the process again, emptying my mana pool over and over. For all I know, I'll manage to get a second level of Masochist for this—if it doesn't accidentally crack my Core as the notification seemed to indicate it might, that is.

CHAPTER TEN

Questionably Dead

By the time the draw from the paranax carcass is lessening, I've managed to increase Flesh-Shaping by one more level, Energy Manipulation by another two, and Meditation by *three*. Clearly, pushing my limits is having a beneficial effect on my Skill levels. Unfortunately, my hopes of earning a second Masochist achievement have come to nothing—the repeated strain I've put my Core under is either not significant enough for the achievement or there isn't another achievement waiting to be earned. Still, I haven't accidentally cracked my Core again either, so I can't be too disappointed.

Eventually, the paranax carcass is saturated. I count up the times I've had to refill my Core and end up shaking my head in a mixture of amazement and dismay. I've probably put more than ten *thousand* units of mana into this small monkey-like creature that only reaches halfway up my chest when it's standing as tall as it can.

The feeling of drops falling on my head makes me look up and tense as my mind automatically leaps to "threat." Fortunately, the reason is far more prosaic. Rain.

It seems that the clouds that had been hovering over the horizon at dusk have spread across the sky and are now releasing their contents. The intermittent drops quickly multiply. I grab the corpse of the paranax and the spread-out crocodile hide and hotfoot it back into the cave. It's starting to get cold outside, anyway, so it's just as well that I go in.

After sneaking back into the alcove, I sit by the fire near Bastet. River's already in the bed and still, so I don't disturb him. Fenrir shifts a little as I go past him, but I send a quick reassurance down our Bond, and he settles back down. Returning my attention to the body of the paranax, I consider the implications of what I've learned so far.

If the amount increases along with size, I shudder to think how much mana the salamander would require. At least it seems like once I've put mana into the body, it doesn't leak out, at least not quickly enough for me to observe. Perhaps I should test that overnight? See in the morning whether it demands any more mana? It could be useful to know.

Even without learning anything else, though, it's been great practice. I can now channel mana directly from my Core to the body even without being "present" in the body. When my mind *is* in the body, I'm not only able to channel the mana, but also to direct the mana where to go—in this case, ensuring that everything was evenly saturated. In other cases, though, my new mana-channeling combined with the newly automatic healing functions of Flesh-Shaping mean that I'll be able to heal simple wounds without losing awareness of my surroundings, which is a big step forwards.

Bastet is awake, made obvious when she shifts closer to me. Now my side is pressed up against her soft feather-fur, warmth coming both through her body and across the Bond. Closing my eyes, I send my mind into the paranax's body. My mind is able to move around the whole corpse with no hesitation, moving as easily there as it can in my own body. It's even easier than it was at the beginning—although there was never any resistance like in River's body, having my mana being pulled away from me was distracting. Now, even that has gone.

Pulling out from the body, I open my eyes, curious about something. I cast Inspect Fauna, wondering if the description might have changed now that the creature is so saturated with my own magic.

> Paranax?
> Tier 1 beast (Unevolved, saturated)
> Dead?
> Mana: 856u (2u per minute loss)
> The body of a paranax that has been saturated with foreign energy for some unknown purpose. An inefficient mana battery: 10u of mana will be required for every 1u of mana stored.

I often find my notifications interesting, and this is no exception. I'm glad that I used Inspect Fauna on the body again, especially when it gives me another level in the Skill. The question marks themselves are particularly intriguing. Do they mean that I could change the species of something since it's now in question? Or by adding mana, have I created something that is not quite a paranax anymore?

And what's up with it being questionably dead all of a sudden? Could I actually bring a creature back to life through this? Or is flooding a corpse with mana what a necromancer needs to do before they can raise the corpse and make it undead? I mean, I'm assuming necromancy is a thing now that magic has been added to the mix, but I don't see why not. Especially if death can be questionable long after the fact.

Looking back at the carcass next to me with fresh eyes, I notice something else. Despite having been around for hours, it doesn't seem to have undergone any sort of deterioration. It doesn't smell worse than it did when I first got it out, maybe even better. Nor has the body become bloated or stiff. I put it in my Inventory too soon after killing it for rigor mortis to set in or for any other effects of decomposition to begin showing. None of those are showing now either.

Touching it, I send my mind into it quickly. Once more moving around its body mentally, I marvel at both the ease and the amount of information that's at my fingertips. Figuratively speaking, if not literally.

With my own magic suffusing its organs, I can now tell instinctively what each of them is for and how they would work if the creature were alive, as opposed to having no idea when I first scanned its body or having only some idea from scanning River's body. I gain information about how its slightly scaled, tough skin works and how so many things interact that I'd never even considered before. As it turns out, the organ that baffled me before is a gland linked to the production of pheromones for mating. Not necessarily information I *needed* to know, but it's good to clear that mystery up.

I marvel at the information that I sense is being imprinted on my Skill. Where Lay-on-Hands seemed to contain all the information needed to heal from the beginning and I just needed to discover it by leveling up, Flesh-Shaping seems to be more an open book waiting to have knowledge recorded in its pages. I reckon that having done this, I'll now have a much easier job healing paranaxes in the future—if I so wish. And even if I don't end up healing any more paranaxes, any other creatures with similar physiologies are likely to be easier for me to deal with.

If that were the only benefit, it would still be good; more knowledge is always useful. However, I soon learn of an even more important benefit: shaping flesh saturated by my mana is a cinch.

With the amount of knowledge I have about the body of the paranax, changing small elements of its body is child's play. I extend its claws and change the shape of its teeth. I thicken its skin and then change the shape of the scales into spikes that stick up from its body.

Emboldened, I try to take some more ambitious actions. Reshaping its legs to ones similar to mine takes some more mana out of me, as I find I have to resaturate the newly created flesh while fueling the actual growth. Pausing for a moment, I consider what to do next.

I'm tempted to try something more difficult, like enhance its heart or brain or something, but I decide not to in the end; with it being dead, it would be hard to discern if my changes were actually an improvement or would have killed it if it hadn't already been knocked off its mortal coil.

In the end, I do something eminently practical: I remove its hide from its body without leaving any scraps of fat or flesh attached. A few minutes and a bit of mana later, I'm holding the paranax's bloodless hide in one hand. Its skinned corpse isn't even leaking any blood on the floor either, since I managed to close every blood vessel that would otherwise have leaked while I was removing the hide itself.

Even though I have no intention of using the paranax's hide for anything—too rough for clothes, not tough enough for armor—I still practically glow with satisfaction. This will save *so* much time. Now I just need to test if I can do the same thing with a section of flesh already detached from the body: the tier-two nere's skin.

Pulling the crocodile-like nere's hide out of my Inventory, where I put it earlier, I immediately set to injecting mana into it in the same way as I did the paranax's corpse. To my pleasure, it works! It still takes a lot of mana, though. I have to wait three times for my mana pool to refill before I succeed in saturating the roll of skin.

It's a bit longer than my height and about two thirds of that in width, so it's pretty big in area. However, since it's only skin with a bit of fat and flesh attached, I reckon that it actually takes a bit less time to saturate than a corpse of similar volume would. I'd have to test it out to be sure, but my impression is that each cubic centimeter of flesh takes less mana to saturate than the organs of the paranax did. Even though I know that skin is actually considered an organ by itself. It does take significantly more mana to saturate than the skin of the paranax, though, perhaps because this is tier two.

When I sense that the hide is fully saturated with mana, I sink my mind into it. Moving through the skin is a bit different from moving through a complete body. There's no depth to my perception, no sense of there being more to discover. Instead, it's skin and not much else.

However, I'm just as able to interact with it as I was the paranax's corpse. I sense that I can toughen the hide at the expense of its flexibility or the reverse. I can even grow the hide to a certain extent, though when I try doing it, I find the process quite sluggish and mana consumptive—much more so than the same actions with the paranax's hide were.

It makes cleaning the hide very easy and far less labor intensive than the flensing I did earlier. I strip the fat and flesh off it in a few minutes and with a small amount of mana. After pulling my mind out of the skin, I toss the fat into one pot and the meat in another; I always need fat for the continued treating of my weapons. Not to mention for making new soap since I'm getting through my block of it rather more quickly than I imagined.

Picking up the hide, I run it thoughtfully between my fingers. Without the fat or flesh attached, it's more supple, more flexible. But there's still no getting around the fact that it's thick armored skin from a beast that was multiple times my mass. It's still far stiffer than the paranax's hide but is no doubt far better armored too.

However, I don't think I'm going to be able to get around the need to tan it. Tanning is necessary to stabilize the skin so that it doesn't rot. I don't want to go and create some armor and then suddenly find that it's rotting off my body. Though, would leaving my mana in the hide stop it from putrefying? Perhaps. But do I want to test that with the crocodile's hide?

Sighing, I'm about to add the hide back into my Inventory when I pause. What if shoving it into my Inventory strips it of the mana I put into it?

Figuring that it's actually pretty likely, I decide to test with something else first. The paranax's hide is sitting on the floor next to me and is still full of the mana I shoved into it earlier. I pick it up and put it in my Inventory. A moment later, I pull it back out and try to connect to it with my mind.

To my dismay, my fears prove true. It starts sucking at my mana just as eagerly as it did at first. Though, I do make an interesting discovery: empty of my mana, I can't feed my mind into the hide like I did with the paranax's body. Does that mean I have to fully or at least partially saturate flesh that is detached from a body before I can work with it? In that case, what counts as a "body"? I'll need to experiment later with that too.

In the short term, it seems like my Inventory keeps proving that it's less useful than I thought. I'm sure there are ways around its Energy-draining properties, but I don't know them—unfortunately, none of the stones I absorbed came equipped with that information.

Staring at the fire, I take stock. So, I have a roll of nere hide full of mana, which will lose it if I toss it in my Inventory but will spoil quickly if I don't. Heck, it might even start showing signs of deterioration overnight, and I'm still a good few days away from actually being able to start the tanning process.

I sigh. While it's possible that my mana will help stop the process of decomposition, there are no guarantees. And if I let it rot and then have to use magic to regenerate the bits of flesh that are damaged, I might end up using more mana than it would take to resaturate the skin anyway. I'm just going to have to bite the bullet.

Before I do that, however, I decide to see if something else works. I put my hand on the nere skin and focus on pulling mana *out* of it, the complete reverse of what I was doing earlier.

My mana inside the hide is sluggish to respond. It's like it's changed in some way, become different as it's made contact with the flesh. Perhaps it has. I've had notifications that have mentioned "healing" magic; there's no reason why this couldn't have become "flesh" magic. Eventually some mana filters back into me, but I can sense that the ratio between what I put in and what I can get out is even worse than the notification said would apply to the paranax.

Actually, that's something I haven't tested yet. I quickly use Inspect Fauna on the skin, only to get back a result that I probably should have expected: none.

The pulse shoots out of me as normal, then takes longer than usual, only to return to me without any more information. Since I was using it on a piece of the hide rather than the beast itself, I'm not really surprised. It would have been nice if it worked, though.

After I've pulled out as much mana as I can, almost refilling my pool with the fifty-three units I was able to access, I put the roll of nere hide into my Inventory with a sense of resignation.

As my last test before finally going to sleep, I take the paranax hide in my hands once more and refill it with mana. Since I'm only dealing with the hide instead of the whole body this time, it takes a lot less mana—just a bit more than my mana pool this time. Since I sense that I'm pretty close to saturating it after I've dumped my whole mana pool in it, I don't wait for my mana to regenerate completely and just add mana points as they start to become available again.

Once it's full, I put it and the body near the entranceway of the alcove—if they start to rot overnight, I don't want the smell to stink up the whole of our sleeping area. And I will be interested to see whether the paranax body has lost any mana by tomorrow morning.

By this point I'm starting to feel *exhausted*, so I swiftly go to lie down next to River on the bed.

Tomorrow's going to be a heavy day, is the last thought to go through my mind as I drift off to sleep.

CHAPTER ELEVEN

If Black Can Be Luminous

The next morning, we set off before the sun has cleared the horizon. We all have breakfast on the hoof—I pull out chunks of raw meat from my Inventory to give each of my companions and feed myself cooked chunks with my other hand.

Everyone has decided to accompany me to fetch some clay. Sirocco is flying ahead to scout, taking Bastet's usual role since the matriarch is riding herd on the cubs. River paces beside me, his spear at the ready, his eyes scanning the forest around us. Fenrir is taking the rear guard since his nose isn't needed right now.

The journey to the clay seems to take less time than I was expecting. I suppose that shouldn't be a shock—in comparison to the journey down to the lizard folk's village, this is nothing. And my physical stats have improved since the last time I walked here. My physical fitness probably has too, even beyond the stats.

I take a moment to survey the site and check that nothing is waiting in ambush, even using my new inspect Skill to check out the environment. Interestingly, the clay patch glows faintly gold. If I hadn't been looking for it, I might not have noticed, the highlight is so faint. But that makes me wonder. Is it glowing gold because the Skill recognizes it as a useful resource or because *I* do? And would it pick up a clay patch that I didn't already know was there?

I guess I'll just have to keep testing the Skill to work out its abilities and limitations. For now, the coast looks clear, so I head towards the clay pit. The section where I dug before is still obvious—without any water running through this area or rain, it hasn't smoothed over. I figure that's a good place to start.

"Here," I say, handing River a stout stick. A shovel would be better, but I don't want to take the time to make one. Not for this. "Like this."

I show him the technique that I learned works best the last time I did this, and he quickly copies me, adopting the new motion with ease. His hands might be clawed, but they don't seem to get in the way of his grip.

The work goes much more quickly with two of us digging up chunks, as I thought it might. The raptorcat cubs come to investigate what we're doing. Trouble, predictably, just gets in the way, stepping on chunks that I've just loosened and somehow managing to always be exactly where I want to dig. Ninja and Stormcloud are more helpful and both get the idea of digging. Storm doesn't seem to like the feeling of clay between her claws, though, and soon moves away to investigate the bushes instead. Fortunately for my nerves, Trouble is attracted by her interest in a small hole that probably belongs to some reptilian mouse or something and also moves away. That just leaves Ninja, who, contrary to her sister, seems to enjoy the feeling of the clay. Her small paws and claws don't do much to help us, but at least she's not hindering.

Fenrir also gets into the spirit, and his bigger paws do a better job than Ninja's at digging up clay. I do have to redirect his focus, though—not all of the earth in this area is useful for me, and he doesn't know the difference between clay and soil. Predictably, Sirocco chooses to sit in a tree and keep watch. Bastet too—not sitting in a tree, of course, but keeping watch, on the cubs particularly.

What is this for? River asks curiously as the holes we're digging get deeper and the amount of clay I have stored in my Inventory increases.

"I need to line a pit to make it more watertight," I explain. "But in the past, I've used this to make the pots that I use for cooking things." River is silent, but I sense his confusion over the Bond between us. "What?"

I . . . Forgive me, but I thought you did not have an Earth-Shaping skill?

"I don't," I reply. Now I'm confused.

But then, how did you create those pots without one?

I pause my digging and look at him with bafflement.

"You don't need magic to shape a basic pot. Just hands and some water."

Such containers are known to be poor for holding liquids, yet I have seen you cooking with them, River explains tentatively. *Only an Earth-Shaper can create vessels that are both durable and do not taint the liquid within.*

Ah. I think I understand why he's confused. In a society without fire, they would be limited to using sun-baked clay vessels, which do have a number of drawbacks.

"That's because I fired them," I tell him, then give a quick explanation about what firing pottery means even as I continue digging. River follows suit and stays silent even after I've finished speaking.

The life-devourer truly has so many uses, he comments finally.

"It's the foundation of the civilization I come from," I admit, thinking about it. Fire and electricity.

And it makes me wonder more about the lizard folk's society. The Unevolved seem to be held in such little regard—maybe this is partly why. If they're reliant on the magic-using Pathwalkers even for something as simple as crockery, then it's unsurprising that the balance of power is so skewed to one side. Yet using fire is such a basic thing to me that it's hard to conceive of a society where it is unknown except as a destructive force.

Perhaps that's something I can bring to them if I take over their village as Kalanthia and River seem to want me to—an idea I'm slowly coming around to.

We keep digging until I've filled four of my Inventory slots. The holes in the clay pit are significantly larger than the one I left before. I may have to find another area to source clay if I want to do any large-scale projects.

By this point, the sun is already heading towards its zenith, and I'm covered in sweat, my muscles tired.

"Let's rest a bit before heading back," I suggest. River shows nothing but relief at the suggestion, interlacing his claws and stretching his back. I watch the movement of the knobbly crocodile-like skin of his back with curiosity. He hands me back the stick I lent him and then happily lies down in a patch of sun. I'd say that he was being a bit too relaxed except for the fact that we haven't been disturbed by anything in the last few hours—anything Sirocco or Bastet have seen has turned around and made the decision not to challenge us. I still wouldn't say it's safe to relax completely, but with my Core and internal matrix fixed, I hope I'm not as much of a danger magnet as Kalanthia warned me I was before.

My own muscles are killing me too. Even with a better physical condition than I had when I first arrived here, digging for hours with a stick is hard work. My shoulders are particularly painful. Part of that is probably from hours of almost constantly leaning over my digging stick. My hands and arms aren't much better, though, and I've got blisters on my palms.

Fortunately, those issues are easily solved with Flesh-Shaping, and I use the damage the exercise has done to heal the muscles just a little stronger than they were before. The blisters on my hands are turned into calluses too, to protect them from future damage.

Once I've done myself and am sure that I haven't caused any problems, I move over to help River. Although there's less damage to his body—I suspected he was stronger than me, and here's the proof—his sigh of contentment and grateful thanks indicate that he's no less appreciative of the healing than I was.

My stomach gurgles loudly as I lean back from my position with both hands on River's shoulders. Now that my hands and shoulders have stopped killing me, I become aware of just how hungry I am—the breakfast I ate hours ago is long gone.

"Anyone else hungry?" I ask all and sundry. Bastet is the first to indicate that she is, and Fenrir is as eager as always at the prospect of eating. River is the next to hesitantly admit to being hungry, though why he thinks I would deny him when he's been working all morning to help me, I don't know. No, that's wrong. I *do* know, but it annoys me that he thinks I might be like those exploitative Pathwalkers of his.

I pull out a carcass for them to eat from. It might not be the best idea, since a bloody carcass might draw enemies when our presence doesn't, but we'll be leaving here soon enough. Predictably, Sirocco turns up her beak at the Energy-less meat that I offer, but I don't feel too bad about that—she swooped off a few times while River and I were digging to find some berries and small prey. I doubt she's hungry anyway.

For myself, I pull out a soup I made earlier from my Inventory. I sip the all-too-familiar taste with a grimace. It fills my stomach, but it's just so *boring*. Two months on these rations has been a bit too much even for me.

Still, with my new Inspect Flora Skill, I should be able to identify some more plants that are edible and thereby expand my diet a little. Maybe I can even do that on my way back. The time that needs to be dedicated to testing each plant is the main reason why I haven't expanded my diet up until now. At least the salt helps season it all a bit.

While I eat, I check my notifications, suspecting that I know what's been nagging at me for a while.

Congratulations! You have worked hard on your Strength (Power) and have earned a point. Would you like to apply this to your status?
Apply point / Refuse point

Bingo. I smile in satisfaction as I accept the point. Curious to see what happens next, I slip into my Core space and watch. For a moment I wonder whether it's actually a bad idea to go into my Core space while out in the forest, but then I'm distracted by what is happening in front of me. I see Energy expand out of my Core and my internal matrix light up in a wave that rushes out from the center to the extremities.

It doesn't travel to the threads that have their ends dangling in midair and instead rushes around those that spool out and then return back to the center, like a wave clashing against the pool wall on the opposite side and returning in the direction from whence it came.

As it returns to the Core, it doesn't actually enter the crystalline structure. Instead, it once more changes direction and heads out again. My focus narrows as I realize that the wave that's traveling around is becoming weaker; the light it emits is less than when it started. I try to work out why.

Focusing on the wave doesn't help—I only start understanding a little when I start looking at where the wave has passed. The area just behind the wave stays bright for a little bit of time before it fades back to its normal light level. Focusing on one of these spots reveals that the light isn't just disappearing into nowhere; it's seeping away into the blackness.

The process rather reminds me of what I do when I'm healing myself with Flesh-Shaping: taking the mana to a certain point in the internal matrix and then forcing it out of the golden thread completely. This isn't exactly the same, though. With Flesh-Shaping, it's far more directed. The mana surrounds the area that is damaged and works on my body at a cellular level. This is more like diffusing the mana equally through my body, and I can't quite tell exactly what it's doing.

The changes are completed before I've finished watching, unfortunately, but this wasn't the only notification waiting for me. With any luck, I've got another point I can add and observe how it works some more.

> Congratulations!
> You have worked hard on your Strength (Endurance) and have earned a point.
> Would you like to apply this to your status?
>
> Apply point / Refuse point

A pleasant surprise, though not exactly hard to work out why I've earned it—the pain in my muscles before I healed them would certainly explain it. It's interesting that I'm getting a point in both subcategories of Strength at once, though. I can only wonder whether that's linked to how I healed myself, using the painful tears in the muscles to build them stronger and more durable than before. Either way, I happily accept the point and then dive back into my inner Core space.

The process starts exactly the same, and this time I focus more quickly on the changes to the space after the wave has passed more than the wave itself. I watch how the Energy or mana or whatever it is feeds into the black area around the Energy channels, making them all so infinitesimally more luminous—if black *can* be luminous.

But it can, as I remember all too soon. Why? Because there is one area that remains stubbornly black. The area that was damaged by the Pure Energy. As the Energy from this stat point starts to wind down, I pay particular attention to what's happening in the space eaten away by the Pure Energy.

When the process stops once more, I return to my notifications and the next message waiting for me.

> Congratulations!
> You have worked hard on your Constitution and have earned a point. Would you
> like to apply this to your status?
>
> Apply point / Refuse point

I take a moment to be a little surprised that my Constitution has improved enough to be increased by a boost of Energy. The only times it's increased by itself in the past have been after fighting for my life or taking some almost fatal wound. This time it's happening after merely a morning's worth of work.

Could this also be linked to the Flesh-Shaping I used on myself? By repairing the small injuries caused by my hard labor with the clay, have I improved my Constitution, if only in a small way? It would be quite useful to know if, with this point, Constitution hasn't reached twenty and therefore maxed out its natural growth. But perhaps it's still worth playing with in the future—I'm only going on what the System lore stone told me to assume: that I won't be able to increase my stats past twenty except with level-up points. What if there are ways to increase them that just weren't included in the stone?

Putting that aside for the moment in favor of discovering more of what's happening in my Core space, I accept the point and dive back in, navigating directly to the section of void black.

As I watch, my fears grow. The same process is happening here as in all other parts of my internal matrix: the Energy is pouring down my channels, leaving a little in its wake, which then seeps into the space around the channels. That's where it ends, though.

Where in all other situations, the Energy illuminated the blackness even if only slightly, here it does nothing. It . . . vanishes. Perhaps the comparison I made to it being a void is more apt than I thought. It acts like a consuming void, a black hole. Like it could take all this Energy and more and *still* not be satisfied.

I suppose I can only be glad that it's not acting like a black hole in other ways. It doesn't seem to have taken more than its fair share of Energy; its gravity doesn't seem to be any greater than other parts of my internal matrix. Thinking about what might have happened if it *had* been able to draw more Energy towards it than it should makes me shudder, despite not having a physical body to move with.

When the process winds down again, I return to my notifications and select the last one to read.

Congratulations! You have worked hard on your Dexterity and have earned a point. Would you like to apply this to your status?
Apply point / Refuse point

I should be happy, and I am. Four points in a single morning is an amazing amount, and earning them when I was just doing a necessary task is even better. I can only conclude that several of them were close to the point of being able to increase by themselves. I suspect that Dexterity in particular is far more a reflection of the various tasks I've done recently, like the flensing by hand of the crocodile skin and the fruitless attempts at needle-making, than a direct consequence of digging up clay. While I have needed to use some fine-motor control in digging up the chunks, it's been far more brute strength than finesse.

Still, I can't help but also be a bit concerned.

Knowing that the percentage of damage to my soul hasn't changed is a different thing from seeing that damage in action. Plus, I can't help but wonder what the issue with that black space means.

Accepting the point, I return back to my Core space to check that nothing is different this time around, my mind only half on my observations. My theory is that the black space is in some way representative of my body. It would certainly make sense when considering how I heal myself. Healing others is different—I see their bodies from the inside, not their Core space. But that I have to manipulate my mana into the blackness around my matrix is, to me, an indication that the blackness and my flesh are intrinsically linked.

When I touched the Pure Energy, I did so with a finger, and it spread into my hand and would have continued spreading up my arm. As I saw afterwards, that was shown in my Core space as if someone had taken an ice-cream scoop and dug out a chunk from the edge of it all. Now, my internal matrix is intact again, but the damage is still evident in the blackness around the new Energy channels, which is as dark as ever.

Clearly, I'm not looking at the flesh itself—the shape of my Core space is most definitely either a sphere or an ovoid and certainly not the shape of my body. However, they are clearly linked, and what is done to one is done to the other.

This makes the black space even more worrying. I've just increased my Strength stat twice—Power and Endurance—and my Constitution and Dexterity stats once each. As I saw in my Core space, those changes necessitated Energy, or mana, being fed into my body. Yet, there was one space where that Energy didn't reach: my left hand.

Does this mean that although my right hand is now stronger, my left is not? Or that my left hand is more vulnerable than my right? Less dexterous? And what about if I accidentally injure that hand or something bites it—will I find myself unable to heal it? Or does it mean that there's a weakness to the whole system rather than just that one area?

The questions are endless and concerning and reduce the excitement I should otherwise be feeling about having increased three stats at once. Reluctantly deciding that I need to investigate more, and soon, I open my status screen, my anticipation returning despite my worries.

Name: Markus Wolfe		Race: Human	Class: Tamer
Level: 12	Energy to next level: 57%	Energy absorption rate: 26u/hr	Energy towards debt: 85%
Intelligence	36	Mana: 450/540	
Wisdom	36	Mana regeneration rate: 900u/hr	
Willpower	42+8 (+20%)	Health regeneration rate: 40u/hr (-20%)	
Constitution	20	Health: 200/200	
Strength	18	Stamina: 100/100	
Dexterity	18	Stamina regeneration rate: 180u/hr	
Class Skills:		Non-Class Skills:	
Dominate – Novice 6		Flesh-Shaping – Initiate 4	
*Companion Bond		Stealth – Novice 1	
Tame – Beginner 7		Animal Empathy – Novice 7	
Fade – Initiate 1		Meditation – Initiate 6	
Inspect Fauna – Beginner 3		Energy Manipulation – Initiate 8	
Inspect Flora – Beginner 2		Sensation Management – Beginner 6	
Inspect Environment – Beginner 3		Spearmanship – Beginner 1	

Sure enough, Constitution has hit twenty points, meaning that the only way I'm going to be able to increase that in the future will be via level-ups. Strength and Dexterity are only two points each away from joining it. And then I'll have all my stats above twenty—rather an achievement, considering what my status screen looked like the first time I called it up!

Leaning back, I frown. I feel a bit . . . different. I've only just noticed it now after being distracted by questions about my soul damage. It's hard to describe, but I'm pretty sure that it originates from when I accepted the Constitution point and the Energy poured through me. I feel . . . steadier. More stable. More . . . grounded.

It's odd and a little bit worrying how I hadn't noticed anything before. A bit like when a pain has become so normal that we only notice it when it's gone. *Is this the consequence of having Constitution so far below the mental stats?* I wonder. The System lore stone did warn of the consequences of having stats too far apart, but it didn't really explain *why* it was a problem. But now I feel more hopeful, more like I have a handle on things, and less like everything is careering out of control.

Would I have been so panicked about Bastet leaving if my Constitution was above twenty? Would I have dealt better with River in our conversation? I guess I'll never know the answer to those questions. But it does make me eager to get Strength and Dexterity over twenty—who knows what effects leaving those below twenty might be having that I don't even realize.

Maybe I should level up as soon as I gather the Energy to do so again. But then, what happens with the blackness? I've seen that the void is unaffected by the Energy that penetrates it. It's possible that a level-up will be able to pierce the blackness and maybe even heal it, but it seems more likely that it won't. And then what? Is the level-up partially wasted? Is my left hand left further behind the rest of my body? What happens if the rest of me is at twenty in all my physical stats and my left hand is not?

Every instinct I have is telling me that I need to address the soul damage first before leveling up if I want to get the full benefits. So far, I don't see any indication on my status screen that the points haven't taken full effect, but I saw what happened when I was in my Core space—or rather, I saw what *didn't* happen.

All I can hope is that I *can* repair the soul damage. The alternative seems rather grim, given what I've just observed.

Some ideas are percolating in my head, but they will have to wait until I get back to the cave—they're not the sorts of things I want to try while I'm in the middle of the forest, not even when surrounded by my Bound.

Sighing, I stare up through the leaves above my head and catch glimpses of the blue sky beyond when the leaves shift in the light breeze that brushes through my hair like gentle fingers. I'm grateful to it—the breeze prevents the forest from becoming humid and airless. I was particularly grateful to it when I was digging. That was hot work, and I didn't dare take my armor off in case of an attack.

Letting my mind wander as my Bound finish their lunch, I find myself staring at the tracery of veins that I see in the leaves above me. The light passing through them makes the lines particularly evident, reminding me uncommonly of a cardio-vascular network inside a living being.

But ultimately, that's what it is: the means by which the tree moves nutrients through its system. It doesn't have a heart to pump blood around its body; instead, if I remember biology at school well enough, it uses the evaporation of water in its leaves to create a vacuum that pulls the sap up from its roots and through its trunk.

Suddenly, I find myself wondering what counts as flesh. Affecting a tree with Flesh-Shaping would seem to be pushing the definition a bit, but why should it? A tree is as much a living being as River or me. It can't walk, no, but it breathes, it cre-ates waste products, it grows, it dies, and it has a body that contains a vein network.

If I can use Flesh-Shaping on trees, that will certainly make my life easier. Firewood, shaping containers . . . I might even decide to use a hollow log for my tanning instead of the clay-lined pit if I can use magic to help me.

Eager to find out, I push myself to my knees and turn around, then lay my hands on the bark of the tree. Then, like with River, I try to push my mana into its "body."

Unlike with River, however, I find that I hit a solid wall. This isn't like when I first moved into his body and felt resistance. It's not even like when I tried to attack the salamander and barely managed to enter its body at all. This is more like . . . the tree doesn't even exist.

I try a few things that I can think of, but none of them gives me any hope that using Flesh-Shaping on trees is possible. After a while, I open my eyes and let my hands drop with disappointment running through me.

Evidently Flesh-Shaping *doesn't* recognize trees as having flesh. A shame, but not unexpected, I suppose. I guess it's back to my original plan of a clay pit, then.

Standing up, I stretch, looking around.

"Have you all had enough to eat?" I check and receive back various replies. Most of them seem to indicate that they have nourished themselves sufficiently—Bastet even swipes at Trouble when he tries to get some more, scolding him with a sense of being greedy. I get the feeling she's telling him that if he eats any more, his reactions will be so slow that he'll be easy prey for any attackers. The cub sulkily sits back down and looks away. "Okay, good. Next stop: the river."

CHAPTER TWELVE

Carving Out a New Life

Digging up the clay was only the start of the job. Even if I'm not planning on firing it this time around, the more stones that are in the clay, the less watertight it will be. And even if I'm hoping that I will be able to learn how to use Flesh-Shaping to do the tanning for me in the future, I do need the water to be able to stick around long enough to do a proper job the first time. Possibly more if the magic doesn't work out. Besides, it needs to be malleable enough to actually coat the walls of the pit and stick there.

Which all means a lot of work down at the river. This time I make sure not to go anywhere near the water before I've used Inspect Environment and Sirocco, Bastet, Fenrir, *and* River have confirmed that they don't see or smell anything nearby. Not that I think Fenrir would be able to smell a nere in the water, but hopefully at least one of my Bound would spot something.

And even then, I don't approach until I've thrown several stones at various spots that I think might possibly hide something. Reasonably satisfied that there isn't anything waiting for an unwary passerby, I kneel on the riverbank, my mace lying right next to me where I can easily grab it.

Would you like some help, Mas—Markus? River asks, joining me. I eye him, then look beyond to where Bastet, Sirocco, and Fenrir are keeping watch.

"Sure." I shrug. "The more the merrier." It will certainly make things go more quickly with help. I pull out a few chunks of clay and then show him how to knead a handful, use water to soften it, and drop out any stones larger than my thumbnail. I'm not looking for crockery-grade clay, so stones smaller than that should still be fine.

River is a little awkward with it at first, but he gets the knack soon enough, and we work in companionable silence. I have to admit that it's nice to have someone to work beside and not to have to do everything myself.

A pang goes through me as I realize that I miss being with other humans. I was never the most social person in the office, but I did enjoy spending time with people from time to time. Here . . . Bastet is great, and I don't know where I would be without her—probably dead—but she's not human. And River, for all the fact that he's humanoid, capable of language and crafting . . . he's not human either. The differences between our cultures are stark—the fact that he's still struggling not to call me "Master" even when he knows that I don't like it is just one symptom of that. And in some ways, the similarities between his people and mine make the differences even more obvious.

I push the thought away as much as I can. There's no point in missing humans. It's still many months until I'll see some again—and even then, it's clear that Nicholas's world is very different to what I was used to in London. *I'll just have to get used to feeling like a fish out of water,* I decide. Easier said than done, but dwelling on it isn't going to help anyone.

With two of us working on the clay and Flesh-Shaping to ease the strain caused by repeatedly squeezing dense clay, we're done by a little after mid-afternoon. Heading back up the hill, the cubs greet Lathani with great joy. The nunda cub reacts just as enthusiastically, and the four of them start romping around as if they've been spending the whole day sleeping rather than trekking through the forest. Then again, the cubs haven't exactly done much—their most physical activity was walking to and from the clay pits. Only Ninja helped with digging the clay, and she got bored of it after a while.

Not wanting to do *more* work with the clay, but at the same time not wanting to waste the daylight, I decide to do something else: tanning frames. I know I also need to consider how to heal my soul damage, but I can do that when it's dark. Wasting the daylight doesn't seem like a good idea, especially when both Kalanthia and River have indicated that the rain is likely to become more and more frequent from here on out.

I pull out the pieces of wood that I cut while out in the forest with River before and lay them on the ground in front of me. A shadow falls over them, and I look up to see the lizard-man himself.

"River? Are you okay?" I ask, wondering whether something's wrong.

I am well, thank you M-Markus. But I was wondering if you would like some more help?

"No, it's fine," I tell him immediately. "You've helped a lot today, thank you. But you can go and meditate with an Energy Heart now if you want."

As you wish, River responds, lifting his chin. *But do not hesitate to ask for my assistance if you would like it.*

"I will," I promise, holding back my sigh. He *is* trying. I can see that. But it doesn't stop his excessive deference from being a bit annoying. As he backs off, I turn my attention back to the frames.

First, I need to chop the two long branches into four shorter pieces—they're too long as they are now. I set to with my axe first and then my knife to trim the ends down a bit, once more grateful for the magic within it. Frankly, I've put it through hell in the time since I've been here, yet it's still as sharp as when I got it. I haven't needed to sharpen it, there are no notches in its edge, and when I've heated it up in the fire, it hasn't warped or shown any evidence of damage. A good thing too—although I could replace it with a number of tools, they'd be both difficult to make and much less effective.

Once the two branches have become four pieces, I set the thickest as the sides of a rectangle and the thinnest as the top and bottom pieces of the rectangle. It creates a shape that is slightly taller than me in length and almost the same in width. To keep it in that position, I hack at the branches a little more to create notches where the branches can slot together—that should make the joint a little stronger. If I were a proper carpenter, I'd be ashamed of the job I've done here. But I'm not, so as long as it holds together, I'll be happy. Finally, I bind the branches together with bark-fiber cord. I contemplate using pitch but decide not to for now. If I need to, I will use it later, but I don't have so much pitch that I want to just use it when it might not be necessary.

In the end, I'm pretty pleased with my work. I can imagine stringing a hide up here after soaking and letting it dry. Though, I do have one question: where will I put it?

I could hang it from a tree branch. That would be the quickest and simplest option. The issue there is that there are no trees on the top of the hill. Hanging the frame from one of the trees at the foot of the slope would make it more vulnerable to an opportunistic scavenger deciding that half-dry hide is exactly what it wants for lunch.

The alternative is that I could create a stand for it so it could be freestanding. That's probably the best option anyway—although Kalanthia may not be too pleased with me, I would then be able to bring the frame inside if it looks like rain is likely to happen. Maybe I can bribe Kalanthia with Energy Hearts or corpses. Then again, if she's going to be hunting as much as she currently seems to be, she's not going to need any more meat . . .

Well, that's something I can figure out later. Right now, I don't even have the means to soak the hide anyway, so wondering where to put it is rather putting the cart before the horse.

By this point, the sun is already halfway beyond the horizon. The days are definitely getting shorter—even without a watch, I can feel the difference.

I pick up the frame and put it in my Inventory for later and then head into the alcove to make myself some supper. I've picked up a few new plants from the local area that Inspect Flora indicated were edible—I'm rather excited about trying them out and *finally* having something to eat that isn't meat, potato, or pondweed.

Bastet has already gone inside with the cubs, so Fenrir, River, and I follow them in. On the way into the cave, Kalanthia hails me.

Lathani and I are going hunting, she informs me. *We should be back by dawn.*

"Thanks for telling me," I reply, nodding at her as she walks out, Lathani trotting at her heels.

River looks at me inquisitively, so I relay the message—apparently, Kalanthia directed it to me specifically for some reason. "Are you hungry?" I check with him, Fenrir, and Bastet—who isn't asleep, just curled up with the cubs near the embers of the fire. I get a series of negative answers from the three. Apparently, they've gorged

themselves sufficiently for now. I suppose I don't need to ask them when there is
a pile of corpses outside—they all know to help themselves. Still, it makes me feel
better to know they're doing okay.

Fenrir stops to curl up near the doorway, on guard as usual. River lies down on
the bed and closes his eyes. I'm feeling pretty tired too—even with Flesh-Shaping
to heal my muscles, I can feel the exhaustion from the amount of hard labor I've
done. Still, *food*.

Not all the plants I identified are edible, and I'll need to give the non-edible
plants to River to have a go at making some of the potions and poisons he knows.
But that can be tomorrow. For now, I have about twenty different plants that were
all edible according to Inspect Flora. I quickly cast it again just to check which bits
of each plant are identified as edible, not wanting to accidentally eat the bits that
aren't.

Using my knife, I separate the plants into leaves, roots, stalks, flowers, berries,
and in one case, the seeds.

"Right, which one to start with?" I murmur to myself. I might prefer a juicy
steak over a side salad ninety-nine times out of a hundred, but even so the lack of
variety in my diet has been very wearing. If Lucy could see how excited I am over
plants, she'd laugh until she cried.

A memory slides into my mind unbidden, one where she and I were mock arguing over choosing which restaurant to go to. She kept jokingly insisting on going
to a salad bar—just because she knew I'd hate it. To get my own back, I equally
insisted on going to Carnivore's Paradise, a restaurant that only served a token let-
tuce leaf to the side of their massive portions of meat and chips.

Of course, to compromise, we ended up going to a completely different restaurant that would suit both of us. One where she could have her far-too-healthy salad
and I could have my steak and chips.

I find my lips turning up at the memory, mirth mixing with the inevitable
pain. Strangely enough, though, I find myself able to concentrate more on the fond
amusement I felt at the time than the regretful agony that I usually feel about any
of the good memories I have of Lucy.

I wonder why that is. Am I getting used to it? Or am I slowly getting over her?
Has being in this world where death is sometimes only a single wrong move or
moment of inattention away helped me put things into perspective?

While I'd love for Lucy to be here with me . . . No, that's not quite true, my
thoughts earlier about missing other humans aside. Part of me yearns for her to be
here, but part of me is also glad she's not. Lucy was no more an outdoor girl than
I was an outdoor guy. I don't know how she'd have dealt with it. Worse than me?
Better? Perhaps there's a little spiteful part of me that is glad she's not here. I've discovered things about myself that I would never have thought existed, improved in
ways I never thought were possible. I don't really want to share that with her.

Here, I'm carving out a new life. It's a hard one, completely empty of so many luxuries I took for granted. But it's mine. Everything I have now is due to my own efforts and the relationships I've built. Yes, I've been given things and my Bound have been absolutely key to what I've achieved. I've also made mistakes—many of them. But if I hadn't made the choices I did, I wouldn't be sitting here. Though some of those choices were a bit questionable, and there was luck involved too, that doesn't take away from my sense of achievement. So far, I've survived everything this world has thrown at me. How is irrelevant.

With that lingering feeling of victory going through me, I pick up the first berry and pop it in my mouth. I hope Inspect Flora is reliable since I don't have a hankering to discover how to heal a poison with myself as test subject. Although I'm not following the proper procedure to check whether a new food is edible or not, I do take a bit of time over chewing the berry.

It's tart, but there's a hint of sweetness, which soothes a craving I hadn't realized I had. I didn't expect that—it's not like I ate lots of sweets or chocolate before coming to this world. I will admit to adding a spoonful of sugar to my coffee on a regular basis and liking the occasional cake or biscuit. But sugar is so much a part of modern life that my body has had to go on a bit of detox since being here, even though I hadn't realized I was so addicted. So the touch of sweetness in the berry is surprisingly welcome.

I let the berry sit in my mouth for a good minute or so before swallowing. Sitting quietly for a couple of minutes, I actually dive into my own body, curious as to whether I'll be able to detect any problems before I would normally be able to feel them.

As it is, it appears that the berry is perfectly fine for me, so I pull out of my body after watching the digestive process of my stomach for a short time. That's surprisingly interesting, actually.

Next, I pick a leaf. Chewing it, my eyebrows shoot up at the taste. It's like something between mint and basil. An odd combination, but one which will definitely add some flavor to my soups and roasted meat. It might even make decent herbal tea. Once more repeating the slow chewing, swallowing, and then monitoring, I'm glad to see that there don't appear to be any negative consequences from it.

One by one, I test the different plants. After tasting them raw, I then cook them one by one to find out the results. I try both boiling and grilling, just to see what happens. For obvious reasons, most of the leaves don't do very well on the grill, and they don't necessarily do that well when boiled either, but I figure it's a good experiment. Maybe a plant with bigger leaves would work better on the grill.

By the end, I have settled on seventeen that I'm determined to collect more of. Some of them are just very tasty and will easily flavor the food I cook. Others are nice enough to eat by themselves, like the berries and another type of root that doesn't taste like much raw, but when I shove it into the fire, it takes on a delicate nutty flavor. One of the leaves that shriveled into practically nothing on the grill actually disintegrated in the water. However, when it did that, it created a surprisingly savory-tasting broth, which I can see being very appealing as the base of a soup.

The last four, which I decide not to bother with for now, are simply either too tough even after cooking, too dull tasting, or, in one case, just taste *bad*. Like rotten meat, I'd say, although it didn't make me sick. I did bother to cook it just in case the cooking broke down whatever made it taste so awful, but to no avail. Ah well. However, I do resolve to give the first three another go at some point. Possibly stewing them will deal with the toughness, and the dull-tasting leaves could be mixed with other, tastier things while still providing some nutrition.

I also test whether there's any noticeable difference between the plants stored in my Inventory and the ones I kept out of it. Honestly, I can't tell any difference. But then, I can't seem to tell the difference between meat I've had in my Inventory and the meat I've carried separately. Not unless I get a percentage towards the next level out of it. I'll check with River tomorrow about whether he notices any differences in his potion-making.

My belly full and my taste buds finally satisfied—I even had dessert in the form of the rest of the berries—I lie down next to the already slumbering River. I'm tired, but I still have one more task to do before I sleep. Well, technically two, but I think I'll sleep on the ideas I've had for repairing my soul damage. Perhaps I'll get some inspiration in my dreams.

Shuffling a little bit to get comfortable, I close my eyes. This time I don't drop into my Core space and instead try to focus on feeling the earth.

I've been trying to do this from time to time to little effect. It's more than a little frustrating. Maybe I'm going about this wrong? *What if I use Meditation at the same time?* I consider the idea but then just shrug; it's not like it could cause any problems, right? And it might even lead to the breakthrough I've been searching for.

Focusing on my breaths, I slip into that calmer state where I become more aware of the world around me and the connections I have to it. The connections I have with my Bound are the most obvious, like fluorescent tubes leading from me to them. They're not the only links, though. Two other strong connections lead off to the side; touching them, I know what, or rather who, they lead to.

Those aren't what I'm looking for. I remember the vine-stranglers and how they had connections that led down into the ground heading for the Pure Energy. They also had other connections, ones to each other, ones to the earth, even ones to the air around. Looking back now, I realize that I saw a lot more at the time than I was capable of truly processing or understanding.

And it makes sense that there would be connections: although the trees clearly fed off the Pure Energy, they also had to take sustenance from the earth below them and from the air around too. Surely I will have similar connections? After all, although I don't take nutrients from the soil, I do breathe the oxygen in the air. And I walk on the earth.

Trying to look beyond the strongest connections, I attempt to feel the slighter ones. Maybe if I start with the air or something, I'll be able to get an idea of what to feel for with earth. Breathing in, I try to feel a connection with the air that enters my lungs. Breathing out, I try to somehow follow it out of my body.

Not knowing if I honestly have a decent idea here or if it's a red herring, I continue trying, figuring it's no worse than repeating the same thing that wasn't working before. At least I'm comfortable; the crackle of the fire is almost music to my ears, and its warmth is pleasant on my skin.

I feel . . . something. I'm not sure if it's the earth or air, though. It feels . . . warm. Hungry. I'm drawn towards it like a moth to a flame. I only realize how apt that analogy is when I start to burn, the crackle of the fire suddenly feeling like it's all around me rather than a meter or so in front of me. Molten heat licks at my skin and sends a mixture of pleasure and pain through me.

As I breathe in, I feel like flames enter my lungs rather than air. Coughing, I'm jolted out of my meditation, my eyes flying open. I haven't moved, for all that I felt like I was sitting in the fire a moment ago.

Returning to settle back in my physical self, I breathe carefully, wanting to see if my lungs are actually burned. A few painless breaths seem to indicate that it was just in my imagination, fortunately. There are no burns on my skin either.

Checking done, I stare thoughtfully at the dancing flames. I mean, being able to control fire would actually be pretty amazing too. *Fire-Shaping? Fire-Dancing? No, Fire-Taming!* I smile at the thought—as if anyone could actually tame fire. I know that there are plenty of people in Nicholas's world who can control fire to a certain extent, but they all seem to just use it for combat purposes.

I can think of so many other uses. Just considering the task I'd like to accomplish of making metal tools, let alone all the other jobs that would be simplified if I were able to shape and direct the fire, it would be *so* much easier if I could somehow control the temperature of the flames. And yes, obviously there would be a combat use for it too; I'd never have to worry about walking through the vine-strangler grove again, for example.

Plus, if I could learn to control fire, perhaps it could give me an insight into how to control earth too? But those are thoughts for tomorrow. Fire is dangerous at the best of times; I'll need to make some preparations in case things go wrong. Besides, my head is already aching and tired; I've learned my lesson about making important decisions while exhausted.

CHAPTER THIRTEEN

Only Two Percent Away

The next morning, I awake excited yet also nervous about my experience with fire yesterday. I don't think it was just my imagination. I'm not that creative—to be able to imagine fire licking at my skin is probably beyond my scope. Maybe I should speak to Kalanthia? It's not "feeling the earth," but perhaps she has some guidance even so.

Kalanthia? Are you awake? I try to project. I suspect that if I get up, I'll disturb all of my still-sleeping Bound, so if the massive nunda doesn't respond, I'll have to do something else. Since it's still dark, I'm limited in what I can do, but I'm too awake to go back to sleep.

Fortunately, it appears that my landlady friend has similar hours to mine or is easily roused, as she responds to me quite quickly.

Yes, Markus Wolfe. I am awake, she responds, sounding a little tired. It's only belatedly that I remember that she went out hunting last night—maybe they haven't been back for long and that's why she's still awake.

Okay, great. I was hoping you could help me a little here? If you're not too tired, that is.

Perhaps, she responds with a hint of curious amusement, sounding more lively. *What is your question?*

Last night I didn't feel the earth . . . but I think I felt fire, I tell her, then explain exactly what happened. When I'm done, she is silent for a long while, but somehow, despite not actually having a Bond with her or even being in the same room, I sense it is a thoughtful silence rather than one of rejection. Perhaps she projected the emotion to me as much as she projected her thoughts so I would know she was mulling it over.

I am not familiar with fire, Kalanthia says finally, thoughtfully. *My mate controls lightning, which is perhaps closer to fire than earth, but I cannot ask him for advice. He is too far away. My own experience with earth was that I felt it under my paws, its firmness, its steadiness, its endurance. Those seeped into my own veins, giving me patience and endurance for the trials I had to face and eventually helped me wait for the opportunity to escape my captors.*

However, whether that is a good approach to take with fire, I know not. Inviting fire to fill your veins seems a risky proposition since it burns indiscriminately. Earth has never hurt me, not even when I have made mistakes. I have hurt myself by reaching for more than I can manage, creating a mana debt that pained me to repay. Yet the earth has always simply been . . . there. Unyielding and comforting in that steadfastness. I suspect that fire will have a very different character.

She is silent for a little longer, but I sense that she has more to say and keep from interrupting. *You will have to find your own path through this unknown battleground. I suggest that you study fire, that you observe how it functions with as many senses as you can. I do not command the earth; I request it cooperate with me as I feed it mana and visualize the forms I wish it to take. Perhaps fire will be the same; perhaps it will be different.*

I wish I could offer more help, she finishes, sounding a little sad at her lack of insight to offer, *but truly my mate would be of more use here.*

It's fine, I say, trying to project my own feelings of appreciation. *Already you've helped me get further than I would have on my own. Perhaps I'm more suited to fire than earth,* I finish.

Perhaps, she agrees. *Good luck, Markus Wolfe.* With that, the sense of her presence withdraws, the conversation clearly done for now as Kalanthia settles back down to sleep. I turn over what she said in my mind.

It would probably be useful to observe the fire with as many senses as possible. Sliding quietly from the bed, I manage to shift closer to the glowing embers in the fireplace without disturbing anyone. Well, Bastet opened an eye as I got close, but seeing that it was just me, she closed it again.

I can't help reaching over to rub at her neck, stroking the proto-feathers behind her ears. A sense of sleepy contentment comes over the Bond to me, and I continue doing it for a few more minutes while I quickly chew on some grilled meat and a cooked potato to ease the growling of my stomach. Then I remind myself that, as pleasurable as stroking Bastet is for both of us, I have another task to do.

The fire is burning very low, the hours without any new fuel meaning that it has mostly consumed the branches that were on there. The heat being put off by the glowing embers is limited and mostly only detectable when I put my hand above them. As I blow, I see the white ash dance into the air and the red glow brightening a little.

The fire triangle, I think to myself, remembering back to GCSEs at the tender age of sixteen. *Fuel, oxygen, and heat.* The coals still have the heat and the fuel, though not too much of the latter. Add a bit more oxygen and suddenly the fire perks up.

Curious, I slip into my Meditation and suddenly view the fire through different eyes. It's still as bright as with my normal vision, but this time it's bright because of the number of connections between it and the environment. It's actually difficult to differentiate the fire *from* the connections. *Maybe fire is more connection than substance?* I wonder even as I try to make sense of it.

The fire has worms of connection that pierce the fuel around it and feed particularly hungrily from the surface. There are also filament-thin connections that wave in the air, sucking heavily, to ensure that it continues to draw sufficient oxygen for its needs. These connections output heat at the same time as drawing in air.

Leaning forwards, I fight to keep viewing the world through this other set of eyes while I blow. I'm not disappointed in my discoveries. The connections brighten, and a set of filaments weave wildly in the air towards me, drawing the oxygen down into the body of the fire. The fire itself expands a little, the network of links chewing hungrily at the coals, increasing their activity until the glut of oxygen has been consumed.

It's strange to ascribe agency to a force of nature like fire, but I can't help but do so. It is hungry—hungry for oxygen, hungry for fuel. Its nature is to consume, and it appears to wish to do that as quickly as possible. It doesn't care that the brighter it burns, the quicker it will flash towards its end.

I remember a verse that has always stuck with me, though I cannot remember its author. *My candle burns at both ends; it will not last the night. But ah, my foes, and oh, my friends—it gives a lovely light!*

Fire knows nothing of conservation of resources, or endurance, or planning for the future. It is all about the present, the enjoyment of the now. What does that say about me, I wonder, if I'm drawn more to this than to the patient steadfastness of the earth?

Then again, fire is steadfast in its own way. While there remain oxygen, fuel, and heat, it will continue burning. It is not like the wind, which blows in gusts and might change its mind at any moment to blow in a different direction—or not blow at all. Fire does one thing alone, but that it does excellently.

It will always do its best, will continue attempting to burn something until either it succeeds or is extinguished. And then, a fire that is almost, but not quite, extinguished may see a resurgence when the conditions are right. One must only consider how difficult firefighters have to work to put out a wildfire or house fire to realize how stubbornly determined fire can be too, even to its own detriment. That, I can identify with. I'm a stubborn ass sometimes, even when I shouldn't be, even when it brings me trouble.

Fire is both creation and destruction. It burns everything it can to ash, but so often that ash offers benefits to others. It helps me in my attempts to create soap, for example. The fertile ash left in the wake of a wildfire in a forest also offers greater growth to the survivors. Fire is a natural part of the cycle of life, though it's one that may offer great pain and loss in the short term. I have burned so many bridges in my life and the process has been painful. Yet in the wake of the inferno, sometimes I've found a path that has offered a new beginning.

With these thoughts in mind, I reach carefully out to the fire in front of me. Kalanthia's words about fire burning indiscriminately drift through my mind, but I don't know how else to start. If I burn myself, I can heal.

I don't plunge my hand into the embers, despite knowing that whatever burns I would gain would easily be healable. Instead, I lower my hand until the heat is on the uncomfortable side of too hot. I watch the way the connections originating from the fire wrap themselves around my fingers and try to feed from the surface of my hand.

How do I move from the fire trying to consume me to obeying me? I wonder as I tilt my hand this way and that and watch how the connections are always densest on the part of my hand closest to the embers. Lowering my hand a little more, I wince slightly as it starts to burn, the connections thickening and multiplying the closer I get. Lifting my hand a little, I move back into the slightly-uncomfortable-but-not-burning range.

Remembering back to what Kalanthia said about how she controlled the earth, I have an idea. She mentioned offering the earth mana and visualizing what she wanted. Perhaps I should try that.

Of course, that requires somehow making my mana leave my body, something else that I wanted to experiment with today. Pulling my hand out of the fire, I decide that I might as well heal the surface burns I've given myself in my exploration. My natural health regeneration will probably clear them up in ten minutes or so, but I need all the practice I can get with Flesh-Shaping.

With my practice yesterday, I heal the burns within a couple of minutes, using two beads of mana to cover sufficient area to heal the whole surface of my hand in one go. Progress.

Now, how can I practice pulling the mana actually outside my body *and* controlling it? The only experience I've had recently of following mana leaving my body took me into Fenrir's head while he was out hunting—not what I'm aiming for.

After pulling myself out of Meditation, I look around to see that faint hints of gray daylight are entering the cave and my Bound have mostly woken during my experimentation. I must have been in that state for longer than I realized. I also hear the soft sound of rain hitting the ground. I sigh—looks like lining the pit will have to wait for a bit.

Fenrir has already left the cave—apparently, he doesn't care about the rain. The sounds of chewing and snapping coming from outside indicate that he has found one of the carcasses left out there and is having breakfast. Bastet is still next to me, pressed against my leg. She's awake, but the cubs are not yet. Sirocco isn't in the cave anymore, though I don't know where she is—I wouldn't have thought she'd have wanted to go out into the rain, but maybe she left before it started. Finally, River is sitting on the bed, watching me curiously.

What were you doing? he asks, obviously interested.

"I was trying to 'feel fire' since it seems to come more easily to me than 'feeling the earth,'" I tell him honestly. "I'm hoping to be able to control it or tame it in some way."

Is it possible to tame the life-devourer?

I shrug. "I don't know. I'm going to try, though."

If anyone can do it, I believe you can, River declares loyally after a moment. I'm touched, but not at all as certain as he sounds. I feel a sudden added pressure to succeed—I don't want to betray his faith in me.

"Thanks," I say in return, feeling a little awkward. "My problem is that I need to work out how to move mana externally. At least, I think that might help. Certainly, I need it for Flesh-Shaping or I'll be stuck using only a fraction of what I think the Skill is capable of."

Can I help in any way? he asks. I'm about to refuse when I pause and think. Actually, maybe there is one way. It isn't exactly what I was planning on doing with my morning, but perhaps learning how to heal from a distance will enable me to learn how to move my mana externally. Which in turn might be exactly what I need to learn how to control fire.

"Perhaps you can," I tell him. "But later. For now, here—I found these yesterday and wondered whether they might be useful for your potions." I pull the plants out of my Inventory, wondering whether to mention about the lack of Energy but decide not to in the end. It will be interesting to see if he notices any differences without being told.

River uses a claw to separate the different plants, eyeing them with interest.

I recognize most of these, he says thoughtfully. *I can create several poisons and one healing potion.*

"A healing potion?" I ask, surprised. River flicks his tail.

Dealt with correctly, even poisons can be surprisingly beneficial.

"Clearly. Well, if you want to experiment a bit while I do some experimentation of my own, that would work. I'll tell you when I'm ready to work with you, and if you're at a good point to stop, we can do it then."

As you wish, River agrees, then pulls his herb box from the corner of the room. I watch as he takes out a wooden bowl and moves to the entrance of the cave. Holding it out into the rain, he lets it fill with rainwater. I realize belatedly that that's a very good idea and pull out a couple of pots to do the same.

I'm definitely going to have to make sure the hides I tan are sealed from the wet, otherwise all my hard work is likely to go to waste the first time I get caught out in the rain. And I need to remember to keep up the oiling of my bow and string or those are going to take damage too. The downside of having things made out of natural materials.

While River gets on with preparing his ingredients, I stoke the fire and then set some water to boil on it. When it starts bubbling, I pour a bit off into a smaller pottery cup and throw in a few of those minty basil leaves so that I can have something other than plain boiled water. After returning the pot to the fire, I add in some meat and potatoes along with some of the plants I tested last night. Not exactly the breakfast of champions but hopefully significantly tastier than what I've become accustomed to.

Even as I sip my herbal tea, I think wistfully of a bottle of whiskey—but then again, maybe better not. While I'm in a much better state, emotionally speaking, than I was before I came here, which seems odd considering everything, having a bottle of whiskey around might be too much of a temptation.

By this point the cubs have woken up and are playing with Lathani in the bigger cave. I can't help but lean in the doorway and observe them for a bit, particularly Lathani. Although her physical appearance hasn't changed, her movements have. Even in the short time since her mom has started taking her out hunting, she's learned an economy and grace of movement that is beautiful to see. And then she stumbles over her own paw and she's the gawky half-grown cub again.

I wonder how long she'll want to continue playing with the cubs. They're so much smaller than her. Though, as I watch them, I realize how much the cubs have grown too. They're more than twice the size they were when I met Bastet a month and a half ago. They're still definitely *cubs*, but their bodies are changing too, lengthening and strengthening.

I should probably ask Bastet how long it normally takes them to mature, though I'm not sure whether I'll be able to communicate the question well enough or whether her answer will be helpful. Perhaps after she's Evolved, she'll be better at communicating. Actually . . .

Bound – Companion – "Bastet"
Health units: 650/650
Mana units: 50/50
Stamina units: 280/280
Progress to Tier 2: 98%
Lifespan remaining: ~1y 6m

I stare in surprise at the screen. Bastet is only *two percent* away from evolving. All right, that settles it.

"Fenrir, can you keep an eye on the cubs for today, please? Alert me if they're about to get into danger or run off into the forest and you don't think you'll be able to stop them, okay?" I figure that they're unlikely to do that while the rain lasts, but afterwards . . . Fenrir agrees happily. "Bastet," I continue, sending wordless thanks down the Bond to the lizog, "I want you to concentrate on getting enough Energy to Evolve. Do you need another Heart?"

The raptorcat sends a sense of denial and gratitude down the Bond, as well as a touch of excitement. I don't blame her; I'd be excited too if I were facing an unknown Evolution. She goes and fetches the much-diminished Energy Heart that she obviously tucked away somewhere in the alcove and settles down with it not far from the cubs. I guess that even with the reassurance that there's another set of eyes watching out for her babies, she's still not willing to leave them completely alone. Fair enough; as long as she is able to concentrate, it's up to her to choose where she goes.

With that sorted, I decide to test out something I was thinking about while walking yesterday. I was considering how if the soul damage is a void, maybe fixing it requires *filling* it. Whether with Energy or mana, I don't know. But I figure it's worth a try.

And as I swig the final bit of my herbal tea and my stew begins to bubble properly, I figure that now is as good a time as any to try.

CHAPTER FOURTEEN

Like an Overgrown Worm

Opening my eyes, I breathe out a harsh, frustrated breath. The difference in the light quality and the hush around me indicate that the rain has stopped and everyone else has gone outside. I look at my stew and curse—it's bubbling sluggishly and practically solid.

Using a couple of layers of cloth around my hands, I lift it off the fire quickly, looking into the pot with dismay. The best I can say is that I don't think it's burned, but it certainly doesn't look very appetizing right now—a thick glutenous slop. I dip my spoon in it and taste it hesitantly. My eyebrows go up. That actually tastes pretty good. It could do with a bit more salt, but appearances are definitely deceiving in this case. A pity I don't have any bread, though—that would go nicely with it.

I put the pot in my Inventory; if I leave it around, I know that something will happen to it—or rather, some*one*. Then, lying back on the bed, I stare at the ceiling and sigh.

It may just be that I haven't spent enough time pouring Energy or mana into the void, or perhaps I'm not doing it correctly, but I suspect that I'm just not on the right track. There was absolutely no noticeable change to the void even after I emptied my mana pool two times over into it and even put in twenty percent of my Energy store.

It feels like being back to square one with the damage to my Core and internal matrix before I worked out how to heal them. And while the soul damage isn't as directly impactful as the damage to my Core, which prevented me from using any magic, I can't help but fear that it's just as damaging in its own way. River asked when I plan to go down to help his village. Ideally, not before I fix my soul damage. But what if I can't? What if I've got to wait until I'm in Nicholas's world to get help for it?

I'll cross that bridge if I come to it, I tell myself sternly. There's no point in borrowing trouble. I worked out how to heal my Core and internal matrix. There's no reason why I can't learn how to fix my soul.

And even if I can't, lying here and feeling sorry for myself won't do anything. River has obviously moved his potion making outside. Maybe he's free for some experimentation in distance healing or can be so within a few minutes. If not, I can get started with lining the pit with the clay from yesterday.

As it turns out, River is right in the middle of creating a nasty-smelling concoction and seems very focused. I decide not to disturb him and instead head directly to the clay pit.

Starting at a random point on the side, I take lumps out of my Inventory and squash them onto the side of the pit, using some of the rainwater from earlier to soften the clay and smooth the lumps together. I don't start at the bottom, because if there's more rain later, I don't want to immediately create a puddle. I'm not looking forward to filling this pit, though—perhaps a good rainfall will come and do some of the work for me.

The work is oddly soothing, and I feel the clenching of my stomach slowly release as I work. I might not be able to do anything about my soul right now, but at least I can mold and shape this clay. And, who knows, perhaps inspiration will come when I'm not expecting it.

By the time River has finished and comes over to greet me, I'm feeling far more optimistic.

"How are the herbs?" I ask him. His tail sways from side to side gently in his version of a shrug.

The poisons seem to be a little weak but effective enough. I have not yet managed to create a healing potion, however. You wished for my help?

"Yes, I did," I confirm. I wonder whether his failure with the healing potion and the weakness of the poisons are anything to do with the lack of Energy in them. It's probably worth experimenting with it. But for now, I have something else I want to try: healing from a distance.

I don't know if it will be possible. I suspect it wasn't with Lay-on-Hands—it's rather in the name—but it would certainly be useful. Not only does running into a fight to heal my Bound put me in danger, but it also limits how many I can influence at a time. Right now, I'm not able to heal multiple wounds at the same time, not even in the same body, let alone different ones, but I'm sure I'll improve as I continue to practice. Even so, I never want to be in that position again, where I have to choose between healing one Bound and healing another because of the distance between us. It's worth a try, at least.

Eyeing the patient River thoughtfully, I wonder how to do this. Perhaps I need to go back to basics and see exactly how I heal a small wound from up close, then try to work out a way of doing it without touching River.

"Are you injured anywhere?" I ask River hopefully.

I am not, but I can make a wound if you need one.

"I do," I admit, "but—" I cut myself off as I watch River brandish his own claw and cut into the softer skin of his forearm without hesitation. "I was going to say that I could find out if any of the others are injured first," I tell him, a little aggrieved. "And if you were going to injure yourself, you could have at least used my knife!" I would have sterilized it too—who knows what foreign bodies have gotten into his wound.

River looks abashed at my scolding, and I immediately feel bad. He's doing this to help me, after all. Blood, thick and dark red, drips down his arm, reminding me that he has an open wound there. I clear my throat and move closer.

"Let's get you fixed up," I tell him, though shoot him a firm look. "Next time use my *knife*."

Yes, Master, River answers obediently. I stifle my sigh and concentrate on the wound. I did say he could call me what he was comfortable with.

Closing the wound is easy, merely the sewing together of a few cells; he didn't dig too deeply, which I'm glad about. As I do it, I pay as much attention as I can to my actions—healing such small wounds as this has become almost automatic, both practice and the Skill itself aiding me now.

As I get to the end, I realize that there's an odd kind of foreign body in the wound. It's not dirt, and it's not bacteria—both of those I'm used to. This is something different. The body breaks it down by itself before I can investigate it properly, leaving me mystified. At least it wasn't doing any damage. It was just . . . there. But where did it come from? And what *was* it? I guess I'll have to wait and see if it appears again later.

Withdrawing my hand and opening my eyes, I gaze thoughtfully at the unbroken skin where once there was a wound. Thinking about my healing in the context of distance, I see two main potential problems.

First, getting the mana into my patient's body—if I can't get the mana in, I won't be able to do anything. At the moment, I feed the mana from my Core through to my fingers and then past the barrier of my skin and into my patient's body. Interestingly, I noticed this time that there is a tiny thread beginning to form exactly where I always force the mana out of my Energy channels. I wonder if one day that thread will extend beyond my skin by itself. Maybe that's how I end up with distance healing? By growing a thread long enough to connect with any of my Bound?

I find myself partly amused, partly disturbed at the thought of having a golden thread extending from one finger and flailing all over the place like an overgrown worm. Or one of those parasites that can grow to several meters in length. *That* thought makes me shudder and divert my mind onto something else.

The second issue I can see is controlling my mana while it's in my patient's body. At the moment, I send my consciousness with the mana and control it from inside the being's body. This makes me lose most, sometimes all, awareness of my own body but enables me to almost see the wound. Well, to see it with another sense that I have no true description for.

But perhaps I can test the latter even if I can't figure out how to do the former.

"I'm going to feed some mana into you, and then I would like to see what happens to it," I tell River. "All right with you?"

Do what you wish. I am yours to command, he promises, and the sincerity in his voice and across the Bond still makes me feel uncomfortable.

After putting a hand back on River's forearm, I push some mana into him—not much, just a big enough blob that I can keep track of easily enough. I relax my hold on it and wait to see what it does. Which turns out to be very little. It shifts around a little but stays together instead of dispersing as it would do in my body.

Taking my hand off the body, I make a discovery: I can still sense my mana, even without touching River. I close my eyes. The sense of my mana is even stronger like this, and I can even get a slight sense of River as well, separate from the Bond between us.

"Don't move," I tell him, then stand up and slowly move backwards. I lose contact with the mana about five steps away. It's like a tenuous thread between us has been cut. When I go back into range, I'm unable to reconnect to it. I move my hand towards River's arm once more. "May I?" I ask, looking up at him, not wanting to touch him without his consent. When he indicates that it's fine, I touch him with my fingertips.

The mana I left in him suddenly rushes towards my fingers and the connection is quickly reestablished—until the mana is reabsorbed into me, that is, and I lose any sense of River's body. I sit back on my heels and tap my jaw.

So, I can leave some sort of tracker, though my range is very limited. Perhaps it could increase with one or more of my stats? More important to me right now is whether I can do anything with the mana while at a distance. I decide to check.

"Stay there again, River," I instruct him, once more moving a little away after pushing some mana into him. This time I don't go as far as five paces, only taking two steps back. Able to feel the connection to the mana, I concentrate on trying to move it. I close my eyes so I can concentrate and sense it better.

After a few minutes of trying, I conclude that I *can* move it but that it's far harder than when I'm touching River. I can't go "into" his body in the same way as I normally do, so it's like I'm trying to complete a 3D puzzle of a statue by feel—possible, since I can feel where the different pieces connect and their different shapes, but difficult.

I take a step back and then another. Each step multiplies the difficulty; by the time I reach the limits of how far I can be before I lose connection, it feels more like I'm trying to complete the puzzle of an amorphous blob rather than of a defined humanoid statue.

Still, when I return back to sit before River, I'm grinning. That I can do *anything* with the blob of mana from a distance is amazing, especially since I don't see any sort of connection created between us. That said, just because I can't see it doesn't mean it's not there—I'm fully aware that there's probably plenty that goes beneath my radar.

What else could this little blob be used for? Well, it could keep track of my Bound, though it would have to have a longer range for that. It could also potentially be useful for keeping track of enemies. Since Bastet, Kalanthia, *and* River have a version of Stealth, I can easily imagine that we might at some point encounter an enemy that uses ambushing as its strategy, jumping away to hide if its ambush doesn't work, then leaping out once more once we've lost track of it.

Or what about those worm-tailed things that spat sticky stuff at me after the encounter with the monster in the salt caves? I can well imagine creatures that might use the underground as a way of popping out to surprise their prey and then retreat back before the prey can react. If I could tag the enemy, I'd know where it was about to come out and could take the creature by surprise instead.

Of course, that would first require me being able to tag it and then not be able to corner it. But if I can get better at affecting the mana inside something, I could potentially tag a dangerous enemy and then play a game of keep-away until I've been able to disable or kill it via the mana invader I planted in it.

I imagine becoming more of a mage fighter—healing my allies and hurting my enemies from a distance that isn't going to get me torn to shreds. Though I've kind of gotten used to regularly being injured, I won't lie and say it's now my preference. Not to mention that despite all the improvements I've made to my health pool and regeneration rate, I'm still barely less squishy than Sirocco, and she's an easily injured bird. So, fighting mostly from a distance would be good.

I'll still need to get in close to plant the mana, though, even if I get good enough at manipulating it not to need constant contact, I think to myself. *Maybe a mount could help?* I can't prevent the image of a knight on horseback skewering his opponent with his lance from coming to mind.

Master! River's voice interrupts my thoughts. I look at him, immediately alert from the urgency in his tone. *Look at Bastet!*

CHAPTER FIFTEEN

Evolution

I twist around, hope and anticipation rising inside me. There's only one reason I can think that might be the reason for his excitement. The sight that meets my eyes almost makes my jaw drop. I scramble to push myself to a standing position and stumble closer for a better look, almost tripping over my own feet. Apparently eighteen points in Dexterity mean nothing when I'm distracted.

Bastet's Evolving, there's no doubt about it. She's wrapped in a whirling cocoon of forest-green sparks that match the lighter shades on her coat. At least, I think they do; the sparks have completely obscured all view of her body. There's a feeling of static in the air that makes my hair feel like it's standing out from my body.

Everyone is watching; even Kalanthia is standing at the entrance to her cave. The cubs and Lathani are gazing at Bastet, rapt, as is Fenrir. Sirocco seems to realize something is happening because a sudden weight on my shoulder reveals that she's winged her way from wherever she was before. I sense more than see River come to join me, standing just behind my shoulder.

We all just watch silently, the quiet of the day allowing us all to hear the soft whirring that the sparks make as they continue their frantic orbit around Bastet. From the raptorcat herself, no sound emerges. *I hope she's okay*, I think, worry grabbing at my throat. I dart a glance over to Kalanthia and am unsurprised when she senses my concern.

Fear not, Markus Wolfe. This is normal. Since the nunda seems disposed to be reassuring, I risk asking another question.

I thought Evolution meant a Core is created. Why is there this . . . cocoon?

Your Bound has accumulated enough Energy. It has been drawn in to condense into a Core, but the pressure is such that it has subsequently exploded out of her. It is a good sign. I frown.

How so? If Cores are supposed to contain Energy, then how is having Energy explode out a *good* thing? Kalanthia sends a sense of amusement to me.

Many things can go wrong when forming a Core: The creature's Energy channels can be insufficient for condensing a Core, so the Energy does not reach a tipping point, and the creature never obtains a Core at all. The Energy gathered can fail to condense with enough force, and the creature's Core is then formed flawed. The Core can be correctly formed, but if the Beast lacks sufficient control, the Energy will dissipate after the explosion; this leads to the creature being weakened temporarily and not gaining the full benefits of Evolution. That your Bound's Core exploded out at all is a good indication that the initial stage of forming a Core has gone well.

This is why this cocoon is a good sign: the larnatis has controlled the Energy well enough to keep it from dissipating. She is now absorbing it slowly, using it to improve her body and channels. The danger now is that she does not understand her own body and limits well enough to appropriately affect her body. I have seen unfortunate Beasts post-Evolution who reached for more than they were capable of and only half transformed themselves or badly transformed themselves. They never last long.

Wait, I say, surprised. *Do you mean that Bastet could look completely different or something?*

Evolution is a time of reshaping, Kalanthia explains. *The wise use it to reshape their Energy channels and to refine their existing bodies. The foolish try to reshape their bodies into something that they were never intended to be. It rarely ends well.*

I kind of regret asking—although her original words were reassuring, these are not. I hadn't realized that Evolution was so dangerous. I thought it was more a case of being able to do it or not; from what River said, I suspect that most lizard folk either fall into the category of not being able to form a Core or just not being able to gather enough Energy to do so.

Then again, Bastet is sensible, practical, I try to remind myself. She's not the kind of person—beast—who would reach for some dream of being a bird instead of a raptorcat. So far everything has apparently gone well; I can only hope that that state of affairs continues.

Slowly, the cocoon reduces in both density and speed of revolution. At first all I can see is a shadowy form inside it, no details. As time goes on and the sparks reduce further, details are revealed piecemeal.

By the time Bastet is revealed in all her glory, the final sparks are being absorbed into her skin. She stands there looking at us; an undeniable smugness is visible in her body language and across the Bond.

At first glance, it looks like nothing has changed. Certainly not any of the changes I was fearing. The raptorcat still has four taloned paws and two wings, a plumed tail rising behind her, and a sharp-toothed muzzle on her feline-like face.

However, when I take another look, I realize how much *has* changed. She's bigger, for one. Before, she used to reach about mid-thigh on me; now she's as tall as my hips. She's grown proportionately—one reason I didn't spot it immediately. Her wings are a bit bigger relative to her body than they were before, though I doubt this means she can fly yet—they don't look that big.

Perhaps she could glide a little or maybe simply reduce the impact of a fall. Or they could be pretty good weapons: with their new size and probable strength, I can imagine them being rather effective bludgeoning tools.

Her talons are sharper, gleaming in the light. When she opens her mouth to yawn a little, I see that her teeth are too. Her feather-fur is glossy, even healthier than before. I hadn't realized that some of it was looking a bit scruffy until seeing what it looks like now. She's holding herself more upright, a stoop that I hadn't even noticed before now absent from her posture. In fact, she looks . . . younger.

With hope making me almost breathless, I open my screen and navigate quickly to my Bound tab.

Bound – Companion – "Bastet"
Health units: 1300/1300
Mana units: 150/150
Stamina units: 460/460
Progress to Tier 3: 0%
Lifespan remaining: ~37y 1m

Bound – Dominate – "River"
Health units: 830/830
Mana units: 70/70
Stamina units: 300/300
Progress to Tier 2: 57%
Lifespan remaining: ~34y

Bound – Tame – "Sirocco"
Health units: 120/120
Mana units: 75/75
Stamina units: 190/190
Progress to Tier 2: 39%
Lifespan remaining: ~16y

Bound – Dominate – "Fenrir"
Health units: 1020/1020
Mana units: 20/20
Stamina units: 380/380
Progress to Tier 2: 35%
Lifespan remaining: ~25y

I focus particularly on Bastet's new stats, though I pay enough attention to my other Bound to see that they've all made progress towards the next tiers. The first thing I look at is her lifespan. The number written in that section lets me breathe a sigh of relief. I guess I won't be losing her in a couple of years after all. And the fact that she gained another thirty-six years by tiering up is excellent to know.

Then I have a look at her stat points in more detail.

"Your health pool *doubled?*" I exclaim, then my eyes widen more at the next line. "And your mana pool *tripled?!*"

The raptorcat, in true feline fashion, just looks smug. I continue looking through her stats, my eyebrows rising in surprise.

"Why hasn't your stamina increased similarly, though—it's increased, but not even as much as double."

No need. My stamina is sufficient. Mana was not. Health was not. I thought that my eyebrows had risen as high as they could, but hearing the low rumble of a sultry female voice in my mind proves me wrong.

"Bastet?" I ask, though I don't need her confirmation to know that it's her. "You're talking?" It's inane and stating the obvious, but I'd otherwise be speechless. I was kind of hoping that she would start talking after Evolving, but I wasn't expecting it *right* after.

Yes.

I nod absently, still trying to take in the surprises. I hadn't known what to expect from this Evolution, but so far it hasn't disappointed. Heck, actually being able to hear Bastet talk to me would have been enough. Although our communication has improved over our time together, I won't deny that there have been times when her being able to tell me something in words would have been far easier.

Though, I also sense that she's still not really using *words*. Not on her side of things. There's a blurred edge to her words, which I recognize from my experience with Kalanthia. It means that she's still sending directed thoughts at me rather than forming her thoughts into words and then sending them to me as River does. And she seems to prefer short phrases over long sentences if that little exchange was anything to judge by.

But the point is that she's *talking*.

After marveling over that fact for a moment, I think over her actual words and notice something.

"Wait, you said that your stamina is sufficient but that your mana wasn't?"

Yes.

"But you don't use mana for anything . . . do you?" Maybe her stealth uses magic? That would make sense . . .

Not before. Now, yes. Before I can ask her what she means by that, she leaps forward, moving with greater speed and lightness than she demonstrated before. Pausing at the edge of the plateau, she rears back onto her hind legs and beats her wings forwards.

I wonder for a moment if she's trying to fly, if she's now going to use mana to overcome the fact that her wings are still far too small for her body, but then I realize that the angle isn't right for that. She's not beating towards the ground but towards the air in front of her.

And then she breathes out and a billow of flame emerges from her muzzle into the air ahead of her, visible because she's angled herself so that we can see it but also not be in danger. The fire is propelled forwards, licking at the air perhaps a meter or so in front of her body. My mouth drops open. *A flame-throwing raptorcat?*

Bastet's status screen is still open in front of me, and I see her pools of mana and stamina start to empty, their rate of use increasing as the seconds tick by. By the time Bastet stops to gasp in some air and drops back to all four paws with her wings tucked on her back, she's used almost half her mana pool and a good quarter of her stamina.

"That attack guzzles mana as badly as a 1950s car," I murmur quietly, my eyes still wide.

Yes, she agrees, trotting back towards us, her expression very much the cat who's got the cream. *Mana was insufficient.*

"I'll say," I agree fervently. Fortunately, I can already see her mana start to tick up slowly. She probably won't be able to get more than two of those attacks per fight, but hopefully, she'll be able to regenerate mana enough to then use at least one in the *next* fight.

Darting a look around at the rest of the audience, I see—and feel—a number of different reactions. Kalanthia is thoughtful, Lathani impressed. The other cubs also looked impressed but are already starting to squabble amongst themselves over a leaf, the lack of continuing action losing their attention.

River is surprised, though I don't get much more from his expression or the flickering emotions I feel over the Bond. Sirocco, surprisingly enough, is a mixture of fearful and *envious.* As for Fenrir, he doesn't seem to have understood exactly what has just gone on, but he recognizes that everyone else appears to feel it's good. Like someone who doesn't actually get the joke and just laughs because everyone else is laughing, his reaction is a little delayed.

I can't help the amusement from tugging the corner of my mouth into a grin.

"So," I say, turning back to Bastet, "did you *choose* to be able to do that, or did it just . . . happen?" A sense of a shrug comes across the Bond.

I wanted another attack. One that could help us against our enemies. This is what happened. When I knew what the attack was, I knew my mana was not sufficient. And I knew before that my health was not sufficient. I could not improve everything at once.

Interesting. I wonder whether fire became part of the attack because she saw me using it against the vine-stranglers, the enemy that, arguably, was the only one recently that she couldn't do a lot against. Or whether it was the salamander that inspired it. Or . . . Another possibility comes to mind.

Kalanthia mentioned that the Energy Hearts are fire-aspected, I remind myself pensively. *All of us have been using them, and suddenly I'm able to "feel the fire" and Bastet has gained a fire-breath attack with her Evolution.* Is it a coincidence, or is there a pattern here? It's hard to say. If the next of my Bound to Evolve gets some sort of fire attack after heavily using the fire-aspected Hearts from the cavern, it will offer more evidence of my theory.

Though, with that being River at fifty-seven percent progress, it's going to be a while yet. *Then again, we've still got a good month before the quest means we have to go back to the cavern; it might happen shortly before then if he keeps hunting and using Energy Hearts.*

"So, what else has changed?" I ask Bastet curiously. She eyes me, and for a moment I think she's just going to let me stew in my own curiosity, make me wait until I see the changes in action. Then she seems to make her mind up to actually throw me a bone. Perhaps because she realizes that revealing things in the middle of a fight probably isn't the best idea.

Faster. A little stronger. Bigger . . . Younger. So, nothing I hadn't already noticed. Well, not the stronger bit, but the other aspects, yes. Though, that doesn't give me any idea of how *much* faster and stronger she's become.

Then an idea occurs to me, and I look between her and my other Bound. Perhaps there's a way of killing two birds with one stone. Or not *killing* per se, and I'm not sure if Sirocco will want to be involved, but . . .

"How do all of you feel about testing out Bastet's new abilities together by . . . sparring?" Silent confusion meets my question, but River just looks surprised.

Mock battles of cubs? Bastet asks, sounding slightly uncertain.

"Kind of. Basically, fighting but for the purposes of practice rather than killing or injuring the opponent. So not ripping out each other's throats, for example. Maybe you've seen River and I doing it with our spears."

I get a mixture of responses, but they seem to get the idea. If they understand by remembering times when they were younger and playing with their siblings before they were able to start hunting for themselves, I'm not going to complain.

Why do this? Bastet asks bluntly. *We are not cubs.*

"No, but you've just Evolved and have increased capabilities. You probably need to get used to using them in a battle, and the rest of us need to get used to them too. As an extra benefit, any injuries will probably be good practice for me to heal." After all, I've only really healed myself and River so far.

Okay, Bastet answers—she seems unconvinced but still willing to give it a go. Fenrir and River send their agreement too. I turn my head to look at Sirocco, still sitting on my shoulder.

"Do you want to take part in this too?" She sends an uncertain feeling to me. I get the distinct impression that she's not exactly against the idea, just not sure what part she can play. "Well, I would suggest that we start with one-on-one pairings, just to get used to it. Then we can try team sparring and a group of us ganging up against one fighter." I'm musing out loud more than talking to them, but it's probably just as well to give them an idea of what I'm thinking. This is the natural extension of my training with River and offers us a variety of options. "Maybe River and Bastet first, then Fenrir and Sirocco? Just remember, small injuries are fine, large injuries no."

I want to get involved in the sparring too, but I figure that it would be better for me to be an observer at first, so if the action starts getting more heated than appropriate for a sparring match, I can quickly call a halt to it.

Without needing more instruction than that, the two opponents face each other. Though, River does have a question for me, it appears.

Should I use a spear or just my natural weapons?

I consider it. "Perhaps your spear this time. You can go without in some other matches, but if Bastet's improved as much as it seems, you're probably going to need it now." He lifts his chin in respectful acknowledgement.

Now prepared, the two square up to each other. For a moment, neither move, and then when they do, it's almost too quick to follow.

Bastet wasn't kidding when she said she's become faster: she leaps forwards and lands an attack on River before he can react. Although she's clearly pulling her strike, she still leaves two three-clawed stripes down his chest that start to bleed sluggishly. Before River can react, she's pushed off his chest and is already a few paces away, crouching, ready to attack again.

River, to judge by the feelings coming through the Bond, is more embarrassed at being so taken off guard than hurt, so I don't call the match there. He seems determined not to be so easily attacked again, his grip tightening on his spear.

This time when Bastet leaps at him, she has to abort her attack as a flint-tipped spear suddenly appears right in her path. I have to admit that my stomach dropped for a moment there—I was worried that she wouldn't react in time and that I wouldn't be able to fix a spear through her heart. *Maybe this isn't such a good idea. I don't want Bastet's first day after Evolution to become her last . . .*

Then again, my worries came to naught and we *do* need practice. If only because we can't expect to become some powerful fighting force if the only practice we have is in the middle of battle—we're too busy just trying to survive at that point to work on or test out technique.

After the initial lightning clashes, River and Bastet have a few almost hesitant exchanges. Bastet feints at River, clearly not wanting to commit and then have a spear strike her; River remains mostly on the defensive, also clearly not wanting to commit to an ineffective offensive.

"All right, stop there," I say. They both do, relaxing and turning to look at me quizzically.

We do not fight until one of us defeats the other? Bastet asks, clearly surprised. I shake my head.

"Not necessarily. The point of this isn't to *beat* the other person. It's to improve your own technique and fighting approach. So, while I check you both over and heal any injuries, think about what you learned from that little exchange."

They settle down willingly, and I first go to heal the six slashes in River's skin, which are bleeding sluggishly. Though Bastet was clearly holding back, they're still quite deep for training injuries—deeper than any I've inflicted.

"Are you all right?" I check with River while I start feeding mana into the wounds. "These aren't exactly shallow cuts."

I have suffered worse, he says dismissively. *If I did not wish to be injured, I should not have let her strike me. Next time, I will do better. It is more than enough that you are willing to immediately heal me.*

While I feel a little sad at the implications about his past, I can't deny that pain is a good teacher. If he's willing to suffer it to improve, then I won't tell Bastet off about being a little careless. Plus, the danger is if she holds back too much in practice, it won't be much use for true fights.

Curious to see whether I can heal River with the mana left in him from earlier, I move closer but don't touch him. Concentrating on the link that remains intact, I focus on sending that little bit of mana to the still-bleeding scratches on his chest. It shifts under my direction but is very quickly used up. The effort still leaves me feeling tired. Distance healing will definitely take some practice, but not now—I don't want to leave River bleeding and in pain for too long.

"May I?" I ask, hovering my hand above River's chest.

Of course, my Bound responds, sounding surprised—again—that I asked. But I've decided that, unless it's a question of life and death, I shouldn't get in the habit of assuming permission to touch my Bound. Not without some other indication that it's desired, like Bastet cuddling into me or Sirocco coming to sit on my shoulder.

Putting my hand over the six rips in River's skin, I close my eyes and work on healing them. Challenging myself in a different way, I try to heal all six gashes at the same time. It's definitely difficult, but I persevere.

When I finish healing River's wounds, I check my status screen, pleased to see that Energy Manipulation has increased a level to Initiate nine, and Flesh-Shaping has increased a level to Initiate five.

"All right, Bastet, your turn," I announce, opening my eyes and turning my head to look at her. She saunters over to lie down next to me. "Are you hurt?" I ask her, not seeing any marks with a quick once-over.

My chest, she says, rolling onto her back. Sure enough, looking closely I can see a little bit of staining on the feather-fur to the left side of her chest.

"May I?" I ask her, and she bats at my hand with her taloned front paw as if to say, "Get on with it." Grinning a little, I touch her soft coat and worm my fingers down to touch the flesh beneath.

Repeating the usual process, I quickly find the culprit. It looks like she wasn't completely successful in avoiding River's spear when she aborted her second attack. Though it didn't pierce her through the heart, it did glance off her ribs, taking with it a chunk of skin.

I'm surprised it didn't bleed more, but to be fair, I can see that the actual amount of flesh lost was limited, and it's already started to heal. Still, this is a wound I haven't actually tried healing yet, which makes it a good exercise for me.

Regenerating flesh to fill the small hole left by the spear takes more energy than merely knitting existing flesh together, but it's nothing in comparison to regrowing River's arm. The challenge this time is that I have to relearn how to grow flesh since the top layers of Bastet's skin aren't the same as River's. In many ways, hers are more similar to mine, though with feathers instead of hairs. River doesn't have pores in the same way—he isn't capable of sweating. When he gets hot, his scales and spikes flush, which must be his body's alternative.

Ultimately, all that means is that I have to carefully examine the sections of skin and feathers around the wound so that I regenerate the missing area correctly. Then, like with River's arm, I have to make sure that the blood vessels are repaired and replaced correctly and any nerve cells are appropriately healed. I decide not to replace the feathers themselves; I want to know that I've correctly formed the follicles that they should grow from. I'll know in a few days if I have or haven't—by then, feathers should have started poking out.

While I'm in her body, I take the opportunity to scan it like I did River's. I reckon that my increased familiarity with his body thanks to the scan was part of what helped me control the mana I left in his body even when I wasn't touching it.

I do find myself lingering a little bit in her wings, finding their construction fascinating. I've always loved watching birds fly. In fact, I used to be interested as a child when I went to medieval-inspired festivals at our local castle and saw the falcons and hawks. Once I saw a "hunt," and the speed at which the hawk dove on the "rabbit" target was amazing.

Though it hadn't exactly been medieval, they'd actually videoed the event and shown the video later in slow motion on a large screen. Watching the way the wings had moved prior to and just following the strike had kept me rapt for a good ten or eleven video loops.

Now, it's like I'm back in that reenactment as I trace the inside of Bastet's wings with my magic, looking at the joints, the way the feathers connect, the tendons that join everything together. *I hope she is able to fly one day*, I think wistfully. *Maybe then I could join her.* After all, if I can use Flesh-Shaping to understand how she and Sirocco are able to fly, then perhaps I could do the same.

Pulling myself back to the present, I turn to my two Bound. I have other things I want to test with them, ideas that sparked during my healing of River, but they can wait for darkness to fall. Sparring can't.

"All right, what did you learn from that short bout?" River and Bastet exchange wordless glances.

Bastet is fast. She prefers to leap at me unexpectedly, River offers. I nod in agreement, having also seen that. *I chose to act defensively to fend her off.*

"And do you feel it was effective as a strategy?"

River hesitates. *It was effective in preventing her from attacking me, but it didn't offer me any advantage in and of itself. I would have to wait for my opponent to commit to an attack in order to gain the advantage.*

In a pack, you would be surrounded, chimes in Bastet, sending me an image of her working with her previous packmates to surround an enemy. One of them would be bait, and then the others would pile in when the target was vulnerable—much like I experienced myself in our first meeting, when I had to hide underneath a tree for the night to avoid being eaten. I forward the image on to River as I did with his comments to Bastet. He tilts his chin to accept her point.

Yes. Though, if I had the numbers on my side, the situation would be flipped the other way, he points out. *I would also generally have some sort of poison on my spear; even a glancing wound might be enough to make me the victor as long as I could survive until it took full hold.* I direct his words to Bastet, the transfer automatic by this point. I seriously hope that when I rank Dominate up next it will offer intra-Bound communications, as having to be the connection hub between them all is going to become increasingly more frustrating now that Bastet is actually verbal.

"And you, Bastet?"

I could not overcome his long claw, she says immediately. *My initial attack was good. In a real fight, my opponent would be dead.*

"But you can't guarantee that your opponent would be dead in one attack," I point out. "The salamander wouldn't have died so easily."

Agreed, she admits. *That's why the pack is important.* She's right—her attacks work better as part of a pack than alone. *And the environment is not ideal. Always in view.* Again, a good point: in the forest, the environment she is adapted to, she would be able to more easily hide and then attack from another angle, even if she was hunting alone.

"So, any advice for each other? Or anything you want to work on?" I ask both of them.

I think I need to practice a bit more of my offence, River admits, looking at me a little guiltily. I understand why: whenever we spar, he tends to take the defensive role. I don't know if it's because he doesn't want to risk hurting me or can't bring himself to attack me, but he seems to have to really push himself to strike at me. I've been encouraging him to do so, and not only for him—I need to practice defense as well—but here's evidence for him that he actually needs to take my words on board.

"That sounds like a good goal," I agree neutrally, trying not to say, "I told you so. What about you, Bastet?"

She tilts her head thoughtfully to one side. *I could be faster,* she answers after a moment. *I am not as fast as my body can be now. Move faster. Change direction faster. Strike faster.* I nod slowly, thinking I understand her point.

"So you want to train your speed. Perhaps you could practice running at things, doing it as fast as possible, and then trying to change your direction at the last minute or something?" I suggest. Not that I'm any sort of trainer, but I've heard of speed runs, and that seems like it might be a good way for her to push herself without needing to worry about her safety.

I'm not a cub, she responds rather crossly. Apparently, she doesn't think it's a good idea.

Fresh off an Evolution, you are not much further advanced than one. Markus Wolfe is right: you must practice. Kalanthia's voice rumbles through all of our heads and we turn to look at her simultaneously. Apparently, she's been paying more attention than I thought. *You have transformed your body with the Energy of Evolution. It would be wise to discover its limits before you enter battle.*

"Thanks, Kalanthia," I say, inclining my head towards her. Thankfully, it seems I'm not as misguided as I feared. Bastet lifts one taloned paw and licks at it, slightly disgruntled agreement coming through the Bond from her. To give her a bit of privacy, I look away to check on the cubs.

It seems like they've taken our actions to heart and are engaging in their own form of sparring. The teams seem to change from moment to moment, at one point being the raptorcat cubs against Lathani, then the next being all of them against Trouble. A few moments after that, it's everyone for themselves. Maybe that's why Bastet was a bit resistant—my suggestion may have seemed to be exactly what's going on there.

"All right," I say, looking at Fenrir. "You and Sirocco are up next, if you're okay with that?" I check with Sirocco, still on my shoulder. She sends me a sense of uncertain agreement. "You saw what it was like before. We're not aiming to kill or even subdue the other in the spar; it's an opportunity for you to see how effective your attacks are. Just please try not to damage each other too much, okay?" I say, looking from one to the other, my short-distance eyesight getting a workout with the bird. "No eye gouges or anything like that."

Both of them send me a sense of agreement, Sirocco almost reluctant where Fenrir is eager. I find myself curious to see how this battle goes.

CHAPTER SIXTEEN

What Did You Learn?

Sirocco takes off from my shoulder and dives at the lizog. Fenrir jumps at her, but she banks her wings and flies out of range before his teeth can snap closed on any part of her.

The ensuing few minutes become even more of a stalemate than the previous battle was, only with one party being airborne and the other earthbound. Sirocco swoops in at regular intervals to land a few scratches across Fenrir's back, and a couple of times he pulls out one or two of her feathers as his jaws close quickly enough.

By the end of the first few minutes, it becomes clear who the winner would be if this were a battle to the death: Sirocco's lack of stamina begins to tell, her dodges happening increasingly slowly. Eventually, she flaps to land on the ground, and I call an end to the spar before Fenrir can lunge to bite her. However, in a true battle, Sirocco would have just left Fenrir far behind long ago.

"All right, that's enough," I say again, and they stop. Fenrir sits. He looks rather pleased with himself, either because he feels that he's the de facto victor here or just because he's enjoying this. "Right, let me check you both out." I check my Bound stats to see which one is the most in need of healing. Although Fenrir has lost more actual health, his pool is so much larger than Sirocco's that he's actually lost a much smaller fraction of his overall pool. I decide to help Sirocco first.

Healing Sirocco is much like healing Bastet—they have the same feather follicles to be aware of. And though Sirocco's body is much smaller, when I feed my consciousness into it, I don't notice much difference.

Honestly, most of the damage is aesthetic: more of her feathers have been pulled out than skin ripped, let alone anything more. Since I don't need to reform the feather follicles, this time I experiment a bit with actually creating the feathers. I find that I can do it two different ways. The first is just creating a feather in the same way as I created bones and claws for River: using another feather as a blueprint and forming it out of my mana.

The other way is by stimulating the feather follicle. That one is actually more interesting than the first method. I can see how the feather follicle draws on the body's resources, even if in a fractional way, and forms the feather from the top downwards, the growth of the barbs pushing the feather out of her follicle. I experiment a bit with how much I can impact the speed of the feather growth and find that there's a limit: I can make a feather grow visibly but not just appear fully formed in the blink of an eye. Not with the second method, anyway.

Given that we're still supposed to be sparring, I decide reluctantly to experiment with that a bit more later. For now, I do a scan of her body too, largely because I'm curious about the differences between her wings and Bastet's—there are quite a few, actually. Perhaps it's similar to how there are significant differences between my skeletal structure and River's even though we're both bipedal humanoids. The structure of her back legs is interesting too. They're something between feet and a tail with no gripping power but the ability to stabilize her when she's perched, whether on the tree or the ground. I look forward to studying them more later.

As I pull out of Sirocco's body, I leave some mana in there too. I can now feel an extra connection with three of my Bound. Fenrir's the only one missing, though not for long.

I dive into the lizog's body and notice that the numerous scratches left on him by Sirocco's claws take longer to heal than the bird's wounds, merely because there are far more of them. They're also rather superficial, though, which makes them a good workout for healing multiple wounds at the same time. Also, I notice an interesting similarity between River and Fenrir's bodies—are they more closely related than Bastet or Sirocco are to them? While their skeletal structure is, of course, very different, they both have similar extra organs or glands in their hands and paws.

Finished healing Fenrir, I return to the question of sparring.

"All right, same question as Bastet and River answered: what did you learn from that bout?" I'm aware that it may be more difficult to do this with the two nonverbal members of my team, but I'm going to try at least.

Fenrir sends across a sense of confusion at the question, but Sirocco seems surprisingly thoughtful. After a moment, she manages to express a sense of frustration that she couldn't seem to do any damage and that she ran out of energy too quickly.

"Your stamina pool is not quite the lowest among us—that's mine—but your attacks seem very stamina heavy." She sends me a series of pictures of looking at a beast from above while sitting in the trees, then swooping down on it, and then sitting back in the trees.

"That's true," I acknowledge. "In the forest, you can use the trees to reduce your use of stamina; here you had to stay in the air all the time. However, we can't guarantee that we'll always be fighting in a forest or a place with lots of perches above. If we can find some way of either increasing your stamina pool or using attacks that are less stamina heavy, then that would be good for when we're in a less ideal environment."

Honestly, I'm going to leave her to think about that herself. I have no idea what she might be capable of doing and feel that any more input from me might be more detrimental than helpful. Still, she's sending a thoughtful feel down the Bond, so perhaps my words have helped.

Turning to Fenrir, I look at him pensively.

"You dealt with Sirocco's attacks very well and were more likely to win that fight just by your better endurance. But can you think of anything that could have been better?" The lizog is very obviously struggling with the advanced concepts of how he could have changed something that is already past and unchangeable, so I try to rephrase it. "If you face Sirocco again in the future, what could help you win more quickly?" This seems to work better for him, as he's clearly thinking about something.

A few moments later he sends me a few images with a questioning feel about them. They depict Fenrir snapping his jaws together just short of Sirocco's tail feathers and then another one with him actually closing his jaws on Sirocco herself.

"You . . . Are you saying you want to be quicker? Like Bastet?" I ask, trying to decipher his message. He sends me enthusiastic agreement. Fair point: he's strong, tanky, and has powerful jaws, but he's not the fastest. Lizogs in general aren't—that's why Bastet and I had enough time to prepare a trap for them the first time we encountered a pack, feeding on the remains of her family.

"Maybe you can practice speed runs with Bastet?" I suggest, not sure if it will help or even if it's a good idea. But knowing how poorly qualified I am as a personal trainer, I'm not going to argue with him. He's identified a possible weakness in his attack style; it's up to him to decide later if that's a good route for him to follow.

Post-spar analysis done, I feel a rising sense of anticipation. Sparring with River is familiar now, but it never gets old.

"River, let's spar for a bit together. Maybe you can practice some of that offence?"

As you wish, River assents a little reluctantly—unsurprisingly, he's not keen on the idea, but since he's the one who raised it, he can't argue. We move to face each other, each of us with a spear. I wait for him to attack, as always trying to focus on the way I hold my spear and position my body. I've already seen plenty of progress, but I know that I still have far to go.

"Let's do this really slowly," I say, looking up at River. "I want to focus on technique just as much as you do. So, half speed? Or even less, perhaps?"

Very well, River agrees, a hint of relief in his voice.

For all his reluctance, I have to admit that when we get going, he does actually put some effort into attacking. It's just as good practice as I thought it would be—I need to block and deflect in a way that I haven't yet had the occasion to use.

As we continue sparring, varying our speeds from bout to bout, I notice River relaxing more and more into it. Perhaps he's stopped being worried that he's going to accidentally hurt me the longer we go without incident. In the end, we even have a proper sparring match, one that leaves me disarmed after a few minutes of frantic fighting.

"Well done," I tell River, clapping him on the shoulder. He looks more than a little shocked and a bit alarmed as he stares at the spear lying on the ground. "I definitely need to practice my defense," I admit ruefully. I'm too used to fighting creatures that only use their natural weapons. Disarming is usually a lot more literal in that situation. But if I'm going to fight other lizard folk, I might end up needing to fight against spears and clubs and who knows what else. *I'll need to find that out from River*, I decide.

You're not . . . angry? River asks, sounding more than a little afraid. I frown, surprised that we seem to be back to that after all the progress so far.

"Of course not. I wanted you to fight well so that we both benefit. Why would I be angry that you did just that?"

I . . . beat you. I . . . Did I hurt you?

"I'm fine," I tell him immediately. It's the truth. I wouldn't count small abrasions on my hands as injuries—they'll only take a moment to heal with Flesh-Shaping. "Are *you* okay?" He seems far more shaken than I was expecting.

River looks up at me for a long moment, his eyes searching. Then he lifts his chin for a longer moment than I was expecting.

I am well. Thank you, Master, he murmurs, his voice full once more of that awe that makes me deeply uncomfortable.

"Okay, good. Another round?" I offer, wanting to change the subject *immediately*.

CHAPTER SEVENTEEN

Choose My Battles

B y midday, it's time for lunch. We finished sparring ages ago, and I've been working on my clay pit ever since. I've made some good progress and am hoping to finish lining the pit by mid-afternoon. After that, it might be worth going out into the forest. I want to get more of those plants that I identified as both tasty and good for me—especially the berries. And we could probably do with collecting more meat for my Bound. If I can avoid putting it in my Inventory, my companions will be able to benefit more from the Energy within it.

Briefly glancing at my other Bound, I see that the cubs are curled up with Bastet, who, in turn, is curled around an Energy Heart. She's consolidating her Evolution, I have to guess.

I was vaguely aware of her grudgingly practicing speed runs earlier while I was sparring with River. I did notice her mood improve as time went on—I think she got a bit into it when the cubs started joining in. Maybe she was able to convince herself that she was doing it for the sake of the cubs. Or maybe she just found it was helping. I don't know—I'm probably humanizing her motivations too much again.

Fenrir also joined in, and Sirocco was doing . . . something. I'm not sure what it was, but it involved a whole lot of aerial maneuvers. By this time, both of them have stopped too and are absorbing Energy Hearts. Interestingly, so is Lathani.

"It's safe for her?" I check quietly with Kalanthia, walking over to her even as I clean my hands with a wet rag. She looks at me as if to ask why I'm even questioning whether she'd allow her cub to do something unsafe. Well, more unsafe than necessary for a young predator who needs to grow up. "I know it must be," I respond defensively. "I'm just a little surprised. And curious."

We have been hunting together. The Energy from her kills has been improving her Energy channels. Some use of these natural Cores will help reinforce the channels that are already there. She will need to do more hunting soon to continue expanding her Energy channel network.

"So, Energy from kills expands the channels but Energy from Cores reinforces them?" I ask, interested.

It is not so clear-cut as that, but yes, as a broad swipe, we could say that.

Interesting. I don't think it works exactly like that for me, but maybe it does? I should see what happens when I kill something, if the Energy starts carving new channels or not. And when I absorb an Energy Heart, I know that the Energy rushes directly towards my Core, but is it reinforcing the channels as it passes through them?

"I'm thinking about going out with my Bound later. Do you think she'd like to come with us?" I ask Kalanthia. I feel like I haven't spent much time with Lathani since we came back from River's village. Either I've been busy, or she's been hunting—or sleeping to recover from hunting. It would be nice to be out in the forest again, this time without the fear of Kalanthia's reaction when we return home.

I don't see why not, the massive feline responds with a thoughtful rumble. *It will be good for her to experience hunting without me.*

"All right, good. I'm planning on going about mid-afternoon. Does that work fine for you?"

I have no other intentions for that time, Kalanthia responds calmly. *I shall speak to Lathani.* With that, she puts her head down on her paws and closes her eyes pointedly. The conversation is over.

I almost roll my eyes at her high-handedness, but in the end, I just walk off to get some lunch. Kalanthia is a true cat—only interested in interacting when *she* wants it.

By mid-afternoon, I'm indeed finished my pit. I've smoothed the sides as much as I can, trying to avoid any cracks. I know that it's likely to crack up a bit as it dries—I plan to cover up or fill in any cracks that appear, but the proof will be when I fill the basin with water. Or, ideally, when the rain fills it. It's a big pit, so I shouldn't need to make it too deep to soak my skins.

"All right, everyone, who's coming into the forest with me?" I ask.

Fenrir happily jogs over, his tail swaying behind him with every step. Sirocco hesitates for a moment and then sends me a slightly regretful rejection. She sends a picture of the Energy Heart. I send her a response of understanding. If she feels like absorbing an Energy Heart is more important for her than coming out hunting, that's fine.

I'll come, Bastet says. *I'll bring the cubs.*

Would you like me to come, Master? River asks. *Or would you prefer that I stay and work on the poisons?*

I consider the question.

"Would it help to get fresh ingredients?" I check with him. He tilts his head consideringly.

Most likely, yes, he admits.

"Then come along."

I'm coming too! exclaims Lathani, bouncing towards us. *Mother says I can,* she adds almost defiantly.

"I know, we discussed it earlier," I reply, taking the wind out of her sails. She stops bouncing and looks sulky. What's *that* about? I eye her warily. I hope that she's going to behave. "Remember, we're going into the forest. This isn't time to play with the raptorcat cubs," I warn her.

I know, Lathani replies scathingly, sending me a superior look. *Mother has taught me* all *about the forest.*

I look at her silently for a long moment. I wonder if it's just me or if there's something . . . off about her. I wonder whether inviting her was a good idea or not, then push the question to one side. I've already offered—it would be mean to change my mind now just because I feel that Lathani's being a little weird. It's probably just that she's just more confident than before, now she's been hunting with her mother.

"That's good," I say finally, neutrally. "But make sure you pay attention at all times—an ambush can come from any direction."

I know that too, Lathani says slightly dismissively, then bounds off to rub heads with Bastet and the three raptorcat cubs—well, juveniles, considering their increased sizes.

We head down into the forest and carefully cross the river. As we move deeper into the forest, I use Inspect Environment to keep an eye out for useful items and then Inspect Flora to check whether plants are edible or not. River works on collecting plants too, though his are probably a lot more lethal than mine. Then again, perhaps he's looking for ingredients for healing potions too.

The rest of our group spreads out around us, keeping their eyes out in all directions. It's peaceful—I don't sense the presence of a single enemy. I'm not sure whether to be happy about that or not. On the one hand, a peaceful afternoon collecting plants is a nice way to pass the time. On the other, I did want to collect some meat.

An hour passes similarly, and Lathani is starting to get restless.

Where is the prey? Mother would have found it already, she complains.

"We're not specifically looking for beasts to hunt," I tell her, this time actually rolling my eyes. "We're collecting resources, and if beasts attack, we'll fight back."

That's boring, she whines. *I thought we were going hunting.*

I stop and cross my arms, staring straight at her.

"Lathani, if you don't like the way we do things, don't come next time. But right now, you're with us, so behave. Or next time we won't even invite you."

She makes a displeased yowling sound. *It's so much more fun with Mother!* She slinks off, clearly annoyed. I sigh. I should have listened to my instincts and not been so concerned about being the "bad guy." I knew *something* wasn't right. And now I have an additional worry to add to the usual concerns of being in the forest.

We continue looking around, pulling up useful plants every time we see them. It's a while later when I spot something that makes me very happy: a whole bush laden with the same berries I had before. I eagerly go over to harvest them. River approaches me and bends down to look at the roots of the bush.

He makes a pleased grunt.

"What have you found?" I ask him, shifting so I can see what's grabbed his attention.

Click-grunt-flash-of-green, he replies, incomprehensibly. Fortunately, he holds it up so I can see. It's a black beetle of some sort, its carapace iridescent where the light strikes it. Curious, I cast Inspect Fauna.

Melanthis
Tier 1 beast (Unevolved)
Special abilities: None detected
Health: 25u
Mana: 10u
Minimum Willpower recommended to Dominate without other impacting factors: 3
A type of insect, melanthis spend their lives eating the roots of various plants. They are capable of eating roots widely considered to be toxic due to their ability to extract and store toxins separately from their digestion system. They excrete toxins eventually, but this process takes several days. This consequently makes them unpopular prey, as it is impossible for most to detect if they have consumed toxic material in recent meals.

An interesting insect. A bit like poison dart frogs, though less brightly colored. I'm pleased with the amount of information Inspect Fauna gave me too—perhaps it's due to leveling it up a bit.

"Are they useful in potions?" I ask River.

Not immediately, but my Mas—Pathwalker Herbalist sent me out into the forest for them multiple times. They offer a much purer and more powerful version of a toxin if they are fed the plant you wish to use in a potion. But since it's necessary to crack them open to extract the toxin, they can only be used once.

A little disturbing, perhaps, but no different than people using insects to make dye. Or hunting. We kill other beasts for food, so why not melanthis beetles for potions?

Either way, River happily pulls out a container from his wooden box and starts packing as many beetles into it as he can. By the end, the beetles within the container are barely able to move—I'm impressed by River's deftness in managing to stop them escaping while he fits the lid back on. He wraps it in a vine from a nearby tree and then tucks it back into the box that he's been carrying on his back.

In the meantime, I harvest as many ripe berries as I can. I consider taking a cutting of the plant, but since I'm not going to be here in a year's time, I decide that there isn't much point in trying my hand at farming.

Finished, I look around, making sure I've spotted everyone. Bastet is near the three cubs, who got bored a while ago and started play fighting. Fenrir is our sentry—needed, considering how distracted the rest of us have been.

Where's Lathani? I wonder with a thrill of alarm. I continue looking around with more urgency. I can't see her, but she's been learning how to be stealthier. Maybe she's hiding.

"Lathani?" I call quietly, not wanting my voice to carry too far.

Bastet, Fenrir, and River have picked up on my alarm. Fenrir sends me a picture of Lathani going off into the bushes. I curse and move towards where the lizog saw her last.

"Come on," I tell everyone. "Kalanthia will kill us if we lose her cub." Never mind that Lathani is the one who's wandered off.

Fenrir takes point, following Lathani's scent. Fortunately, she hasn't gone too far, and my heart finally calms down when I see her poking curiously with her paw at a burrow.

"Lathani! Don't do that!" I reprimand her. She looks up at me, her ears pulled back and a slight snarl on her face.

You're not my mother! You can't tell me what to do!

"While we're in the forest together, you're my responsibility, so hell *yes* I can tell you what to do!" I volley back at her. Lathani's lips rise higher, and she starts growling. For the first time, I wonder if she might actually be a *danger*—and one I can't deal with as I would any other type of threat. I'm abruptly glad that River has followed close behind me. I might need his help to restrain her if she decides to actually attack me.

But before the situation can devolve any further, a sense of urgency suddenly hits my mind. I feel something moving quickly towards me and I duck, only for the ball of mud to hit River instead. I quickly look at where it came from, and my eyes narrow. Fantastic timing! Not. Well, perhaps it's time for another rematch. Though, if these are the same ones I fought before, they've had some additions.

"We meet again," I mutter darkly at our new assailants, even as I shoot a hard look at Lathani. "We're being attacked. Find cover." The nunda juvenile doesn't move. "Now, Lathani!" I order, then stagger as a ball of mud strikes my shoulder.

I want to fight! Lathani actually *argues* with me. Completely done with her attitude, my hand lashes out and grabs her by the scruff of the neck. She's surprised by my actions and barely resists as I drag her towards the bushes, where I don't see any of the velociraptors waiting. "River, grab their attention," I order the lizard-man quickly. Without a word, he does exactly that, roaring loudly as he runs towards the greatest concentration of feathered velociraptors.

We're surrounded by them, both on the ground and in the trees. The ones on the ground are bigger, but the ones in the trees are capable of launching sticky mud towards their targets. With River's diversion, that's him.

He succeeds in getting every eye fixed on him, and I quickly take advantage of that to duck into the bushes. Releasing Lathani, I glare at her.

"Obey orders or stay here," I murmur to her, pressing as much intensity into my voice as I can. I can only hope that she will pay attention this time, but I don't have much hope given her attitude so far and the fact that she's gone stiff with anger. But I can't pay more attention to her—these beasts are too dangerous to take lightly. We could try to escape, but they would pursue us, and our retreating backs would be easy targets. Besides, we need the meat, and these will do nicely once they're dead.

I Fade into the background. Temporarily hidden, I do a quick recon to get an idea of the situation. The velociraptors have mostly surrounded River by this point, both ground and tree-bound attackers shifting to get around him.

My Bound is doing well; the spear that is never far from his clawed paws thrusts at them skillfully. The velociraptors have clearly learned that it's dangerous: after two were left bleeding heavily from well-aimed thrusts, the rest of the ground attackers are being much more careful.

In fact, I consider with my eyes narrowed, *the velociraptors may actually be using the ground attackers as a distraction to allow the tree-bound ones to slow him down with their mud.* Where the mud is coming from, I don't know; last time I was too focused on defending myself to ask the question, but now I can see that the velociraptors in the trees are just . . . producing it. After a short period of making motions like they're about to vomit, the mud appears in their mouths. They then pull their heads back briefly before pecking forwards and spitting the stuff. Yuck.

I know from experience that it'll take a bit of time for the mud to start to have an effect on my Bound, especially since his Strength is probably significantly higher than mine was when I was last ambushed by these creatures. But he could still do with some help.

Fenrir, go help River, I order, hoping that Fenrir will hear my thoughts well enough. Apparently he does, as he emerges from where he was hiding and joins River. The lizard-man takes his new partner's assistance in stride, and they soon get a good strategy going. While River distracts the velociraptors, Fenrir lunges forwards to grab one and pin it down. River then uses his spear on the downed beast, Fenrir releases it, and they repeat. I suspect that I'm seeing the strategy they've used when hunting together—it looks too well practiced to be a new invention.

Of course, that doesn't deal with the beasts in the trees, but that's my job. I feel like I've got a plan that should work—it's simple enough, at least. I pull back the string on my bow and quickly release an arrow at one of the ranged velociraptors. It hits dead-on, and the raptor is dead before it lands heavily on the ground. I freeze as the dead velociraptor's companions turn around and look in my direction. I focus on staying hidden, staying invisible. The raptors scan the area, but when they turn back to River, I figure they haven't seen me. Excellent.

Bastet, how are you at climbing trees? I ask, sending my thoughts at her.

It is not my preference, but I can, she answers simply.

Okay, then you take the velociraptors on the right side, and I'll take those on the left, I instruct, indicating with an image what I mean by "left" and "right." She sends me wordless assent, and I sense her moving away. When the first velociraptor is sent falling to the ground, Bastet becomes a target. My heart is in my mouth as I watch balls of mud fly towards her, but she turns out to be adept at shoving other velociraptors into the path of some of their allies' attacks and dodging the rest.

Once a velociraptor falls to the ground, either from Bastet's actions or because of friendly fire, the three raptorcat cubs leap on the downed predator and are surprisingly vicious as they make short work of it.

Relieved that that side of the battle is going well enough, I turn to my own side of the battle and work on picking the raptors off there. By shifting from bush to bush, I vary the angle the arrows are coming from and prevent the velociraptors from escaping.

With the attacks on the tree-based attackers, the ground-based ones have less backup and are suffering under the combined onslaught of River and Fenrir. It's going well.

Which, of course, is when I see spots in the exact place I was just about to shoot an arrow. I jerk at the last moment, and the arrow I was in the process of releasing is diverted to the side. I curse loudly.

"Get the hell out of the way, Lathani!" I yell in frustration, then curse again when my raised voice attracts the attention of all the velociraptors not currently fully occupied—apparently, Fade doesn't work if I shout. Good to know. The next few moments are entirely full of dodging, and I don't manage to avoid all of the disgusting dirt-vomit missiles. I finally manage to hide in a bush that's sufficiently dense enough to act as an obstacle in the eyelines of those attacking me. That allows me to reapply Fade, which enables me to sneak to another bush without the velociraptors noticing. From there, I gaze at the battle in frustration.

Seeing as Lathani is basically doing what Bastet is, I start picking off the velociraptors that have fallen to the ground. I use my bow since I haven't yet got an archery Skill, which probably means I need to do more focused practice. Seeing as the battle seems mostly under control, I dare to take a little more time over each shot than I would normally, focusing on exactly *how* I'm using my bow.

With everyone's combined efforts, it's not long before I hear the same kind of signal to retreat that ended our last encounter.

"They're retreating!" I shout, once more breaking the effect of Fade. But seeing as the velociraptors are all turning to run, that's not a big deal. I get two arrows in the air before any of the velociraptors manage to escape. One hits; one misses, its target shifting just before it lands. A beat later, everyone else explodes into faster, more focused motion.

Bastet is no longer actually attempting to kill; she's just doing her best to bat as many tree-based velociraptors off their perches as she can before they flee. The cubs are getting a real workout and are proving themselves surprisingly deadly. Their hunting practice is showing clearly.

River is moving at almost double the speed as previously, abandoning efforts to conserve stamina in favor of speed. In three thrusts, there are three velociraptors lying at his feet. One gets too close, and he releases one paw from the spear to reach down and grab it. He brings it up to his jaws and uses his sharp teeth and strong jaws to rip its head off. Fenrir does his best too, but he's just not built for speed.

Still, he focuses more on laming the creatures than going for the kill, which speeds things up a little.

I'm not idle either and aim for the now-fleeing ranged attackers, then watch in satisfaction as they fall to the ground one by one. Lathani is the only one who hasn't changed her tactics in the slightest and who seems surprised when she looks around to find no more attackers nearby.

Battle over, with only a handful of attackers living to fight another day, I move to execute the last of the velociraptors that Lathani knocked out of the tree. I'm filled with grim satisfaction as I see the carnage surrounding us. Why they thought they could take us on, I don't know. Maybe because of their numbers? Maybe they only saw Lathani and me and thought that we were vulnerable? Well, they definitely bit off more than they could chew.

"Is everyone okay? Any injuries that need healing?" I ask. I'm angry with Lathani, furious even. She put us—and herself—in danger *twice* by not following orders. But reprimanding her can wait until I'm sure that everyone is safe.

A few scrapes, but their teeth weren't particularly effective against my hide, River answers promptly. I beckon him over nonetheless to quickly check him out with healing magic. Like he said, there are a few slices on his lower legs—the velociraptors couldn't reach much further up. Fenrir has similar wounds, though his slices are higher since he's lower to the ground than River is. His scales are pretty tough, though, so most of the damage was deflected. Bastet has a few slices too, as do the cubs—not all the velociraptors that fell were stunned by their fall, and a few got in a bit of a fight before the cubs ripped them apart.

Still, most of them are fairly minor wounds, so it doesn't take too long before my Bound are all surrounding me, whole. Then Lathani approaches me. I run my eyes over her body in a visual examination. She's not limping or protecting any part of herself. She does have blood on her fur, though most of it doesn't appear to be hers. I see a few scratches that the velociraptors got through on her, and one of her ears is a bit torn. She's much like Bastet, perhaps a little bit more scratched up. And there's mud in her fur too—she wasn't as good as Bastet at avoiding the missiles, it seems.

And me? she demands, nudging me demandingly. *Heal me.*

"If you hadn't gotten involved in the *damn battle* when you were ordered not to, you wouldn't be hurt!" I throw at her.

I'm injured! Heal me! she demands, stepping forwards with hackles raised and her teeth bared. Maybe I should be concerned about the imminent threat she seems determined to pose, but with the rest of my Bound around me, uninjured, and my own abilities, I'm not afraid that Lathani could do much to me before she's stopped. And almost anything she *does* do to me can be healed.

But though I want to leave her with her injuries just to emphasize how *stupid* she was and how easily she could have been killed, maybe that's just my anger talking. We have to journey back through the forest, and having her stinking of blood is likely to attract trouble. Besides, how would it look to return to Kalanthia with her cub covered in blood and scratches while my own Bound are uninjured? I can explain, sure, but I don't know if Kalanthia would agree with my explanation.

"Fine," I agree through gritted teeth, stomping forwards. I reach out to put my hand on her head, but she backs away from me, showing her teeth. "You want me to heal you? I need to touch you, Lathani!"

She eyes me for a moment and then lifts her paw. I stare at her incredulously. *Seriously? Whatever.* The longer we stay here, the more chance there is that something else is going to come investigating the smell of blood.

"Collect the bodies together, please," I instruct the rest of my Bound. At least if they can start clearing the area, it will save time later. In fact . . . "River, if you could prepare the carcasses for transportation, that would be great." I want to be able to offer my Bound some Energy-rich meat, meaning my Inventory is out.

Sending Lathani another glare, I reach out to touch her paw and send my magic and mind into her body.

It's hard, far harder to do than with any of my other Bound. The resistance against my presence is almost enough to push me out, and it feels like she's fighting me every step of the way. By the end of it, I've used more than three times as much mana as I used on any of my Bound. Even the cubs weren't that bad, though they were more difficult than Fenrir, Bastet, or River. The Bonds I have with them clearly make a big impact, though I don't understand why Lathani is so much harder to heal than the cubs, who don't have Bonds with me. Does sapience make that much of a difference?

Once I'm done, Lathani drops her paw and stalks off imperiously without a word. Not even a thank-you.

"You're welcome," I mutter sarcastically in her general direction. *What is up with that nunda?* She's not the friendly, playful cub I babysat, nor the subdued melancholic juvenile we brought back to her mother. I know she and I haven't spent much time together in the last few days, but it hasn't been *that* much time since we traveled through the forest.

Shaking my head in exasperation, I turn to see what my Bound have been doing. River is crouched over a stick and using vines from the forest to tie the tails of the most intact velociraptors to it. The others are in a different pile; Fenrir, Bastet and the cubs are filling their faces with the organs in particular, and Lathani is sauntering over there to do the same. My lips tighten as I see her growl at Storm and use her bigger size and weight to push the raptorcat off the organs she was enjoying. Why is she suddenly throwing her weight around? It's not like there aren't plenty of other piles of meat to enjoy. And the rest of her behavior too . . .

I sigh and push it out of my mind for now. We need to get going. I can think about why Lathani is being so obstreperous once we're out of this place. Preferably when we're back home. Hopefully, she won't cause any more problems until then.

Focusing on the bodies, I consider how I'll need to put the least intact carcasses in my Inventory; if we tie them to the stick, they'll drop bits off everywhere on our way home. I just have to hope that the lighter blood scent given off by the less damaged bodies won't be enough to bring half the forest onto our tails.

When I raise that concern with River, he doesn't seem worried.

I have smeared the stick with a certain odoriferous herb. It is one that puts off a scent similar to a dangerous forest beast. We often use it when we have beasts in the cages that are likely to draw predators. He falters for a moment, both of us remembering that I was one of those beasts all too recently. *Combined with the scent of blood and death, it will deter most creatures from investigating.*

"That's good thinking," I praise him, determined not to take my annoyance at Lathani out on anyone else. River's spikes color a faint pink.

Thank you, Master. Markus, he corrects himself, looking away. I decide to ignore it.

"Come on, let's finish up here and get back home. It's probably about time to make our way back anyway, if we want to be back before dark."

It's only when I'm busy tying velociraptor tails to the stick that I realize this might be the first fight I've been in where I wasn't injured at all. It just shows how much safer being an archer is, I guess, but I like the flexibility of being able to fight at both long and short range. There's no guarantee that I'll be able to choose my battles in the future, after all.

CHAPTER EIGHTEEN

You're Not Good Enough to Make Me Try

"All right, time to go," I say to everyone as I hoist one end of the stick onto my shoulder. We've cleared all the carcasses, and I've collected all my intact and damaged arrows. We need to get going. River hoists the other end of the stick, and we prepare to move out. Well, most of us do.

Of course, Lathani decides that she's going to studiously ignore me in favor of an apparently *fascinating* plant at the base of a tree. "Lathani! Come here!" I shout at her. She doesn't react at all.

Exchanging an exasperated look with River, I replace my end of the stick on the ground and stride towards the nunda juvenile. "Lathani, come on. If we don't go now, it will be dark before we're back." She doesn't react, and I reach towards her nape again—if she won't come when I ask her to, I'll haul her home the way I hauled her into the bushes. I'm not returning back to the hill to face questions from Kalanthia about where her cub is.

But before I can touch her, Lathani lets out a blood-chilling snarl, a sound I've never heard from her and one that instinctively freezes me in my tracks. The look on her face is one I've never seen before either. Almost like . . . she's looking at me as a target. As prey. I've seen it on her mother's face before, but not Lathani's.

"We need to go," I tell her more weakly than I would like as my hand drops to my side. She glares at me and then looks away pointedly.

I look back at the rest of my Bound, feeling a little lost. This isn't a situation I was expecting or have any idea how to deal with. If she were an enemy, I would attack or Bind her, but she isn't. Maybe I can bribe her.

"If you come and behave, I'll give you some yummy meat when we get home," I offer, feeling more than a little off-balance.

She eyes me, interest sparking. I feel a bit of hope.

Give some to me now, and then maybe I'll come with you, she offers imperiously. I hesitate, but if this will get me what I want . . .

No. It's not Lathani who speaks; it's Bastet. The raptorcat approaches us, exasperation running through the Bond. *Don't do that,* she scolds me, but I don't know why. I listen to her, though, and don't pull out some of the roast meat for Lathani. The raptorcat matriarch stalks forwards, goes up to Lathani, cuffs her over the head, and then growls at her.

Don't be stupid, I hear her say, her "voice" muffled—because she's not directing it at me, I guess. *Pack Leader gave an order. You follow.* Lathani growls at Bastet, her tone still unhappy.

Bastet is apparently not taking any backtalk, though, and instead shoulder-checks the nunda, sending her stumbling off-balance with something more like a squawk than a growl. They're almost the same size, so I'm a little surprised that Bastet manages to shift her so easily. Then again, I suppose that experience wins out every time.

While she's off-balance, Bastet pounces on her, rolling her over in a tumble of limbs. The contretemps comes to an end with Bastet leaning over Lathani, her paw on the young nunda's throat.

You may be bigger, but you are still a cub. Follow your elders' orders without question, she instructs Lathani with finality.

There's a silence for a few moments as the rest of us look on with interest.

Yes, Elder, Lathani says grudgingly. Bastet steps away and lets her up. She pushes herself to her feet quickly, then licks at her ruffled fur with a sense of embarrassment. Bastet steps forwards and licks at some ruffled fur near her ear.

Good. Listening to your elders is how you become an elder yourself in time. Then you can teach the same lessons to your pack's cubs.

Lathani doesn't reply in words to that, but she seems to like the idea, if the hint of pleasure coming off her and the way her fur starts lying flat again is anything to judge by.

Sorry, Elder, she says finally to Bastet when she's gotten rid of the leaves and small twigs that were caught in her fur during the tumble.

Forgiven, Bastet replies, then nudges her towards me. Lathani darts a look at me, then another at Bastet. The raptorcat growls softly, the tone a warning. Lathani slumps, then pads towards me, looking like she's going to her execution.

Sorry, Elder, she says finally, her tone more than a little begrudging, her gaze fixed defiantly on mine, her ears back.

Bastet growls and comes over to cuff her on the head.

Try again, she orders the nunda cub. Lathani makes some grumbling noise. *Now.*

Sorry, Pack Leader, she says finally, but her teeth are still slightly bared, her eyes are on mine, and her ears are still back. Something's not right here.

Forgiven, I say, following Bastet's lead. The nunda then stalks off, her body lined with anger. At least she's moving in the direction we need to go to get home, but if we don't get moving quickly, she'll be the one leaving *us* behind.

I stare at Bastet, not sure what to make of the whole thing. From what I saw, it looked like a dominance play, but I thought it was dogs who needed a clear hierarchy, not cats. Then again, nundas aren't cats, for all that they look like felines . . . I give myself a shake. We need to go.

I walk over to pick up the stick end again, and we get moving through the forest in the wake of the moody nunda. Bastet and Fenrir seem to have switched roles: the lizog scouts ahead while the raptorcat paces by my side. The cubs stick near her most of the time, though they do wander off from time to time to inspect something in the local area.

What is going on with Lathani? I ask my raptorcat matriarch mentally, hoping that the nunda won't pick up my thoughts. I don't know how much difference distance makes to her ability to pick up mental projections, especially ones not directed at her. *She's being so . . . difficult. I almost thought she was about to attack me,* I confess as quietly as I can. *Is this some sort of . . . thing about dominance? Working out who's who in the pecking order?*

Bastet walks closer to me and butts at my hip, rubbing her head against me affectionately.

It's a difficult age, she says to me. *She is old enough to start wishing to be independent but not old enough to truly be so. She must be reminded regularly that her elders are still stronger and more capable than she is.*

So, what, beat her into compliance? I ask, more than a little disturbed by the notion. Bastet eyes me.

Humans are odd. Your thought carries strange nuances. No, it is not "beat into compliance." She sends back the same thought I sent her, complete with the nuances of abuse and victimization that I hadn't realized I'd attached. *It is proving that we still have more to teach. When she can overcome us, or even simply stand against us in defense of her desires, she will have demonstrated her ability to be independent.*

I shake my head not in negation, just in confusion.

So, what, I didn't prove that I had more to teach or something?

She has been testing you. You have failed the tests.

I frown. *What tests?* Though, even as I ask it, I have a feeling that I know at least a couple of them—that final moment was one of them for sure. Lathani kept pushing me, and I kept moving my boundaries and complying with her. The healing was probably another. She demanded that I heal her, and I did. I even accepted touching only her paw instead of putting my hand over the wounds as I would usually do. Maybe this is why there was so much resistance to my healing.

Ever since we left the den, she has been testing whether you are the leader or whether she is. I was right—it *is* a dominance play. Though, the realization doesn't exactly fill me with joy. *Her decision to move far away from us was, intentional or not, a way of seeing whether you would follow her or whether she would have to return. You failed that, leading to another challenge when the enemies arrived. Forcing her into the bushes was a good move, but you then did not give her any task to do that recognized her strengths, leading to her becoming restless and getting involved anyway. Which in turn led to another challenge. She threatened you to see if you would fight back. Instead, you tried to appease her. So she tested to see how far she could push you with the appeasement. I stepped in when you seemed on the verge of giving her tribute. You are pack leader. You must make sure that she understands that.*

I wasn't giving her tribute! I just wanted to calm the situation down. Kalanthia would kill me if Lathani got hurt, so I didn't want it to come to a fight.

If you do not prove yourself worthy of being listened to, Lathani will not do so. That could prove more dangerous than demonstrating to her that you are more powerful, Bastet warns me.

She has a point, I realize. All I need to do is think about how Lathani decided to attack the velociraptor that I was about to shoot—and the arrow that almost hit her. If I'd noticed where she was a moment later, if she had been angled wrongly, it could have ended up with an arrow through the eye. Even with Flesh-Shaping I might not be able to heal something like that, especially with the resistance I felt when healing the scratches.

I sigh. Now that Bastet's pointed them out, I can see all the moments when Lathani was testing me. I knew she was just being difficult but didn't realize that it was an intentional attempt to provoke me—or that my responses were just making things worse. And with this other perspective, I can see why the situation just devolved. I need to remember that I'm not dealing with a logical being here but an emotional one. Apparently, nundas are more canine in this way than feline—I've never had a dog, but several of my friends who do have said that it's important that the dog knows who's boss according to the human's behavior.

What should I do now, then? I ask, feeling a bit lost. *How am I supposed to prove that I should be her pack leader?*

Something similar to what I did. Demonstrate your superiority and why she should listen to you. Then, demand she appease you. If you wish her to listen to you in the future, you must do this now. Otherwise, she will only obey you if her mother or I ensure her compliance. She pauses for a moment and then continues a little tentatively. *It is about . . . respect.* The last word is very blurry, mostly a series of images and feelings.

Okay, I can kind of understand that.

But why is it only coming up now? And why don't you seem to have the same problem? I ask her in frustration.

As I said, it is a difficult age. Not quite a cub, not quite an adult. All right, a teenager, then. *As for me, it is different. You earned my respect long ago, and my cooperation with it. I do not need demonstrations of superiority to recognize that it is better if you are pack leader.*

Well, that's good to know. I suppose if I think about Lathani being a teenager, it makes a little more sense—humans are known to go through an . . . interesting period of time when they feel a strong urge to defy all types of authority. Maybe it's the same for Lathani now. Will the raptorcat cubs go through this period too? I can't help but feel apprehension at the idea.

How am I supposed to prove my superiority? Am I supposed to just go up to her and roll her over like Bastet did? Not really my style. And given how she bared her teeth and flattened her ears at me, I suspect she would fight back, which would probably end with one or both of us getting injured.

I'd like to ask Bastet for more advice, but I have a feeling that she might tell me to go figure it out for myself.

As we walk through the forest, I find myself distracted by the question of what to do about Lathani. My eyes keep getting caught by her figure stalking through the bushes ahead of us. She loses the angry lines within a fairly short space of time, but every time she drops back because her attention has been caught by something, she sends a look over to me and then hurries forwards again, as if letting me go first would be conceding a battle.

Since I don't feel like appearing like a teenager, I don't try to one-up her by dashing ahead myself—the stick I'm carrying with River would fall if I did that, anyway. Instead, I just think and plan for when we get back. By the time we climb the hill and reach the plateau, I have a couple of ideas of what to do. But I feel that I need to speak to Kalanthia first—I don't want to overstep with her cub.

I leave River to get started on untying the velociraptors and walk over to the massive nunda basking in the evening sun. I feel surprisingly nervous about it all.

When Kalanthia opens her eyes to reveal her golden orbs, I quietly explain what happened while we were away, projecting my thoughts for her telepathy to pick up. *Bastet seems to feel I need to do something to . . . uh, establish my authority,* I finish nervously, eyeing her to see how she will take it.

She surprises me a bit when she seems to take it completely in stride.

Indeed. Do you feel you need my permission or some such?

My eyebrows raise, and I fumble a little with my response. *Kind of, I suppose. We do have the agreement about not offering violence, after all.*

That is true, though I suspect that your aim is in fact to prevent harm to my cub, Kalanthia points out. I nod absently.

I could have shot her accidentally today. And we might not have ended up in the fight at all if she hadn't run forwards too fast for us to properly observe our surroundings.

Then it seems like establishing your authority is overdue, Kalanthia answers very seriously, the hint of amusement that frequently laces her mental voice completely absent.

All right, I answer, a little taken aback at her sudden soberness. *And if she is injured?*

Assuming you do not cause any damage you cannot heal, pain is the best teacher.

Huh, is all I can say, feeling like I've just been given a carte blanche, which I didn't actually want. If Kalanthia had required this to be kept to only minor cuts and scrapes, that would be one thing. Having the only requirement be to inflict nothing I can't heal . . . By this point, that basically means just keeping her alive.

Go make things right with my cub. I trust you will not take it too far.

With those slightly ominous words to accompany me, I walk over to where Lathani is prodding at a beetle. I'm reminded of the time she poked at a beetle while I was digging my firepit and was bitten by it. The memory of her panic when this tiny thing wouldn't let go brings a smile back to my face even now. It puts me in a better mood for what I apparently need to do.

"Right, Lathani," I say to her. She sends me a glance and then seems to remember that she's not talking to me and returns to what she's doing. "Let's have a bout, you and I." She ignores me. "Lathani, I'm not asking," I tell her firmly. "I *will* attack you in a moment. I am giving you fair warning, but you do not have a choice here." Lathani wants, needs me to be firm and decisive? Then she'll have to live with it when I am.

Perhaps my tone of voice registers, as she looks up at me suspiciously, her eyes going to the spear I now have in my hands. "First to be pinned or to give up loses. You want to know who is more powerful between the two of us? Here's how."

I know that I'm gambling a bit here—if she wins, she'll probably be worse than ever. But if she loses . . .

She looks at me calculatingly.

You are much bigger than me, she comments challengingly.

"Are you submitting to me without a fight, then?" I ask with my eyebrows raised. "Are you saying that your teeth and claws are not capable of making up the difference? That I am automatically superior to you because of my size?" I feel stupid saying it, but I can't think of any other way.

Lathani yowls angrily, pinning her ears back and lifting her lips slightly.

No! I am powerful. I am deadly. You have the blunt claws and blunt teeth of the prey Mother and I eat.

"Then there should be no issue with facing me in a fight," I point out, then shrug. "Prepare to fight." I level my spear at her.

She springs forward quickly, even as the spear materializes in my hand. I swing my weapon at her, butt end first. The blow knocks her off course, and she lands a little heavily to the side.

That hurt! she complains. I raise my eyebrows at her.

"Are you so weak that something as small as that will take you down?" I ask her.

That, apparently, is a red rag to a bull.

I'm not weak! she refutes with a snarl and leaps for me again.

Once more I swing my spear butt, and once more she's knocked off course with a calculated blow to the ribs. I find myself relaxing a little bit as the fight continues.

It's a bit like sparring with Bastet. A much younger, less adaptable, less canny Bastet. Lathani is practically the same size as her and has a similar tendency to pounce with her claws and teeth bared. But where Bastet very quickly works out that a technique isn't working and tries another, Lathani seems to subscribe to the mentality that if something hasn't worked, she'd better try, try, and try again.

I soon realize that my nerves when I started the spar were for naught. It's not that Lathani *mustn't* win, it's that she *can't*.

She doesn't have the right kind of technique to get past my weapon. She doesn't have the ferocity to just shrug off pain. She isn't adaptable, and while she's quick and strong, I'm quicker and stronger than she is. The only thing actually going for her is that she has plenty of determination; she hasn't yet given up despite the constant failure.

I actually start using the opportunity to continue practicing my spear technique, playing a bit of a game. At first, I keep hitting the same spot every time she jumps at me, then practice hitting different spots each leap. It starts feeling like a normal spar, a notion that's enhanced when I realize that have an audience: all my Bound have formed a large circle around us and are watching. Kalanthia too, of course.

On the one hand, the situation is good for me: Lathani's inability to fight works to my advantage in this particular fight. On the other, it's worrying: how am I going to help her stay alive when she's this poor at fighting? No wonder she picked up so many scratches from the velociraptors—I can only be grateful that the ranged ones seemed to have been less physically capable than the ground ones.

Then again, was I much better when I arrived in this world? If I can learn, then Lathani, who is by nature a powerful predator, should pick it up much quicker.

The nunda juvenile pauses after her most recent attempt to jump at me and glares hotly.

You're not even trying! she whines. I glare back at her.

"You're right—I'm not. You're not good enough to make me try." That hits home. I see her lips curl back from her teeth in anger. I bare my own teeth, letting my worry turn into righteous anger. "How have you managed to kill *anything* if all you can do is pounce?"

It's always worked so far, she argues sulkily. I suddenly wonder whether Kalanthia has had anything to do with that—perhaps she's been making the hunt easier for her cub. But if so, then she's given Lathani a false sense of her own capabilities. Given her earlier words, that doesn't make sense, so maybe this is the first peak of overconfidence shown by the Dunning-Kruger effect—Lathani has had a few successful hunts, so now she thinks she knows everything about hunting and fighting.

"And what happens when it doesn't, eh? What happens when you pounce on an enemy and they aren't where you expect them to be? What happens when they avoid your attack and then return their own?"

So saying, I shift my footwork forwards quickly and then jab at her. My spear point pokes the fur of her breast. She jumps back, and I pursue with quick steps. She leaps sideways, but I just shift my spear around to follow her. She jumps at me again, perhaps hoping that my movements have put me off-balance, but this time I knock the wind out of her with the butt end of my spear as I bring it sweeping around.

You're bigger than me and can attack me long before I can reach you! she protests, pawing at the ground with frustration. Since she's not attacking, I decide to give her a moment.

"So?" I demand. "You've been there when I've fought creatures bigger than myself or more numerous than us. The point is that you *adapt*. You use what you *do* have to your advantage. You work *with* your packmates. And you never"—here I jab at her with my spear for emphasis, making her dodge back—"never go against the plan mid-fight without a good reason, especially if the plan is for me to *shoot damn arrows* at them." Yes, I'm still angry about what she did with the velociraptors.

She bares her teeth again at me, but this time it looks more defensive than angry—the rest of her body is huddled into the ground, doing its best to present a smaller target. I sigh and try to soften my tone.

"Look, you're young and inexperienced. Survive long enough and neither of those will be true anymore. But if you're coming out with my party, you *listen to me*, capiche?" She doesn't answer me verbally. Perhaps she needs a little demonstration. "Bastet, come here, would you?" I say, not taking my eyes off Lathani. I don't doubt that she'd quickly take advantage of any distraction on my part. Which she should—it would probably be the best move she'd made all fight—but I wouldn't want her to accidentally win on a technicality.

Yes? Bastet asks, stepping forward to stand next to me. There's a sense of amusement in her tone—I have a feeling she already knows why I asked her to come forward.

"Let's show Lathani how it's done," I tell her, then look back at Lathani. "Watch and stay put, or I'll have River sit on you." After the uncomfortable look each of them sends me, I have a feeling that I'm not going to have an issue with her disobeying right now.

Locking eyes with Bastet, I settle back into my spear stance, leveling the point at her. No using the butt here—I can heal the wounds I cause to Bastet, and just being knocked sideways wouldn't do anything more than give her another platform to jump from.

The raptorcat attempts to trick me with a feint, leaping forwards as if to go for my throat while instead aiming for my front leg. I see the shift of movement, though, and spot the trick in time—the sparring we did this morning is already paying off.

Stabbing down at her, I miss actually hitting my Bound by a hair when she aborts her attack in the nick of time by flicking her wings. Instead of backing away as Lathani was doing, she pushes herself to one side and then attempts to leap at me from that angle.

My spear is out of position; I have to scramble to hit her with the butt. The force of the impact shudders through both of us but pushes Bastet more than it does me. She turns the tables on me, though, by twisting her head to bite at the spear shaft.

We engage in a tug-of-war as we both struggle over control of the spear. I'm about to drop the spear and attempt a different approach when Bastet beats me to it. Already braced to drop the spear myself, I don't fall over as I might have done otherwise. I do lose my balance a little, though, and Bastet takes quick advantage.

She leaps at me and bowls me over to land on the ground with my arms and legs splayed.

Knowing that she's not going to actually hurt me, I don't panic. Instead, I grip my spear with both hands and pull it down to separate us. Then, using my greater body weight, I twist us around so I'm on top with my spear pressed against her throat.

"Stop," I say, and we both freeze. A moment later, I pull my spear away from her throat and push myself off her. I'd probably be considered the victor here—I could easily have crushed her throat. However, I wouldn't have come out unscathed.

Bastet can't retract her claws like Lathani can—her paws are more like a bird's talons than a feline paw. Nonetheless, she did keep them away from me as much as possible, which I appreciate—wounds can heal; my clothes, on the other hand, would have been torn to shreds. So while I would have won even if this were a real fight, I would have had a lot to heal afterwards, risking bleeding out before succeeding in closing all my wounds.

After pushing ourselves to stand, I scratch at Bastet's head as she rubs herself against me.

"Good fight," I praise her. "I wasn't expecting that tug-of-war with the spear."

I saw Fenrir do it with River in their spar earlier, Bastet admits.

"Even better, then. That's what these spars are for: learning from each other." Looking over at Lathani, I pin her with a pointed stare. "Do you see what I mean? Bastet had the same issue as you, but instead of just doing the same thing over and over again, she adapted. She tried different things. She took risks, but calculated ones. In short, she turned what you felt was an impossible fight into one that would have ended with me severely injured if she'd used her claws."

Lathani has left her defensive stance and is now sitting properly, her eyes and ears clearly showing how intently she has been focusing on our demonstration.

I understand. But how does she know what to do?

I glance at Bastet and then turn back to the nunda juvenile, shrugging. "How do any of us? Practice. You saw us practice fighting against each other this morning, and it's something we're going to continue. Otherwise, for each of us it has been from getting into real fights and coming out the victor, or at least not getting too hurt to continue." I add the latter thinking about Fenrir and his fights with his packmates.

Can I join? Lathani asks, her attitude abruptly different from what she was showing me earlier. I raise my eyebrows at her.

"That depends. Do you accept that we still have things to teach you? That *I* have things to teach you?"

She looks down at the ground and her ears relax. *I do.* She darts a glance up at me, then returns her eyes to the ground. *Pack Leader.*

I move over to her and crouch down beside her slumped form. Reaching out, I rub her fur behind her ears.

With a noise of pleasure, she pushes against my hand, then stands and rubs herself against me with enough force to almost send me sprawling.

"All right, then," I say, both pleasure and relief going through me that this whole thing seems to have worked out. "I expect to see you joining us during our sparring every day. Unless your mother has something else for you to do," I quickly add, looking up at the massive nunda.

You're okay with that, right? I send to her, realizing that I might have overstepped. Fortunately, her response sets me at ease.

I am glad she will have an opportunity to learn in a safer environment. It is a privilege few of us have.

After spending a little more time bonding with Lathani again, I push myself to my feet. Time for supper—I want to see if I can make something tasty with the plants we harvested in the forest.

CHAPTER NINETEEN

Lesser Healing Potion

Entering the alcove, I see Bastet curled up near the hearth, the three cubs pressed against her as usual. Fenrir is keeping watch, but his eyes are half closed. He reacts as I walk towards them, pushing himself to his feet. I'm not sure where Sirocco is, though I sense that she's still awake—probably in a tree nearby. She sometimes stays inside with us but usually remains outside; she prefers the freedom of the outdoors.

River, surprisingly, isn't lying on the bed trying to sleep. Instead, he's kneeling in an area of relatively clear space, frowning over a bowl full of blackish liquid. Next to him are two vaguely familiar plants, which I'm pretty sure he found today, along with another couple of bowls.

"What are you doing?" I ask quietly so as not to disturb my other Bound. "Experimenting?"

I am . . . frustrated, River replies. *I know that this combination works—I have seen Herbalist do it many times before—but every time I make it, I end in failure. It should not be the quality of the plants. These have not been in your storage space, and I have collected these many times for Pathwalker Herbalist, so it is not my collection skills at fault. It's possible that it is the lesser Energy density up here, but that seems unlikely. It is far more likely that I'm missing something.*

I move over to kneel beside him, enjoying the touch of warmth from the still-glowing hearth fire. The nights are beginning to get a little nippy; winter is approaching, I guess. Turning to the fire, I start stoking it up—I did want to get some supper going, after all.

"Not that I know, well, *anything* about herbalism, but can you tell me what you're doing? And what you saw the herbalist do? Maybe I can help you pick out the difference." I speak quietly, not wanting to disrupt the sleeping raptorcats or keep Sirocco or Fenrir from their own rest, but I have a feeling that River won't be able to go to bed until he's made *some* progress.

The lizard-man shifts, and he points to one of the plants lying next to him. It has angular, almost spiky leaves, a thin stem, and surprisingly tuberous roots.

This is aslebellum. It is a plant that grows near the river. Its leaves are poisonous, but its roots are the reverse. Even just chewing on them helps one's wounds heal a little faster.

River points to the next plant. I think I recognize it—I've probably used Inspect Flora on it before, as I have with most of the plants River uses. Unfortunately, the

descriptions aren't saved in some sort of mental reference guide. I use my inspection Skill again, but the pulse goes out without returning any information about
the plant in front of me. It's almost like the plant no longer exists to the Skill. I try
doing it on the other plant he has next to him with the same result.

It seems that there's a limited amount of time between the plant being collected
and when Inspect Flora stops working. Why this is, I don't know, but I suspect it's to
do with Energy—that seems to be the answer to everything these days. Oh well, it's
a shame, but if I'm that curious, I'll just have to find the plant growing in the forest.

Interestingly, when I try Inspect Environment, it still lights the plants up in
halos—the aslebellum in red, the other in a faint gold. Clearly Inspect Flora looks
at something that is lost soon after the plant is picked, while Inspect Environment
uses something different to get its information. I wonder briefly about the implications before returning my attention to the matter at hand.

The second plant is more like grass, its long and flexible leaves all emerging
from a single stem. Its roots, in comparison to the previous, are thin and stringy.

*This one is called harash. Its roots can be eaten but do not offer much benefit; the
leaves are what I am using here. However, the healing properties are difficult to get at, as
the leaves themselves are very fibrous. To that end, I have to use this.*

He gestures at a black liquid in one of my smaller earthenware bowls.

"What's that?" I ask, curious. I sniff at it and recoil, its acidic tang hitting my
nose harshly.

The venom of a grunt-click-flash-of-orange. Not a creature I'm familiar with, then.
The accompanying image of something that looks almost identical to a scorpion
but with two tails doesn't spark any memories either. It doesn't look very big, but
from how strong its venom smells, I'm glad I haven't encountered it.

"So, what, that eats into the fiber of the harash?" I ask, not seeing any other
reason for using the venom.

*Yes, exactly. But therein lies my problem. The resulting potion has the healing nature
required, but it also retains the acidic quality of the venom. It shouldn't do that.* I feel his
frustration emanating across the Bond. I understand it—I've encountered plenty of
moments like that myself.

"How does the herbalist overcome that, then?" I ask.

I don't know! River exclaims. *I have been trying to mimic exactly what she does, but
I keep encountering the same problems.*

"Can you demonstrate for me?" I ask. Perhaps I will be able to spot something
or ask the right question to make River realize whatever he's doing wrong. "Explain
what you're doing as you do it."

Very well, River says with his equivalent of a sigh. *First, I mince the aslebellum
roots as small as possible.* As he says it, he takes a root and does exactly that, his
wooden knife doing a surprisingly decent job at the task.

Once the pieces are minced, resembling grains of rice more than the root they
started as, River takes the next plant.

I then slice the harash into slivers as thin as possible. So saying, he wraps the leaves of the harash into a tube and slices from the bottom, like I might do with a leek. Once he has a small pile of leaf slivers, he collects them and places them in a wooden bowl. I wonder if the material of the equipment might make any difference to the product.

"What kind of containers did the herbalist use?" I ask. River's tail sways in his equivalent of a shrug.

Whatever we could find, really. We still had some containers remaining from before the Earth-Shaper died, but not many. Otherwise, we used carapaces, or shells, or hollowed-out roots, or bowls the Wood-Shaper created.

"Does it make a difference?"

Some ingredients must be in a shell, as they may eat through wooden bowls. This venom is an example of that. It's why I have used your earthenware and the carapaces.

So, that's a probable "no" for the container being the problem.

River continues working, pouring a little of the venom on top of the pile of harash slices and swirling the bowl about.

I have poured the scorpion-lizard venom onto the harash leaves and am agitating them to encourage the fibers in the leaves to break down. He then places the bowl onto the ground and holds his hands above it for a long moment. Then, dropping his hands, he reaches for the pile of minced aslebellum. *I now take the—*

"Wait, what were you doing when you held your hands above the bowl?" I interrupt. River looks thoughtful for a moment and then shrugs.

It is something Herbalist always did with this mixture. I don't know why.

I nod slowly even as he continues his explanation about dropping the aslebellum into the mixture and combining them by swirling the basin. I think I might have an inkling about what's going wrong, but I save my thoughts for now.

And so, you see, River finishes, *although the two plants have been correctly dissolved by the acid of the venom, the concoction remains acidic.* The lizard-man clicks his teeth together in frustration. *I just don't understand it. I've used exactly the same amount of each ingredient that Herbalist would use. I've prepared it in exactly the same way. Unless I am forgetting something.*

"I have an idea," I start slowly, "though I may easily be wrong."

River grunts loudly. *Any guidance would be appreciated, Master.*

I smile humorlessly. "Unless it sends you in the wrong direction. Just . . . take my suggestion with a pinch of salt, okay?" River just waits, a sense of impatience coming over the link even as he regards me silently. "So, I remember you mentioning before that the herbalist is capable of using shards of Cores to infuse potions. Right?"

Yes, though this is not one of the combinations that requires such treatment.

"It's less about it being relevant to this potion and more about evidence. I'm thinking out loud here." River tips his chin up briefly before eyeing me again. "So, all the other Pathwalkers appear to be able to use mana. Is that right?"

It is.

"You held your hands over the concoction for no real reason, only because you've seen the herbalist do it." River sends affirmation over the Bond. "What if the herbalist does this because she's using mana on the potion to get rid of the acidity?"

The lizard-man looks taken aback, the thought clearly not having occurred to him. It wouldn't have occurred to me either except for the fact that I've been contemplating the mana in everything around me for the last few weeks.

But if that's the case, then I won't be able to make this concoction, he tells me, crestfallen. I shrug.

"Maybe, maybe not. First of all, you *do* have mana. Perhaps you could learn to use it." The Bond communicates River's doubt.

That's what the Pathwalkers do, not the Unevolved, he points out. I shrug again.

"Maybe that's how it's always been, but does that mean it *has* to be the case? I don't know, but don't ignore that it might be possible. If you try and it doesn't work, then it's not the end of the world. Still, for all we know, it will increase the chance that you will become a Pathwalker instead of a Warrior upon your Evolution. Then you'll be able to do it however your herbalist does."

I can try, my Bound replies, doubt still filling his mental voice. *But that doesn't help much right now.*

"If that's the issue in the first place," I remind him. "But I do actually have two suggestions about things to maybe try that don't require mana." River perks up in interest.

Please tell me, Master!

"Okay, first of all, perhaps use less of the venom." River looks at me in confusion. *But if I don't use the venom, the concoction* definitely *won't work.*

"I didn't say don't use *any* of it. I suggested using *less*. Where I come from, we understand that acid can be neutralized, but only if it's used in the right quantities. Perhaps if you use less acid, more of it will be used in the process and won't remain to cause an issue with the final potion." I shrug. "Like I said, it works where I come from; that doesn't mean it will work here—the rules do seem to be quite different in some cases. If you do it that way, you'll probably have to swirl it longer, maybe significantly longer, as it will take the acid more time to break down all the fibers in the harash. And you'll have to test through trial and error how much venom to use."

I see, River says slowly. *You mentioned two suggestions?*

"Yeah. The second is a bit more . . . based on guesswork," I say, hesitating. "So, you said that the purpose of the acid was to eat away at the fibers that compose the leaves of the harash, right? What about boiling them instead?" The idea had occurred to me when he first mentioned why he was using the acid.

I'd automatically thought how awkward it was to use acid when boiling was exactly how humans have dealt with tough plants for thousands of years. Then I remembered that the lizard folk haven't yet discovered fire, and it started to make a little more sense to me. My guess is that the acid is used despite its downsides because there aren't any other better' options. And when magic can deal with the residual acidity, it turns from a possible solution to a realistic one. But without that magic . . .

Of course, I don't know if boiling the plants will destroy whatever makes them beneficial for healing; River will need to test that for himself.

Will you show me how to do this . . . boiling?

"Of course," I smile. "Let me just get my supper going, and then we can use the fire to the side of my stew to test this. And anyway, my stew has to boil—it's the same idea I'm suggesting you do." I can live another night with just the usual stew. I'm too curious about whether boiling will actually help to delay things enough for me to make something more interesting. At least I have those berries waiting for me as dessert.

As you wish.

While I chop the potatoes and leaves that I found earlier today and put them into my pot with chunks of meat, I spend the time thinking about how to start experimenting with fire. I decide that River learning how to make fire himself is probably a good idea—if this turns out to make any difference, he may want to experiment with other potions. In fact, he probably *should* experiment a bit to see if fire can make a difference to other concoctions, regardless of its effect on this one. It occurs to me that in doing so, I'm giving fire to the lizard folk for the first time in history—as far as either of us knows. Does that make me Prometheus?

Then I consider exactly what that unfortunate titan's fate was and shudder. With my own increased ability to heal, having my liver torn out every morning only for it to regrow by the next doesn't seem as far-fetched as it used to.

Perhaps it's better not to tempt fate.

"Ready to make fire?" I ask River, who's been spending the time getting the ingredients ready for new experiments. A mixture of trepidation and nervous excitement comes over the Bond. It seems like his fear is outweighing his anticipation—for now, at least. I think it might do him some good to actually gain some control over the terror that imprinted itself on him as a child. Or hatchling, or whatever they call themselves.

"Don't worry about it. The worst that will happen is you burn yourself a bit and I heal you. No, actually, the more likely worst-case scenario is that you don't manage to set light to the fire at all," I try to reassure him, my tone amused.

I trust you will keep me safe, Master, River replies, and his honesty takes my breath away for a moment in a mixture of joy and pain.

"I will," I promise instead, my voice suddenly a little thick. *I can't free him and offer a Companion Bond,* I remind myself. *Not yet.* But abruptly I ache to do so, to find out how much of our relationship is real and how much is caused by the Bond.

I cough to clear away the physical indications of my feelings and then indicate the area in front of the hearth.

"All right," I start, trying to make my tone professional and businesslike. Fortunately, I have practice in both covering and suppressing my emotions. "This is what you're aiming to make. For now, we'll use the space just in front of the hearth for you to learn how to make a fire, and then you can use the one in the hearth for your experiments. First you need to build your fire."

I show him how to construct the fire with a mixture of materials—from the dried mosslike plant that I often use as tinder, to the thin dry twigs that I use as kindling, all the way up to the thicker pieces of cut firewood. I've put significant effort into building a stockpile of these over my few trips into the forest.

"You need to make sure that there are lots of gaps," I emphasize as I place the last, thickest pieces in a pyramid shape above the rest of the kindling. "Fire requires oxygen to burn, which is in the air around us. At the same time, by placing these branches above the fire, we make it easier for them to catch light. This is because heat rises, and the hotter something is, the more likely it is to ignite."

I understand, River replies, watching intently.

When I next deconstruct the fire and ask him to recreate it, his actions are slow but steady, moving almost without error. Certainly, his first attempt at the physical construction of a fire is significantly better than mine. I don't think the lizard folk know how to write, so their powers of observation are probably a whole lot better than most humans'.

Once the fire has been remade, I take out my fire starter.

"Okay, so this is called a fire starter, and it makes our job a *lot* easier. You've seen me use it before, I'm sure."

Yes. You strike one piece against the other and little lights fly off.

"In essence, yes. You have to get the right angle, and the little lights are called sparks. Sparks are actually tiny pieces of the material that have become hot enough to ignite. The aim is to get those sparks to land on our easily ignited kindling and then to coax it into a fire. Come on, let's try."

I pass the fire starter to River and help correct his grip until he's managing to strike the right sort of angle. It's fortunate that his hands are almost as agile as mine—only his claws get in the way sometimes. It does take him a number of tries before he manages to strike his first spark and then several more until he's getting a small shower of them.

After that, it takes even more time before he gets the idea of aiming them onto the small patch of dried moss. Once he's managed that, blowing on where the spark has landed is the next challenge—it turns out that having a lipless mouth makes blowing rather difficult. In the end, we settle on making a fan out of one of my books, though I warn River not to let it burn on pain of his life. I hope he realizes I was joking. Mostly.

Ultimately, the point is to get the air moving over the spark; how that happens is irrelevant.

I didn't realize it took so much effort to start a fire, River admits when we're finally sitting back, watching the fire start licking at the twigs. He is fanning it, but the fire's now doing most of the work.

I find it interesting that he's now able to say "fire." Or perhaps it's that our understanding of fire is now overlapping sufficiently for the Bond to be able to translate it correctly.

I don't understand how the life-devourer attacked us if making a fire is so difficult, he says next, sounding a little confused. I shrug.

"It doesn't always take as much effort as this. And sometimes it takes more. Basically, where I come from, we talk about the fire triangle. If all three elements are present, a fire will happen. If one is absent, it won't. Can you work out the three elements now that you know more about fire?"

River looks thoughtful. *You talked about gaps in the firewood, and we needed to move the air around the spark. So, air is one?*

"Well, oxygen, but yes, essentially. So, one way of stopping a fire is to smother it—pile earth or another substance on it that stops air from reaching the burning elements. That's one. What's the second?"

River considers it for a few moments. *We needed to supply firewood or other materials. Those are the second element?*

"Fuel, yes. Fuel comes in a variety of forms. The ones we use here are solid, but if you remember the massive salamander, it used a flammable liquid to project its fire. There are also gases that ignite and can be very dangerous. Good so far. What's the third element?"

This one seems to have River stumped. He eyes the fire, then me, then the fire again. After a bit of time, he holds up the fire starter.

Is it this? he asks hesitantly. *But then I don't understand how the life-devourer started. As far as I understand it, you were not present three years ago.*

"No, I wasn't," I confirm. "Wait," I continue after a beat as the implications of his words register. "I thought that you were a . . . hatchling when this happened."

I was, he agrees easily. I blink.

"So you're, what, four years old?" I ask incredulously.

Almost, he replies. *I hatched in the first few days of the sun's return to strength.*

Spring, I interpret that to mean, according to my knowledge of the seasons. I can't seem to get my head around this. He's only three years old? At this age, human children are still unable to be left without supervision, practically incapable of doing anything for themselves. Whereas for the lizard folk, three years old is clearly an independent adult.

Well, I suppose the relatively short lifespan makes a bit more sense, then—River's expected life span is only thirty-seven years in total. Hopefully, his lifespan will increase as significantly as Bastet's. Actually, what about mine?

The memories I have from the System lore stone do seem to indicate that lives of people on Nicholas's world are longer, but I'm not sure if that's a result of leveling or if they're a different species of human with a longer lifespan than mine.

You seem surprised at my age, Master, River interrupts my thoughts with a tentative statement. *Did you wish for one younger than me? Or older and more experienced?*

"No, no, it's not that. It's just that my kind only reach adulthood in . . ." I chuckle. "Well, it depends on what you consider adulthood. We're technically able to start having children at thirteen or fourteen years of age, sometimes a bit earlier, but that isn't a good idea for many reasons. Generally, we're considered to be of adult age at eighteen, though some places consider twenty-one the age for full independence. Heck, in the past, sometimes it took until *thirty-five* before a person was considered able to make all decisions for themself."

River stares at me.

How has your species survived? he asks wonderingly. *To have to wait even thirteen years between hatchings would spell the death of our village. As it is, only five or six hatchlings survive in each brood, and then there are always deaths of Unevolved adults, which whittle down our population further. And that's with yearly hatchings.*

I hold up a hand.

"Now, that's one key difference. We don't have to wait for each child to grow up before having another. In fact, technically, I think it's possible to have a child every year and a half or so. In the past, some women had ten or even twenty children."

You only have one child at a time? River sounds even more surprised, which, again, I understand. The lizard folk seem to have the same scattergun approach to progeny as do most reptilian species: have many in the hope that a few will survive.

"Yes. Well, usually. Multiple births like twins or triplets do happen, but they aren't as common. We put more effort into ensuring children survive—one or both parents generally dedicates decades of effort to raising them. In the past, child mortality was a lot worse than now, but I don't think it ever exceeded fifty percent as an average. I mean, there were plenty of things that killed adults then too, but even so, apart from a few outlier events, our population has only grown over the centuries.

"In the last century, it's exploded—better health care means a reduction in deaths by natural causes, and fewer wars are killing us off." I grimace. "Unfortunately, though all those things have helped us as a species, our effect on the world hasn't been so positive." After a moment, I shake the morose thoughts. "Anyway, that's irrelevant. I think we've discussed lightning before?"

River eyes me for a moment and then clearly concentrates on trying to remember.

Yes, he says slowly. Then his expression lights up—literally: his spikes start flashing an almost lurid green. *I remember you suggested that as the cause of the life-devourer the first time I saw you make fire.*

"Yes, exactly. The third element of the fire triangle is called 'heat' or sometimes the 'ignition source.' So this"—I point at the fire starter—"gave us the ignition event for our little fire here. There are a number of potential causes for a forest fire, but it's often lightning. On a hot day when there hasn't been much rain, a storm builds, and lightning strikes a tree and sets fire to it. If it's close enough to other fuel, such as dry wood, the fire can spread. Due to the two entrances in this cave, there's plenty of air available, so all three conditions are present for a fire, which, unfortunately, will rage until one of the elements is removed."

I understand, River says thoughtfully. *And now we can try boiling the concoction?*

"Yes. Let me show how to extinguish your fire first, and then we can put your potion on the main fire."

By the time I've explained and demonstrated how to extinguish a fire and gotten River to help do so, my own stew is just about done. I pull it off the fire and let River put his own container on—I lent him one of my earthenware pots since wood isn't likely to do well on a fire.

While I eat the stew, River and I watch the concoction start to boil. I feel like we're a pair of witches ready to cackle over their cast iron pot. *Double, double, toil and trouble. Cauldron burn and cauldron bubble, and all that,* I think with amusement to myself, my boyhood participation in the Scottish play coming back to me abruptly. I feel a sudden urge to turn widdershins and spit but suppress it with a wry grin. Who would have thought that I'd *actually* be brewing a magical potion in a cauldron?

Well, sort of a cauldron. Of course, it's not a cast iron pot—I need to do a lot more work with the metal ore in my Inventory to be able to create one of those. *But that's something to add to the list,* I decide. And it's just a couple of plants that have been stewing long enough to color the water they're cooking in a faint green.

"So, how are we going to test it?" I ask River.

I'll cut myself a little and then take a mouthful, he tells me decisively.

"Would you like me to do it?" I offer, as clearing poison is easier from my own system than anyone else's. He sends a sense of negation over the Bond.

No, you have never used the original concoction or tested any of my previous failures. It would be hard to know how this new technique compares.

Understandable—he needs a fair trial. He picks up the bowl and tilts it towards his mouth.

"Wait!" I interject, but a little too late. He jumps as the boiling hot liquid touches the inside of his mouth and some of the scalding liquid splashes out of the bowl. Although he has the presence of mind to carefully place the bowl back onto the floor, he makes disturbing noises of pain throughout.

I grab my canteen from my Inventory, filled with cold water that I haven't yet boiled—fortunately.

"Drink this," I order him, passing him the canteen. He does, splashing the water particularly on bits of his mouth that are already going red. I see that, despite his scales, he's also showing small signs of injury to the areas where the water splashed over the edge of the bowl.

Placing my hand on his shoulder, I send my consciousness into him, taking a chunk of mana with me. Healing the burns to his scales isn't difficult—the injury is only slight. The injuries to his mouth are worse since the tissue there is softer and more vulnerable, but I've had enough practice with Flesh-Shaping by now that it's easy enough.

I pull out of his body and glare at him balefully. Disturbed by the commotion, Fenrir and Bastet do the same.

"*Don't* drink scalding hot water. Honestly!"

River just looks at me, his expression dismayed. *I . . . I didn't think,* he finishes lamely.

"Clearly!" I breathe explosively, throwing my hands up in disgust. Is this a case of disjointed thinking? He knew that fire was hot and could burn but didn't realize that hot water could also burn? Ah well—lesson learned now. "Just for future reference, anything that is heated by a fire can itself cause damage. That's why we used those rags to take the bowl off the heat in the first place. And the contents of a pan heated on the fire will need time to cool down. And the more of a substance there is, the longer it generally takes to cool, especially if it's a liquid."

I will remember, he promises. I believe him. Maybe I shouldn't be so hard on him—I've had to learn my own sharp lessons from experience too. And I've made stupid errors with far more serious consequences than drinking boiling water.

River makes a second attempt. This time he's clearly taken my words to heart about more substance taking longer to cool, as he tips the bowl to allow a small amount of liquid to fill another, smaller bowl. This, he eyes cautiously.

How do I know when it is safe to drink? he asks me warily. I shrug and point at the steam rising from it.

"That's often a good indicator that it's hot, though not always completely reliable. The warmer the day, the hotter something has to be to steam. Equally, the colder the day, the lower the temperature needs to be before it will produce steam. Heck, on really cold days, even our breath steams like we're dragons. Have you seen that?"

A dragon? River asks, surprised.

"No, your breath steaming," I clarify. The lizard-man looks thoughtful.

Once, perhaps? We did not leave our huts that day; we were too uncomfortable. We just huddled together and shivered. We thought we were being attacked by spirits, that they were summoning our very souls with every breath we took. Shaman blessed us the next day, returning our souls to us, she said. Those who survived, that is—not everyone did.

Depressing.

"Well, this isn't anything about souls or spirits," I tell him, doing my best to be cheerful. "It's just about difference in temperature. So, if something steams, approach with caution. You can also hold your hand nearby. If you don't feel much heat, try holding your hand above it. If it's still not too hot, you can lower your hand and then eventually dip your finger in the liquid to test its heat." I eye his scaled and clawed hands. "Though, I'd see how good your ability to sense heat is first—it's not a good idea to accidentally burn yourself because your scales are so protective that they don't allow you to feel it's hot. Basically, just try different things, but approach it with caution. In this case, you can blow on the liquid, as that hastens its cooling."

Blowing on it? Is it some sort of magical technique?

"Not magical, just . . ." I sigh, wondering how on earth to explain about energy transfer between atoms. Then I give up. "It just works, okay?" Of course, as we've established before, blowing isn't quite so easy for the crocodile-mouthed lizard-man. "Or you can wave a fan at it. Any air movement works."

After that little discussion, it doesn't take long before the small quantity of liquid is cool enough for River to drink. He does so with more caution than before. Then, taking his knife, he makes a small cut in his inner forearm. *Funny that that seems to be a soft spot for both of us.*

Watching intently, he waits until it's fully closed before pronouncing his judgement.

"So?" I ask, impatient to know.

Weak, very weak . . . but it does have the effects of the original with none of the downsides of the venom, he concludes.

A sudden bout of curiosity seizes me. The brew is entirely made of plants and water. *Could I . . . ? Inspect Flora.*

I feel the pulse of mana go out from me, hit the bowl of mixed aslebellum and harash, and return to me. There's no notification, but the pulse *does* return some information to me. It's confused, however, disjointed. I get hints of healing, and edibility, and health, but nothing clear. *Hmm.*

Tapping my chin with a finger, an idea occurs. I consider it for a moment and then mentally shrug. Might as well see what happens. *Inspect Flora, Inspect Environment.*

This time I feel a double pulse of mana go out from me, one directed at the bowl, one expanding out from me in all directions. When they return, I feel a moment of acute discomfort. It's like . . . I'm listening to music, but there are two pieces playing at the same time. They're discordant enough to actually hurt my ears, but some instinct tells me that they are actually meant to fit together.

The information I get is much the same as the first time. Interestingly, though, it's a little clearer, the aspects of health, healing, and edibility more definite. The golden glow around the bowl is stronger than usual, too, while the glows around the plants themselves and the venom—gold and red respectively—are significantly weaker than normal. It seems like even if Inspect Environment expanded all around me as usual, it didn't do so equally.

Deciding that there's no point stopping there, I next activate all three, trying to do them as quickly as possible, as I'm not quite able to do them simultaneously. This time when the pulse returns, I actually get a notification. Kind of.

Po!&o% §ame: Les(%? &eal+$%
I#gre!§ie&@s: Aslebellum, harash, water
Ef"/§s: &eal+$% for 6u of h%§lth o#&! 5 m§?ut<s
S§&e ef"/§s: none

"Well, that's a bit of nonsense," I murmur.

Master? River asks in confusion. I wave at him distractedly.

"Just a weird notification," I explain.

Notification? is his next confused question, but I ignore him for a moment, trying to work out what I'm looking at here.

The only words that are clear are the three ingredients of the potion and "none."

"Les something eal something"? What could that be about? I stare at it, my mind working over the problems. *"Les eal." For something that heals. Could it be saying "Less something heal"?* I count the number of indecipherable characters. *Actually, could it be "Lesser Healing"?*

Things start slotting into place. *"Po!&o%" might easily be "potion." It has the right letters in the right places and the right number of characters overall. I'm not sure about the second word, but maybe "name"?* So, the potion name is "Lesser Healing." That makes sense.

As for the next line, being able to read the ingredients makes it very clear what the word preceding them is.

The third line is a bit of a blighter, but having worked out healing, I see that the same indecipherable characters are repeated. Though, given that % is used as the *n* at the end of "potion," and then as the *g* in "healing," I don't think the symbols are themselves used as any sort of code. Unless I'm wrong about "potion," but I don't think I am.

"So, 'healing for six units of something something five something,'" I think out loud. "Hmm, could that last one be 'five minutes'?" I wonder, eyeing the vague shape of the word. "And if that last one is 'minutes,' it would seem that it's talking about the 'effects,' which would work with the beginning of that line . . . What about the other two words?" I look at "h%§lth" and think that I might know what it is. After that, the final word falls into place.

So, "Effects: healing for six units of health over five minutes." Makes sense. And that simplifies the last line, which says "S§&e effects: none." Side effects, I'm sure.

I dismiss the screen, a grin of pleasure on my face at managing to puzzle that out. It's good to know what the effects of this potion actually are. Though, it didn't say anything about whether the effects are stackable or if there are any cooldowns involved, I note. I guess we'll have to test that ourselves. It's also illuminating to realize that the three Skills used together are able to offer more information than each used separately, or even two used together. It's not something I've tested up until now, but I make a mental note to do so—when I have time.

"Okay, sorry about that," I tell the patiently waiting lizard-man. "I have this . . . thing . . . that gives me information sometimes. This time I had to put more work into deciphering it. Anyway, apparently this offers six units of health over five minutes, which . . . is pretty weak." My first Lay-on-Hands did better even than that, even if it is above my original natural regeneration rate.

Yes, I noticed that, he comments.

"Exactly. I have a couple of ideas that you might like to try?" He just watches me expectantly. "All right, first, you could try reducing the mixture and see if that strengthens it," I tell him.

Reducing?

"Continuing to boil away the liquid until the contents of the bowl are concentrated. It makes a stronger-tasting stew; it may concentrate the healing power of a potion, for all I know."

I don't know either, River replies thoughtfully.

"And perhaps you could try grinding the leaves with a mortar and pestle," I suggest next. "Do you have one of those?"

This? River asks after turning to his wooden box and pulling out a smooth stone and a vaguely bowl-shaped stone.

"Yeah, that looks about right," I tell him, not too surprised that the lizard folk might have discovered this particular tool—it does seem to go hand in hand with alchemy. Or herbalism, or whatever.

I shall try your suggestions, River tells me with an enthusiastic glint in his bronze-colored eyes, his clawed fingers already reaching for more ingredients.

"Sure, but maybe we should get some sleep now—it's getting late."

Very well, River answers, looking rather disappointed.

"We'll have time tomorrow," I tell him, feeling a little sorry for interrupting his fun.

It will be better to work on this with a clear mind, I agree, River sighs, and apparently, that's that. Well-fed and tired from the day, I fall asleep partway through my Meditation.

CHAPTER TWENTY

Noticeably Growing

The next morning, I wake up and continue the Meditation that I failed to complete last night. When I'm done, feeling more than a little frustrated at my lack of progress in that area, I check my status screen only to realize that, somehow, I've gotten to a hundred percent progress towards the next level again. I guess it's the natural accumulation over the last two days in addition to the flood from the velociraptors. My debt hasn't shifted at all, though, indicating that I didn't get much more than what I needed to reach a hundred percent.

Name: Markus Wolfe		Race: Human	Class: Tamer
Level: 12	Energy to next level: 100%	Energy absorption rate: 26u/hr	Energy towards debt: 85%
Intelligence	36	Mana: 450/540	
Wisdom	36	Mana regeneration rate: 900u/hr	
Willpower	42+8 (+20%)	Health regeneration rate: 40u/hr (-20%)	
Constitution	20	Health: 200/200	
Strength	18	Stamina: 100/100	
Dexterity	18	Stamina regeneration rate: 180u/hr	
Class Skills: Dominate – Novice 6 *Companion Bond Tame – Beginner 7 Fade – Initiate 2 Inspect Fauna – Beginner 3 Inspect Flora – Beginner 5 Inspect Environment – Beginner 4		Non-Class Skills: Flesh-Shaping – Initiate 6 Stealth – Novice 1 Animal Empathy – Novice 8 Meditation – Initiate 6 Energy Manipulation – Initiate 9 Sensation Management – Beginner 6 Spearmanship – Beginner 3	

Several of my Skills have increased a little, my inspect Skills particularly. None have gotten to the point of ranking up, though Energy Manipulation is on the edge of that. I'm still two points off twenty in both Strength and Dexterity, the last two stats trailing behind, but overall, my status looks fairly healthy.

This issue is, as always, the fact that I'm still suffering the consequences of absorbing too much Pure Energy. The twenty percent reduction to my Willpower, and thereby my health regeneration rate, is a constant specter that I don't seem capable of exorcising.

From what I saw when I earned points to Strength and Dexterity, I'm losing part of the Energy that rushes through my inner world to the black void that is the result of the Pure Energy. I think it's logical to say, therefore, that every level-up I do while still suffering the reduction is partially wasted.

That's simply not something I want to keep doing. I've already lost who knows how much in leveling up to twelve, most of those levels while suffering the effects of the Pure Energy. I didn't have any choice then—it was level up or explode. I do have a choice now. However, I'm not making much progress on fixing it, either. Which is to say "none," despite trying everything I can think of.

That's what makes me wonder whether I should at least try leveling up. Maybe watching how mental or soul stats affect my inner world will reveal something I can use to help me figure out how to solve my issues with Willpower. Watching the Energy make changes to my Strength, Constitution, and Dexterity was very interesting, but it hasn't given me any inspiration for how to fix my Willpower.

My issue is that although I'd like to spread my points out evenly between all three stats, the nature of my level-up doesn't seem likely to tell me much if I do it. I was lucky when I was able to see how Strength, Constitution, and Dexterity changed my inner world: I earned each of those points individually and therefore didn't need to dedicate a whole level-up to each of them to see their effects. Unfortunately, my mental and soul stats are all high enough that I won't earn any points to them through effort, so if I want them to increase, I have to dedicate level-up points to them.

On level-up, I think that all the changes essentially happen at once. Meaning that if I increased all three of my mental and soul stats, I'd end up seeing the effects of *all* the changes at the same time, rather than knowing which ones applied to which stat. While that might help me anyway, it would be less clear than if I could see each stat at a time.

But the problem there is that I'm not sure if I'll be able to earn another level-up before I'll need to go back down into the valley. If I were going out hunting every day, I probably would be able to, despite the much higher Energy requirements per percentage point now that I'm level twelve. With me mostly spending my time crafting and Meditating, though . . .

A thought suddenly occurs as I think about Meditation. *Actually, I know what happens if I Meditate while my mana pool is empty, but what happens if I Meditate when it's full?*

It's an interesting question. I sink into my inner world and just watch my Energy channels for a while. I'm intentionally not Meditating, not properly. I've noticed the difference as I've increased my capabilities both with Energy Manipulation and Meditation itself.

Although entering my Core space is only possible with Meditation, now I'm capable of doing it at a much . . . greater level of awareness, I suppose. I remember when entering my Core space meant I was basically unaware of what was going around me.

Now it's not like that. Or it doesn't have to be, at least. I can dip into my Core space and watch the movements of Energy while still being aware of a conversation and of movements around me. I still can't use my physical eyes and mental eyes at the same time, but perhaps I'll get there.

Of course, there are consequences to not being so deeply engaged. The slowing down of time that I experience when I'm deeply engaged in my Core space is not present, which means that changes and fluctuations are a bit harder to see—they happen too quickly for me to notice everything. More relevant, it also means I don't trigger true Meditation and therefore don't gain its benefits of increased mana regeneration.

After watching a bit, trying to get a sense for the flow of Energy coming in, I focus on calming my mind and body and triggering Meditation. My mana pool is full, so if Meditation simply works to fill my mana pool and then stops working, I shouldn't see any change. If, however, it pulls Energy in regardless of whether my mana pool is full or empty, the flow of golden Energy through my channels should increase.

Of course, given that I'm now experiencing the relative speeding up of my perception, that makes it a little difficult to tell if the flow has increased or stayed the same. The flow only reduces slightly in my estimation, but I have to guess that, in fact, it has sped up.

By this point, with my bonuses from Beginner and Novice levels, my Energy increase should be more than twice what it was before. Shame I can't check my status sheet in this state to see for sure. My speed of perception is probably three or four times faster while I'm deep in both Meditation and my Core space. Therefore, I conclude that Meditation is most likely helping me absorb more Energy than I otherwise would.

If I do earn Energy faster while in Meditation, I muse idly, *perhaps I need to see if I can access some sort of meditative state when I'm doing other things too.* While I might not get the full 135 percent increase to my rate, if I could even get a fifty percent increase, it would help.

I might even manage to earn another level before we need to go finish that quest. Which brings me right back to where I started. Leveling up.

It would certainly be advantageous to have more stat points, I muse. Especially if I can get two level-ups under my belt before heading off into the valley. I've already made significant inroads into my debt and still have over 250 days before it will come due, so that's not a reason to delay. And potentially I could learn more about how to fix my soul damage from the experience . . .

It seems like my subconscious has decided that leveling up is a good idea, despite the potential risks. The question now is where to put my points.

I automatically cross out Strength and Dexterity: they're still under twenty, so I can still earn those points through enough hard work. Besides, given that I've already seen how they act on my Core space, I doubt that I'd learn anything that might help me with Willpower.

I think about Constitution for a moment. It clearly has a link with health; maybe it has a link with health regeneration that I'd be able to use to heal the damage to my Willpower stat. Or maybe not. Maybe I'd just suffer some invisible reduction to whatever Energy I dedicate to that stat as part of the level-up goes into the black hole of my damaged soul.

If I were to go down that route, I might as well put all my points in Willpower. That's the one that's damaged, after all. It's probably too optimistic to hope that leveling up with Willpower would solve the issue entirely, but it's possible that putting points in it might show me the route to getting rid of the reduction. It's an idea, and I put it to one side for later consideration.

I dismiss Intelligence after a moment's thought. More Intelligence would be great, sure. The way it improves the functioning of my mind is definitely a point in its favor, and the mana points it would give me would be great, especially with how they now give me fifty percent more bang for my buck each time.

But I'm not sure that more mana would help me in any way. I haven't gotten anywhere with as much mana as I have; do I really want to gamble that ninety more mana points would solve all my issues for me?

Wisdom, however, is another strong contender. As far as I've worked out, Wisdom seems to be linked to connection. Certainly, it was healing the Energy channels in my Core space that removed the penalty I gained to that stat after my encounter below the vine-strangler forest.

While most of those connections were woven in with each other, connecting to create the ever-flowing mandala of my internal matrix, there were a handful that reached out and then . . . stopped. I have a sneaking suspicion that those are the ones that absorb Energy from the outside and direct it to my Core. If I'm right, then Wisdom has a big impact on my Energy absorption.

That's another reason I feel that adding all six of my level-up points to Wisdom might be a good idea—if I'm wrong and it doesn't directly help me either to remove the final reductions to my Willpower, at least it might help me gather the Energy I need for leveling up again that much faster. And, for all I know, it might also help me learn how to use either Earth-Shaping or Fire-Shaping faster.

I take a moment to consider Willpower again, but it's not long before I settle on Wisdom as the best choice for now. The main problem I have with Willpower is that it's a gamble. With it damaged the way it is, putting points there could show me how to repair it . . . but it also might just waste the Energy. Or worse, potentially actually damage my soul further—I'm pretty sure leveling up again before I fix my Core would be a bad idea, for example.

Having made the decision, I refuse to hesitate any longer. Activating the level-up—something I feel I haven't done for a long time—I'm almost surprised when the box comes up to ask me about subcategories. I hadn't thought of that.

Breadth or Depth, it asks. Good question.

Before all of this, I had no idea what these might mean in practical terms. Now . . . I have a couple of ideas.

What if it's referring to my internal matrix? What if Breadth is about spreading it wider and Depth is about enhancing what is already there? And which would be better in this situation?

Breadth might easily give me more Energy absorption per point spent, but Depth is more likely to give me information I could potentially use to heal myself. The latter is a bit of a gamble, though—it might just as well mean that it is more likely to lose Energy to the hungry black void within my Core space. Breadth, on the other hand, might help my efforts to connect with fire.

Do I have to choose? I question myself. Choosing one stat to put all my points into makes sense to me. But when it comes to choosing the subcategories in the same stat? Choosing to split my points evenly might mean I get a bit less information about what each of the subcategories do, but I should learn more about Wisdom as a whole.

Decided, I plug three points into Breadth and then three points into Depth. If I'm lucky, the changes will happen chronologically, and I'll actually be able to see the difference between them anyway.

My last point chosen, I quickly dive back into my Core space with Meditation engaged and my perception speed increased as much as possible. I don't want to miss anything that's about to happen.

I enter my inner world before anything starts happening. At first glance, nothing is different. Then, as I look at my Core, I see that the light within it is growing in intensity, the usual fluctuations moving faster and faster until my whole Core is a steadily glowing heart of heatless light.

I normally compare my Core to being the star at the center of the solar system that is my inner world, but only now can I see just how wrong I've been. *Now* it's a star. A source of light so bright that I feel even my mental eyes should be burned out by its intensity.

When the luminance increases beyond anything I thought possible, there is a pause. For a heartbeat, it feels like time has stopped, like the world is taking a breath. And then with the exhale, it all begins.

Like the strident first notes of a symphony when every instrument plays simultaneously, the light explodes out of my Core in a tidal wave. An ocean of light forces itself through my narrow channels. I don't understand how it's possible for such a huge amount of Energy to fit in them, but somehow it works.

Normally almost completely detached from my bodily sensations, I still feel the echoes of the intense pleasure that usually pours through me during a level-up. Now inside my inner world, I can see what causes it.

The Energy, at first so uniform, has shattered into a thousand or more smaller movements. Like a wave that encounters rocks and becomes a raging mass of white spray, the tsunami that ripped through me is now ricocheting around the mandala.

Getting closer, I investigate what's happening in more detail. Every time the Energy passes through my mandala, the channels widen just a fraction more. Unlike with the Strength and Dexterity points, I don't notice much Energy seeping through the channels themselves into the blackness beyond.

There is some, but it doesn't appear to be doing the same thing as the Energy that leaked out during the individual Strength and Dexterity points. It also appears a little different from the rest of the Energy passing through me. Dimmer, perhaps? More bronze than gold.

At least it's not much. I'm satisfied at the thought that I'm not losing a whole load of my level-up benefits to the ever-hungry void that surrounds part of the mandala—just as I'd hoped.

As I investigate my internal matrix, I realize that there's something else happening. The Energy isn't just washing around my mandala; it's also pushing in rhythmic waves through the channels that lead outwards.

Worried that I might be losing Energy to my surroundings, I go to see what's happening. I see that I probably *am* losing some Energy to my environment, but the majority of it is actually being used. Each pulse of Energy extends the threads outwards just a bit more. The channels are noticeably growing—I'm surprised at just how much.

Considering that I've only added six points to Wisdom, in comparison to the thirty-six I had previously, I wouldn't have expected it to have as much effect as I'm seeing here. By the time the pulses of Energy start slowing down, the threads extending from my mandala must have put on a good third more growth compared to what they had when I first arrived.

I'm not complaining, but I do have to wonder why. Is it because I committed so many points to Wisdom all at once? Or is it because the points become more "valuable" as I increase in level and they themselves move past certain thresholds? Certainly, less Energy is required to add a partially earned point to a stat with fewer than ten points than to one that's approaching twenty, like my Strength and Dexterity now. Presumably, that means more changes were made with each of the stat points. Is that what's happened here? Or is getting above forty another threshold value of some sort?

Perhaps I'll find out when I add points to my other stats.

The pulses of Energy have slowed down significantly by now, the ripples moving much more slowly and sluggishly than they did at the start. My matrix in general is dimmer, not as under strain as it appeared to be earlier. Looking at my Core, I note how it seems a lot dimmer now too. Not in a bad way—in fact, if anything, I would say it looks in better condition at this level of brightness. The patterns of movement inside are more relaxed, and it just simply looks under less stress than before.

I'm not too surprised at the observation—it was the Pure Energy's forcible filling of my Core that both caused the damage to it and gave me no choice but to level up again and again. Actually, I'm a little surprised that I didn't cause damage to my internal matrix as a whole: now that I've seen what happens when I level up, I imagine that starting another level-up before the last one has really finished would cause overloading of the internal matrix itself.

Well, maybe it would be good for me to go through my matrix with a fine-toothed comb just to make sure. Nothing is showing on my status sheet about it, but that might just mean any damage isn't serious enough to appear.

Not right now, though.

Thinking that it's all over, I'm surprised when the remaining ripples within my internal matrix suddenly reverse direction. Where before they were ricocheting around my mandala, now they concentrate back on my Core, moving back to encircle it like a halo. I wonder whether some of the Energy is actually going to be reabsorbed, but I'm quickly proven wrong.

Instead, it explodes outwards, a sudden wave of light going through my internal matrix. When it reaches the outer loops of my mandala, it actually feeds into the luminous blackness, continuing to expand out to the limits of my Core world.

As it does that, it seems to collect those motes of bronze light I noticed earlier, which, interestingly enough, haven't diffused into the blackness the way I was expecting.

At the edges of my inner world, the wave seems to diffuse through the edges of my Core space and then . . . vanishes.

Perplexed by this finale, I pull out of my Core space, only to be hit by a sudden wave of nausea. I'm quickly reminded of something I forgot happened at times like this, not having leveled in a while. For all the pleasure during the leveling up itself, the aftermath isn't fun. Not to mention something else: the smell.

It's not actually too bad. I don't think I even vomit this time—I don't see any evidence of it, anyway. Perhaps my body has gotten rid of the majority of its toxins, or perhaps a non-physical stat causes less purging, I don't know. Is this what that final explosion of light did?

Of course, less purging doesn't mean none—I've still sweated dark brown stuff and currently stink to high heaven. The stench wakes those of my Bound who haven't already woken, and Fenrir actually retreats from the alcove entirely, distress coming through the link. I probably shouldn't have leveled up indoors . . .

"Sorry, everyone," I say, hurrying outside before any of the disgusting waste coating me can sink into the floor and make the cave stink forever more. When Bastet comes out, she doesn't look too happy with me, though the cubs seem unbothered. River has discomfort rippling through his spikes as he emerges too.

Does that happen frequently? he asks me, a little trepidatiously.

"More frequently than I'd prefer." I sigh. "I need to go wash in the river. Would you like to come with me?"

I am always happy to accompany you, River tells me earnestly, though I have a feeling that he'll make sure he's on the upwind side of me. *Besides, I have run out of water to use for my experiments, so I need to collect some.*

That's a good point. I should make sure I bring all my pots with me to fill. Though, I probably best ask River to get them for me—I don't want to risk making the smell linger even longer than it should.

River seems to agree, as he doesn't object in any way to being my gofer and soon returns with all the empty pots I left in the alcove.

"We're going down to the river," I announce to everyone. "Who wants to accompany us?"

As it turns out, everyone does. Surrounded by my Bound, I walk down the hill, doing my best to feel the differences between before and after leveling. Apparently, six points in Wisdom all at once makes a noticeable difference.

I haven't yet checked my status screen, but I definitely have more of a sense of . . . connection to my surroundings. It's like there's a sixth sense that is slowly being awakened. I'm not limited only to my eyes anymore, though my new sense is nowhere near as clear as my other senses. It's more instinctive, like a flicker in my peripheral vision or the hint of a scent.

I also feel less like an outsider. More like I . . . belong here. It's odd to say, but I feel a kinship to the creatures and plants around me that was missing before. Curious about how it might be affecting my inspection Skills, I cast Inspect Environment.

There's a qualitative improvement—I feel the pulse go further and impact more plants and hidden creatures than it did before. Interesting.

"Just one moment," I say to my companions. They stop and look at me curiously as I cast Inspect Flora on a plant by my feet. It's one I recognize, one I've cast on before. I'm doing that intentionally: I'd like to see how it's changed.

Common plant: Sycopsis franguloides
Edible: Yes (leaves, roots after being exposed to high heat, berries after being frozen)
Alchemical uses: Unknown (leaves), unknown (sap)
Medical uses: Burn treatment (unknown)
This plant is an evergreen that may have specific properties when exposed to extremes of temperature. It has multiple alchemical and medical uses.

The answer is that yes, there is significantly more information. Where before only leaves were identified as edible, now the roots and berries are marked as edible too, but only after they've been exposed to a certain temperature. There's also more information about the alchemical and medical uses—clearly the leaves and sap are the most useful when it comes to alchemy. More experimentation will be needed to find out which part of the plant is good for treating burns and what needs to be done to make it into suitable medicine.

Still, it's a lot more information than I had before, proving the immediate use of adding points to Wisdom. Looking up at River, I tell him about the new properties that the Skill revealed to me. He looks interested and leans down to pick the plant.

"Why don't we come back this way and grab a few then?" I suggest. "That way we don't have to carry them for long. You can experiment when we get back."

Very well, River agrees, standing up straight again.

We travel the short distance to the river, and I use Inspect Environment again just to make sure there are no more of those crocodile-like neres hiding in the water. Fortunately, the only thing the pulse picks up is a quickly retreating shape in the bushes, which disappears out of range before I can get a proper look, let alone use Inspect Fauna.

I wash off the level-up gunk and then collect some water from upstream. It isn't too long before we head back up the slope, with a brief detour to collect some of the plants I inspected earlier. I'm relieved to have had a peaceful trip into the forest for once. Not that we went far, but distance doesn't seem to influence how much trouble we can get into.

Up on the plateau, I detour past my clay-lined pit and check its drying status. It's hard to the touch but still feels a bit clammy. I suspect it will take another day to get fully hard, assuming it doesn't rain tonight. I make a mental note to prepare the tanning solution today—that way it will be ready for tomorrow.

Today, I have other things to do. Preparing the hides for tanning, for one. Seeing what else we can do with River's potion-making for another. I have also had some inspiration from increasing my Wisdom and am eager to see whether it might lead to any improvements in my Willpower. Then there's sparring between my Bound and attempts to earn an archery Skill. And that's not including the arrows that broke yesterday, which I need to fix or replace, or the flint-headed spear that I still need to create. Lots to do and not much time to do it in.

Mentally rearranging the day, I decide that sparring is probably the best to start with—that's the one that requires us all to be present. After it's done, everyone can then split apart to do their separate tasks.

"All right, everyone," I announce, getting the attention of all my Bound. "Get ready to spar." I look over at Lathani, who's peeking at us from behind her mother as if shy. "If you want to join us, you're welcome," I invite her warmly. The nunda juvenile doesn't need telling twice and bounds towards us, clearly keen on the idea.

Now, who should go first?

CHAPTER TWENTY-ONE

Make a Difference

After our sparring session, I continue working on my archery. I finally get the reward I want in the form of a Skill notification after at least an hour of practice holding the bow correctly and shooting from several different positions. I think the final trigger for the Skill is when I manage to shoot a leaf I've convinced Bastet to throw into the air for me—apparently, shooting at stationary targets just isn't enough. However, shooting at moving targets doesn't count either unless I'm actively doing my best to shoot *well*—and making some noticeable progress in that regard.

> Archery
> You have taken the first step along the path to Master Archer. You have displayed an understanding that wielding a bow means more than simply setting a string to a stick, pulling it back, and letting it go. Continue practicing techniques designed for the more efficient and effective use of a bow in order to advance this Skill. Gain 2% to the effects of Dexterity per level in this Skill when using a bow.

Two percent to the effects of Dexterity isn't much when my Dexterity is only eighteen, but every little bit helps. And by the time it ranks up to Novice, I'll have earned an eighteen percent increase, which might actually make some difference. But what exactly it means by "effects of Dexterity," I'm not entirely sure, though I can make some guesses.

While I've been practicing my archery, River has been working on his potions. I decide to check on how things are going. As I walk over to where he's set up a station, not far from my clay pit—which is drying well thanks to the cloudless sky today—I see the evidence of multiple tests, both with the venom and without. He has a fire going too, which he's obviously been using to test the impact of boiling.

"Any luck?" I ask.

Well. The, uh, reducing seems to strengthen the potion, but it also reduces its quantity.

"Expected," I comment since that basically is the idea of reducing—getting rid of the dilution doesn't change how much active product is in the brew.

Yes. He holds up a small bowl of liquid, which is the same shade as the one I inspected earlier but more opaque. *This is what I was able to produce. The same mouthful seems to work at least three times as fast.*

"All right, let me see if I can get any information about this," I say with interest. As before, I trigger all three of my inspect Skills and receive a notification.

%otiµ% n&§e: $?ss¤r H%@l+n%
#n?&edie&t§: Aslebellum, harash, water
/§ff"cts: H%@l+n% for 11u of he§l§: #v&r 2 /@nu!es
S§&e /§ff"cts: none

Still a lot of gibberish. I sigh. *And not even the* same *gibberish.* If I thought there might be some sort of code within the messages, that hope is gone now as I compare the two notifications to each other. Even the words that are clearly the same don't have the same symbols, nor are they made difficult to read in the same way.

I add trying to make my inspect Skills play more nicely together to my to-do list. Still, at least it appears that the same *actual* words have been used, so it doesn't take me too long to work out what this notification is saying.

It seems like this potion is still classified as "Lesser Healing," though its effects are definitely better. Eleven units of health over two minutes is a *lot* better than three units over five minutes. In fact, it's even starting to verge on being useful—the healing is equivalent to one of my original Lay-on-Hands casts, though significantly slower.

Assuming it can be used in conjunction with my Flesh-Shaping, it could help in the situation where I'm just not able to channel healing fast enough. Or if I have multiple injured Bound, it could be enough to keep the less injured one in the game while I deal with the more injured one.

"Not bad," I say to River. "Eleven units of healing over two minutes." He makes a face of disgust.

Still very poor, he comments. *Herbalist could make concoctions with at least four times the healing power of that one with her eyes closed.* I shrug, passing the bowl back to him.

"She was probably using magic to do so," I point out.

Which I cannot use. River sighs. I stay silent, but the thought triggers an idea: what if he could? River doesn't seem to notice my distraction as he continues speaking. *I have tried your other suggestion of reducing the amount of venom.*

"Has it helped?" I ask in interest. He makes his equivalent of a shrug.

Some. There are still the side effects. He holds up two bowls, both with black, lumpy liquid. Appealing. Not. *This one is with half as much venom as I originally used. This other is with a quarter as much.*

I use my inspection Skills on the first potion and once more roll my eyes at the gibberish that appears.

P§tiµn n&m!: Ac!?ic #?a§in@

§?gre&#e&ts: Aslebellum, harash, venom (unknown)
Ef§"c&s: #?a§in@ for 25u of he§l§: #v&r 2 mi?u!§s
§id& ef§"c&s: 6 acidic d#m!?e e/e%y mi?u!§ /or 4 mi?u!§s

"It's no longer classed as a Lesser Healing potion," is the first thing I say. Squinting, I try to work out what it *is* classed as. *Ac something ic. Ac-ic. Acidic!* Well, that makes sense, considering what River said.

Interesting that the venom is identified as "unknown." Because I haven't identified the creature it comes from? Perhaps.

The healing on this is much better even than the reduced health potion: twenty-five units over two minutes. But there's something written in the side effects section. It takes me a little time to work my way through.

"Six acidic . . . *d, m, e* . . . damage? That would work. So, six acidic damage something minutes? No, minute—there's no *s* at the end. Six acidic damage *over* . . . no, *every* minute for four minutes? Yes, that makes sense." Which really sucks. Twenty-five units of healing for twenty-four units of damage.

I wonder why it's not outrightly saying "health damage." Maybe some creatures would be resistant to acid damage, so drinking this would be like a normal health potion? Perhaps.

I check the other potion, but it's much of the same, just lower healing and commensurately lower damage.

"Seventeen health points healed over two minutes, but fifteen points of acidic damage in total over three minutes," I tell River. He looks a little depressed, but not surprised.

Much as I thought, he comments a moment later, shaking his head.

"Well, keep trying," I say in the end. "Maybe experiment with different concentrations of each substance, or even leaving something out?"

As you wish, River agrees. *I will need more ingredients.*

"I imagine that some of the others have finished their meditation by now," I reply. "I'm sure that we can find a group to go with you."

The others have been meditating since sparring this morning, though Bastet has been watching the cubs instead. I'm sure by this point some of them wouldn't mind going out—hunting is necessary to maximize their gains, after all.

It only takes a few minutes to check with my Bound, and soon I'm watching the backs of River, Bastet, and the cubs disappear down the hill. Fenrir and Sirocco both stay with me—Fenrir because he apparently wants to guard me, and Sirocco because she wants to absorb more of her Energy Heart.

I decide that it's time for me to test the inspiration I gained when I added those six points of Wisdom during the level-up process.

I feel like it might be a bit of a long shot, but what if the pattern of waves I saw going through my Core space during the level-up could help me saturate that black space? Perhaps the issue with my previous attempts to saturate the void was less to do with quantity and more to do with *how* I was doing it. It's worth trying—it's not like I have any other ideas.

Settling in a sunny spot that will become shady as the day wears on, I close my eyes and try to figure out how to make my Energy ripple.

It's evening. I missed lunch and I'm *starving*. I pull some cooked meat out of my Inventory and tear at it with zeal, partly because of my growling belly, partly because of the frustration I feel.

I can't do it. Whatever happens with the Energy I collect during a level-up doesn't seem to be so easily replicated. Maybe it's that I need more Energy—I just leveled up, so all I was working with was my mana and what little Energy I could gain through Meditation. Maybe it's just that my Energy control isn't good enough to be able to replicate it. At least my efforts have been rewarded with Skill levels. Meditation has gone up two levels to Initiate eight and Energy Manipulation has actually ranked up to Journeyman.

I pull up the notification again to have a proper look while I finish my predinner snack—extensive Core space manipulations make me far hungrier than they really should, considering I'm just sitting down during them. Before, I just noted that I ranked up but hadn't wanted to distract myself too much from what I was doing. Now I have the time to actually think about it properly.

Congratulations!
You have advanced a Skill past Initiate. Energy Manipulation is now Journeyman 1. You previously focused on Energy manipulation within your internal matrix, but recently, you have been exploring controlling mana outside of your internal matrix, both internally and externally. You have also been improving your ability to precisely control different types of Energy, even when multitasking. You continue to earn 1% Energy efficiency per Journeyman level in this Skill. In addition, you will gain +4% Energy control while mana is not in your internal matrix and a further +2% Energy control while mana is within the domain of a consenting target per Journeyman level in this Skill.

The description takes me a little time to get my head around, but when I do, I'm pleased with the improvement. Although only getting a single percent increase in Energy efficiency per level isn't as good as before with two percent, I'm currently sitting at a forty percent Energy efficiency increase. That means by the end of the Journeyman levels, I'll be at fifty percent Energy efficiency, which is a pretty good level, I reckon.

The real benefit is the other four percent increase to Energy Control *per level*. What does it mean when it says it's not in my internal matrix? Is that linked to what I was trying to do earlier with pushing my Energy or mana out of my internal matrix and into the void? Or is it more related to what I do when I heal my Bound? Or both? Either way, it seems likely to be useful within a few levels.

As for the additional two percent improvement in Energy control within the domain of a consenting target, which I'm sure means when I'm controlling mana in my Bounds' bodies, I'm hoping it will enhance the improvements that I already have to healing with my Flesh-Shaping upgrade. I guess I'll see the next time I heal one of them.

That my afternoon hasn't been a dead loss is a relief, though I certainly haven't achieved what I wanted to. I look over at where River is staring into a bowl with frustration and somehow think that I'm not alone in that.

I push myself to my feet and walk over to him, detouring only temporarily to stroke Bastet and then Fenrir. I was vaguely aware of the party returning from their hunt—which doesn't seem to have been very fruitful if the single carcass I see is any indication. It's another beast I don't recognize. Not that that's too surprising, considering how little time I've spent in this world. It's about twice Fenrir's size, so a decent meal for the group but not much more than that. It seems like today has been destined to be of limited use for all of us.

"Things not going well?" I ask River, coming to sit next to him.

The lizard-man sends me a sense of frustrated negation.

The concoction has improved but not enough. When I test it on myself, it doesn't even come close to what I experienced with Herbalist's creation.

"And boiling it doesn't help enough?"

It helps, but it doesn't solve the issues. In fact, boiling the harash on its own until it is practically yellow makes a more effective potion than combining the harash and the aslebellum does, but even that is weak in comparison to what it should be.

Yellowy-orange irritation flickers through his spikes. I understand entirely—it's immensely annoying to know *how* to do something but be unable to actually do it. Almost as frustrating as knowing I need to do something and not being able to figure out how to. And not being able to ask Google.

"Perhaps I should see if Flesh-Shaping can make any difference," I muse out loud, this other possibility having occurred to me during the day. "And if so, maybe I can teach you how to do it for yourself." Assuming that I can explain how to use Flesh-Shaping well enough for him to actually translate that into something that works for him.

I greatly appreciate the offer, Mas—Markus, River starts with both hesitance and gratitude flowing across the Bond between us, *but I fear that it is unlikely I will be able to learn magic before I Evolve. I would not wish to waste your valuable time on such a fruitless endeavor. Nonetheless, it could be advantageous if you were able to recreate Pathwalker Herbalist's efforts.* He is very careful with his wording; dipping a little into our Bond indicates to me that he's doing his best not to offend me. I sense that he's indeed grateful that I might offer to help him learn magic—and that he's fearful there would be consequences if I spent the time trying and then he still failed.

"Listen, I don't mind trying to teach you, and it might actually help me too even if you don't manage to learn. They always say that one learns something best by teaching it to someone else. But you're right that I should probably see if I can do it at all before even considering teaching you." Though, thinking about it, having someone else able to use Flesh-Shaping would be good. He's probably right that he needs to Evolve first, though—hopefully, if he ends up as a Pathwalker, his mana capacity will expand significantly. At the moment, even if he does manage to gain Flesh-Shaping, the seventy mana units he can hold at one time is barely enough to fix even a scratch—Flesh-Shaping is very mana heavy.

But as I've just established, that's a later consideration. For now, I need to try it myself, and I figure that that starts with me testing what I can actually do with the materials. I suspect that the herbalist affects the concoction directly, though—she probably has a particular Skill for it, or whatever she'd call it.

To that end, I pick up the harash and try to infuse mana into it the way I would with a carcass.

It's not all that surprising when it doesn't work; I was more than half expecting that result. After all, my attempts to infuse other plants with mana haven't succeeded, so why would this be any different?

Nonetheless, in the pursuit of being thorough, I pick up the aslebellum and do the same. With the same result.

All right, I say to myself. *How about the venom?* This attempt I give even odds. It's an animal product, which might mean that it's able to be affected by Flesh-Shaping. On the other hand, it's not the whole body, only a small part, and not really flesh at all.

A flicker of hope lights inside me when my mana isn't just automatically rejected. At the same time, it isn't absorbed as easily as into the crocodile skin, for example. It's almost like my mana is reluctant to move forwards. Like it's uncertain whether it should do this or not.

If it's possible for mana to have an opinion, of course. Which I really hope it doesn't, because I'd hate to know what would happen if my mana decided it didn't like me . . .

Either way, I press forwards, trying to overcome the reluctance of my mana with my will. Slowly, begrudgingly, it enters the venom and starts to spread within it.

I suddenly realize that I understand why it dissolves everything around it—it's not dissimilar to my own stomach acid, but several times stronger. If I remember correctly, stomach acid is usually hydrochloric acid and strong enough to dissolve food as it is. Why it's black, I put down to the other substances that are mixed in with the acid. What they're for, I can't tell.

Once my mana fully saturates the venom, I sense that I have just as much control over the liquid as I do over skin or a carcass. I test it briefly and add in some more mana to increase the quantity of the liquid. I'm tempted to test whether I can change the concentration but decide that I better separate it out for that.

Actually, if I do separate it into two amounts, will both parts be equally saturated or will my mana only stay in one?

To test that out, I take one of my earthenware and separate some of the acid into it. To my pleasure, separating the liquid changes nothing: I have equal control over both quantities.

A few more tests to the liquid in the bigger earthenware pot reveal that, yes, I can increase or reduce the concentration of the acid—to a point. I suspect that I can increase the concentration about two or three times. Reducing the concentration, funnily enough, is actually harder, and I can only reduce it to perhaps half of its initial concentration at most.

I do find something else interesting. If I increase the concentration of the acid and then rapidly reduce it, I can reduce the concentration to half of the original acid. If, however, I increase the acid's concentration and then wait for a few minutes, the new concentration becomes the base value from which the half concentration is calculated. I have to guess that that indicates the mana actually changes into the physical components of the acid but takes a little bit of time to do it, even if the effects are immediately evident.

My tests done for now, I turn back to River, who is waiting patiently. It must be pretty boring for him—although I can sense all the differences I've made to the venom, for him it must have been like watching paint dry.

"Let's give this another go. I haven't been able to affect the plants at all, but the venom is a different story. Perhaps that will be enough to make a difference."

Perhaps, River replies, equally cautious, but his eyes tell a different story, as does the excitement in his movements.

He chops the harash and aslebellum. Why he didn't do that while I was testing the venom, I don't know—perhaps the freshness makes a difference? Or he thinks it does, at least. After putting the harash slivers in a bowl, he reaches for the venom. This time when he pours it in, I'm immediately able to feel what happens.

The acid in the venom starts reacting with the harash and breaks the outer layers apart. Even as it does that, parts of the venom itself are transformed. Some of that is the acid itself—being neutralized, I suppose—but the other components of the venom, the elements I wasn't able to identify the function of, are also being affected.

So, there goes the idea that it's purely the acidity that makes a difference to this potion.

Clearly the acid *is* important, and I guess the plants themselves are a large part of the function of the potion. That is evident from the fact that boiling them *did* work. However, I now have to theorize that the venom is important in some way to *enhance* the healing aspects of the plants.

Or perhaps the reactions that are going on here, besides the immediate effects of the hydrochloric acid, are actually detrimental. Could they be the reason why the potion is almost as harmful as it is helpful? But then, that's clearly not a feature of the original potion, so the herbalist must have some way of getting around it.

I just observe while the reactions continue. I even swirl the bowl a little when the speed starts to die down to make sure that the venom that has not yet had a chance to come in contact with the plant pieces is able to do so.

Finally, it seems like the mixture has stabilized; even when I swirl it around, no further reactions take place.

"Okay, add the aslebellum, please," I tell River. The lizard-man jumps a little, perhaps startled by me suddenly speaking after having been silent for a rather long time.

He wordlessly obeys, not asking any questions even though his curiosity and impatience are coming across the Bond. All I can say is that he's *far* more patient than me. There's no way I'd have been able to keep silent all this time. Even so, I don't say anything right now—I don't feel like I've learned enough yet.

When the minced aslebellum enters the liquid, a new explosion of frantic reactions takes place. Once more the acid itself dissolves the new pieces of plant, and the substance that was already changed by the harash is interacting now too.

Maybe changing the order of plants would make an impact on the potion produced, I think to myself. After all, venom that has reacted first with the aslebellum wouldn't necessarily react in the same way with the harash, and that might have unknown effects.

As before, once the reaction speed starts dying down, I swirl the bowl to speed it up again.

By the end, I'm left with a liquid that is quite different from what it started as. Interestingly, I maintain control over the liquid as a whole, even though it has fully encompassed the plants that I was previously unable to affect. I suddenly wonder whether it's because my mana has been present since the start.

Curious, I turn to one of River's previous attempts with the venom and try to sink my mana into it. I fail, just as I did with the plants. My magic clearly doesn't recognize this as a space it can affect in any sort of way.

Well, that answers that *question. Now only . . . hmm, a myriad more?*

The concoction done, I quickly cast my combined inspect Skills. Once more, gibberish comes up, but I'm familiar enough with it now to verify that nothing has changed just from me adding my mana: it still offers twenty-four damage for twenty-five healing. That verified, I pick it up and take a mouthful.

Master, don't— River exclaims, reaching out for me. Too late.

The potion is *nasty,* and I grimace as I swallow it. Though it doesn't *taste* like stomach acid, it's certainly got that same burn to it. The actual flavor isn't particularly nice either, earthy and bitter at the same time.

I immediately close my eyes and focus on being able to see what it's doing to my body. As expected, the acid remaining in the liquid burns the lining of my mouth and throat, then hits my stomach like a punch. Since my stomach is already designed to deal with strong acid, it's not as impactful there as in the other places, but I have a feeling that if I ingested too many of these potions without being able to heal myself, I would develop a stomach ulcer before too long.

At the same time, though, I sense the other aspects of the mixture getting to work on the damage the potion caused. Once that damage has been healed, a little of it is absorbed into my body and heads towards the aches from practicing my archery that I haven't yet bothered to heal.

When the small amount of substance—healing mana?—reaches my over-used muscles, it goes to work on healing them, but it's used up in a second and makes no noticeable difference to my muscles.

That's the point of healing above the damage, I say to myself in amusement. Opening my eyes, I see River looking at me anxiously.

"I'm fine," I reassure him. "It didn't taste nice and felt worse, but it actually healed its own damage."

You should have given it to me, he chides me grumpily. It's the most critical I've seen him, and it makes me feel exasperated that it's over me hurting myself.

"One, I made it, so I should test it. Two, I wanted to see its effects, and of the two of us, I know my own body best," I say with a shrug.

Did you learn anything? River asks, losing his grumpy demeanor in favor of excitement.

"I learned lots of interesting things," I tell him obligingly, "but whether they will be useful to improving the potion's success, I don't know."

He looks a little depressed, perhaps assuming that that means we're not going to go any further. That, of course, is far from the truth.

"Do you have plenty of ingredients now?"

Yes, Master, River answers. *Markus,* he corrects himself with some chagrin.

"Then let's do some more experiments. I'm sure now that I can affect the potion; it remains to be seen if those changes are improvements, of course. And then, if they *are* improvements, whether you can do them."

River doesn't look entirely convinced that the latter will be possible, but he seems open to exploring it.

By the time we call it a night, the sun has already set, and my stomach is threatening to go on strike again. Bastet has already retired for the night with the cubs, though Fenrir remains outside with us, loyally on guard.

In the end, the most effective method for the potion-making turns out to be relatively complex. I have to first double the concentration of the acid, then, before the new concentration "sets," I have to return it to its original concentration. Repeating that a few times while swirling the mixture seems to do a good job at making the reactions happen quickly.

And making the reaction happen quickly between the harash leaf slivers and the venom seems to be key to increasing the number of health points the potion offers.

After that, I actually *reduce* the concentration further—in comparison to the harash leaves, the aslebellum root seems to work better with a longer dissolution time. I've also discovered that as long as enough time passes after I reduce the concentration, I can actually reduce it further.

Therefore, my final step is to reduce the concentration by half again as soon as I can, then by half a final time when the reaction between the aslebellum and the rest of the concoction is complete.

The final product that I come out with is a lot more satisfying than what we started off producing.

```
!o+on §&me: @cid%c Heal§?!
Ingre&ie&ts: Aslebellum, harash, venom (unknown)
E§§ec!s: Heal§?! for 39u of heal%*: ov/r 2 ?!nute§
Sid# e§§ec!s: 2 acidic dama§e e/e%y ?!nute fo% 4 ?!nute§
```

The healing and the damage time haven't changed, but this new potion only loses eight units of health for the thirty-nine that it provides, which gives a net benefit of thirty-one units of health. Significantly better than the one unit of net benefit that we had before. Though, it does leave faint burns in the stomach since the damage lasts longer than the healing effect.

My other experiments mostly offered better results than the initial potion, though a few were worse, but this is definitely the best of them all. The downside, of course, is that I have to be involved in it.

"No luck?" I ask River. He gives his equivalent of a sigh. While I've been experimenting, I've been trying to help River get in touch with the small pool of mana he has somewhere inside him.

No, Master. I'm sorry.

"It's all right," I say, though I sigh a little myself. The problem is that River is failing at the first hurdle: he's unable to even enter his Core space, or whatever the equivalent is for lizard folk. Either my instructions are exceedingly poor, or it's because he's only tier one. Or both.

What do you wish me to do? River asks. I consider the question for a moment.

"Well, for tonight, sleep. But in the future, keep trying," I say in the end. Surely it won't hurt? "But don't spend too much time on it. I will try to create a few more of these potions for backup, but you keep making ones with boiling water. Try to improve the concentration as much as possible by reducing them, maybe try grinding the leaves and roots too, but don't worry about matching the venom exactly, or even getting rid of the venom entirely. If you can find a way to concentrate the effects of just the harash leaves, that will create a healing potion, albeit a weak one."

My reasoning is that even if they're weaker, he'll be able to create them by himself. And, who knows, perhaps by reducing the concentration of the water significantly and grinding the herbs, he'll be able to make a potion that has at least thirty-one units of health. If it has more than that, he'll actually be beating the Acidic Healing potion for effect.

But for now, it's time to turn in. I take a moment to check on my clay pit. Today's sunny weather has been perfect for it. Tomorrow, I'll need to take multiple trips to the river to collect enough water to be able to submerge my hides. I'll also need to use Flesh-Shaping on the hides to rid them of the remaining fat, blood, and meat.

Preparing the tanning solution will require brains. I already have a good few in storage, but it might be a good idea to collect some fresh ones too—plus more Energy-containing meat for my Bound and perhaps some hearts for me to help accrue Energy towards my next level just a little faster.

While I make my plans, I pull out some more food. I don't have the mental energy to actually cook anything—a premade stew will have to suffice.

Once again, there's a long day ahead. I better get to sleep. Before that, though, I have one more thing to do: Meditate on fire. And this time I've decided that actually observing the fire might be a good starting point.

Sitting cross-legged in front of the fire burning in my hearth, I stare into its heart, not looking for anything in particular, but rather trying to see as much of it as I can.

I've always loved seeing the flames dance, and as I relax into my observation, this time is no different. I watch the different colors—the shades of orange and yellow, the white that appears occasionally, or the odd flash of blue or green from trace elements in the fuel that feeds it.

And suddenly, I realize that all kinds of connections are slowly coming into focus. At my realization, they sharpen, as if they were just waiting for me to mentally acknowledge them before appearing before me fully. It's amazing the amount of difference my increased Wisdom seems to be making. Honestly, it feels like when I gained Meditation in the first place—the change has opened up a whole world to me, one that I hadn't even realized I couldn't see. And just like when I first gained Meditation, I wonder again at what greater depths there are that I still can't see but that I may be able to gain insight into later.

The fire is at the center of the almost translucent tendrils waving in the air, reaching out into the air, into the ground, even into my Bound—and me. I find the latter particularly curious. Is it drawing something from me, or is this a representation of the heat that I feel on my skin? Can I touch the connection somehow?

With all my practice recently in sending my mind either deeply into myself or into someone else, it shouldn't be so surprising that I find myself able to both touch the connection and actually follow it with my consciousness in the way that normally only happens with Flesh-Shaping. I don't know if I'm seeing this with my physical eyes or if I've closed them and am seeing this with my mental eyes, but I somehow get closer to the fire without actually moving.

Looking at it this way, the fire appears immense. The little blaze that I set light to a while ago and nurtured into the fire that warms my sleeping area is now an inferno that fills my full vision. Its flames are not themselves visible, but the tendrils that wave in the air and burrow into the fuel below are reminiscent enough of the physical appearance of fire that it makes little difference.

I see the connection I'm following disappear into the heart of the fire. Following it with my mind, I'm almost surprised when I don't actually get burned. In this state, the fire is not hot, but there are other dangers. One of the tendrils passes through my presence and I abruptly feel a sense of suction.

Instinctively rejecting the sensation, the tendril falls away—but not before another has come to try to investigate. I move hastily on, a little unnerved despite myself.

Into the heart of the fire I go, and there I find the end of the connection. It doesn't end abruptly; instead, it breaks into multiple threads, which surround a single ball of light—the fire's heart, I guess.

It's odd to think about from a scientific perspective. I wasn't aware that fires *had* hearts, though I suppose they have areas of particular heat. But these change as the conditions do—the fuel that previously offered plenty of burning potential is used up, and so the fire moves. That's what a forest fire does, after all—sweeps through a forest, constantly burning new material as the old is consumed and left behind as ash.

But then, maybe this fire heart isn't actually physical. As I observe what's happening, I notice the heart shifting about, jumping from place to place. At one point another heart develops, and my connection sends new strands to weave in with that one too. Then it flickers out and my connection returns to this one.

It's a fascinating view, and I could honestly watch it for hours, but I do need to sleep. Gently pulling back, I return to a greater awareness of my physical self. I stretch, feeling oddly stiff and slightly burned, as if I've been in the sun for too long. Which I probably was, but I wasn't feeling it until now.

Lying down on my bed, I close my eyes and focus on the warmth of my hearth fire once more, the sensation of heat against my skin more than a little soothing. Once again, I reconnect with the tendrils that tantalize and stroke against me, though this time I don't follow them anywhere. Instead, I wrap them around myself, the sensation of heat almost like sinking into a hot bath—oh, that sounds wonderful. With flames licking at my mind, I'm enveloped by the warm blanket of sleep.

That night my dreams are filled with fire.

I dance amid the flames, the flames licking at my skin. Sometimes the fire burns, sometimes it caresses. It feels like I'm dancing with a partner, one who is always a hair's breadth from choosing to immolate me. There's a thrill to the danger that I've never felt before.

I speak to my partner, but my words are lost in the crackle of the flame so thoroughly that even I don't remember what I said. I am walking on fire, surrounded by it. It forms the hall around me, a ballroom of white-hot pillars and vaulted arches of red and orange, constantly moving.

We spin and my partner dips close enough to whisper in my ear, but all I hear are the snap, crackle, and pop of the flame in her voice.

"I don't understand," I whisper back. Her expression becomes frustrated, and she speaks again at a normal volume.

This time her voice is the roar of an inferno but is no more understandable than the first time.

"I'm sorry, I don't understand," I tell her, genuinely distressed at my inability to communicate with my wonderful dance partner.

A third time she tries to talk to me, stopping our dance and shouting, her expression twisted in frustration and anger. Her voice is the crack and rumble of something unable to take the intense heat and finally giving way. A house that has withstood an era being consumed by a fire; a rock that has endured for eons being melted and broken in a lava flow. It's an awesome sound, yet still not one I can interpret.

Wordlessly, I shake my head.

My partner erupts into incandescent rage, the fire of her being turns white-hot and blue-tinged. I cry out as what before was simply the threat of burning becomes the reality of it.

CHAPTER TWENTY-TWO

To-Do List

I jerk awake as the pain mounts, only to discover that the inferno wasn't only in my dreams.

Cursing, I beat at the fire, which has set light to the fabric I'm lying on. Fumbling for my canteen, I pour it on the flames licking at my clothing. Fortunately, since most of them are from synthetic fabric, they're resisting the heat. Annoyingly, though, it has caught on my cotton jacket.

After a few moments, I've managed to get the accidental blaze under control. There are still some hints of fire that I fear might erupt anew into a conflagration. Then I have a thought that I wish had come sooner: what about my Inventory? It puts out fire on torches, so wouldn't it deal with the flames on my clothes too?

Putting action to thought, I start piling the fabric in. Then, my head cocking to one side, I pause. Am I seeing something here? Looking at the marks in the fabric that was around me while I slept, I start to see a pattern. Did the fire actually erupt from my body? It looks like it—although the line of burned fabric is blurred thanks to both the fire spreading and my own efforts to beat it out, I can see the shape of my own body.

I finish putting the fabric into my Inventory, wondering at how exactly I managed to set light to everything around me without actually burning myself or even setting light to the clothes I'm wearing. I vaguely remember a dream of some sort. I was dancing? In a ballroom? Or was it in a fire? And I don't really remember *who* I was dancing with, but I do remember feeling sad about something.

Anyway, that I was apparently able to create fire is good; that it was completely uncontrolled is not.

As I look at the burned remains, I become aware of several pairs of wide eyes looking at me. *Oh hell, I forgot that I wasn't alone in this cave!* I twist to find River pressed against the back wall looking—and feeling, now that I'm paying attention to the Bond—rather terrified. I remember him telling me about the poor experience he had with a forest fire. Being roused by licking flames probably wasn't the best wake-up call . . . I'm surprised he didn't run away completely.

By the door, Fenrir is less afraid but more wary, poised to run—either out of the cave or into the alcove to drag us out. Bastet, standing warily by the hearth, is equally wary, posed in front of the cubs protectively. The cubs are peeking around her legs, more curious than afraid.

"Sorry, guys," I say, a bit shamefaced. "I'm not quite sure what happened there, but I don't think it will happen again." I cross my fingers behind my back. That said, I am actually fairly confident that the reason this happened was because I was playing with the connections spooling out from the fire before I fell asleep. Hopefully, if I just go to sleep normally, I won't have any accidental eruptions in my sleep. At least, none involving flames.

At my reassurance, Bastet and Fenrir both settle down, Bastet licking a couple of cubs, who make a few quiet noises of complaint or question but then settle down too. River, on the other hand, while relaxing a bit, doesn't lie back down.

What happened? he asks.

"I'm not entirely sure," I admit, not wanting to lie to him. "But I think it was connected to some exercises I was doing before I went to sleep. I'm not going to do those exercises again now, so it should be fine. Go back to sleep." River slowly tilts up his head and, with just as much reticence, lies down again but doesn't close his eyes. "You can sleep outside if you'd prefer," I offer, not wanting him to be uncomfortable.

I sense him weighing up the decision: inside, where there might be fire but it's warm, or outside, where it's cold, but the risk of fire is much lower. He eyes me again.

What do you intend to do now?

Good question. I don't know how long I've been asleep for, but I'm not feeling particularly tired right now. I walk quietly to the entrance of the cave and look out at the sky. It's cloudy and dark, not offering any indication of time. I shrug and step carefully back inside the alcove.

"I'll think through my to-do list," I tell him quietly, deciding while I speak. "Then maybe do a few experiments, but nothing with fire. Or go to sleep if I start getting sleepy again." For now, I'm definitely too awake to do that.

Very well, River says. *I shall stay inside for now.* I get the sense that if he wakes up to fire again, he'll probably choose to brave the cold instead of risking getting burned.

"All right. I'll see you later, then," I agree. He turns onto his side to face the wall, presenting me with his back. Knowing that it's a gesture of trust more than an affront, I don't take offence. Instead, I lie back down and think, staring at the stone ceiling.

The first thing I think about is the time-bound task hanging over my head: that quest. I search through my notifications. *I wish there was a Quest tab or something!* I say to myself in frustration. Then I remember how I was able to make my Bound's stats appear in a tab and wonder whether I could do the same here. Focusing, I'm pleased when it suddenly appears next to my Bound tab. Opening it, I see a few entries.

Quests
Active Quests: The Vine-Strangler Grove II

Completed Quests:
The Vine-Strangler Grove I
Available Quests:

Focusing on my only active quest brings up the information about it.

In the course of your adventures, you explored the center of the Vine-Strangler Grove and defeated its guardian. Upon investigating the guardian beast's lair, you discovered a route down to one of the Ley Lines of the planet, running unusually close to the surface. However, you do not seem to have been the first to make this discovery. You have realistically theorized that a beast may have tunneled down to access the Ley Line and blocked the stream. You have posited that a side effect of this may have created the stagnant pool of Pure Energy, the Cores, and the tunnel you first encountered.	
Quest: The Vine-Strangler Grove II	Quest type: Regional
Objective: Find evidence to prove or disprove the reason for the formation of the underground tunnels. Objective: Rectify the situation with the exposed stream of Pure Energy and return the area to its previous state.	
Time to complete Quest: 45 days	
Suggested difficulty: Journeyman	Reward: Uncommon Silver Chest → Rare Silver Chest (rarity increased due to previous rewards being passed over)

Eleven days have already passed since I got the first one and seven days since I got the second, and I still have a lot to do. *I wonder if I could have some sort of note-taking tab?* I think to myself. *It would certainly be useful to be able to write a to-do list.* Figuring that I might as well try, I focus hard on what I want to achieve.

There's a bit of resistance this time. I don't know if it's because the System, or whatever is controlling this display, doesn't know what I mean, doesn't want me to have this facility, or if there's some other reason. However, I just double down on my visualization.

I want a blank screen that I can add words to by thinking at it, which I can then access later. I visualize a blank page on a computer screen and a keyboard input that allows me to only add what I want; no more or less.

As my brain starts to hurt, the System gives way. Slowly, a screen forms in front of my eyes, exactly as I imagined it. At the top where I can see "Quests," and "Bound," and "Status," there's now a new entry: "Notes." There's even a QWERTY keyboard input at the bottom of the screen, which, surprisingly, reacts to my finger movements rather than my mind directly. Maybe it's running off sense memory rather than actual touch since I certainly can't feel anything beneath my fingertips. It was probably because I was concentrating on how it felt to write on a Word document.

Still, I'm not upset about that; if anything, it makes writing easier. I have a feeling that I'd otherwise struggle to keep my thoughts disciplined. I'd hate for my new note-taking software to be filled with nonsense because I started thinking about one thing and ended up with another—I had enough of that kind of rubbish when taking notes during quick-paced university lectures.

Actually, if I can get a Quest tab and a note-taking tab, why can't I get a clock? Excitement fills me as I think of another option too—if my quest can count down the days, can't I get some sort of indication about when my Energy debt will be due?

Since they're two different ideas, I focus on them one at a time. I start with the idea of my Energy debt showing a countdown first; that's probably more important than me knowing exactly what time it is.

There's a little resistance, but not as much as when I was attempting to get the Notes tab to appear. In a short amount of time, I see a number appear in my status screen below the Energy debt. Two hundred and sixty. The number of days remaining, I imagine. Huh, longer than I thought. Better that way, I suppose, than shorter.

When I try to get a clock, however, I find that there's some sort of impassable block. It doesn't matter how much I focus or on what image I settle, no clock of any sort appears. Eventually, I give up. I have the countdown to when I'll be leaving this world; that will have to do.

After returning to the Notes tab, I check that what I write on the tab remains even when I switch to another tab or close the screen completely. I'd hate to write my whole to-do list and then have it disappear as soon as I click away . . . Fortunately, my experiments prove successful. My touch-typing is a little rusty since I haven't touched a computer keyboard in a couple of months, but I did it for enough years that after a little practice, I'm soon back to my previous ease.

So, a to-do list.

I've only got forty-five days until the quest timer reaches zero, which I assume means I'd fail the quest automatically; what that means in terms of consequences, I don't know. Losing the potential rewards, for sure. Would there be more consequences than that? Possibly. Either way, I'd like to at least try. And frankly, it's probably a good idea for me to head down before the quest timer ticks down to zero—solving the quest will take time. It might even be possible to solve the quest before the timer runs out. For all I know, that might earn me extra rewards.

However, before I do that, I want some decent armor and better weapons. Hopefully, I will be able to use Flesh-Shaping to make the creation of the former easier and, potentially, better. I know I can affect an animal when it's dead and remove its hide or affect the hide once it's off the animal's body. What I still need to test is whether I can speed up the tanning process or even tan something purely with magic. Then, I also need to know whether I can affect a tanned hide. As I experienced when experimenting with River, being able to affect ingredients and being able to affect the sum of those ingredients aren't necessarily the same thing.

And I *do* need to tan it. My experiments with the roll of paranax hide I saturated a few days ago have proven that it *does* deteriorate even when full of my magic, though much more slowly. Possibly I could actively cut bits off and regrow them to solve that issue—like dead skin shedding to allow new cells to come through—but that would require regular maintenance and weaken the protection as it starts deteriorating. If tanning can create something more enduring, that would be better.

Still, I'm hopeful that magic can help me. I'm planning on using brain oils to make the hides more supple since the hide itself is heavily armored but stiff. My experiments with River's potions seem to indicate that I'm able to affect ingredients that originated from living beings. So, there's a good chance that I'll be able to learn how to create the effects of soaking in a tanning basin for days with only the raw ingredients.

But that will require me to do the first batch manually so I can actually see the differences. Going into the forest tomorrow will hopefully supply me with enough brains to soak the Tier-two crocodile hide, paranax hide, and maybe a few others. It would be good to get a view on the differences between how the tanning solution affects the hides of different creatures. If I have time, that is—whether using magic to strip the hides from the bodies or physically doing it, the process takes time.

After that, I'll need to find some way of smoking it to seal in the tanning and make the hides waterproof—something else to see if I can replicate with my magic. I might test boiling weaker hides too. From what I can tell from the memories I absorbed, boiled hide is stiffer and tougher than tanned leather. It might work better as armor, but I'll have to see.

Once the hide is tanned or boiled, what I do next will be rather determined by how much control over the flesh I subsequently have. If I have control, I can easily shape it to my needs, though I'll probably still put on a non-magical fastening so that if I run out of mana, I'll still be able to put it on and take it off. If I don't have any control because it no longer counts as "flesh," I'll need to take more time cutting and shaping it, probably using sinew to sew the pieces together.

I'm planning on making something like a tabard. Since the roll of crocodile hide that I have in my Inventory is a bit longer than I am tall, I'm intending on making a hole in the middle for my head so that it should hang down about mid-thigh on both sides of my body. That might still offer some vulnerabilities to my sides, but maybe I can do something to help with that. Of course, that will only be once it's tanned. I also need to make a soft underlayer and some new trousers—I've got very few clothes that aren't rags by this point, and I want to keep *some* of my old outfits if I possibly can, if only as a memento.

I've only made one tanning frame at present, and if I'm lucky, that's the only one I'll need if I manage to do everything with magic on future hides. But again, I'll have to see for that.

So, that's armor. Weapons are another topic.

I've got the iron ore in my Inventory, but it's going to take a lot of processing to render it into a useable form. While both metal tools and metal weapons would be an immense upgrade, I'm not sure whether I'm going to have time to do that as well as the tanning before I need to go back down into the valley. After all, the quest timer isn't the only time commitment I have there—River's village is facing the incursion from the vine-stranglers, and the more days that go past, the more likely it is that they will be engulfed by it.

It takes two days—well, a day and a half—to get to the tunnel down to the Pure Energy stream with no delays and then a further day to get to River's village. I'll need to build that travel time into my calculations. Ultimately, the earlier I can get down there, the better, but I can't see it happening for at least another week, probably more like two. And that's assuming my experiments go well with my tanning and I don't have to start over.

Considering I also need to continue to dedicate time to try to solve my Willpower issue, I think it's highly unlikely I'll be able to create metal weapons. Primitive techniques are as tediously time consuming as they are laborious. Once more I heartfully wish for an interdimensional Amazon. Heck, I'd even take an interdimensional DHL at this point. At least they might be able to take an order and bring it to me.

There's a huge amount of processing I need to do even before I get usable ingots of iron. Making charcoal, for one thing, to get the furnace up to the right temperatures. Even the most simplistic method will take time to collect or process enough wood, chop it into the right sorts of sizes, build it into a mound, and cover the mound with mud. Then there's the actual time that the wood will take to char until it becomes useable charcoal. That last alone will take a couple of days. So, all together, it's probably a week of work just in that.

Then there's all the processing of the ore itself. Another good week or more of effort when I consider all the time it takes to create the tools as well as actually do the job—I'll need to build a kiln and hollow a log to make bellows. And then even after I've actually got a lump of rudimentary iron out of the process, it'll take a good amount of time to turn the unformed metal into the shaped tools I'll need to even *begin* creating the arrowheads and spearheads that are my first priorities.

So, we're looking at about twenty to thirty days of pretty consistent effort before I can expect to be able to make some better-quality weapons. And that's just the blacksmithing work. For arrows I'll also need to make a balanced arrow shaft, fletch it, then attach the arrowhead. Not to mention that the tools and spear will need handles or shafts, all of which take time to create.

It's a process that's far too long to do this side of going into the valley. Which means that, as I thought earlier, I need to make sure I'm sufficiently supplied with primitive weapons. At least the longer days on this world and my reduced need for rest and sleep do mean I can get more work done than the average person on Earth.

Of course, I have other aims in mind too. I want to explore more of the connection I feel to fire. Obviously, I don't want to have unexpected events like what just happened, so I need to work out how to exert some control over it. Perhaps applying some of what I've learned with Flesh-Shaping could help? Certainly, being able to control the temperature of the iron would make my task of processing the metal significantly easier. So, I definitely want to work on both of those.

In addition to Flesh and Fire-Shaping, I do still want to work on Earth-Shaping since I reckon that would be very useful too, especially with my plans for the future. It being both practical for daily life and useful in combat, I'm keen to find a way past the obstacle stopping me from "feeling the earth," whatever it is.

And then there's weapons training. As I've learned in recent days, actually taking time to focus on technique is a good way to earn new Skills that offer good benefits to using specific weapons in combat. I might get a mace Skill if I work with that for a bit and perhaps a knife Skill if I try fighting with that too. That means continuing to dedicate time to sparring.

Part of making new clothes for myself may involve making needle and thread for sewing the hides together. It's possible I won't need to sew things together if my Flesh-Shaping proves up to the task, but if not, I'll need to add a needle and thread onto the list. So far, my attempts to create a needle out of bone have proven rather . . . fruitless. I just don't have either the knack or the patience to work bone so thinly.

And then I feel like facepalming. I've overlooked something *very* obvious. I pull out a bone from my Inventory and focus on pouring my mana into it. Since I specifically retrieved a small bone, it doesn't take long until it's saturated, taking less than a quarter of my mana pool. Once it is, it only takes a matter of moments and mental focus to reshape it. Less than five minutes after I started, I have a perfectly serviceable bone needle.

I haven't gotten any Dexterity points out of it, that's for sure, but it's good to know that I won't have to struggle with using a flint stone to very carefully knock off shards of bone and hope that I don't accidentally snap it again. Thread is another question, but if I don't find anything better, there's always the option of growing my own hair to extraordinary lengths and then creating thread out of that. I tuck the needle into my Inventory for later if necessary.

Finally, there are all the normal daily tasks. Fetching water. Cooking food. Hunting. Collecting Cores for River's debt. Helping more of my Bound to get closer to their Evolution. Not to mention helping the new additions become comfortable with the rest of us. Plus, my experience so far has taught me that I get restless when I do one activity for too long. *Then again,* I think ruefully, *I suppose that with as many things as I'm adding to my to-do list at the moment, I'm not going to have to worry about running out of different things to switch between.*

Ah well, at least River's poisons and potions add another element to our fights, plus my bow is only just now starting to reach its full draw with my current Strength. When I increase my Strength, I'll have to either find another material or a different construction method to enable it to cope with me. Or change to a weapon that will more directly translate my Strength into damage. An atlatl, perhaps? It's worth considering; I haven't dedicated so much time to a bow that I couldn't switch to a different weapon right now. But whether it's a good idea or not, I'll have to decide later. Besides, I like my bow.

It's a lot to do. Fortunately, I do have my Bound to help out, especially when it comes to hunting, collecting resources, and, in River's case, some of the processing too. A plus point to having a sapient, humanoid Bound, even if the whole thing leaves me with a knot of guilt in my stomach now when I think about it.

Feeling a little better at having written my to-do list, though already exhausted at the thought of all the work ahead, I wonder if I can fall asleep now and close my eyes.

Perhaps half an hour later, I open them again—sleep is still evading me. Sighing quietly, I shift to move next to the banked fire, most of it reduced now to embers. I add another few thick sticks to help it keep going longer.

Bastet shifts closer to me and presses her head against my knee. She's clearly awake too.

"Did I wake you?" I ask in a murmur.

Yes. But it is fine. What troubles you?

I switch to speaking mentally so I don't wake anyone else. *Nothing particular, just . . . restlessness. There's a lot for me to do, and River's village to help, and the quest to achieve, and I don't even know how I'm going to do half of it.*

Bastet is silent for a long moment, then rubs her head against my knee again.

Do one thing, and then the next, and then the next. You will either succeed in doing it or not. If you don't succeed and it does not kill you, you can try again later.

I can't help grinning. It's just the pragmatic sort of response I should have expected from her. And she's right—I can't do everything at once. I have some things I know how to do and others that I can at least try to accomplish.

We're silent for a while, just content in each other's company. Slowly, a thought comes to mind, something I've considered at other times but never at the right moment to actually test it.

Bastet?

Yes? she responds after a moment, turning to face me with curiosity in her eyes.

Do you mind if I test something?

What? she asks again immediately as a hint of wariness comes across the link. Not wariness because she thinks I'll hurt her intentionally, but caution caused by having just lived through the recent fire episode. I don't blame her.

It should be fine, I try to reassure her. *I just want to feed a load of my mana into you and see what happens.* The feeling of skepticism increases despite my attempt at soothing her worries. *Look, I'm not going to ask the mana to* do *anything. I just want to . . .* I trail off, figuring that "see if you can become a magical battery for me" wouldn't sound great. There's silence between us for a few seconds.

If this causes a problem for me, I expect you to correct it, Bastet tells me finally.

I promise, I say, meaning it. After all, if Bastet had any sort of problem, caused by me or not, I'd do my best to sort it anyway.

Then I'll allow it, she consents, turning her head back to the fire and leaning into my knee more heavily.

I feed mana through my hand and into her. With all the practice I've had recently, I find that I'm actually able to do it without even fully entering my Core space. That will certainly make healing her easier, though I may still need to go into Meditation to actually do the healing bit.

After channeling most of my mana pool into Bastet, I cast Inspect Fauna on her.

Raptorcat: Bastet

Tier 2 beast (Evolved)

Special abilities: Fire breath

Health: 1300u

Mana: 150u

Minimum Willpower recommended to Dominate without other impacting factors: 41

Bound (Companion) of Markus Luke Wolfe. Most commonly used weapons are its natural features of teeth and claws, though this beast may use the wind generated by its wings and its magical ability of fire breath to gain an advantage. Social beast with strong capacity to form bonds. Will not quickly or willingly give up previously formed Bonds.

This is the first time I've used Inspect Fauna on Bastet since her Evolution. Maybe I should have used it before, but I didn't think of it. It's interesting seeing the changes. Nothing I didn't know, much like River's, though.

That tickles, Bastet tells me a moment after I use the inspect Skill on her.

You felt it? I ask, my eyebrows rising up my forehead.

It ran through my Energy channels and poked at my Core, she adds. Huh. So that's why it could potentially enrage Tier-two creatures, I guess.

Did you feel anything from my mana? Or now?

I get the impression of a shrug from her. *Warmth. Nothing more.*

Well, at least it doesn't hurt her. I shrug too. I didn't see anything about Bastet becoming a mana battery or anything like that. Maybe it only happens if I saturate the target with my mana. Considering that Bastet is significantly bigger than the paranaxes, it'll probably take another several hours to do that. I don't feel like dedicating that much time right now. Maybe later.

I do leave the mana I already transferred, though; even if she isn't identified as a "mana battery," if I can withdraw the mana I put in her later, she could act as one in a pinch.

All right, thanks, I say to Bastet. *Let me know if you feel anything odd or uncomfortable at any point, okay?*

Yes, she assents easily, then lays her head back down on her taloned paws. I'm actually starting to feel tired again. Emptying my mana pool several times in a row and then Meditating to regain it has that effect on me.

Trying not to disturb anyone, I lie down on the piled fabric next to River and close my eyes. This time I'm out like a light.

CHAPTER TWENTY-THREE

An Important Function

Waking up as the sun lights the sky with the magnificent colors of sunrise never gets old, though this morning I have to admit to feeling a bit groggy. The longer nights here might mean that I can usually wake up at dawn and still feel completely well rested, but it turns out that burning the midnight oil for a few hours rather cuts into that. Still, my body is used to waking up with the dawn, and the stirring of my Bound would rouse me even if it weren't.

I boil some water for drinking and add in some of those faintly minty leaves to make the water taste a little more palatable since I'm not going to give it time to cool down. Meanwhile, I make a breakfast out of berries, those nutty-tasting roots, and meat.

I wonder if I could find some eggs, I muse to myself. That would certainly be a change, but perhaps it's not the season. If I *can* find eggs and maybe make some sort of flour out of the potatoes or nutty roots I can collect, I might even be able to make something like pancakes. *Mmm, berry-covered pancakes.* It sounds like a dream, but it might be possible—potato flour is a thing, isn't it?

After breakfast, I go over to check my clay pit. It seems fully hard to my touch, and it hasn't cracked badly at all. There are small cracks, of course—that was inevitable—but none of them seems to go deeper than a few millimeters, so they shouldn't compromise the watertight nature of the pit. I fill them in with a bit of extra clay anyway.

Unfortunately, since it hasn't rained, the pit is empty. I tip in the other containers of water I have in my Inventory—on our trip later, I'll fill them up again. At least my Inventory makes carrying water so much easier than it would be otherwise.

Once my Bound have eaten, we all engage in some sparring, though I cut it a bit short after only four fights each.

"I need to go into the forest to do some hunting," I offer as an explanation. "Who wants to come with me?"

It doesn't take long before I get a response from everyone. Bastet has decided to stay home with the cubs today—I think she wants to teach them some techniques and have them practice before they go back into the forest. It seems that she's taking the idea of sparring to heart. So in the end, it's River, Fenrir, and Sirocco who join me as I troop down the hill.

As always, I use my inspect Skills at regular intervals to spot any interesting plants or potential dangers. Unfortunately, there is no record of what Inspect Flora says in my status screen, so I'm going to have to rely on my own memory for the plants I spot that look interesting. I approach the river only when I'm almost certain that there's nothing waiting for me there and fill all my containers except the one containing my tea.

Then, we continue deeper into the forest looking for prey, though I do take the opportunity to collect some of the most interesting-looking plants, as does River—much to Sirocco's annoyance at our slow pace.

"Go and scout ahead, then, if you're restless," I tell her with slight annoyance when she once more sends irritation down our Bond as I stop to collect more potatoes. Ruffling her wings huffily, Sirocco does just that. I focus back on the potatoes, tucking them into my Inventory. River is using his box to store the plants he's collecting—his experiments have proven that using ingredients that have been stripped of their Energy by storage in my Inventory make particularly weak potions and poisons. The hard box is a bit awkward for him to carry, though. Once I've got some tanned hide, making a backpack for each of us definitely needs to be on the agenda.

While we continue walking, I think back to something else I tested this morning—Bastet's use as a mana battery. Unsurprisingly, there are differences between the results of feeding mana into a live body and into a dead one. Primary among those is that the mana disappears out of her body far more quickly. The paranax's hide still held most of the mana I put into it in the morning, whereas Bastet's body held no trace come this morning.

Before we started sparring, I tested it again, though I didn't fill her this time. Instead, I put four hundred units in—almost all of my mana pool. I then tried to pull it out and discovered something interesting: as an immediate-use battery, Bastet is *much* more efficient than the paranax's carcass, which only yielded a single mana back for every ten units spent. For the 400 units I put into Bastet, I got out 395.

However, that didn't continue. I put another four hundred units in before we started sparring and then pulled it out again just before leaving, and I was only able to withdraw about three hundred units. I will need to test more, but I suspect that I would have been able to use that mana for healing—certainly, the way I was easily able to reconnect with it by touching her briefly indicates that.

Which means that it might be a good idea to fill my Bound with mana when I know we're about to go into a difficult situation where they will likely require healing. Of course, doing it much ahead of time is pointless, as it will just disappear, which lessens its use as an emergency mana storage. But in a situation like with the salamander, shoving a chunk of mana into each of them for use in a later healing session might be a good idea—things might not have gotten so dire with Bastet if I'd been able to tap into a store of mana I'd left in her earlier.

By the time Sirocco comes back to tell us excitedly about a group of prey animals further into the forest, I've amassed a good collection of plants and each of the two inspect Skills I've been using have increased by another level.

The animals are . . . odd. Kind of like large—very large—beetles. The smallest are about the size of a dinner plate; the largest are about three times that. They're quite flat, their tops only about fifteen centimeters off the ground at their highest, and their legs are more sideways squat than holding them up tall. In fact, their legs rather remind me of a cockroach's, even if the actual shape of the thing isn't particularly similar. Instead, they're round with no obvious head.

I realize why that is a moment later: their mouths must be underneath them, as I see them leave a trail of destruction as they move slowly across the ground. Generally bizarre.

Not wanting to miss the chance to use my Inspect Fauna Skill, I quickly cast it.

Pylobus
Tier 1 beast (Unevolved)
Special abilities: None detected
Health: 90u
Mana: 10u
Minimum Willpower recommended to Dominate without other impacting factors: 10
Invertebrate species subsisting on loam and other detritus. Important for the health of the forest as a whole.

Basically worms, I conclude, *except with an exoskeleton.*

"You want to hunt these?" I ask Sirocco dubiously. Not only are they not likely to be much good for Energy considering how little health they have, but bottom-feeders don't tend to taste good. Yes, I know that many people like eating the rubbish bins of the ocean—namely shellfish such as oysters and mussels—but we don't tend to eat worms or beetles if we have a choice.

Sirocco, however, seems to be of another opinion. She sends a series of images to me of her finding a much smaller one once, picking it up, and letting it fall on a rock to crack open the exoskeleton. Apparently, she really liked the taste of the meat inside. I'm rather more impressed at her ingenuity in finding a solution to getting through their hard outer covering.

"All right," I agree quietly. I pull my mace out of my Inventory, then pause. Maybe a mace would be better for crushing, but perhaps these things have a softer underbelly. They certainly have a mouth, so that indicates that there might be some easier way through the exoskeleton. If I can flip them over with my spear, I might be able to make the fight easier than it's already likely to be—I can't imagine that these creatures are going to offer our group much threat. Then again, I have been wrong before.

Pulling my spear out, I look around at my group.

"Ready?" I ask, then receive a range of affirmative responses. "Then let's go."

Since the creatures don't seem to have identified our approach despite the lack of stealth we've been practicing, I don't bother to engage it now. Though, on second thought, maybe I should have used it anyway; it's not going to increase in level unless I use it, and what if I fail against a more perceptive opponent because I didn't use it when I could have?

Anyway, too late for that. The beetles—pylobuses, apparently—become aware of our approach when we're only a few steps away. They scatter, darting into the bushes as quickly as they can. Which turns out to be pretty fast when they have a mind for speed.

I use my spear to try to flip as many of the creatures as I can, figuring that even if I don't kill them immediately, either one of my Bound can, or I can come back later to deal with them. I reckon that they'll take a few moments to right themselves either way.

It takes me a couple of tries to get the right angle to flip the pylobuses I target, and in the end, I only manage to get three onto their backs by the time the rest have disappeared into the bushes. True to my expectations, they rock back and forth in place, their legs waving madly. Definitely a design flaw, that one.

When I look at what they were hiding on their undersides, I can't help my face from screwing up in disgust. While the pylobuses' tops are covered by a dark brown carapace, their underparts are a nondescript beige color and segmented. Though it still looks too hard to easily pierce with a beak, I'm right that this is their weak point.

The pylobuses have legs set all around their bodies, emerging from joints at the edge of their carapaces. Right now, they are all waving in the air, the pylobuses clearly trying to gain some sort of purchase somewhere. It's hard to get a proper count with them moving so much, but I reckon that there have to be around twenty to twenty-five legs on each, though the bigger ones appear to have more legs than the smaller.

The disgusting bit, however, is their mouths. They're a mess of tendrils that remind me more of an anemone or a parasitic infestation of worms than anything else. With them stuck on their backs, even their mouths are doing their best to reach out for anything they can grab. I can't help turning to Sirocco again.

"You *really* want to eat these?"

Sirocco sends an impatient assent, clearly making it obvious that she's already answered that question. Then she wonders whether I'm going to kill them or not.

I shrug and pull out my spear, holding it above the closest pylobus. Then, before I stab it, I suddenly wonder whether using Inspect on different members of the same species makes any difference. Mentally shrugging this time, I decide that it's worth a try. Casting Inspect Fauna, I discover that the biggest of the pylobus is actually Evolved. *I wonder if it has a Core,* I think to myself with interest.

Then, focusing on moving and holding the spear correctly, I kill the helpless pylobuses. The one that was identified as being Evolved already had double the health points as the others, so it required four strikes where the others only needed two. Considering that I'm still only using a sharpened stick here, their mouths must be an especially vulnerable bit.

Looking over at the others, I see them already tucking into their own kills. River appears to have used his spear too, as it's lying next to him. I don't know how Sirocco and Fenrir killed theirs, but when Fenrir senses my curiosity, he sends a quick image of him flipping them and Sirocco pecking them to death with her toothed beak. Fair enough.

In total, we killed eight pylobuses. That it hasn't even made a noticeable impact on my Energy store is not a surprise: these probably would have only given me a couple of percent each when I was at level one. By this point, I'd probably have to kill the whole . . . herd? Pack? Swarm? Anyway, I'd have to kill a lot of them to gain any sort of progress towards my next level.

Don't you want to eat some, Master? River asks, his head cocked to one side. *Sirocco is not wrong: the meat is surprisingly tasty and very tender,* he adds. I suddenly realize that I've been standing here like a lemon for too long, just staring into space. I eye the dead beetles, a squirmy, sick feeling in my stomach.

Remember tortoises, I say to myself. *Considered by Darwin to be extremely tasty, and they're creatures in shells like these ones.* But somehow the limp, ichorous tendrils coming out of the creatures' mouths are just so off-putting. Not to mention those *legs.*

"No, it's okay," I say finally. "I've been collecting plants to eat; it's only fair that you guys have something tasty too."

Very well, River responds, though he gives off the distinct impression that he thinks I'm a little mad.

"If you find a Core, can you give it to me, please?" I say, turning away from where he's starting to dive into one of the ones I killed. While they dine, I use Inspect Environment on the area around.

Interestingly enough, the Skill points me to a number of still circular objects half buried in the ground underneath the bushes. I only see them because they're ringed in red, but once my attention is drawn to them, I realize what the pylobuses have done: they've disappeared under the bush to break my line of sight and then settled themselves into the forest loam. They might even have some sort of Stealth Skill or ability to go unnoticed as long as they don't draw attention to themselves since no one spotted them before.

I don't draw my Bound's attention to their hiding places, though—I figure the pylobuses have earned a break. It's not their fault that I have a Skill that can spot their hiding places. And they're fulfilling an important function in the forest: waste disposal is always necessary.

Besides, I hardly feel it would be fair—a bit like attacking the baby porcupigs all the way back in the beginning. Though, to be honest, with what I know now about them, I reckon I might have come off worse in that fight if I'd gone for it.

I do resolve to take the carapaces of the dead pylobuses with me, though. I think they'll make pretty good bowls or plates.

By the time my Bound have finished munching on their treats and I've packed all the carapaces into my Inventory, the sun is already more than halfway on its journey towards its zenith.

"All right, let's do some proper hunting. Preferably things with *heads* this time," I comment wryly—though getting meat for my Bound is part of the objective, harvesting brains for my tanning solution is the main reason I'm here. The pylobuses, even if a delicacy to my Bound, were unfortunately short on any recognizable brains. "Can any of you detect anything bigger than these?" I ask all and sundry, knowing that they all have different ways of finding prey. I get a series of thoughtful but negative responses. Then the last—Fenrir—seems to indicate an uncertain positive. "What is it, Fenrir?" I ask him specifically.

The lizog offers me a sense of a group of big two-legged creatures somewhere to the right of us. If my interpretation of his message is correct, he's not sure where they are or how far away they are; although he caught a faint hint of scent, it wasn't strong enough to give him much information.

Well, that's more than we have to go off otherwise. I decide that we might as well investigate. Directing Fenrir to lead us to the creatures, I wonder what it is that he's taking us to—something I've already encountered or something new?

While we travel, I continue using my inspection Skills on a regular basis—Inspect Environment and Inspect Flora more often than Inspect Fauna, but even the last gets a bit of a workout whenever I see a creature scurrying away from our party. The forest is alive, but I feel pretty safe walking through it. With the four of us together, we kind of out-level the area.

While there are still creatures around that could pose a risk to us, most are not likely to choose to start something. Since they don't look particularly appetizing or likely to offer much Energy, we don't attack them either.

I frown as we head back into an area that seems very familiar—weren't we here ten minutes ago or so? I pull up my Map, but since I didn't look at it before, I can't tell whether we are going in circles. I do, however, notice that we're heading back down towards the valley, though the general downward trend of our route could have told me that anyway.

Over the next few minutes, I check my Map several times. We're moving at a medium pace—something like a quick jog or a slow run. It means we cover ground reasonably fast without chewing into our stamina too much. It also means that I can tell Fenrir is leading us on a bit of a meandering path, though always in a certain direction. *Is he trying to triangulate the scent?* I wonder. I'd love to hop back into his head to work out whether my guess is correct, but that would mean I'd have to stop moving so I could concentrate. I suppose I'll have to live with my curiosity for now.

As it is, I notice that the meandering on our route seems to reduce more and more as we move further down the valley. Soon, we're not meandering at all but running almost directly towards something.

The creatures, whatever they are, are further away than I was expecting; I'm rather in awe of how sensitive a lizog's nose is. Bastet was right when she gave me the sense of the lizogs being able to follow us all those weeks ago when I first Dominated her.

Finally, though, Fenrir slows and sends warning that we're close. By this point River seems to have identified something too if his intent focus is anything to go by.

"Sirocco, can you go scout for us?" I ask the bird. She sends an indifferent assent and wings her way through the trees towards whatever the rest of my Bound can detect. Personally, my senses are still too dull; I can't see anything, but if I concentrate, there is a quiet sound of rustling and cracking up ahead.

The bird doesn't take long to do her scouting and return. Upon landing on my shoulder, the impact surprising considering her slight weight, she sends me an image of what she saw. I immediately recognize the creatures: the two-legged odd mixture between an ostrich and diplodocus that I've creatively named ostridocus. I'm able to count this herd at between twenty and thirty individuals.

We won't need to kill even half that amount: they're big enough that a single corpse should feed at least two of my Bound for a couple of days. If we each kill one, we'll have enough meat to last us for a few days. If we kill more than that, I'll probably have to put the meat in my Inventory; even if that will strip the Energy away, it still provides important nutrition, which makes it better than starving. And even better, they have good-sized heads.

This is also a good opportunity for us all to practice our fighting in a relatively safe scenario. Not completely safe, though: the ostridocuses are not exactly defenseless. However, considering that Bastet and I took them on and killed a good few with only us two and without suffering significant injury, we should be able to do better than that with the four of us.

Plus, we can actually try to work together. The fight with—or rather, slaughter of—the pylobuses didn't have any strategy to it; it didn't *need* any strategy.

"All right," I say quietly to my Bound. "Here's what we should do." With that, I outline my thoughts. "Any comments?" I ask after my explanation.

If I may summarize, River asks, then continues when I nod at him, *Fenrir will be the visible threat, driving the bulk of the herd towards our trap. You and I will be the true damage dealers, the jaws of the trap that close on the herd. Am I correct?*

"Yes," I affirm, "and Sirocco will be keeping an eye on things from above. There's no need to kill every member of the herd; we only need to grab two or three each to easily satisfy our requirements. Any other questions?" I receive a series of negative responses. "All right, let's do this."

Moving off, we quickly get into positions. At first, the plan goes exactly as intended: the appearance of a lizog serves to spook the herd. I imagine that since lizogs run in packs, they think that the first lizog is only the herald of more to come. If they are thinking at all, of course.

The members of the herd quickly move away from Fenrir, who, as intended, drives them straight into our trap. The panicked ostridocuses—or bisonisans, if my Inspect Fauna is anything to judge by—are easy targets, and I manage to get in a lethal spear strike on two of the stampeding creatures with no issue. In fact, there's more indirect risk of being knocked over and trampled than direct risk of being attacked.

A quick glance to my sides tells me that River and Fenrir are also having success—at least two more bisonisans are down near them. Satisfaction goes through me. I judge that we've got more than enough meat and brains for our needs.

That, of course, is the moment when a feeling of alarm from Sirocco comes across the Bond. If I could put the feeling into words, I would only need one: incoming.

CHAPTER TWENTY-FOUR

The Law of the Jungle

What's coming? I ask Sirocco sharply over the Bond at the same time as sending out a wordless warning to my other two Bound. The bird sends me a picture of a running creature snapping at the heels of the herd. The picture is blurry, though—I don't know if that's because it's fast or because Sirocco's not focusing enough on its details or on sending a clear picture of it to me.

Fenrir confirms her message at the same time with his own image of a much larger silhouetted figure running past him. Evidently, it chose to ignore the lizog for now; why, I don't know. Because it doesn't see him as a threat? Because it doesn't feel he'd offer enough meat to make the fight worth it?

By this point, both River and I have closed ranks, our spears in our hands, the other ostridocuses—bisonisans—ignored. As the last of the herd moves past our sightlines, we are able to see what's chasing them.

Though Fenrir's perspective is affected by his own short stature, the creature *is* big. Its shoulders are level with my own, above even River's. On top of that, it has a long neck that puts it at least a head taller than me if it stands up completely straight. It has four limbs but only runs on two of them: the other two are flightless wings, which nonetheless play a role. I watch as it flaps its wings to add speed to the strike at the bisonisan in front of it.

Its jaws are long and toothy, its tail surprisingly weighty; I would have imagined it to have a thin one more like Sirocco or Bastet, but it turns out that it's more like the prey it's chasing in the tail department. Its skin is scaly and barely feathered except on its wings, which have a bit more plumage. In fact, it kind of looks like an allosaurus if the dinosaur's small front legs were small wings instead.

It chases the bisonisans towards us. I grip my spear more firmly, prepared to defend myself. It gets closer and closer, its jaws opening.

And then it's past us.

I exchange a dumbfounded look with River even as Fenrir trots up to us, having been following the newcomer at a safe distance. Turning my head to watch the predator continue snapping at the heels of the bisonisan herd, I dare to use Inspect Fauna on it while hoping it's not too far out of range.

My hope proves to be in vain, though: clearly my inspection Skills have quite a short range. Since the whole group of creatures are now practically out of sight, I just shrug and stoop to check on the creatures we've killed. I got two; River managed to get three. Five bisonisans are likely to be enough meat to satisfy us for a couple of days at least. I reckon that this hunting trip can be considered a success.

Just as I'm starting to tie the feet and tails of the bisonisans to a couple of long branches I had in my Inventory, I hear a familiar thudding. It's a bit like thunder, except there aren't enough clouds in the sky for a storm. Plus, the sound isn't coming from the sky above but from the forest in front of us. And it's the same noise I heard only a few minutes ago.

As I look up, I realize what's happening: the whole load of bisonisans are running at us once more. *Why?*

"Sirocco, what's happening?" I ask urgently. She takes off from the branch that she's perched herself on and skims over the top of the herd of frantic prey animals. She sends me a picture that looks rather like the one she sent me earlier of the new predator chasing the bisonisans. The only difference here is that there are *three* of the creatures.

Suddenly, I realize what must have happened: two groups of predators have targeted the same herd of bisonisans and with the same strategy. While Fenrir was strategically driving the herd of bisonisans towards us, the other predators must have been doing exactly the same thing. That would explain why the predator ignored Fenrir and us and was only snapping at the heels of the bisonisans rather than actually properly attacking them.

Which means that at best, we're about to be overrun by bisonisans and their hunters, or at worst, caught in a pincer move between these hunters and any that might have run ahead of the herd to catch them a second time. Neither of which sounds like a good position to be in.

"We need to get out of here," I tell my Bound urgently, eyeing the swiftly approaching line of bisonisans. Apparently, I don't need to tell them twice: before I even fully get the words out, they're all hurrying off to the side.

I run after them, pushing myself to make it past the line of charging prey beasts before they overrun me.

Succeeding—by the skin of our teeth—apparently doesn't mean we're out of danger. The hunters are seemingly less keen on just letting us be observers this time. Oddly enough, they seem to decide to give up on the chase. Are they that territorial or do we somehow look like better prey than the bisonisans? The three of them approach us, their heads down and hissing menacingly. As they stalk towards us, every inch of their demeanor is that of menace.

I send a few quick messages to my Bound and take hold of my spear in a grip that my sparring practice has taught me is an appropriate one for combat. With any luck, I might even get levels in my Spearmanship. I also take the opportunity to cast Inspect Fauna—this time they're within range.

Kiina
Tier 2 beast (Evolved)

Special abilities: Unknown
Health: 920u
Mana: 100u
Minimum Willpower recommended to Dominate without other impacting factors: 45
These intelligent group predators are a dominating force in their local territory. Forced to migrate into areas with lower Energy density due to their previous territory being overtaken by an explosion of aggressive flora, these beasts are hungry for both meat and Energy.

Interesting . . . A moment before the hunters come in range to strike, I decide to change the plan a little. I send a mental message to my Bound, and we prepare for the attack.

As the kiinas approach, Sirocco flies at their heads and rakes at their eyes. She's careful not to get too close to their toothed maws, but then, her purpose isn't really to do any damage: she's more of a distraction than anything else.

While the three kiinas are momentarily distracted by the flying threat, Fenrir, River, and I attack. Fenrir goes in to bite at one of the kiinas' legs; River and I both move in with our spears, going more for the kill.

Of course, when we're dealing with creatures that are taller than me, that's easier said than done. On the other hand, it's not a giant salamander, either. Without any real idea of where its heart might be, and with its head far too mobile to make a target, getting a kill in a single hit seems unlikely.

We both aim for the chests of the two other kiinas, hoping that perhaps they will contain the hearts or lungs or other vital organs. I purposefully don't aim for the center of the chest, as the slight ridge under the scaly skin indicates that there is probably a chest bone protecting the vital organs there.

My recent practice with a spear comes in useful as does my increase in Dexterity, allowing me to hit almost the exact area I was aiming for. Eighteen points in Strength is no joke, either, even if more than half of them are in Endurance rather than Power. My spear sinks deeply into the kiina's chest, wrenching a screech of pain out of it.

Sirocco forgotten, it swipes at me with its wing. I wasn't expecting the blow and barely manage to react in time to raise an arm to protect my face. I'm knocked off balance, and my spear falls from my hands. My arm explodes in pain, but I don't think it's broken. At least, I don't feel the nausea that accompanied the agonizing pain when the crocodile broke it.

However, whatever the kiina has done has clearly damaged it in some way, as when I reach to grab the spear still stuck in the kiina's chest, I struggle to fasten my grip around its shaft. It doesn't help that the kiina's movements are making it swing in and out of my range. With my right hand mostly out of action, using my bow is also removed from the list of possibilities. Maybe I should have started with that instead of my spear, but too late now.

Here's where Flesh-Shaping has its drawbacks: with Lay-on-Hands I would already be pouring healing magic into my arm, hopefully bringing it back into the fight within a short time. With Flesh-Shaping, I'm unable to apply sufficient focus to even start the healing process. But that's life, and if I spend too long mourning could-have-beens, I'll lose my future.

So, using my nondominant hand, I pull out my mace from my Inventory. The spear stuck in the kiina's chest is hampering its movements—a plus in my favor. Approaching it, I bash the wing that swings at me and then the toothed maw that tries to snap at my face.

My blows feel clumsier than they would be with my right hand, but they're far more fluid than they were at the start of my time in this world. I start to get in the rhythm of defending from the alternating wings and bites, my mind searching for a way to break through the deadlock. It's not doing damage to me, but I'm not doing much damage to it either. With my spear in its body, it's not even bleeding much, though the weapon must be causing a significant amount of pain.

Then the kiina changes tactics. I had gotten used to two wing beats and then a bite, but the kiina suddenly claps both wings together *behind* me and then lunges forwards. *A trap!* I realize it only when I automatically try to dodge backwards and am stopped by the barrier of the wings.

On the other hand, it's also an opportunity. At the last moment, I drop my mace and summon my knife out of my Inventory—I've discovered that I don't actually have to have the Inventory open to pull things out as long as I can visualize them sufficiently. Using my damaged right arm to deflect its toothed maw sideways, though earning *more* damage to that limb in doing so, I lunge forwards and bury my knife in its throat. Using my eight points in Power, I yank at the blade viciously and open as wide of a wound in its airway as I can.

When it tries to flinch away, I step with it. This close, it can't do much: its wings can't bend that far, nor can its mouth reach me when I'm so close. It tries to lift one foot, maybe to kick me away, but that just puts it off-balance and makes it easy to tip it over sideways.

Once on the ground, I throw myself on top of it and stab with my knife until it stops moving, though it continues to twitch. Looking up, I see that River has dealt much more skillfully with his opponent. Although he's not quite done yet, the kiina looks to be on its last legs—well, leg. It's limping fairly significantly.

Fenrir, however, is still attached to the leg of his own target, which, instead of trying to attack, is now attempting to run away. Since this kiina is also limping, I have to guess that at some point Fenrir chose to switch legs. Having two mauled legs is a significant injury to a bipedal creature. I almost wince at the thought.

I hoped that Fenrir would be able to keep the third one alive—that's why I asked him to do his best to subdue it rather than kill it. I knew that we'd most likely have to kill the others; that River has managed to lame his own opponent rather than kill it is a testament to how much more skillful he still is with a spear than me.

But now the battle is pretty much done, and I move eagerly over to River's opponent. The lizard-man trips the kiina so that it falls heavily to the ground. For a moment, I feel a moral qualm. *Should I do this?*

They attacked us, I remind myself. We would have been perfectly happy just to get out of the way of the kiinas' hunt, but *they're* the ones who clearly decided that we would make better prey than the bisonisans. They're the ones who broke off their own hunt to come back to attack us. The law of the jungle is brutal.

I'll offer them the same choice as I've done before, I decide. *If they refuse . . . I'll have to judge whether I'm willing to risk them attacking us again afterwards or if I should just kill them before they can continue to try to kill us.*

My moral qualms quieted, I crouch and grab the toothed muzzle as it bites at me. The kiina is strong, but it's already exhausted and at the end of its rope. Looking in its eyes, I invoke my Skill.

"Dominate."

Once more entering the space that has become increasingly familiar, I face the kiina. The pressure beating against me is strong but has a sense of . . . tiredness to it. And fear.

I was gambling a bit: the recommended Willpower to Dominate is forty-five points according to my Inspect Fauna Skill, and while I technically have fifty points in Willpower, I'm also suffering from a twenty percent reduction to that stat. Whether that impacts my ability to Dominate, I don't know—I'd have to guess it does, but I don't know for sure. However, I was hoping that by proving ourselves stronger than them, I might be able to reduce the requirements to the point that I can still Dominate them despite my reduced Willpower being below the minimum threshold.

My first impression is that my guess is accurate. The fear and fatigue hollow the pressure that pushes me back, making it feel like a paper bag is pressing against me instead of the usual jet of water. The air inside is strong, but the bag itself is weak, and a single harsh move from me will tear a hole and deflate it completely.

What "tearing a hole" would entail when we're talking about a sense of metaphysical pressure rather than any real object pressing against me, I don't know. What I do know is that, as always, all I can do is press forward until I can communicate with the other party. Which actually happens sooner than I thought.

Normally I need to push to halfway between my starting point and the creature to find the moment we start to be able to communicate mentally. This time I only need to press forward about a third of the way. Is this the difference between the first and second tiers?

Why have you not killed me?

Another surprise is the clarity of the communication. It's not dissimilar from the mental messages I receive from Bastet now, though still not quite as clear as what I receive from River. Although this space facilitates communication, and the kiinas probably aren't capable of such communication by themselves in the real world, it's still likely that these creatures are able to communicate between themselves in some way given how practiced this feels. However, the slight blurriness does indicate that, though Evolved, these creatures are not used to communicating in words—or whatever I should call the combination of sounds and colors that River's people use.

"I wanted to offer you an opportunity," I say honestly. "You and your companion."

You killed one of my mates. You may still kill the other. Your mate could kill me at any time. What opportunity do you think to offer me? It's very clear that this creature is capable of a wide range of thought and emotion. Perhaps even as much as River or me. At the same time, it's as straightforward as Bastet, its fear not preventing it from speaking its mind.

Though I can communicate with the kiina at this distance, I can't really feel its emotions; its ability to send mental messages is good enough that very little emotion actually accompanies the thoughts themselves. I take a few steps forwards, pressing against the paper bag.

What are you doing? No! Stay back! the kiina cries, its mental voice laced with panic.

The pressure between us resists me, almost halting my progress. And then I push just a little bit more and the bag tears. The pressure practically disappears in a moment. The kiina lets out a wounded cry of despair, of hopelessness. I stop immediately, hoping I haven't gone too far.

This battle has not been similar to any other in my experience, and I'm a little at a loss for what to do. However, with the pressure having almost completely disappeared—only the ambient pressure remains—I'm certain that I could stroll over to the kiina and complete the Bond easily. However, that's not what I want. I still refuse to Bind someone completely unwilling.

Anyway, I've succeeded in my goal. With the bursting of the resistance against me, the kiina's emotions flow over me unhindered. She's in pain and scared, her fear almost making me feel nauseous with its intensity and omnipresence. I frown and concentrate as I try to work out exactly what is frightening her.

My battle with Fenrir was over so quickly that I wasn't able to really notice the difference in comparison to before my stats had such a dramatic boost, and subsequent battles have been rather more distracted. This time, though, I realize that with my significant increase in mental stats, I'm able to detect nuances in the sea of emotion that surrounds me. That's to my benefit: if I can reassure her, I'll be more able to convince her to accept the Bond willingly.

She's fearful of our strength, that's clear. Both the strength of River in being able to overcome her when she believed him to be easy prey, and my strength here in demonstrating how easily I can overcome her resistance. I mean, *I* wouldn't say it was easy, but her impression of me is that it was.

She's also sorrowful about her dead mate and fears the death of her second mate. Tied up in that is a fear for her unborn children: the eggs that are growing within her, soon to be laid. I actually take a step back in surprise when I realize that she's pregnant, or sort of—is it still "pregnant" if we're talking about an egg-laying species?

And then, of course, there's the fear of death, which exists in any thinking species, and the desire to find a way out of the problematic situation. I can work with that.

"Look," I say to her. By this point, although she's unable to move, I get the sense that she would be hunched up if she could. Her eyes are glassy and despairing. "First of all, I promise that as long as your mate, your children, and you don't try to attack me or my companions, we will let you go."

I'm actually less worried about these two than I should have been about the snilepede. The snilepede wasn't in a battle with us; this one is badly injured, and her mate is half-lame. If they try to attack, it will be easy to take them down. Besides, I was able to kill one almost completely by myself, and they know that. It would be suicide if they attacked us again; they're intelligent enough to realize that.

Either way, the hope actually brings light back to the kiina's eyes, especially when I support my statement with a sense of the genuine intention behind my words.

You would let us go? Then, why attack us? Why bring me here?

"*You* attacked *us*," I point out, my eyes narrowed. "Don't forget that. We were hunting the same prey, but we had already gotten what we needed and would have cleared out of your way. *You* chose to pursue us."

You seemed weak. Good prey, the kiina retorts.

"How did that work out for you?" I ask a little sarcastically. She doesn't reply. "So, as I said, I will let you go if you reject my offer. However, I hope that you'll see the benefit of what I suggest."

Which is?

"Strength in numbers," I say straight up. "You clearly already see the benefit of that: you were traveling around in a group of three. Yet you've also seen how easily we took you down, and that's because we were able to apply our strengths to your weaknesses," I tell her honestly. "Being different species, we're able to cover each other's weaknesses and offer an all-rounder group without significant downside." *Or significant strength,* I think but don't say. Still, I'd rather be part of a jack-of-all-trades group than a glass cannon group that can only handle half of what is thrown at it.

"And that doesn't mean that we don't also offer individual strength: one of our group has recently Evolved, and the rest of the group are on their way to it, advancing quickly." The kiina looks at me keenly, her attention now focused entirely on me, interest beginning to quicken the emotional cloud around me.

I am injured, significantly. How can you offer me strength when you have taken it from me?

"I can heal you," I say confidently. While it might take more than one session, I'm confident that I can heal her entirely. I wouldn't have offered the Bond otherwise.

"It's true," I insist. "Look." I shove the painful memory of River missing his arm at her and then replace it with an image of him a moment ago with both arms fully intact. I throw in the memory of the tail end of Bastet's Evolution for good measure, proving my words about one of our number having undergone it.

The skepticism I feel is replaced by further interest. Not, I sense, specifically for herself, but more for her unborn offspring. Like Bastet, her concern turns towards her young.

If I allow this chain, if I accept binding myself to your path while it still benefits us both, what will happen with my eggs? I sense that, like with Bastet, this is a make-or-break question.

"We are already looking after the young of one of my companions," I tell her honestly as I shove an image of the three raptorcat cubs playing together at her. "She keeps them under control. When they reach adolescence, I intend to offer them a Bond. If they refuse, they will be allowed to leave with no hard feelings. If they attack any of my Bound, they will be driven out forcibly, though I will still try not to kill them if it's at all possible to avoid. Or they may choose to take the Bond and be able to stay with the rest of us. Does that sound acceptable to you?" I ask.

The kiina considers the offer for a short time before responding with a sense of uncertainty.

My offspring will not stay with me until adolescence. I will protect my eggs until they hatch, then bring them their meals for the first few sun cycles. When they are able to move easily and are capable of hunting for themselves, they will be responsible for themselves. I would not want them to be trapped before they had any experience of the world.

I consider the question. It's true that it's a different situation than with the raptorcats. I don't think I'd be comfortable Binding babies not now knowing how much a Bond impacts a creature, willing or not. Thinking about Binding the raptorcat cubs as they are now actually makes me feel a bit uncomfortable.

"How much time are we talking about here?" I ask. "I mean, how much time would you or the eggs need to be protected?"

The kiina hesitates. *My eggs will hatch before the rains start fully, and they will be independent a number of sun cycles afterwards.* To be fair, that she's capable of giving me even that precise of an estimation is pretty good. To expect her to be able to tell me how many days with numbers is probably unreasonable. Still, we're talking about at least a few weeks and probably not more than two or three months of time.

"Then I will not offer a Bond to any of your young before they leave the nest," I decide out loud. Yes, it will be annoying to have one or more of my Bound tied up in looking after the young, but the raptorcat cubs are unlikely to be fully grown by that point anyway. Even though they've grown in the month and a half since I Bound Bastet, they aren't even as far along as Lathani is now, so it's going to take a while yet. That said, what happened to Lathani wasn't exactly natural growth.

So, we'd have to be protecting the cubs anyway; protecting some baby kiinas isn't going to be much more work. "If we come across them later, though, when they're old enough to make their own decisions, I'm not making any promises," I warn her. I get the sense of indifference from her; I have a feeling that after the hatchlings leave the nest, she's not too concerned with what happens to them.

"And if any choose to stay with us until they *are* grown, I'll decide that on a case-by-case basis," I add, considering what to do if they choose not to leave at all. This elicits more discomfort from her, but I don't get the sense of outright rejection. "So, what do you say?" I ask. "Do you wish to join us or not?"

She considers the question for a few moments more, but I'm already sure of what she's going to choose. Sure enough, a moment later, she answers with what I expected.

I wish to join you. You will offer this to my mate too?

"I will," I confirm. "But be warned: if you become part of our group, you are *part* of it. We share what we have—need, not greed. We help each other where necessary, knowing that we will be helped in our turn. Basically, what I'm saying is to expect to give at least as much as you take." I fix her with a serious stare. "If you can't deal with that, tell me now." A sense of impatience comes from her—not what I was expecting after my little speech.

That is normal. All right. I've definitely got a second Bastet here.

"Okay, good," I finish, a little nonplussed. Then, with a little shrug, I keep walking forwards. The kiina keeps her eyes on me until I'm standing within arm's length. I will her to accept the Bond; she lowers her head and does.

A moment later, the misty gray space vanishes and we're back in the real world. *Right, one down, one to go.*

CHAPTER TWENTY-FIVE

Collecting

By the time we get back to the cave, the sun is well on its way to the horizon—we went further than I thought and then had to spend a fair bit of time healing the kiinas so they could travel with us without attracting unwelcome attention. Not to mention the unexpected double Battle of Wills, though the second one can't really be counted as much of a battle.

The female requested a few moments to communicate with her mate before I started the Battle of Wills with him. Though I was a bit wary, I figured that she wouldn't gain anything by betraying me at that point, so I gave her the time. As it turns out, that was a good decision. Clearly, she somehow communicated what had happened, as her mate very quickly accepted my Bond when I initiated the Battle of Wills.

She is my mate and carries my unborn offspring, he'd told me. *I will follow and protect her now and in the future. Since she has decided to accept a Bond with you, I must do the same.* There was no resentment, no antipathy. No sorrow, actually, about the loss of the other kiina; I have to wonder what their relationship was like—allies, rivals, or a mixture of both. Either way, I think it was probably the shortest Dominate I've ever conducted. The shortest successful one, anyway—the failure with the salamander probably set the record for the shortest overall. It was even faster than Fenrir's.

I'm feeling pretty happy with the trip, despite not now having much time to work on the other tasks I wanted to do. Not only do we have two new members of our group, who I suspect are going to fill important roles, but we've also got a fair number of bodies to feed all the hungry mouths. In addition to the five bisonisans that River, Fenrir, and I downed, we've also brought back two of the three bisonisans that the kiinas took down before they decided to attack us. The third has already been consumed. In total, that means seven big brains, which is plenty for my purposes.

The uneaten bodies are tied to a couple of branches that River and I carry between us. I considered using the kiinas as pack beasts too, but I decided against it, considering that they're not completely healed—I prioritized getting back to safety over healing them fully.

So, we have meat for at least a couple of days, especially since none of my Bound who came out with me are at all hungry by this point. I am a bit, especially since I didn't eat the hearts as I normally would. I decided that it was better for my Bound to make progress towards Evolving by eating the Energy-dense meat.

With what happened to Bastet, I'm keen to see how the others will change once they reach that point. The kiinas, of course, are already Evolved; it will be interesting to see what happens to them in the future. Actually, I haven't yet checked out their stats.

Bound – Dominate – "Persephone"
Health units: 613/920
Mana units: 100/100
Stamina units: 565/600
Progress to Tier 3: 17%
Lifespan remaining: ~32y

Bound – Dominate – "Hades"
Health units: 721/880
Mana units: 110/110
Stamina units: 529/550
Progress to Tier 3: 19%
Lifespan remaining: ~31y

Yes, I decided to call them after the Ancient Greek power couple. After the loyalty Hades showed to his mate, willing to follow her into a Dominate Bond just to continue protecting her, I figured it would be a good name. I briefly considered Artemis and Apollo—that would have suited the female quite well, with Artemis being the goddess of hunting, but Apollo wasn't so appropriate.

Besides, Apollo and Artemis were siblings, not lovers, so Persephone and Hades sounded like a better option. The kiinas didn't have a preference—they seem rather indifferent to names, to be honest. It's interesting how each of my Bound has had a different response, considering most of them weren't used to having names before I came into their lives.

Now it remains to be seen how they each fit into the team. I'll need to see them in action to get a better idea of what their advantages are—they clearly weren't used to fighting against creatures with weapons, which put them automatically at a disadvantage. Maybe some sparring will help; though, I'll have to be sure that they understand what "sparring" means.

In addition to the new members of our group, as well as the meat and the plants we collected, I managed to gain another three percent in progress to the next level. Though it might not seem like much, the amount of objective Energy I actually need to gain to raise it by a single percentage point just speaks to the killing spree we've been on this afternoon. By this point, I have just enough Energy that if I manage to half earn a point towards Strength or Dexterity, I should be able to speed up the gain. Maybe if I run up and down the hill a few times while collecting water from the river I will earn something. I might as well do it while it's light—the water I brought back this time is barely enough to create a small puddle at the bottom of the pit. Even if I haven't worked on the other hides, if I get the tanning solution boiling while I fill the pit with water, I should be able to get the crocodile and salamander hides starting to soak overnight.

My thoughts are interrupted when Bastet trots over to greet us, rubbing her head against my thighs and then moving on to do equivalent actions with the rest of our group.

Good hunt? she asks and sends a questioning feeling over with a picture of the kiina. Clearly, she's realized that they are new additions to the team. I'm glad not to sense any antipathy from her towards them since she wasn't present to weigh in on whether she wanted them to join us.

"Yes, it was a good hunt," I respond with a smile and a reassuring feeling. *That's what I love about Bastet*, I realize suddenly. *She just accepts what I throw at her and does her best to roll with it.* I'm far more used to complaints and resistance to suggestions. As for what would happen when I had to deliver an edict to the office workers that didn't even come from HR but from the board? I'm suddenly glad I'm here—being attacked by rabid beasts in the forest seems positively relaxing in comparison.

River approaches her and holds out an item.

A gift for you, Bastet, he says, and I transfer his words to Bastet without thinking about it.

For me? Smells yummy! I look away as she starts tearing into it. The item is, indeed, a pylobus that River saved for her. By this point the Energy must have practically disappeared from the body, but she seems to like it well enough.

As I planned, I also have the carapaces of the other pylobuses, and I resolve to clean them out and turn them into serviceable bowl-plates. I was already using one to carry the pile of plants I collected that were unable to fit in my pockets and that I didn't want to put in my Inventory.

Moving over to Kalanthia, I pull out three Cores from my Inventory. Two of them are from the pylobus and the bisonisan we killed. The last is from the other kiina. Persephone expressed discomfort with the idea of cannibalism but was indifferent to others eating his body. Perhaps she's like Bastet: sorrowful about his death, but not trying to deny it like humans usually do.

I regret, in a way, that I killed the third kiina. Not only would Persephone have been happier to have her other mate here, but having three kiinas is sure to be better than having two. Then again, I'm not sure if I could have conducted another Battle of Wills—after doing two in a row, I was feeling rather fatigued in a way that doesn't seem to be related to stamina. Not physical stamina, anyway.

By this point, I'm feeling fine again, but it took me most of the way back to get to that state. I wouldn't have wanted to begin a third Battle of Wills in such quick succession for fear of not having enough energy to see it to its conclusion. Besides, my battle with Persephone might have been harder if we hadn't so clearly revealed our power by killing one of them.

Still, it's good to know that there's a limit to how many Battles of Wills I can do in a certain period, especially with Kalanthia's suggestion about River's village. Unless something significant changes, I won't be Binding all of the members of the village in one go. Then again, perhaps this could be a symptom of the damage to my soul from the Pure Energy. Maybe when I fix that, the limit will disappear.

"For payment of River's debt," I tell Kalanthia about the Cores. She eyes them speculatively.

A little small, she comments, most likely about the pylobus's Core. It's true that it's more of a big marble than a fist, but the kiina's Core is slightly larger than she asked for. I point that out to her, and Kalanthia rumbles speculatively. *If you will give Lathani one of those beasts, I shall accept it,* she concludes finally.

"As long as I can have the brain, fine," I agree. In a way, we've almost got *too* much meat at the moment, so I won't begrudge her that.

Very well, Kalanthia rumbles, pushing herself to her feet and padding over to choose one, which she picks up in her massive mouth. Sometimes I forget just how big she is. When she's lying down, her head is about level with mine. But when she stands up and towers above me, when she's able to pick up something that probably weighs close to a tonne without looking overly burdened, I remember.

Still, that's good progress towards River's debt—seven out of nine Cores. We should be done soon. Persephone and Hades back away fearfully as Kalanthia walks past them with her prize in her mouth.

It's okay, I send to them mentally. *As long as you are my Bound and you don't attack her or her cub, you'll be fine.* Persephone sends a feeling of mistrust down the Bond to me—it's understandable since we've only been allies for a few hours. Bastet had difficulty too. Heck, so did River, but that was for another reason. And Sirocco. In fact, only Fenrir has taken Kalanthia's presence with complete equanimity.

You've been collecting, Binder, Kalanthia sends to me, a hint of amusement in her mental voice. I shrug.

It was a good opportunity. And they're already Evolved.

Yes. It's unusual to see members of their species this high in the valley.

I think the vine-stranglers have chased them up the mountainside, I tell her, based on what I read in the description from my Inspect Fauna Skill.

That seems like a likely explanation, Kalanthia remarks as she lays the carcass down at the cave mouth. She sends a mental message that I can't decipher, but a moment later Lathani comes running out. She rubs against me briefly in greeting, then leaps straight at the body.

I nod at Kalanthia and then move away. Time's marching on and I still have use for the remaining light. Before I go and fetch water, I probably best heal the kiinas fully. Or maybe I can combine the tasks a little: heal the kiinas while I have mana, then go fetch water when I run out. I could even use the time to experiment a little with Meditation to see if I can access it at even a shallow level while moving.

Deciding that that's a good plan, I walk over to the two kiinas, rubbing the heads of the three raptorcat cubs en route. They're already eating one of the bisoni-san carcasses still tied to the branches.

"Can you get these knots undone?" I ask River. "If you can aim not to cut the cord, that would be good." Then I remember him trying to do such a thing a few days ago and failing. "If you can't do it, let me know, and I'll get to it when I can," I add.

As you wish, he responds, lifting his chin briefly, then stooping to get to the task. I send him the feeling of my appreciation down the Bond.

"Thanks to both of you for your help," I say to Fenrir and Sirocco, turning to them next. "Do you need anything?" Both of them send across feelings of negation, so I reply with feelings of gratitude, then walk off to my newest Bound.

"Okay, my mana has regenerated a bit, so I'll continue with your healing." I can tell that Persephone in particular is in pain. Hades's injuries were mostly dealt with on site, though I do want to do another round on his bones. I suppose I ought to be glad that Flesh-Shaping *does* seem to consider bone as "flesh." Then again, I suppose its use would be pretty limited if it didn't.

Fenrir did a number on Hades's legs, and although they weren't snapped, they've certainly been cracked a bit. Plus, it seems that bone takes more mana to repair than flesh; natural, I suppose.

As for Persephone, my mana pool only managed to seal the worst of her wounds so they didn't keep leaking; I didn't really manage to properly deal with them.

Sitting down and directing them to come down to my level, which they do with some reluctance, something putting them on their guard, I put my hand on Persephone's chest and get to work.

CHAPTER TWENTY-SIX

A Good Day

F inally, I'm done. I lie back and close my eyes with a sigh of exhausted satisfaction as a pulse of pain goes through my head with every throb of my heartbeat. Mana exhaustion is never fun, no matter how many times I've done it.

Healing Persephone and Hades has taken a lot of mana, and I've had to empty and refill my pool multiple times. Flesh-Shaping is *definitely* more mana hungry than Lay-on-Hands used to be. But I don't begrudge them the effort—I can feel myself improving as I practice, and Flesh-Shaping has even gone up two levels to Initiate eight. And the time spent waiting for my mana pool to refill in between has allowed me to fill the clay-lined pit halfway with water. Given that it's a pretty big pit, that will be enough to submerge the rolls of hide.

River was very helpful in removing the brains from the bisonisans, and I mashed them up with the others in my Inventory. The solution is currently boiling away on my hearth fire—under guard by Fenrir to stop a troublesome cub from spilling it—and should be ready by the time it's fully dark.

I was pleased when running up and down the hill carrying water did indeed half earn me a point to Strength (Endurance). It was a good choice to maximize my efforts by carrying two of the containers by hand. Unfortunately, running through a forest didn't test my agility enough to earn a point in Dexterity, apparently, but perhaps it's gotten me closer. Though, it could also be that I'm now down to practically no Energy—previous experience has indicated that the System that governs my stats doesn't offer me a point if I don't have the Energy to pay for it. Hopefully, I'll either fully earn it soon or earn enough Energy to pay for the "shortcut."

When accompanied by Sirocco to serve as an extra pair of eyes, the journey to and from the river proved itself perfect for a different kind of growth too. Although I haven't developed some sort of walking, let alone running, Meditation, I *have* made some steps towards it. *Heh, steps.*

It requires allowing a sense of peace and tranquility to take a hold of me, which is why I can only do it when Sirocco is there—without her presence, I'm too wary to reach the state of serenity I need to achieve. Knowing she's there and watching our environment intently is reassuring enough to allow my thoughts to focus inwards. Oddly enough, the state isn't as hard to reach as I thought it might be.

I wonder if it's a result of my increased Wisdom, but when I actually pay attention, the life and peace of my surroundings make it surprisingly easy to sink into an awareness of my present, paying far less heed to the past or future than I usually do. And apparently, that's the state I need to be in to draw in Energy faster.

It's not nearly as noticeable as if I'm sitting down and Meditating, but increasing the speed of my mana regeneration by twenty percent or so still helps. And the level I got in Meditation to bring it up to Initiate nine indicates that I'm on the right track.

Today's actually been a good day for Skill levels. Finally hopeful that I can open my eyes without feeling nauseous, I crack them before committing to opening them fully. Then, satisfaction running through me, I pull up my status screen to remind myself.

Name: Markus Wolfe		Race: Human	Class: Tamer
Level: 13	Energy to next level: 2%	Energy absorption rate: 26u/hr	Energy towards debt: 85% (260)
Intelligence	36	Mana: 17/540	
Wisdom	36	Mana regeneration rate: 900u/hr	
Willpower	42+8 (+20%)	Health regeneration rate: 40u/hr (-20%)	
Constitution	20	Health: 200/200	
Strength	19	Stamina: 110/110	
Dexterity	18	Stamina regeneration rate: 180u/hr	
Class Skills:		Non-Class Skills:	
Dominate – Novice 8		Flesh-Shaping – Initiate 8	
*Companion Bond		Stealth – Novice 1	
Tame – Beginner 8		Animal Empathy – Novice 9	
Fade – Initiate 2		Meditation – Initiate 9	
Inspect Fauna – Beginner 3		Energy Manipulation – Journeyman 3	
Inspect Flora – Beginner 6		Sensation Management – Beginner 6	
Inspect Environment – Beginner 5		Spearmanship – Beginner 4	
		Archery – Beginner 1	

Dominate went up to Novice eight—two levels in one go. I guess it's because I Dominated beings who had already Evolved since I doubt that at this point just the act of Dominating any creature would be enough to increase the level once, let alone twice. My spear work also earned me a level in Spearmanship. Even Animal Empathy went up a level to the cusp of Initiate. Energy Manipulation has gone up two levels too, though I can't say whether it's my use of Flesh-Shaping or my efforts with Meditation that has earned that. Perhaps a bit of both.

Tame went up at some point, though I doubt that was today. Perhaps it's just the increasing closeness between Sirocco and the rest of us since she's the only one with a Tame Bond at the moment. Both Inspect Flora and Inspect Environment have gone up too—another result of our outing, I guess. I'm a little surprised that Inspect Fauna hasn't gone up too, but I suppose I only used it twice.

Apart from the Skill levels that Dominating and then healing the kiinas got me, I now have a significantly better understanding of their bodies. In fact, I'd say that I know them better than any of my other Bound apart from River. And my own body, of course.

Starting from their heads, they have a relatively long muzzle, about the length of my forearm. It's something between a pterodactyl's and a crocodile's, with the bit near its head narrower than that of a crocodile but not as narrow as a pterodactyl. When closed, the teeth interlock but are angled a little inwards. Their heads are relatively small and they have binocular vision. Like most of the creatures I've come across, their pupils are slits within dark bronze irises—no indication of any whites.

Their skin is scaly in the way of a fish rather than a crocodile—unlike River's, theirs is smooth, with each scale dappling from darker green at the root to lighter green at the tip. The exception is a stripe of black that runs from their crests down their spines and to the tips of their tails, and they seem to use this to communicate with each other.

Their wings are similarly colored, their feathers a bit brighter green than their scales, but only by a shade or two. Like Sirocco, their "wrist" joints have a talon protruding from them, which I experienced firsthand when one of the kiinas tried to use it on me. Unfortunately, as that battle proved, their wings are not flexible enough to be able to use the talons on themselves—or on anything clinging to them. However, I imagine they're pretty useful for grabbing onto prey to stop it escaping. And, as I also experienced, the wings themselves are good as weapons in their own right.

While their chests are relatively narrow, with most of the muscle being around their shoulders, their hips and thighs are thick and muscled. Their torsos are shorter in comparison to mine, and their hips are actually at mid-stomach height on me. Running is a particular strength, as we saw.

Though their natural pose seems to be leaning forward with their necks, backs, and tails forming an inclined chair shape, they're capable of standing taller with their backs almost vertical. The latter seems to be the best pose for them to use their wings as weapons—at least, that's what I experienced.

Their legs descend into a four-clawed foot: three claws forward, one shorter claw behind. Their tails are thick at the base of the spine and continue to be fairly thick along the length. As a result, they're relatively short, probably only about a meter long or so, but the thickness appears to be enough to counterbalance the rest of the kiina.

When running, they lean forwards a bit and tuck their wings in close to their bodies—unless they're using their wings to add a bit of extra forward momentum, of course. In that respect, they're much like Bastet. As it turns out, their special ability from Evolution is being able to use their wings to send a blade formed of air. I don't know if it's common for the same species to share the same special abilities; certainly, it doesn't seem to be that way among River's people.

Persephone helpfully demonstrated her air-blade for me on our way back from the hunting area. It's pretty efficient, as it only uses a fraction of her mana pool at a time—perhaps ten mana units or so.

I have a few ideas I'd like to try in combining that attack with our team, but I'll need to think about them for a bit. If we could somehow combine Bastet's fire breath with the kiinas' air-blades, that would be pretty awesome. I also have some perhaps too-hopeful ideas about potentially riding on one of them. They're big enough; the question would be whether they're strong enough. And whether they'd agree to it.

Famished again from the mixture of magic use and exercise, I pull out some meat and munch on it.

"So, you were driven out of your normal area, right?" I ask, sitting up slowly and looking over at the kiinas—I'm feeling significantly better now that my mana has ticked up a little again. Still, I don't feel like doing much. The last few hours, heck, the whole day has been busy, and I could do with a rest. Still, this is something I've been wondering about since I met them.

We had to move away from our territory, yes, Persephone answers. From my short experience with them, she definitely seems to be the leader of the pair. Hades is a quiet, attentive presence. I know that Dominating a creature automatically forces the inclination to protect and obey me, but I have a feeling that Hades's instincts of protection towards his mate are stronger even than those. Then again, I don't get the sense that they've undergone the same kind of reshuffling of priorities that River described. Maybe it's because they're a different species?

Either way, I wouldn't want to test which of us he would side with if it came to a conflict between us. I suspect that I'd lose unless I actively used the Bond against him. And I would rather not do that, since it would build up resentment between us given how intelligent the kiinas have turned out to be.

"Why?" I ask, following up on Persephone's answer.

The trees around us started trying to eat us. So, it's as I thought: the vine-stranglers drove them up the mountain. I wonder how many other animals have been displaced by the sudden explosion of carnivorous trees. And how many more are going to attack us. Being from deeper into the valley, there's a good chance they'll be Evolved like Persephone and Hades are. *Good sources of Cores*, I say to myself thoughtfully.

Looking up at the sky, I realize just how late it's getting. There's still a touch of light on the horizon but not much of it. I need to get my hides soaking for the night. But before then, I should probably work out the sleeping arrangements for the kiinas—somehow, I don't think they'll fit in the alcove.

"We normally sleep inside in an alcove," I start, "but it's already pretty full. Are you two okay sleeping out here for now? If you'd rather sleep down in the trees, that would be fine too." They eye each other, and I get the feeling that they're communicating in some way that I'm not quite capable of understanding. I probably could if I invaded one of their minds, but that would probably break their burgeoning trust—which is fragile enough as it is.

We shall find shelter under the trees, Persephone says finally. I nod.

"All right. I hope to change our living situation in the future, but for now I guess that'll have to do. Are you hungry?"

No, is the short but prompt reply.

"Then I'll see you in the morning. Please return here when the sun rises. And don't hesitate to call for help if you get attacked by anything." At this Hades shifts, his wings lifting a little and his feathers ruffling. I get the sense of surprise, irritation, and affront. I'm confused for a moment, but then as I look at how he's standing protectively in front of Persephone, I think I understand. "It's not that I think you *need* our help, but we're a team now," I continue, pretending not to have noticed. The sense of affront reduces, though the surprise remains. "Anyway, I'll say goodnight."

Persephone and Hades don't seem to be ones for polite conversation—unsurprisingly—and immediately turn to make their way down the slope. Sirocco wings her way over my head and sends me a quick thought. I send one back to her in gratitude; she indicated to me that she's going to keep an eye on them. Although I suspect that Persephone will put the safety of her unborn children first, that doesn't mean that she will definitely call for me soon enough for me to actually help. It eases my heart to know that Sirocco will be there.

"All right," I say to my other Bound. "I'm just going to sort something, and then I'm off to bed."

I take the boiling brain mush off the fire and tuck it into my Inventory for the journey—no need to tempt fate and risk badly burned hands or accidentally tripping over something or someone.

"Thanks for guarding this, Fenrir," I tell the lizog, and he sends pleasure running through the Bond between us. And is that a twitch in his tail I see? I know I think of him like a dog, but he doesn't typically wag his tail. Maybe I'm just reading things into a muscle spasm or something. It doesn't stop me from patting him like he's a dog, though, and he wriggles with pleasure as I stroke his scales.

Returning outside, I make sure my hands are well covered before I pull the hot pot out of my Inventory. After tipping the mixture into the water below, I set the pot to one side to cool down a bit. Then, taking a long stick, I mix the brains into the cold water in the pit. Taking the crocodile hide out, I shove it in and use the stick to ensure all parts of it are below the surface. Then, pulling the salamander hide out, I hesitate. If something goes wrong, I can't replace this one.

After a moment of thought, I tuck it away again into my Inventory. I might as well test it out with the nere hide first—there are probably more of those creatures lurking in the river. More of them than the salamander, anyway.

Hoping that nothing will think a soaking hide is a good meal, I head back inside. Kalanthia's taken Lathani out into the forest, so the empty cave echoes oddly as I step through it to reach the alcove. My den, warm and full of my companions, is far more welcome.

CHAPTER TWENTY-SEVEN

One I Control

U sing a stick, I poke at the hide stretched on the frame in front of me. Prodding carefully, I stretch the crocodile skin in multiple places, then walk around the frame and start doing the same to the other side.

I've already done this process several times in the last few hours and expect to do it several times more. The hide is bound to the frame with my bark-fiber cord threaded through holes around the edges of the skin. Normally, I would have made those holes with my knife, but this is where my Flesh-Shaping has come in handy: with holes shaped instead of cut, there should be less chance of the hide ripping free. As it turns out, even with it saturated with oils, I'm able to sink magic into the hide and control it perfectly well.

The frame is standing in the middle of a cave that Kalanthia made for me at my request. It cost me—River's debt hasn't yet been paid off, since I needed to offer Kalanthia the Cores I would have otherwise used to do so. I still feel a bit guilty for that, but having a space to allow my hides to dry out is important for making the armor I need before going down to help River's village, and Kalanthia point-blank refused to have them in the main den.

My new crafting cave is shaped a bit like a bubble in the rock except that it has a channel from the highest point that leads to a ventilation hole about two meters above the entrance. The entrance itself is low, intentionally so, and requires me to bend double when entering or exiting, but it should help when I need to smoke the hide—my next step.

Since I only have one frame, I'm working on the crocodile hide to begin with. Once the crocodile hide has started to smoke, I'll be able to replace it with the sala-mander hide. As it turns out, even though I can't just magically saturate the hide with brain oils, I *can* speed up the saturation process. I did this by submersing the mana-saturated hide in the tanning mixture and then essentially sucking at the oils in the surrounding liquid. Doing it that way, I can draw them through the hide and coat its inner fibers; instead of the three days it took for my crocodile hide to become sufficiently saturated, it took me half an hour or so to do the same to my salamander hide. It's back in my Inventory for now—I don't want to risk it deterio-rating while there's no frame available, and making another frame seems like a waste of time when the first frame will be free soon enough.

After another two pokes with my stick, I'm done for this round. I feel the skin, then nod in satisfaction—the drying is coming along nicely. The fire I have burning cleanly at the end of the cave is doing exactly what I'd hoped: pulling in a strong draft from the door and sending its smoke out of the top hole. The wind helps the drying go faster, as does the warmth that fills the cave. The hide is more supple than it used to be, but I don't think that it's lost any of its defensive capabilities.

Putting my stick down on the ground, I walk back over to the fire, then sit down next to it and close my eyes.

Since it's my first time actually tanning something, I have to admit to feeling some anxiety over making sure everything goes well and as a result, I don't want to go too far from my skin. Obviously, I also don't want to waste time. I figure that trying to improve my magical abilities is a good use of the time between needing to stretch the skin, now that I've done as much as I can to prepare weapons for the upcoming trials.

In the last five days, I've made sure that my stock of arrows is plentiful, that I have *two* backup flint spears in addition to my main weapon and River's one, and even created a back-up mace just in case. It's not as good as my main one—instead of a stone head, I've just carved another wooden one. But in an emergency, it will work well enough. I'm thinking about making a shield too, even if I don't tend to use one, but I have decided to see how well the armor comes out first. Maybe I'll use some boiled leather for the shield instead of wood—my Flesh-Shaping would make that far easier to create, as I've verified that I can still shape cooked flesh.

It's been a lot of hard work, but I've benefitted from it: I've finally managed to bring both Dexterity and Strength to twenty points each even if that basically ate all of my progress towards the next level. And that's not the only change that's happened in the last few days.

Name: Markus Wolfe		Race: Human	Class: Tamer
Level: 13	Energy to next level: 11%	Energy absorption rate: 38u/hr	Energy towards debt: 85% (255)
Intelligence	36	Mana: 540/540	
Wisdom	42	Mana regeneration rate: 1050u/hr	
Willpower	42+8 (+20%)	Health regeneration rate: 40u/hr (-20%)	
Constitution	20	Health: 200/200	
Strength	20	Stamina: 120/120	
Dexterity	20	Stamina regeneration rate: 200u/hr	
Class Skills:		Non-Class Skills:	
Dominate – Novice 9		Flesh-Shaping – Journeyman 1	
*Companion Bond		Stealth – Novice 3	
Tame – Beginner 8		Animal Empathy – Novice 9	
Fade – Initiate 2		Meditation – Initiate 9	
Inspect Fauna – Beginner 6		Energy Manipulation – Journeyman 6	
Inspect Flora – Beginner 9		Sensation Management – Beginner 6	

Inspect Environment – Beginner 8	Spearmanship – Beginner 5
	Archery – Beginner 3
	Blunt Weaponry – Beginner 2
	Knife-Work – Beginner 2

Several of my Skills have advanced by one or more levels, most of them because of use during sparring or hunting in the forest. Only Flesh-Shaping has ranked up, though. Fortunately, all the non-healing work I've done recently has expanded the scope of the Skill once more. It was a relief when I saw the rank-up description.

Congratulations!
You have advanced a Skill past Initiate. Flesh-Shaping is now Journeyman 1. You have become a confident user of mana in both your own body and that of others. You have focused on healing with some exploration of non-healing purposes. You have saturated the bodies of both living and dead creatures and discovered some of the different effects possible as a result. While your Skill remains more healing focused, it has grown to include more non-healing modifications. Scanning a body now gives more information about the body of your target and the functionality of different aspects. You are more able to memorize this information and automatically use it to achieve your goals. The previously narrowed focus of your Skill has widened once more, opening up options that you have not yet tried.

Of course, it doesn't say what those other possible applications of Flesh-Shaping are, but I suppose that discovering those for myself is rather part of the point.

In addition to Flesh-Shaping ranking up, I've earned two more Skills, thanks to focusing on different weapons while sparring. Interestingly, though the first is much like Archery or Spearmanship, the other doesn't seem to focus entirely on a single weapon type and instead seems to be linked to a *class* of weapon.

Blunt Weaponry
You have shown a more nuanced approach to the use of a blunt weapon than simply swinging it at a target. Improve this Skill by continuing to practice techniques designed for the more efficient and effective application of force with blunt weapons. Gain 5% to the effects of Strength (Power to Endurance = 4:1) per level in this Skill when using a weapon that principally deals blunt damage to a target.

This Skill has required some testing, particularly in relation to its weighted percentage bonus to the effects of Strength. It's hard to see exact results since even if I have Blunt Weaponry up to Beginner two already, that still only means it's two points of extra Strength, and only a fifth of those are supposed to be applied to Endurance, which makes it hard to test whether I can fight for any longer than normal. I think I've noticed some difference in the power I can apply to a target, though. Of course, I have more points invested in Endurance than Power—twelve as opposed to eight—since most of my earned points have been from pushing myself to the limits of my endurance. I don't know whether that makes a difference.

The percentage increase for Blunt Weaponry is significantly better than for Archery or Spearmanship; the downside is that it seems to take a lot more effort to level it than the more specific weapon Skills. The time it's taken me to level Blunt Weaponry is at least double the time it took me to go from Beginner two to Beginner three in Archery.

My other new Skill is simpler and clearly relates to my more conscious use of my knife.

Knife-Work
You have taken the first step along the path to Knife Mastery. You have displayed an understanding that wielding a knife means more than simply jabbing or slashing it at a target. You have used your knife in both combat and everyday life and have become more proficient at controlling its angle and the force you apply to it. Continue practicing techniques designed for the more efficient and effective use of a knife in order to advance this Skill. Gain 2% to the effects of Dexterity per level in this Skill when using a knife in or out of combat.

This one is interesting in that it seems to apply to my everyday use of my knife as well as to combat. And although I haven't exactly felt the difference that two percent, or even four percent, to my Dexterity earns me, the fact that it's already leveled up despite me barely using it in sparring since earning the Skill is notable. It indicates that just making dinner might help it progress. Then again, I suppose that the skills are transferable—the cuts I make to slice meat off a bone can be used against an enemy just as easily as to prepare my stew.

Unfortunately, I haven't yet managed to deal with my soul damage or earn either of the Skills I really want, despite my best efforts. Although I'm a bit stuck on the Willpower issue, since I've run out of ideas to try, I've been doing my best to advance in the other areas. I've been trying to observe fire and earth, to reach out and touch them in my Meditation, to try to control them. And while I've learned a lot about fire, and practically nothing about earth, I haven't managed to actually control it in any way.

Still, I think that fire at least is coming along a bit. Each time I sit and stare into the fire's heart in contemplation, I feel . . . Well, it's hard to say "progress" when nothing has changed. Yet somehow, each time I still feel like I *understand* the fire just a little more. Controlling it is still out of reach—every time I try, it slips away from my mental grasp like fire evading confinement. But maybe it won't be too long before I succeed.

At least I feel like I'm further ahead with fire than earth—while I've been able to see the connections that reach out from every fire into the environment around it, I haven't even begun to see them within the earth, despite my best efforts.

I console myself that Energy Manipulation has gone up not one, not two, but *three* levels in the last five days. And considering that it's already at Journeyman, that's quite an achievement, I think. I *know* from past experience that the higher ranked a Skill is, the harder it is to level, so my rapid progress with Energy Manipulation makes me very satisfied. I reckon that it's because I've been using my mana in a variety of ways—healing, growing, saturating, examining, reaching out, observing . . . Between Flesh-Shaping and my attempts to get Fire or Earth-Shaping, my mana has definitely been getting a workout.

And possibly my work with Meditation has also helped. It's been a struggle to learn how to use Meditation even when I'm moving and even more of a trial to learn how to keep a constant low level of Meditation going, but it's something that I've been working on any moment I can. And with some success. Though I don't get the full ninety percent boost that I do if I Meditate while not moving, and the sense of peacefulness is limited, a forty-five percent boost to my ongoing passive Energy absorption has still made a big difference to how much Energy I've managed to accumulate in the past few days. Testing it with the Energy Hearts has proven that it actually works to extend the time I benefit from the incredibly high Energy rate—I guess by making my absorption a little more efficient or something. I still haven't managed to quite work that out.

Of course, it *does* take a small amount of concentration to keep Meditation going, which means that I haven't yet been able to work out how to do it while I sleep, and it usually lapses in combat too—my focus becomes too distracted. Still, having it active while walking through the forest actually helps. It seems to improve the feedback I receive from my inspect Skills even if only by a little.

Since I'm currently sitting down, activating Meditation to its full extent is easy enough. I focus on the fire before me and decide to do something different.

The dream that I had almost a week ago has been playing on my mind ever since. At first, I was excited—I'm pretty sure that the fire emerged from me, which means that I managed to actually shape fire. The problem is that I was unconscious at the time, and I've failed to replicate the event. Of course, River and Bastet are both very relieved that we haven't had a repetition of the midnight fire explosion, but by this point I'm almost frustrated enough to *want* it to happen in hopes that I might gain some clues that I can actually use.

Sighing, I try to engage with the sense of peacefulness that usually comes over me when I go fully into Meditation. Getting frustrated will only be counterproductive.

Maybe I've been thinking about it wrong. In the dream, my partner, who I've concluded can only be some personification of fire, seemed to be trying to invite me to dance, to join her. Maybe instead of controlling fire as an outsider, I need to try to . . . become the fire?

It sounds like some sort of martial arts monk bullshit, but I'm in a world of magic and impossibilities. Maybe martial arts monk bullshit is exactly what I need.

Opening my eyes, I look at the fire, but this time, instead of focusing on its heart, I just stare at the fire's physical appearance. Flickers of connections shift at the corner of my vision as the flames almost perfectly hide the world I can normally only see with my mind's eyes. Almost.

Thoughts go around my head, but I don't try to direct them much, merely let them come and go, my gaze soft and my mind unfocused. It's like stargazing: try to look at them and they vanish. So instead, I just . . . relax. Invite them to be seen, to be known. To be acknowledged. But coaxed, urged, not ordered.

Slowly, like the first hesitant licks of fire caressing a new piece of fuel, like the initial tentative connections built from the fire to its surroundings, ideas coalesce. My mind is taken back to talking through the fire triangle with River. Fuel, oxygen, heat. Necessary for a fire, and just as necessary for me.

Are we that different?

I suffocate as easily as a fire if I am buried below earth or my openings are blocked.

I starve just as a fire does if all my fuel is taken away from me.

I will freeze and expire if I have no heat to keep me moving and working.

Instinctively, I reach a hand out to the fire. I'm not afraid, not fearful of being burned. Because we're the same, and I've learned that all fire is ultimately the same fire.

The flames lick around my hand playfully, the dance of the physical matching the movement of the connections that I now see plainly, even with my physical eyes.

But all of that is irrelevant. The only thing that matters is that we are one.

A bubble of excitement rises inside me, a desire to dance, to make merry, to enjoy the present. For what is the past? What is the future? There is only the present. And in the present, we have everything we need, so why not dance?

We move together as the heat warms but does not burn. Why would it burn? We are fire. We do not burn; we cannot. Everything else burns in our presence, but we ourselves are exempt.

We realize that there is more fuel nearby, enveloping us. Hungry, always hungry for more, we start munching it happily.

But something is wrong.

What is wrong?

What is this "wrong"? Wrong does not exist. We feed, we consume, we live. That is all.

But no, something is *wrong*. The coverings are not fuel, are not food.

We hesitate for a long moment as we war with ourselves. All that burns is fuel, yet this can burn but is not fuel?

We pause and in that pause become suddenly aware that we are not we. There is an outsider. Or we are an outsider?

Like a brick wall suddenly giving way to the heat of a house fire, my sense of self returns and fills me with cold fear.

I'm kneeling in the fire, having somehow crawled close enough to it to actually be *in* it. The flames that were licking harmlessly at my skin suddenly burn me.

I yelp and push myself backwards. My clothes have caught fire, so have my hair and beard. Doing the old drop and roll, I keep going until I'm sure that all the fire is out.

A nasty smell fills the air—burned hair is never pleasant. I suddenly can't bear to be in the cave and quickly make my way out of it.

River is the only of my Bound present—the others have gone out hunting. I can tell they've been doing well: I'm already at eleven percent towards my next level when I was at ten percent when they left.

Are you well, Master? River asks with a hint of concern, glancing up from where he's stirring a pot over his own fire. More concern goes through him as he looks at me properly. *You've got something here,* he says as he raises his clawed fingers to brush under his long muzzle.

I lift my hand as a mirror image and find that I have a much shorter patch of beard on one side. I pull my hand away from it quickly, not liking the reminder. Maybe I'll have to properly shave just to get rid of it. Although I brought my razors with me, I've fallen out of the habit of shaving since I don't need to present a professional appearance anymore.

"Yeah," I say, brushing myself down with slightly shaky fingers. It's not every day I almost lose my sense of self completely. "How are your experiments going?"

River eyes me but decides to go along with my obvious desire to change the subject. *I have made some interesting discoveries with one of the poisons I know. Boiling the berries I use nullifies it completely, but warming them up to just above body temperature before combining them with the other ingredients seems to increase the lethality of the mix.*

I eye the small lizard lying limply in a small cage to one side. The enclosure is formed of branches bound together with vines and bark-fiber rope and took River half a day to build. On his other side is another cage full of lizards just waiting for their turn to be test subjects. I still don't feel good about using test subjects, but at least River rarely kills them—he sees it as a good opportunity to test his healing potions as well as his poisons. Then again, I'm not sure that living while being used as a test subject is exactly a gift, even if the creature doesn't have to suffer the damage for too long.

I reach forwards and touch the lizard's tail through the bars. It's still alive, so I feed mana into it. It's not one of my Bound, so there's significantly more resistance, but at the same time, it's not particularly strong, so the resistance isn't enough to prevent me from checking on its injuries. On *her* injuries, if my scan is accurate—which it is.

The healing potion that River gave her has nullified the poison and healed most of the damage but not all of it. I clear up the rest of the injuries and then pull my hand away. The lizard pushes herself to her feet and starts running around the cage frantically. I look up at River.

"How many times have you tested things on this one?"

This was the third time.

I nod in acknowledgment and then open the door of the cage. The lizard takes a moment to realize that there's a route to freedom, and then she zips through it almost too fast to see. She scurries away into the ground cover and disappears from view.

When I look up, I see River looking at me with an odd expression.

"What?" I ask, feeling slightly defensive. I'm already feeling a bit raw from my earlier experience and his incomprehension isn't helping.

Nothing, Master, River answers quickly, tilting his chin up.

I sigh and try to control myself. "I'm not going to be angry, I promise. What is it?"

It's just . . . River hesitates before continuing. *I still do not understand why you limit the number of times I can test something on a creature. Or why you let it go. These lizards taste good enough, though they are rather bony. Unless you fear that they will still be poisoned?*

"No, it's not that. It's just . . ." I sigh again. "It's something that I need. To feel better about what we're doing here." It's not logical; I know it isn't. My Bound kill creatures every day for meat to eat and for Energy towards their Evolutions. And my own hands certainly aren't clean either. It's just . . . at least then they have a chance of fighting back. I accept the need to test potions and agree that I'd prefer not to test them on myself or my Bound until I know that they won't kill or maim us. But at the same time, even the little lizards are arguably capable of gaining sapience at some point. And in the meantime, they're perfectly capable of feeling pain and fear. Catching them, putting them in a cage, and then essentially torturing them is, to my mind, far crueler than engaging them in a battle.

I know, they end up dead either way, but I can't help but feel the *means* of dying matters. So, I'm trying to find a compromise: one that allows River to test the potions while limiting the number of times he can test on a particular individual and ensures that individual is released if they survive the tests.

River doesn't understand, and I recognize why. In the lizard folk's way of looking at the world, anything in the forest is a resource for them to draw upon to fulfil their own needs. Heck, from the sounds of it, the ruling class are barely better when thinking of their own underclass. So testing potions on small lizards caught in the forest makes absolute sense to them—getting sentimental about it, on the other hand, doesn't.

As you wish, Master, River answers finally, once more giving way to my expressed need despite his lack of understanding. That he keeps *trying* to understand is something I appreciate.

River continues by updating me on the various discoveries he's made—apparently, fire is as much of a game changer as I thought it might be, though he still hasn't succeeded in making a particularly potent healing potion. He's been having fun, though—boiling, frying, charring, heating . . . He's even tried experimenting with the ashes of ingredients rather than the fresh ones, but with limited effect as far as I can tell. Still, he's discovered plenty of useful strategies as well, ones that almost make up for his lack of magic.

After he's finished updating me, I eye the cave again but decide that I'm feeling a bit too antsy to continue attempting to shape fire and too distracted to do anything that requires concentration. But there's always something to do—in this case, it's moving my store of firewood under shelter.

I haven't done it before because there was no space in the alcove, and I didn't want to overflow into Kalanthia's area. I don't think she'd be happy with that. And putting it in my Inventory means that it isn't able to dry any more than it already has. But now that I have this convenient little space, keeping my firewood dry is actually feasible. That will be especially useful in the rainy winter—in the last five days, we've had one rainstorm and two short showers. The rain is definitely coming more often and, apparently, will increase in frequency even more. At least my clay pit has filled up fully as a result.

The physical activity of shifting wood is perfect for contemplation. It takes almost no brainpower to move firewood, only the little that's reserved for making sure the logs are stacked in a way that means they're not likely to fall. The rest of my focus can therefore be on working through what just happened to me.

Deciding that ripping the bandage off is the most effective solution, I focus on the core of the issue, the thought that sent me reeling away from the fire with my hands shaking and my legs feeling weak: I almost lost my sense of self and became part of the fire. And I can't help but think that it might have even been permanent.

But what does that mean? If it hadn't started licking at my clothes and jarred me out of that state, what would have happened? Would my body have dissolved into flames? Or would it have been left there, mindless, as my consciousness lost all connection with it?

And what would have happened when the fire went out? Would my mind have returned to my body, assuming it had still been present? Or would my mind have been snuffed out with the flames?

Perhaps it's not useful to think of such what ifs, but I feel like I *need* to. Like I need to work through what could have happened emotionally.

I could have lost everything. Because, ultimately, without my sense of self, what am I? I can replace tools, clothes, furniture, shelter. But I can't replace friends. And I can't replace myself.

I suddenly sense that I'm touching on something with that thought, but it vanishes even as I chase after it.

Giving up after a few fruitless attempts to follow the idea, I sigh and return to the issue at hand.

I feel like . . . It's almost like some part of me was pulled adrift, askew—like a tablecloth tugged sideways off a table. It's still on the table but not as it was before, not hanging evenly on all sides and smooth across the top. The physical activity and contemplation are helping, like somehow each minute that passes twitches the tablecloth back into position, its well-worn creases settling over the edges and corners of the table as always.

Though I'm not done yet, I can't help settling on the ground near the entrance to the cave. Closing my eyes, I drop into my Core space.

The movement of Energy is like a pulse, like the internal matrix truly is the network of blood vessels that I've compared it to many times and my Core is the heart. The golden light rushes towards my Core in a small wave, then rushes away from it as if pushed. It's not all that dissimilar to what happened when I leveled up, actually, just on a much, much smaller scale.

Curiosity suffuses me. I know this isn't what I came here to do, but I can't help wanting to satisfy my desire to *know*. Pulling out of my Core space, I take a moment to slow my breathing, to calm my mind.

And then, instead of diving into my Core space and appearing there abruptly, I . . . drift downwards. Like an ember floating through the air.

The ultimate destination is the same, but I feel different about it. As I am now, I'm calmer than before, more peaceful. And interestingly, I feel the connections leading out of my body more strongly. I'm inordinately tempted to follow the connections that I sense are my Bound and perhaps repeat what I did with Fenrir once.

Later, I promise myself. *When I've at least warned them that I'll be trying something.* I wouldn't want to accidentally disrupt them in the middle of a fight, after all. The thought sobers me, and I return back to the center of my Core space from where I was drifting at the outer reaches.

There, I'm struck by a thought. *If I'm now able to maintain Meditation when barely even thinking about it, when moving, and now even when I'm mostly disconnected from my physical body, what about healing?*

At present, although my use of Flesh-Shaping has improved significantly, I still have to be still, close my eyes, and focus fully on it. *But what if I could develop it even further to be able to heal while doing something else?* I'll probably have to work up to it, but being able to use healing in combat may require me to be able to defend myself at the same time. Being able to continue fighting will make a big difference to how much use I can be in a fight, especially since my explorations with distance healing indicate that perhaps one day in the future, I'll be able to heal as easily from a distance as when I'm touching my target.

After my recent realizations, I'm eager to try it, if only as a distraction. And isn't it fortunate that I have some burns to practice on?

After pushing myself to my feet, I keep my eyes open while I work on healing my burns—more than half the challenge is being able to move mana through my internal matrix without "looking" at it.

It's hard, very hard. It's just as difficult as trying to heal my Bound at a distance, though in a different way. That's difficult because it's like trying to use a long pole with a pen on the end of it to write on a board—the fine detail becomes increasingly trickier the longer the distance. This, however, is difficult because it requires me to split my attention in a way I'm not used to. Like trying to have a conversation with someone at the same time as trying to solve complex math problems. Possible, because they're two different subjects and use different parts of the brain, but not easy. It's more like trying to Meditate while moving, though it's not exactly the same as that either.

Still, the chances are that practice makes perfect, so the more I do it, the more likely it is that I'll be able to use this in a combat situation. Ultimately, that's what I need to aim for in order to be at least as effective as I was with Lay-on-Hands.

So, despite the way it makes my head feel like it's being split with my own stone axe, I refuse to close my eyes as I clench my fists, furrow my brow, and try to cope with two different sets of inputs at the same time.

I don't know if I'm surprised, relieved, or simply unmoved by my success, because as my burns start healing, I'm just concentrating too hard to take note of my emotional reaction. By the time I've moved onto the third burn, it's starting to get easier. Perhaps because having done one burn, it's simpler to do others. Or perhaps I'm getting used to it—I never realized that directing healing with my mind would be comparable to working out in the gym, but it is.

As the task becomes easier for me to do, I challenge myself further by beginning to actually move and continue my task of shifting the firewood logs between one pile and the other.

This is even more of a challenge, and I mostly move on autopilot even as the odd disruption of logs dropping on my feet or splinters piercing my fingers threatens to tip this delicate balance. But I keep going doggedly until, finally, my fingers grasp at empty air and my mana fails to heal.

It's only then that I realize I've both moved all the firewood and healed all my burns. I sit down where I am, surprisingly tired.

The corners of my mouth tug upwards. I have a splitting headache, like someone truly has taken my axe and gotten their kicks out of cleaving my head with it. But I've made progress. I consider trying to use mana to deal with the headache, but I refrain. Something tells me that this kind of pain isn't actually anything that mana is going to be able to fix. If I'm unlucky, it would actually make things worse.

I do want to make sure that I haven't accidentally done myself any damage, though, both from this particular activity as well as from the fire earlier.

Dropping into my Core space—without Meditating this time—I do a quick scan over myself.

No problems as far as I can see, I conclude after completing my inspection. My Flesh-Shaping Skill seems to have grown a little, taking up just a touch more space than it was before. I examine it a little longer, moving around so I can see it from different angles. I can't work out exactly what's changed, but I wouldn't be surprised if just that little exercise has gained me a level in the Skill.

Interestingly, Energy Manipulation—or the dense interwoven lines I'm pretty sure belong to that Skill, anyway—has grown too. I guess that's normal. I don't think I've received any notification, though, so it obviously hasn't crossed from Journeyman into the next rank yet.

A quick look over to the void area proves that nothing's changed in that region either, as frustrating and worrying as that is. I can't just hope to stumble across the right solution before it becomes a major problem, but nothing I've tried has worked so far.

I open my eyes and pick up my stick to poke my drying hide a bit more, eyeing the fire. Risks aside, both physical and mental, I do feel like I've made a bit of a breakthrough with my understanding of fire. Where it will take me, though, is another question. Where I *want* it to take me is again a separate matter.

Honestly, I'd still like to try for Fire-Shaping. I can think of so many applications for Fire-Shaping, both in combat and outside it. And ideally, I want to get it before my armor is ready and it's time for me to head down to River's village.

The reason I have for wanting Fire-Shaping before then is linked to the vine-stranglers. They are both an obstacle in my way and the threat to River's village—dealing with them would kill two birds with one stone.

Since they seem so flammable, fire is the obvious solution. But I have no desire to create another forest fire. A fire like that is indiscriminate and will hurt friend just as easily as foe—judging by River's own experience with a forest fire, I could end up hurting lots of lizard folk in my attempt to save them.

While killing off the whole village arguably solves the issue with Kalanthia, I have a feeling that River would be . . . upset. And it's not like that would be any better of a solution than just letting her take her due from the village in the first place.

So, if I start a fire, it needs to be one I can control.

The risks are worth the potential benefits, I decide, unconsciously nodding in agreement with my own thoughts. But hopefully, forewarned is forearmed; I don't want to experience the same realization I had while kneeling in the fire.

That I could have lost it all and not even known it.

CHAPTER TWENTY-EIGHT

The Universe Is Laughing

I'm hungry, so I decide to take a break. I'm also eager to eat one of my more recent experiments with food.

It's a sort of flat cake, which I made with ground roots, water, and one of the five eggs River managed to find for me on one of his hunting trips into the forest. I was a bit dubious about them at first, but they turned out to taste much like the eggs I'm used to, though a bit more strongly "eggy," perhaps. Either way, the egg seems to do the job I wanted it to of holding my cake together.

Paired with some of the berries, the cakes are not bad at all. I wish I had some sugar or honey to put in them—or, even better, maple syrup—but even just with the berries they're pleasant enough. And, most importantly, they're not soup, stew, or chunks of meat.

While I enjoy my little almost-pancakes, I bask in the sun and try to sense where my Bound are at the moment.

Though I'm unable to pinpoint exactly where everyone is, I can get a vague sense of both direction and distance. It doesn't take me too long to realize that they seem to be on their way back. It makes sense: it's already getting towards mid-afternoon, and they've been out since we finished sparring this morning.

As I suspected when I first thought about the idea, Hades and Persephone have taken a bit of time to get used to the idea of fighting seriously without the intention of maiming or killing their opponents. Unlike the rest of my Bound, they're new to the group and a bit wary of everyone to begin with. They're starting to settle down now, and the hunting trips into the forest have definitely helped them integrate with the group, but for the first couple of sparring sessions, they seemed more than halfway convinced that their opponents were actually trying to kill them. Needless to say, my Flesh-Shaping got a bit of a workout the first few times.

Side note: much like regrowing an arm, it turns out that healing a gouged eye is possible with Flesh-Shaping; it just takes a *lot* of mana. Fenrir was rather happy with that discovery, as was I, for all that I'd rather not have experimented with it on him.

After the daily sparring, we tend to all get on with other tasks. River, of course, works with his potions, but Fenrir has been taking his guard duties seriously and uses the time when he's not going into the forest to patrol the area close to the den for the scent of any threats. He's also been an excellent protector of my once massacred samova beans. They're finally getting the chance to recover thanks to Fenrir chasing down the small mouselike creatures that were coming to nibble any shoots they dared to sprout.

Bastet tends to spend time with the cubs and has been hard at work on their hunting education—they've gone out into the forest the most out of everyone, and even when they're back at the den, I've seen her teaching the youngsters various techniques.

Sirocco disappears for long periods of time but is never uncontactable. Still, that doesn't mean that she will necessarily come back to go on a hunting trip, though I always send her an invitation. What she's doing, I don't know, and she refuses to tell me.

As for Hades and Persephone, they've been slowly relaxing around us, though I feel that there's still a distance between them and us. Maybe that's the result of bringing an existing couple into a group—they have less interest in integration. Since team-building exercises other than combat practice seem likely to backfire, I decide to leave it until or unless it proves to be a problem.

Lathani has also been going out into the forest a lot, though only with her mother. We've been working together in the sparring sessions, and she *seems* to be listening to me now, but I've only gone out further than the river a couple of times, and she hasn't asked to come along with me then. Nor have I offered, but I might do so soon if the sparring sessions continue going well. She's at least been becoming more affectionate again, which I consider a good sign.

Finishing my meal, I find myself hesitating over what to do next.

The return of the hunting group offers me a welcome distraction for a few minutes as I greet all of my Bound and inspect the carcasses they've brought back. It's fewer than I would have, of course, but that's the natural consequence of none of them having an Inventory or agile hands that can tie carcasses to a stick for carrying. Nonetheless, it isn't long before I'm once more left at a loose end as my Bound disperse to either sleep off their exertion or meditate with an Energy Heart.

Hades and Persephone are particularly enthusiastic about being given Energy Hearts, but they appear fearful when I come closer—perhaps they think I might take the Hearts away from them. Once I sit down again, they relax and huddle together with the glowing rocks nestled between them.

Although there are always physical tasks I *could* do, most of the ones I need to do ahead of going down to River's village are already complete or need time before my next intervention. Sure, I could start pounding the iron ore chunks to make the sand I'll need when trying to extract the iron from them, and yes, I could create more equipment or go searching for wood to turn into charcoal. But the fact is that I have more urgent, less physical objectives.

After my experience with the fire earlier, I feel reluctant to go too deeply into that again any time soon. Instead, I want to work on something that desperately needs to be solved and that might actually help me with my efforts anyway.

My soul damage.

The problem is that I've already tried several methods and they just haven't worked. I've tried feeding Energy into the void, and it's just been consumed. I've tried extending my matrix further in that area, but though I succeeded in doing that, it had no noticeable effect, and my extensions were slowly eroded away unless I continued reinforcing them consciously. I've even tried forming my mana into healing mana and using that. No luck.

Perhaps the issue with the methods I've been trying so far is that they're what worked to heal my Core and internal matrix; that doesn't mean that they'll work with my soul.

So this time, instead of trying immediately to think of a solution, I take another approach and attempt to start at the root, at what caused the problem in the first place.

Obviously, it was Pure Energy, and I don't know enough about Pure Energy for this line of thought to be at all helpful. What I *do* know is how it felt to have sustained the damage in the first place. Even a few weeks after the event, it's still vivid in my memory.

Before coming here, I wasn't even sure I had a soul at all; after suffering the pain and damage to it from the Pure Energy, I became convinced that I do.

I close my eyes and bring to mind that moment, that feeling of pain in something I recognized on an instinctive level but could never have discovered on my own. Part of me recoils once again, as if flinching at the memory.

I attempt to pounce on it like Bastet would an unsuspecting beast, but I'm just as disappointed as she would be when it escapes my mental grasp.

I try a couple more times, but it seems like my soul—if I'm even succeeding in feeling it—quickly becomes inured to the traumatic memory and stops reacting. Or perhaps it's because *I* am more used to it.

This isn't working.

I sigh and add it to the list of *other* things that haven't been working. Opening my eyes, I stare up at the blue sky. There's not a cloud to be seen today, but the slight haze that obscures my view of the valley indicates that this is not a state of affairs that's likely to continue.

Somehow, the blue sky, the same clear color of my father's eyes, reminds me of something.

I have a Skill that deals with the soul. Two, actually, though only one might possibly be able to help me here.

After all, what can the Battle of Wills be but a battle between two souls?

I'm putting words to a thought that's been percolating at the back of my mind for a while. Maybe this is what I almost grasped when I was considering how the fire could have consumed the essence of who I am. My soul. Ever since the first Battle of Wills with Spike, I've been wondering about what that space actually is. With all the evidence of subsequent Battles, that it is some sort of soul space is the only thing that makes sense.

Point one: Kalanthia said right at the beginning how Bonds affect the soul and that the sundering of a Bond, willing or unwilling, leaves scars upon it.

Point two: when I'm engaging in a Battle of Wills, I have the same access to my opponent's emotions as I do with a full Bond—as long as I move close enough. But that could be because our souls have to be within a certain distance of each other.

Point three: we are unable to feel what's happening to us physically while in this space, even though time continues to pass for our bodies. I mean, I'm assuming a little bit here, but I was unable to feel how close to drowning my own body was during the fight with the crocodile. Equally, the crocodile appeared unable to defend itself while it was engaged in the Battle, given how River didn't have any injuries. That time passed is certain—I wasn't sure at first whether it had, but given that River was able to kill the crocodile in the middle of our Battle, I think there is sufficient evidence that time doesn't stop during a Battle of Wills.

Actually, that latter is very important to know. It means that I mustn't use Dominate on an opponent that is surrounded by allies—not unless I have my own allies to defend me while I'm vulnerable. Otherwise, next time it could be me who disappears mid-Battle. Which in itself seems to support the Battle of Wills being either a mental or soul projection since it disappears with the death of the physical body.

Though it might be a mental projection rather than a soul one, with what I know from Nicolas's world's experiments about Willpower being connected to the soul, I think there's a strong likelihood that my guess here is correct.

But who knows? What if the crocodile was so indomitable because I'm suffering a penalty of twenty percent to the stat that governs the success of the Battle? Perhaps if I didn't have the damage, I might have made more headway against the water dweller. Then again, perhaps not. Obviously, I wasn't able to inspect it before it was dead, so I have no idea what the minimum recommended Willpower level for it was.

Anyway, that's somewhat irrelevant to the matter at hand. If I'm right, that gives me a new avenue to explore to heal my soul damage.

But how to use it? Can I enter that space again by directing it at one of my Bound? I doubt it, somehow, but decide to give it a go. That, of course, raises the question of who.

I look around. Bastet is sleeping with the three cubs cuddled around and on her. Hades and Persephone aren't good targets for multiple reasons. River is intent on his potions, and I'm reluctant to disturb him. Sirocco is probably a bad idea—since she's connected to me through Tame, that could have some unintended side effects. Which leaves the indefatigable Fenrir.

"Fenrir, could you come and help me here, please?" I say out loud as I turn my eyes to where he's gnawing on a bone. I suspect it's less because he's hungry and more because he just gets some sense of pleasure at crunching bones to broken shards.

He perks up at my words and comes trotting over, his side of the Bond emanating eagerness.

"Do you remember when we first met? The space we entered?" Fenrir cocks his head and sends a sense of confusion along with a few images. The pictures are of us fighting in the cave, of him feeling weakness suffusing his limbs, and of seeing me stand over him, much larger than life. "Yes, and then after that, do you remember what happened?"

This time he sends a picture of gray mist, and the feelings attached are far more informative than the picture itself. The emotions are those of fear, of sensing something much larger and more powerful than himself come closer. Of being offered safety and belonging. Of his eager acceptance and the immediate brightness of a connection being formed. Of him feeling an instantaneous sense of loyalty, hierarchy, and pack.

So, he *does* remember it, though somewhat differently from me. It's interesting to see how he's connected the automatic feelings of loyalty and obedience to the usual expectations within a pack. Unlike what happened with River, I get the feeling that this isn't so foreign to his personality—fortunately for my sense of guilt.

On that note, maybe once River has surfaced from his current experiment, it might be worth asking what things were like from his perspective as well and compare to see if it's the same as Fenrir is describing.

"I'm going to try to do something similar to what happened in that memory of yours," I tell Fenrir. "I don't know what will happen, but are you okay with me trying?"

He sends a sense of confusion but willing acceptance of whatever I wish to do across to me. Praying that this won't mess things up more somehow, I look him in the eyes.

"Dominate," I say firmly.

As if the universe is laughing at my previous trepidation, nothing happens. I try again but then shake my head. It's not working.

Clearly, the Skill detects that a Bond is already in place and stops it from triggering. Or something like that.

"Thanks, Fenrir," I say, trying not to let my disappointment leak across to him. "You can go back to eating." With a hint of confusion, he trots away.

Well, that was a letdown.

My throat is dry, so I pull out my sneleon shell full of water. As I drink, I see the blue sky and my own face reflected in the surface. I suddenly pause.

Could that work?

CHAPTER TWENTY-NINE

Challenge Initiated

I t's an idea. Is it a good one, though?

Although using Dominate on myself might offer the potential of healing my soul, it might also cause some significant problems. What would a Bond with myself entail? Who would I even be facing? My shadow self? My evil twin? My *good* twin?

Or would something else happen? What if triggering Dominate on myself causes some catastrophic failure that essentially renders me brain-dead? Or what if I successfully finish the Battle of Wills and some perpetual feedback loop eventuates, which traps me in the role of the Bound at the same time as the Binder and unable to be either?

The potential downsides are almost enough to make me dismiss the notion as an option at all. The only thing that stops me from deciding to move on to another idea is that I don't *have* any other ideas.

I've spoken to Kalanthia, and she has no clue—soul damage is not something she is at all familiar with. I've checked with River, and even Bastet. No dice. I've tried everything I can think of, and none of it has worked.

The only thing I haven't yet tried is leveling up and committing all my points to Willpower, then looking to see what happens to the Energy and trying to mimic it. The problem with that is that I'm still a long way from earning enough Energy to do that. I check my status screen; my progress is at twelve percent.

I suppose that if I spent time in Meditation, I would gain more Energy . . . but as of yet, I can only move slowly and do actions that don't require much thought to maintain the state. I have a lot of things to do that will take my full concentration, meaning I can't be in Meditation for them.

My Bound's hunting does help, of course, as does my natural daily absorption. By using Meditation as much as possible, I suppose I might be able to level up in ten days or so. But what if that doesn't work? What if I pour my six level-up points into Willpower and don't learn enough to heal myself? What if some or all of the points get lost by the Energy being sucked into the blackness? Or worse, what if it damages me further?

I agonize over the decision. Using Dominate on myself is so uncertain. The potential consequences I'm considering may not even be realistic—I simply don't know enough about this Skill and its effects.

My estimation of the potential consequences of leveling up and putting points in Willpower are based a lot more on what I've seen and what I feel. I've seen Energy disappear into the void; I've sensed that increasing my Willpower, especially so significantly, has a non-negligible chance of doing more damage.

Trying to mitigate the damage by only adding a couple of points to Willpower isn't something I consider for long—it's unlikely to give me the information I will need. Besides, the tidal wave that crashed through me when I leveled up last time might easily be enough to knock something loose even if I only add *one* point to Willpower.

Racked with indecision, I end up entering Meditation and slipping slowly into my Core space. Drifting over to the knot of Energy channels that make up my Dominate Skill, I eye them, wondering if they might give me an indication of what might happen if I try to use the Skill on myself.

Of course, it would be a massive disappointment if, after all this time spent going over whether to do it or not, I chose to do it, only to find that it's impossible to conduct a Battle of Wills with myself just as it was impossible to reinitiate it with Fenrir. Honestly, when I think about it, that's probably the most likely result.

In my meditative state, which has followed me even into this other space, I go over the Energy channels, tracing them like I might trace an etching with my fingers. And as I trace the Skill, holding the question in my mind of whether I can safely try Dominate on myself, I find that an answer starts coming to me.

Or, not an answer, exactly. It's not like my Skill starts speaking to me and telling me what will happen. Instead, I become more and more convinced that it's possible and without immediate risk. I do get the sense that there probably is some risk attached but nothing that's likely to be lethal.

So perhaps no feedback loop of brain death.

The fact that I still feel like there are probably some risks to this process isn't so heartening, but I suppose there are risks to everything. Certainly, my only other idea of leveling up is risky too.

I pull out of my Core space and open my eyes. I'm still feeling the floaty, peaceful sense of being in a light meditative state—somehow, it's a little easier to consider the decision without all my emotions of fear and dread attached.

My fears about an immediate failure, catastrophic or otherwise, when first activating Dominate seem to be unfounded. However, that still leaves the questions of who exactly I'd be facing and what the consequences of a successful Battle of Wills would be.

But without the fear of immediately lobotomizing myself the moment I activate Dominate, I'm more willing to give it a go. After all, if I feel that I can't or don't want to move forward, I can always exit the space—assuming that aspect stays the same, but I don't see why it wouldn't.

And, who knows, perhaps just being in the space will allow me to work on my soul damage. Perhaps I don't need to actually Dominate myself successfully to do it.

My mind made up, I stand and go into the alcove. I brought my shaving kit with me—not that I've used it, despite my vague plans of evening my beard out from where it's half burned—and there's a mirror inside the box. It's only when I open the box that I realize there's also a block of shaving soap there.

I slap a hand to my forehead—all that work to make some soap when I'd actually brought some with me in the first place! I haven't bothered trying to shave since being here, so this is the first time I've opened the box and reminded myself of its presence.

I make a mental note that it exists, not wanting to forget about it again, but withdraw the mirror from the box for now. I go back outside and take a seat.

Butterflies flutter in my stomach as I meet my own eyes in the mirror. *Am I really going to do this?* I ask myself a final time. Then, my resolve firming again, I focus and speak quietly.

"Dominate."

The space is different from usual. That's immediately evident.

I'm not facing myself—or anything, actually. Instead, I'm alone in a gray, featureless area. I can't tell how far it extends, since it starts becoming misty from the tips of my fingers outwards; only the area directly around me is clear. It feels like I'm standing in a fogbank, but even the ground beneath my feet is gray. It feels solid but doesn't appear to be . . . I quickly look back up, unnerved despite myself.

Turning on the spot, a nasty thought suddenly occurs. If there's nowhere to move towards, there's also nowhere to move away from. How am I supposed to exit this space?

I try to move one way, then the other. The area of clear space moves with me, the misty area around me unchanging, making me feel like I'm walking on a treadmill. I'm starting to panic when a screen suddenly appears in front of my eyes that looks much like the notifications I'm now accustomed to.

Challenge initiated: Level one
Commence challenge / Leave arena

"Challenge? What challenge?" I ask, though the words come out strangely. Instead of vocalizations I can hear with my ears, they seem to resonate with something else.

To my utter lack of shock, there is no response from the box in front of me. However, its presence is comforting. First, it offers me a way out. Second, the fact that it's there at all suggests that this is actually a legitimate use of Dominate—I haven't gone completely off piste and into pastures new. Given how much else I've learned that wasn't in the information from Nicholas's world, this is reassuring.

I shrug to myself and choose to commence the challenge. I've come this far; why not see what else this new use of the Skill has to offer? I suspect that picking the other option would just take me back to my body, so there's no point in doing that right now.

A new box appears in front of me.

> Error
> Existing damage to the soul detected. Risks of further damage to the soul as a result of the challenge are therefore multiplied tenfold.
> Do you wish to commence the challenge regardless of the damage? Yes / No

I hesitate but then shake my head, frustration and disappointment mounting inside me. So, this is a legitimate use of Dominate, but I can't do it with my soul in the state it is. I don't know what the original risk was, but for it to be multiplied tenfold is just too much to chance.

After selecting "No," another box appears.

> Challenge declined.
> Do you wish to remain in the soul space or leave it? Note: you are able to leave at any time by stating "leave soul space." If you decide to commence the challenge again, you must leave the soul space and reenter it.

My flagging spirits perk up at this. So I don't have to leave entirely? Now I know that it's possible to leave, I find that I don't want to. When I spoke, I felt something resonate, something that I've only felt twice before. I'm suddenly convinced that this might be the key to my problem.

After choosing to remain in the soul space, the box disappears. The gray mist, once so foreboding, is suddenly alluring, seeming less like it's hiding dangers and more like it contains secrets waiting to be revealed.

Still not focusing too much on what is beneath me, I settle down to the ground in a cross-legged position.

Right, let me see what I can do here.

CHAPTER THIRTY

Push the Boundaries

O f course, deciding that this is the perfect place and time to work on my soul doesn't mean that I automatically know how to do it.

Without any other ideas, I try entering Meditation, but that doesn't seem to be available to me. I enter a calmer and more peaceful state of mind, at least, but I don't transition into my Core space or start being able to see the connections around me with my mind's eye.

However, as I allow the meditation to continue, I start feeling . . . something. A vibration in the world around me. I'm reminded of when I spoke out loud and how the results were very different from what normally happens when I speak.

"Hi?" I say, testing. The world vibrates around me, but only for a moment. *I need a longer sound*, I decide. "Aah," I say next, drawing it out. This time the vibrations are far easier to feel. But there's still something not quite right.

I suddenly remember the stereotypical sound that Tibetan monks are apparently supposed to make when meditating on the universe. *Well, it's worth a try,* I say to myself with a shrug. Feeling a bit stupid, I even shift myself into a lotus position—my new Dexterity actually makes that possible.

"Ommmm . . ." I say, drawing out the sound as long as I can make it. This time, the vibrations around me are so much deeper and feel like they touch on something almost transcendent. The vibrations of my voice reverberate around the gray space, somehow amplified instead of deadened.

My sound continues long after I feel like I should have run out of breath. Maybe I don't actually have lungs here? Or maybe the sound has been so taken up by the environment around me that whether I make a sound or not makes no difference.

And in that vibration of sound, I feel a dissonance. An area where the sound is not echoed, where it is absorbed and not reflected back. *Is that the damage?* I wonder. Opening my eyes, I see no difference, but I can *feel* it.

The question, though, is whether actually being able to feel the damage means that I can heal it. It's got to be a better start than not even being able to detect the damage, though.

Focusing on the damaged area, I use this new vibration sense to feel at its edges. It's a very odd feeling. I'm kind of hearing it, but in hearing, I also see? It's almost like I've got that condition—synesthesia, or something. Either way, I find I get something of an image in my head that's created by the vibration, as long as I don't actually open my eyes. In exploring the area with sound that somehow translates to sight, I find out something interesting: my soul damage is already healing.

That's the only explanation I can think of, anyway. There is evidence that the damage was made with clean slices: some edges of the injured areas are completely smooth. But not all of them are still smooth—some have a faint clouding, which partially reflects the sound. I can only take that to mean that whatever substance my soul is made from is replenishing itself.

I feel a sense of relief go through me, my emotion so strong that it cuts through even the peaceful state of my meditative trance. If I'm right, and I'm pretty sure I am, even if I don't find a way of healing my soul, it will sort itself out eventually. I don't know how long it will take—the repairs that have happened so far are slight enough that I didn't notice until I started examining the area closer—but I will be whole once more, someday.

Of course, if I can speed up the process, that would be great. Walking around with a twenty percent debuff to my Willpower doesn't really improve my odds of surviving to see the end of the year. Especially since that's one of my key stats, if my Class Skills are anything to go by.

It's still relieving. And the removal of some of the pressure I've been feeling doesn't reduce my motivation to do the job. Instead, it fills me with hope that it's possible.

How is another question, of course. But at least I'm further ahead than I was.

The key must be in these vibrations. It's the only thing so far that I've tried that has affected the fog-like substance at all. Though, actually, when I open my eyes, I realize that it's not the fog that is being affected. I thought it was, but instead it's something that is filling the space directly around me. I thought it was empty, but as I hum "om," I notice that the area directly touching my skin is . . . thickening . . . instead.

It's like the air around me in the "real" world. The air is completely transparent, invisible, and undetectable if you sit still and just look at it. However, its presence becomes clear on a windy day when it blows stiffly against the skin, or on a cold day when breath plumes into it, or on a hot day when it shimmers and creates mirages just above the surface of the road.

In this case, it's the vibrations that are making it become denser, hazy. Now able to properly see what I have to conclude is my soul, I also finally see the damage with more than just my mind's eye. While the haze everywhere else is so dense that it's practically becoming physical, the damage is an absence that even the fog doesn't fill.

Oddly enough, it's not at all the same shape as in my internal matrix. There, it was like an ice cream scoop had taken a hemisphere out of my being. Here, it's more like a four-sided pyramid, with the tip centered on my elbow.

Shifting my arm, I notice how the damage moves with it, though in a sort of delayed reaction. A bit like how quickly moving one's hand leaves afterimages in the air, the damage to my soul takes a little bit of time to catch up with my movement.

Interesting, though I'm not sure whether it helps me much. Oh well. When I know as little as I do, any knowledge has to be good to have, even if it doesn't ultimately prove to be of much immediate use.

Holding my arm still, I inspect the damage with my eyes. I notice similar things to what I've already sensed with the vibrations. I confirm that it looks like my soul is healing itself—it's starting from the tip and moving outwards, but from the looks of it, the rate is *very* slow. If I leave it to its own devices, I might heal by the time I'm due to go to Nicholas's world, but not very long before. Having my most important stat crippled until then is not exactly ideal, even if it's a relief that it will heal itself at all.

Since vibrations seem to have been key so far, I hum again, this time putting as much force into it as I can.

I notice how the visible density of my soul thickens further, though I can still see all parts of it at the same time, in a strange contradiction of the normal laws of reality. I try not to think about it too much—it's helping me, and that's what's important.

The healing that has already happened to my soul thickens too, but it doesn't seem to spread. Instead, it just swirls gently on the spot, not pushing at its boundaries.

I reduce the hum and relax a bit as I try to think about a possible next step. What am I doing wrong here? Or what am I not doing here that I should be?

After sitting with the question for a little while, a thought slowly bubbles up from under the surface. Everything I've done with magic so far seems to have needed intention as well as action. When earning a Skill, I have to *intend* to do what the Skill's objective is and then make an effort to achieve the goal without the Skill at all.

Take Stealth, the very first Skill I earned by myself. I had to intend to make as little noise as possible, and then I had to make an effort to walk quietly. As a result, I gained a Skill that enhances my ability to move quietly through the forest. Or take my weapon Skills, where I had to focus on improving with the weapons themselves to earn the Skills—though, it seems likely that I needed that achievement first to open the door for me.

It even applies to my Skill rank-ups. I've long noticed the connection between the new developments of a Skill and what I've been using it for. That's intention and action combined.

So, what if this is the same?

Determined to test it, I once more start humming. The sound never completely disappeared, but now it returns with renewed vigor. I focus on the damaged parts, in particular the ones where healing has already started, and project my intention that they heal.

Nothing happens, but I'm not daunted.

Instead, I redouble my effort, straining all my will to make those swirling areas of haze extend until my whole being starts to ache.

Nothing happens.

I huff a tired sigh, a little dismayed. I realize now how sure I was that my idea would work.

Perhaps it should but I'm missing something. Once more, I close my eyes and just breathe. I don't care whether I need to in this space or not—the action is familiar and calming.

An indeterminate while later, I open my eyes again. By this time the vibrations have almost disappeared and the area around me is clear once more. I don't mind—I know how to make it solidify again.

The thought that occurs to me is about fuel. Fixing my Core required using Energy. Fixing my internal matrix involved using mana. What does fixing my soul need?

It's possible that it could consume either Energy or mana, just like one of the others, but something inside me doubts this. Which leaves two other resource pools I could draw on: stamina . . . or health.

Given that Wisdom, and thereby my internal matrix, is linked to mana regeneration and I needed to use mana to fix that stat, I have to guess that the most likely option for fixing my health regeneration stat will be health.

However, I'd still like to test with both Energy and mana since I'd much rather use those than my health directly. What if I pull too much and empty it entirely? Could I accidentally kill myself? No, I have to hope that either Energy or mana will be able to heal the damage.

Actually accessing my resource pools while in this state is another question. It takes a lot of trial and error to succeed in touching my mana pool at all. It takes me even longer before I'm able to pull at my mana while focusing on the damage done to my soul. And when I *do* succeed, I find that it doesn't work.

Feeling a sense of inevitability, I nonetheless attempt to pull at my Energy store, but this seems to be impossible. I try for double the time that I attempted to access my mana pool, but when none of my efforts work, I eventually give up.

Resigning myself to what I suspected would be the result from the outset, I turn my attention to pulling from my health pool.

That's easier thought than done, of course. However, with my recent experience of managing to touch my mana pool, I find that it takes me less time to access my health pool than it might have. In fact, most of the difficulty is in trying to work out where to *find* it.

I'm used to accessing my mana pool—I know it's mostly held within my Core, and I've become relatively adept at pulling it out and directing it through my internal matrix. My health pool is a different story.

I'm aware that it drops when I am injured and is replenished when the injuries are healed. I'm aware that it increases slowly over time even if I don't actively heal myself, my injuries knitting together with my natural health regeneration. I'm even, unfortunately, aware of how a severe enough injury can permanently reduce the pool I have to draw on—that's what happened with my eye when my natural regeneration and potion were unable to heal it.

I think about more recent experiences and recognize what's happening to my Core space when I add a Constitution point, the stat that determines my health pool itself: most of the Energy is fed into the blackness around my internal matrix rather than into the golden weave itself.

All of that together implies to me that my health is very much grounded in the body. That might seem obvious by the fact that it's what's most affected when I sustain an injury, but I feel that it's an important foundational point to make clear.

So, instead of trying to touch on my Core as I did before, I do my best to touch my body. In this strange gray world, my body feels very far away and difficult to access. It's a bit like I'm reaching for something but can't see because of a blindfold, and I can only feel the most obvious aspects because I'm wearing thick gloves.

It probably would be easier to leave the space, work out how to access my health pool, and then enter it again, but I'm uncertain I'll even be able to make it back to this exact space. I should—it seems like it's part of Dominate—but what if because I couldn't take the "challenge," I'm barred from entry until my soul is whole again?

It's probably unlikely, but not impossible. Having finally found a way of properly accessing the damage to my soul, I'm reluctant to do anything that might jeopardize it. So I choose to take the harder route of fumbling around blindly.

Eventually, after a lot of trial and error—mostly error—I manage to grasp the fact that my health seems to be held in the opposite manner to my mana. My mana, as far as I can make out, is kept under pressure in my Core along with the Energy I absorb. The effect of this compression within my Core is that when the mana comes out, I have to actively work to keep it together. If I don't, it will quite happily either dissipate or rush out of my Core space entirely. Conversely, my health is diffused throughout my body, and the challenge there is to gather enough of it to even be able to detect it, let alone work with it.

Now I've made that discovery, it makes complete sense—enough that I feel like I should have realized it at the outset. When I was force-fed Energy, it threatened to fracture my Core and then actually did damage it when I leveled up too many times. I have to guess that the Core didn't have enough time to adapt to the greater amount of mana it was being forced to hold. Perhaps I wouldn't have done as much damage to myself if I'd chosen physical stats instead of my mental and soul ones on each level-up—the Energy might have been disbursed rather than concentrated.

Or maybe I would have just been injured differently. I guess that flooding my body with mana could have done just as much damage in a different way.

The most important discovery I make is that my health is just another form of energy, no doubt deriving, as my mana does, from the Energy I absorb. It suddenly makes so much more sense! My body naturally absorbs Energy through the tendrils of my internal matrix that extend outside me—perhaps I should call it my "external" matrix. That in turn must determine how much health and mana I regenerate.

If my mana pool isn't full, some of this Energy is transformed into mana. Kalanthia has indicated that it's linked to the soul, but I don't know if that's a difference between beasts and humans. From what I can tell, it's my *health* regeneration that is determined by my Willpower stat, which implies that my soul must be an important part of that and not my mana regeneration, which depends on Wisdom. Though, for all I know, Wisdom is also linked to the soul in some way. Equally, if my health pool isn't full, some of the Energy I absorb is transformed into health, replacing what was lost with my injury.

I suddenly start wondering if my stamina is actually the same. Though, why then would its pool size be determined by Strength and its regeneration by Dexterity? I decide not to pursue that line of thinking at this moment—it probably makes more sense to do it when I'm not in my soul space and able to examine myself a bit better.

Pausing for a moment, I consider the implications of the fact that at least two, maybe all three of my resource pools are derivatives of Energy.

Shouldn't I have noticed something about my Energy absorption rate fluctuating? I think to myself. Or maybe not my actual Energy absorption rate, but the amount of Energy I'm actually accumulating in my store. After all, if I'm absorbing, say, thirty units of Energy per hour, but I've got a deficit of three hundred units of mana and fifty units of health, then wouldn't I earn less Energy towards my next level?

Then again, I continue the thought, *given that all I have to work on with my Energy store is a progress percentage, perhaps it's happening and I don't even realize it.* I resolve to pay better attention to what I can actually see on my status screen. Because if getting injured and using my mana actually slows my progress to the next level, I need to know about it.

Then again, I don't generally *intend* on getting injured, and I need to use my mana to keep myself alive, one of my Bound alive, or deal with an attack. I suppose I could use mana less for things like skinning a carcass, but if I avoid using it too much, my Skills won't increase as fast. So maybe it doesn't matter too much if my progress to the next level *is* affected. Ultimately, if I want to increase my rate of progress, the method is still the same: earn more Energy. It would still be good to know, though.

Returning once more to the question of health in comparison to mana, I find myself wondering what would happen if I found a way to transform Energy into health and force more of it into my body. Could I increase my health pool beyond its normal limits that way? Or would it damage me? Perhaps it's worth an experiment.

But not now. For now, once I figure out how to access my health pool directly, I'll start trying to apply it to my soul damage.

This proves to be the easiest part of the process. Now using the correct "material," all I have to do is focus on expanding the mist into the areas that need it. The most difficult bit is multitasking as I keep my hum going even while I focus on pushing the boundaries of the mist.

I realize at one point that I'm not actually breathing; apparently, in this space I don't need to do so to speak. I suppose it's additional evidence of me not actually being here physically.

Too soon, my health runs out. It becomes harder and harder to draw on the energy in my flesh, like what happens when I continue sucking on a straw when only the dregs of the drink remain. I feel a sudden weakness take over, even in this non-physical space—an ache that fills every inch of my being.

Guess that's my signal to stop, I think to myself weakly as I fold limply onto the ground. As I look at my efforts, though, I'm a little dismayed. I felt like I was making progress.

Actually, I *have* made progress. Just not as much of it as I thought. I've filled in the tip of the pyramid, but not much more. From what I can see, I'm going to have to do this many, many more times.

But my health pool is tapped out from what I can tell. I sigh. At least I've discovered that there is a natural limit stopping me from killing myself. But what if I continued pushing past the weakness? Not that I'm intending on doing that. Actually, it was probably pretty reckless of me just to keep pulling at my health like that . . . Hindsight, and all that. More to the point: right now, if I wait for my health to refill naturally, this is going to take a *very* long time. Though, *do* I have to wait for it to fill naturally?

I push myself more upright as I consider that thought. If my theories earlier about health just being another form of Energy are correct, could I use mana to replenish my health directly?

Certainly, Lay-on-Hands and now Flesh-Shaping are able to replenish my health when I've lost it through an injury. But does that mean that I can replenish my health energy even when I haven't actually sustained an injury? It would be focusing on doing something that usually only happens incidentally, but the fact that it happens at all means that it should be possible, right?

All I can do is try.

Once more, it takes me a fair bit of time to figure out *how* to convert mana into health, but I eventually succeed. By that point, my health pool has actually regenerated almost halfway by itself, indicating that a good couple of hours have gone past in my testing. And when I figure out exactly what I have to do to turn mana into health, I can't help cheering.

The conversion seems to cost two mana units per health unit, but I'm pretty sure that that's only because I'm being inefficient in the transfer. After all, I got Lay-on-Hands to offer over twenty points worth of healing per cast, the cost of which had reduced to five units of mana by the end. And that was with some of the mana being used for the actual healing bit, not just replenishing the health that had been lost. I set myself a goal to get the conversion down to at least one mana for three health units by the time I finish this task.

With a feeling of achievement, I quickly refill my health bar. And then I proceed to empty it again. And then refill it. And then empty it.

Caught in the repetitive actions, time passes without me noticing it. Draw on my health, push the boundaries, draw on my health, push the boundaries. Empty on health? Convert mana into health. Full health? Draw on health, push the boundaries . . .

I only come back to myself when pushing suddenly becomes far harder. Not impossible, but harder. Coming out of my fugue state, I blink, then realize that the whole pyramid-shaped wedge has been filled in, and I'm now pushing at the boundaries of my soul itself rather than just filling in what was damaged.

I stop, suddenly feeling incredibly fatigued, but make a mental note to come back here if I can to test further. After all, although it feels a lot more difficult to do, it doesn't feel impossible. Could I improve my Willpower or soul without actually leveling up?

Exiting the space is easy. However, my exhaustion is so great that I barely even register that it's full dark around me before I drop like a stone into sleep.

CHAPTER THIRTY-ONE

Master

P*ack Leader, are you truly waking?*
    I rise from the darkness to the sound of a familiar voice rattling around my head. I blink—the world when I open my eyes is not much different from when they were closed.

Pack Leader, Bastet sounds relieved. *Are you well?*

I blink again, a little owlishly. What happened?

My recent memories take a little bit of time to filter back in, but when they do, I sit bolt upright. Hissing in discomfort, I become aware that my whole body is aching. Throbbing, more like. I try to determine what's causing the pain, but my answer is inconclusive. From what my magic is telling me, it seems like it's *everything*.

"Ow," I groan as I try to send magic to at least reduce the pain but don't really know where to even start. "I'm fine," I say belatedly to Bastet, realizing that I never answered her question. I hope I'm telling her the truth. My voice is surprisingly croaky.

What happened?

"That's what I'd like to know," I mutter more to myself than to her. I sigh. "I was testing something. Hopefully, it worked and has been worth the effort." Then something occurs to me. "Why were you so concerned?" Okay, it's obviously been a number of hours, but they're used to me Meditating for long periods of time.

You have been unreachable for three dawns and four dusks, Bastet informs me. I stare at her, my jaw muscles going slack in shock. Three and a half days? Am I understanding that right?

How am I alive? I'm pretty sure that humans are supposed to die after three days without water. Or at least be in a very bad state. I mean, I'm ravenous and parched but otherwise fine.

"Three days?" I ask, more in disbelief than to actually question her words. I automatically reach for my canteen from my Inventory to quench my thirst. It's amazing how good water tastes when you apparently haven't drunk any in three days.

Yes. And then some time ago but during the same dark period, you suddenly started moving and then collapsed completely. We all felt a shift a few beats ago and pain from your side of our connection. We were worried.

Sure enough, I realize it is "we" as I look around. All of my Bound are present, encircling me. Although I can only see the vaguest of silhouettes in the darkness, I sense their presence and feel their worry through the Bonds. Even the kiinas actually appear a little concerned—clearly the sparring we've been doing together is helping build an actual bond between us. That or Persephone is worried about not having a safe place to have her eggs and Hades is mimicking her.

Anyway, that's beside the very important point: somehow, I've completely skipped three days without knowing it. Maybe when I replenished my health points after using them as fuel to repair my soul—or, at least, that's what I hope I was doing—I undid the damage not having any water or food would have been doing to me? That's the only thing I can think of for why I wouldn't be half or fully dead at this point. Or my Constitution being at twenty points means that I'm more able to undergo starvation and dehydration. That's possible too.

I suddenly realize that I'm actually inside my alcove rather than sitting outside where I remember starting all of this. It's a bit of a squash with everyone inside—the kiinas in particular take up a lot of space. Though their concern is apparently soothed by me being awake and talking; they soon leave without a word.

We moved you in when you started changing color, River says, my question clearly going over the Bond. *The Great Predator said that when humans change color, it is an indication that something is wrong. Though, I thought that was only when you turned blue, not red?* he asks, his relief giving way to curiosity.

I can't help but laugh a little.

"I turned blue in the fight with the nere because I wasn't getting enough air. I probably turned red because I was in the sun for too long." Then I consider for a moment. "I turn green when I feel sick, too, and can go white for a number of reasons—fear, shock, blood loss, illness." River eyes me carefully.

I thought you did not use color to communicate like we do. I laugh again, the convulsive movement making my aching worse. I stop quickly.

"It's not voluntary! It's just how my body reacts." Speaking of my body, I really need to check out what's happened to it. "Thanks for your concern, everyone, but I promise I'm okay. I just need to eat, drink, and check out the changes."

The rest of my Bound take that as their cue to settle back down to sleep, it apparently being somewhere in the middle of the night. River doesn't move, though. I lean forwards to rekindle the fire and am surprised to find that there are still glowing embers present, rather than it being completely cold as I would expect from three days of no attention.

"Did you look after the fire?" I ask a few minutes later. Having put some more fuel on and blown it a bit, the flames are now starting to grow and lick at the sticks.

Yes, Master, the lizard-man confirms. *I know you do not like it going out fully.*

"Thank you," I tell him gratefully. I would have otherwise had to go without any real light—possible, but not preferable.

I pull out another pot of pre-boiled water—I've already finished the contents of my canteen—and swig at it thirstily. When I eventually feel like I've had enough liquid, I pull out a handful of cooked meat, not even caring about the taste as I devour it. Piece after piece disappears down my gullet until I finally start to feel a little less like my stomach is trying to affix itself to my spine.

"Why don't you sleep?" I ask River in between my slower bites.

I was curious about what you were doing, he answers. *If you would care to tell me, of course,* he hastily adds.

"I don't mind. Just let me check what's actually happened. I was . . . experimenting," I say hesitatingly. "Flying by the seat of my pants" is probably more accurate, but it doesn't sound as good.

Pulling up my status screen, I stare at the changes. *Wow.*

Name: Markus Wolfe		Race: Human	Class: Tamer
Level: 13	Energy to next level: 17%	Energy absorption rate: 40u/hr	Energy towards debt: 85% (252)
Intelligence	36+1 (+5%)	Mana: 555/555 (15u/IP)	
Wisdom	42+2 (+5%)	Mana regeneration rate: 1100u/hr	
Willpower	43+10 (+25%)	Health regeneration rate: 53u/hr	
Constitution	22	Health: 142/330 (15u/CP)	
Strength	20	Stamina: 120/120	
Dexterity	20	Stamina regeneration rate: 200u/hr	
Class Skills:		Non-Class Skills:	
Dominate – Initiate 2		Flesh-Shaping – Journeyman 4	
*Companion Bond		Stealth – Novice 3	
Tame – Beginner 9		Animal Empathy – Novice 9	
Fade – Initiate 2		Meditation – Journeyman 4	
Inspect Fauna – Beginner 6		Energy Manipulation – Master 1	
Inspect Flora – Beginner 9		Sensation Management – Beginner 7	
Inspect Environment – Beginner 8		Spearmanship – Beginner 5	
		Archery – Beginner 3	
		Blunt Weaponry – Beginner 2	
		Knife-Work – Beginner 2	

"So many things have happened . . ." I murmur to myself.

The first and most important is that I was not wrong: what I was doing in that different space *was* healing my soul. I have *finally* gotten rid of that reduction to my health regeneration—and probably to my effective Willpower too, even if that was never indicated on my status screen.

However, the rest of it . . . I decide to switch to my messages in hopes that they will enlighten me to all the differences. Like how, suddenly, I have half again the health units that I used to have and a five percent multiplier to Intelligence, Wisdom, and Willpower. Or the two extra points to Constitution. Not to mention the single Skill that has now gained Master rank.

The first message that comes up is actually about Dominate. I hadn't realized when I quickly scanned through my status—too distracted by the percentages and health and *Master-ranked Skill*—but my Class Skill has now ranked up to Initiate.

Congratulations!
You have advanced a Class Skill past Novice. Dominate is now Initiate 1. Due to your uses of this Skill, two new effects have been discovered.

Effect 1
You have used this Skill to build connections between your Bound, seeking greater cooperation and collaboration between them. You have even sent your Bound away to work together without your presence. Henceforth, any of those Bonded to you will be able to communicate with each other via the Bond. You will be able to access any of these communications but will not be obliged to do so. Note that Tame Bonds may not automatically allow these connections to take place, depending on the conditions set during the Taming.

Effect 2
You have sought self-mastery and have taken the first step along this path by using the access to the soul space that Dominate can offer. You will henceforth be able to access this soul space at will and can explore the challenges that you are offered to increase your self-mastery.

Well, that will make organization significantly easier, I think to myself as I read the first effect. My Bound managed to make hunting and so on work through body language, but being able to communicate with each other as they do with me will probably be so much simpler.

The other effect is also welcome, even though it doesn't seem to offer me much more than I was able to do by staring into my reflection and casting Dominate. Though, perhaps that method is risky in some way or being able to access my soul space without using Dominate has benefits.

Either way, it's a nice improvement and a welcome one, but it doesn't explain the crazy things I saw on my status screen.

I pull up the next message. Another rank-up, as it turns out—and the longest I've ever seen.

Congratulations!
You have advanced a Skill past Initiate. Meditation is now Journeyman 1. You have extended your understanding of your inner world, recognizing that your body and your internal matrix are inextricably linked. You have succeeded in accessing your soul space and have entered a deeper level of meditation within it. You have repaired damage to your soul, an achievement only a very rare few

can boast. At the same time, you have also succeeded in maintaining a light level of Meditation even when moving and doing other activities. You have therefore unlocked different levels of Meditation, each with different rates of Energy gain.

Light Meditation
At this level, you are able to move and do a number of simple tasks while maintaining a clear and focused mind, with additional Energy gain. Speed and complexity of tasks will increase with practice. Extra Energy gain: 15–50% (+5% per level past Journeyman in this Skill).

Medium Meditation
At this level you must be stationary, but you are aware of your surroundings and able to react to danger. Awareness and speed of reaction will increase with practice. Extra Energy gain: 45–90% (+10% per level past Journeyman in this Skill).

Heavy Meditation
At this level you must be stationary, and you will be unaware of your surroundings. You can, however, engage in work in your Core space or within your domain and maintain the benefits of Meditation. Ease with completing activities in your Core space will increase with practice. Extra Energy gain: 70–130% (+15% per level past Journeyman in this Skill).

Deep Meditation
You may only achieve this level of Meditation when meditating in your soul space. This will offer you greater capacity to repair or expand your soul. Warning: you will be completely unaware of your surroundings and of time passing. Sufficient pain may alert you to a problem. However, it will take time for you to surface from this Meditation and disorientation may occur directly afterwards. Ease when manipulating your soul will increase with practice, and disorientation after exiting Deep Meditation may reduce with use. Extra Energy gain: 100–200% (+20% per level past Journeyman in this Skill).

My eyebrows rise higher and higher as I read the information about each new level. Like most of the Skill evolutions, it's nothing terribly new. In a way, I've done each of those types of Meditation before. But this is concretizing it, offering paths to grow, and officially stating the benefits and limitations of each.

It also seems like there are two metrics going on here—at least, that's what I've interpreted. I gain more Energy in each of the levels when I increase my overall level in the Skill. However, my ease and ability to use each of the levels seems to improve if I practice them individually.

Though, I may be wrong about that. I'll have to find out when I use them.

Honestly, it's a pretty amazing upgrade. It offers me everything I had before and more. Not only can I continue to use Meditation when moving slowly, which offers the potential of being able to use it the whole time if I practice it sufficiently, but I have a level of Meditation that, if my assumptions are correct, offers me up to 280 percent more Energy absorption at my current rank of Journeyman four. My current basic rate is forty units per hour, which means that in Deep Meditation, I could be earning up to a 152 units per hour. Suddenly, level fourteen doesn't seem so far away.

Pulling myself out of my daydream of once more steamrolling through the levels, I remind myself that there are other things to look at.

And when I open the next message, I realize that it's a doozy.

Congratulations!

You have advanced a Skill past Journeyman. Energy Manipulation is now Master 1. You have achieved this feat by gaining an in-depth understanding of at least one aspect of your Skill.

You have come to understand that health, mana, and Energy are all intrinsically linked, to the extent of being able to convert one to the other. You are henceforth able to convert Energy to mana intentionally, and your efficiency in this increases as you practice it. However, your understanding is still limited, and you must research and explore further to potentially unlock other effects of your new discoveries.

The path to Sage is long and hard. Do you have the will and inspiration to stay the course?

Not only is it my first Skill to reach Master level, but the wording of the message makes it appear that it requires crossing some sort of threshold. Also different is the message at the end. *So "Sage" is the end goal?* I wonder. *How many steps are there between Master and Sage? And what are the requirements for it? Evidently "will" and "inspiration," but what else?*

The way the message tells me that I achieved Master level in Energy Manipulation by "gaining an in-depth understanding of at least one aspect" of my Skill indicates to me that crossing from Journeyman to Master isn't as simple as continuing to practice the Skill—I actually need to *understand* it. That could be useful to know in the future: two of my other Skills are already in the Journeyman ranks—Meditation and Flesh-Shaping—so this may become directly relevant soon.

It also seems to give me a path forwards too, and not the one about becoming a Sage. It very clearly states that my understanding of converting one form of Energy into another is flawed and must be corrected and expanded. Perhaps this is how my Skill will progress from Master to Grandmaster. Or perhaps I need to advance my understanding just to move through the levels in Master itself.

I suppose it makes sense: one can reach a Journeyman's level of understanding by being able to *do* things with a Skill, but they cannot become a Master of it. To do that, one must actually understand *why* it works. Perhaps that's why it's described as a "feat"—I can imagine Journeyman nine being a bottleneck for many people. Heck, it probably would have ended up a frustrating obstacle for me, too, if necessity hadn't forced me to develop the understanding required to get past it.

Still musing on the implications of that message, I click to the next.

***

Achievement awarded: Masochist II

If the odds of successfully gaining a single Masochist achievement are low, the chances of gaining a second are vanishingly small. Not because few attempt it, but because the process of gaining it kills the vast majority of those who do. Nevertheless, you have successfully managed to not die, despite reducing your health to one unit over fifty times within three days. Either you truly are a masochist, or someone really wants information from you.

As a result of draining and replacing your health in such quick succession, your body now has an increased health capacity. Each point in Constitution now offers 5 more units of health.

***

Well, that explains the sudden increase in health. I shake my head a little at the message text. Most of the notifications are written quite neutrally, but the Masochist achievements seem to have a remarkably chatty tone. It makes me wonder what exactly is producing the messages.

I was thinking it was some sort of automatic message, something like a computer would offer whenever something triggered a specific routine. Even the way the text relating to rank-ups seems personalized could be explained by an artificial intelligence generating it. But to have snark? Either the computer is *very* advanced or there's someone somewhere sending these messages.

Both options make me feel rather uncomfortable, the hairs sticking up on the back of my neck at the thought of something—or someone—being able to see my every move, my every thought.

And then I remind myself that whatever or whoever it is, there's simply no way that I'll be able to do anything about it. *I can't even wear a tinfoil hat,* I joke to myself. No point in wasting time thinking about something I have zero chance of being able to affect. Not now, anyway. Besides, even if I could block out their observations, I probably wouldn't, since it would most likely require me to give up the Class that has allowed me to achieve superhuman stats. I don't value my privacy *that* much.

Having achieved two Masochist achievements, I suddenly start wondering whether I could either upgrade them or get a third for stamina. Or both. After all, my rank-up in Energy Manipulation mentioned health, mana, and Energy, but it didn't mention stamina. What if it didn't mention my third resource pool simply because I haven't found a way of converting Energy into it? If two of the pools are simply different forms of Energy, why would the third pool be any different?

And if my body gained an extra ability to hold health because I emptied and refilled my cells over fifty times in three days, what if I could empty and refill them over a hundred times in three days? Or less. Would my body be able to hold even *more* Energy?

Suddenly, it doesn't feel so much an achievement in the sense of a reward for attaining something, but more of an achievement in the sense of winning a race or obtaining an objective.

Clicking onto the next message, my eyebrows rise again. *Another achievement?*

Achievement awarded: Healer
You have succeeded in healing damage to your Core, Core space, and soul. To have suffered all three types of damage at the same time is unfortunate; to have successfully repaired all three areas in full is incredible, requiring insight, inspiration, and perseverance in large measure as well as the vitality to survive whatever hurt you long enough to find the solution.
In light of your remarkable achievement, you have gained +5% to Intelligence, Wisdom, and Willpower, and +2 to Constitution.

That's . . . a pretty amazing reward, I think to myself, a smile stretching the corners of my lips. That explains the percentage increases I saw on my status screen as well as two of the additional points. Honestly, I'd have been happy with just being whole again. Heck, gaining Masochist II in the process was enough of a reward. I'm not going to turn it down, though. Or even think too loud about not needing it—if Big Brother knows my every thought, he might decide to take it away from me just to teach me a lesson about ingratitude.

I close the message, and the screen vanishes from my vision, leaving me staring at the fire thoughtfully.

There were a few other changes that were obvious in my status screen but that weren't actually highlighted in my messages. I've gained a couple of levels in Flesh-Shaping—not unexpected—and in Sensation Management as well. Again, that makes sense.

What doesn't make sense is the point I gained in Willpower. Prior to this experience, I was sitting at forty-two base points in Willpower. Since it's already far above twenty, I wasn't expecting to gain anything to it except what I put in when leveling. However, somehow, Willpower has gained a point.

How? That's the question I find rattling around in my head. By me accidentally continuing to push even when my soul was completely healed?

The most important factor, I feel, is the clear evidence that what is believed to be true in Nicholas's world is *wrong.* The System lore stone I absorbed was very clear that twenty points in each stat is the highest a human can naturally achieve without having a Class and using Energy to gain levels. But somehow, I've just gained a point without leveling up at all.

I don't know if it used Energy, though—my Energy store is higher than it was when I started my Meditation, but it's also been three and a half days, apparently. I frown as I try to work out whether it's more likely it did or didn't use Energy.

First of all, I have my daily absorption rate to take into account—probably with a significant percentage increase considering that I was in Deep Meditation for the whole time. Heck, I'm already in Journeyman four in that Skill, so I clearly didn't just gain it at the end. It's probably been affecting my rate of absorption for at least a day.

Secondly, my Bound may easily have gone out hunting without me—even if a couple stayed with me to guard me, the others probably didn't. So I have an unknown amount of Energy absorbed from their kills to account for as well.

In short, it's impossible to know for sure.

What I do know, though, is that I'm going to do my best to recreate it—if I'm able to gain stat points between levels and it's "cheaper" to do it, of course I want to know. But . . . I might work on something else for a bit. I think I've had enough Deep Meditation for now. I've lost three days of the time before the quest is due. Usefully spent, but lost all the same.

As I gaze into the flickering flames, my thoughts slow a little—most of my questions were answered upon seeing my status screen, and the others aren't answerable without further testing—and I slowly become aware of something else.

It's not an obvious change, not one that was mentioned on my status screen. Yet I can't help feeling that something *has* changed. I stretch towards the fire with my interlaced fingers and turn them so my palms face outwards. Then, releasing the interlacing, I twist my wrists and wriggle my fingers. I clench my hands into fists and then open them wide.

There is a difference, I note. My left hand feels . . . fuller than before. It's very hard to put into words, but it feels like there was something missing, something that I hadn't even truly known was absent, and now it's present. Like it's heavier, more vibrant, denser, but all in a very, very good way.

At the same time, although I still ache all over, the rest of me feels more settled, more comfortable in my own skin.

I feel a bit like I sometimes do when I've finally been forced to release my emotions. Like when I've sobbed until my tear ducts were dry, or screamed until I went hoarse, or was so pent-up with energy that I punched a cushion or, once, a wall. Though, that latter didn't actually result in this feeling, since the pain on the outside just added to the pain inside. But in the other situations, after venting my emotions, I suddenly felt exhausted but that by ridding myself of the heavy feelings, I had finally cleared some space for myself again inside me. Cathartic, I believe it's called.

That's how I feel now. Although the soul damage was a void in my Core space and an area without mist in my soul space, it feels more like I've just gotten rid of something than filled in a hole. I hadn't realized how displaced I was feeling until now, when I feel *re*-placed. With all my stats now twenty or above, and all the damage healed, I feel better than I have for a long time—perhaps ever.

Exhaustion suddenly hits me, and I turn back toward the bed. Catching River's eyes, I belatedly remember that I promised to tell him what I'd been doing.

Sorry about that, I say to him, realizing he's just been sitting there patiently, waiting for me. Since the rest of my Bound are currently trying to sleep, I try to respect that by communicating mentally.

It is no problem. He hesitates. *It's good to see you back with us. We were . . . worried. Especially when your eyes and nasal holes started bleeding.*

My eyebrows rise at that. *I was bleeding?*

Yes, at regular intervals. But you didn't seem to be worse for it. Not that there was much we could have done about it if you were.

Is it just me or were those words rather pointed? Then I think about what the consequences of my death would have been, and I realize that he has good reason to be a little annoyed at me. Angry, even.

After all, he's thrown in his lot with me, hoping that I will hold the key to helping his village. Me dying kind of scuppers *that* plan. And perhaps there's an element of emotional attachment too—though, that might just be wishful thinking.

I was trying to heal my soul damage, I say abruptly, wanting to justify myself. *I found a way to do it and was worried I would lose the chance if I stopped. I didn't realize I was bleeding.* I didn't realize it could kill me, is what I think but don't actually say, even if I know it's not entirely true. Perhaps the message and the remorse travel across the link without me intending them to, as River softens in some way.

Did you succeed? he asks, letting me off the hook—probably being more forgiving to me than he should be. At that, I smile.

I did. Those words somehow manage to encompass the whole of what I've just achieved, satisfaction rolling through me like a cat stretching luxuriously.

Then that you achieved your goals and came back to us is what is important, River finishes. *You must be tired.*

I am, I admit. Without another word, River shifts to lie down, turning his back to me, and curls his tail up to his chest. I'd never noticed before, but he actually holds the tip of his tail to his neck, like a child might hold a teddy bear. Is it for the same purpose, or just to keep it away from harm? I'm not going to ask, though.

Instead, I happily take the invitation and lie down too, my exhaustion hitting me full force once more. About to fall asleep, my eyes abruptly fly back open as a thought hits me like a lightning bolt.

If I've been meditating for three days, what's happened to the hide I was drying? If it's been ruined, I'm going to be *furious.*

CHAPTER THIRTY-TWO

Mad Scientist

When I wake up the next morning, the first thing I do is to go check on my hide. It's still on the rack, now completely dry. Testing its stretch with a hand, I frown a little in confusion as I feel its flexibility. Although I did lots of stretching before going into my meditative trance, the hide wasn't quite dry, so I was expecting to feel some stiffness. But no.

The slight scrape of a claw behind me alerts me to the presence of someone else. Turning around, I see River has followed me in, the entrance no doubt at least as awkward for him as for me.

I had seen that you were poking at this hide with a stick at regular intervals, so I continued doing it while you were unconscious. Was that the right thing to do? he asks uncertainly.

My eyebrows rise a little in surprise. I hadn't realized he'd seen me at it and certainly not enough to notice that I was using the stick on the hide regularly. That he did seems to have worked in my favor this time. I'll have to remember that he's more observant than I anticipated. Perhaps I should have known that he would have good observation skills—he's survived in a dangerous forest environment a lot longer than I have. *It's a miracle how I've managed to stay alive this long, as often as I've found my head in the clouds while traveling through the forest,* I think to myself ruefully.

"Thanks for doing that. It's perfect," I answer, realizing that he's still anxiously anticipating my response. "I was a bit worried that it would be ruined when I heard just how long I meditated. What else happened while I was . . . away?"

River gives his equivalent of a shrug, nerves playing across the Bond.

Nothing much different from usual. That first day, we were all worried about you, but apart from a bit of bleeding, you didn't seem to be distressed or hurt, though the sensations we received over the Bond were a little strange. After trying to rouse you a few times without success and then monitoring your state for a while, we went hunting as usual. I was uncertain about leaving you here without all of us, considering how vulnerable you clearly were, but Bastet convinced me that you would prefer us to continue advancing. We made sure to leave you with at least two of us at all times to guard you, though, he finishes, looking at me anxiously. Even without saying it over the Bond, I feel that he's seeking reassurance.

"That sounds like a good compromise," I tell him a little soothingly—it's much as I expected, actually. Though, there is one thing that makes me a little surprised. "Wait, what do you mean, Bastet convinced you? Could you speak to each other already?"

Yes. Shortly after you fell unconscious we discovered that we could communicate with each other even as we do with you. It has certainly simplified things!

Well, that's pretty clear evidence that what I suspected is true: the effects of leveling up are felt even when I'm not yet consciously aware of them. Still, I'm glad of it—I wouldn't have wanted my absence to mean that my Bound were thrown into chaos. Kalanthia might have been able to help them communicate between each other; whether she would have been willing to do so is another question. At least it wasn't an issue.

On that note, I wonder how my Bound are doing; it's been a while since I checked on their progress to the next level.

Bound – Companion – "Bastet"
Progress to Tier 3: 2%

Bound – Dominate – "River"
Progress to Tier 2: 71%

Bound – Tame – "Sirocco"
Progress to Tier 2: 59%

Bound – Dominate – "Fenrir"
Progress to Tier 2: 51%

Bound – Dominate – "Persephone"
Progress to Tier 3: 20%

Bound – Dominate – "Hades"
Progress to Tier 3: 21%

To my pleasure, I see that all of them have made progress, even those who are already in Tier two. Obviously, theirs is a lot slower—two or three percent in comparison to the others making ten to twenty percent progress. River is almost in the home stretch: his progress is sitting at seventy-one percent.

"Have you guys run out of Energy Hearts?" I ask, suddenly remembering that they're all in my Inventory and inaccessible to anyone but me.

Fenrir still has his, but the rest of us need more, River confirms. I sigh in annoyance—I feel the pressure of time enough that I'm frustrated at losing these few days. *It is no issue,* River continues, perhaps feeling my self-castigation at not leaving them a small store before accidentally going unconscious.

Not that I would have known that I needed to—it was *accidental*, after all. But it's probably a good idea for me to leave a small pile of them in the corner of my alcove so they can help themselves. That way if something happens or a creature manages to steal them, we'll still have some more in my Inventory.

"I'll put a few in the alcove so this doesn't happen again," I voice my thoughts to River.

That's probably a good idea, but honestly, it doesn't matter too much. Bastet explained that we need to do plenty of hunting as well as absorbing Energy Hearts to prepare for Evolution.

"Oh?" I ask, interested. "Did she explain why?" It's good that Bastet is offering some direction. Her own Evolution went very well, according to Kalanthia, so if she can help the others to achieve similar results, that would be excellent.

I didn't entirely understand what she told us, River admits, *but apparently the Energy from the Hearts is different from the Energy from hunting, and we need at least twice as much of the latter as the former when starting the Evolution process.*

Well, that fits with what I've learned so far about the whole thing. "So, what are your plans for the day?" I ask. "Hunting again?"

Sparring first. We continued it while you were absent but were a bit more cautious about it, not wanting to cause an injury that we could not heal without you. Then yes, the majority of us will probably go hunting. Unless you have other preferences?

I shake my head. "No, that sounds good. In fact, I'll come and join you for sparring now. After so long meditating, I could really do with some physical exercise!"

By the time I get back to my hide, the sun is more than halfway to its zenith and my body is feeling pleasantly tired. I was also pleased to see the progress of my Bound when it came to sparring—both River and Bastet got the better of me, and it was a close run with Hades. I'm clearly going to have to up my game to not be overtaken by them. Once I have my armor, I fully intend to test it out by going on a hunt.

Persephone is a bit slower, and her midsection is starting to show some faint lumps—the eggs, I guess. She's therefore being more cautious and protective. Actually, it was fortunate that she only took part in two rounds of sparring since I could see that Hades was unable to concentrate on his own battles while she was fighting.

As for Sirocco and Fenrir, they've both progressed too, but their strengths don't yet allow them to overcome mine, particularly since my reach with most of my weapons permits me to keep them at bay without risking injury to myself. Though, it was a lot closer when I used my knife.

Thanks to working with all my weapons, I've gained a level in each of my related Skills except for Blunt Weaponry, which is still stubbornly sitting at Beginner two.

Since my hide is now completely dry, I lean the tanning rack down and work at the knots. It's only as I'm pulling the hide free—my fingers aching from struggling with the bark-fiber cord—that I realize I could probably have just used magic to do so.

Once it's on my lap, I send magic into it anyway. As suspected, a good portion of the mana I saturated it with before has vanished—three days is definitely too long for all the magic to stick around. Still, I sense that only about a quarter of the magic has been lost, proving that this hide has a much slower rate of mana loss than anything else I've experimented with so far.

It takes a bit of time to refill, but by using Heavy Meditation, I find that my mana regenerates significantly faster than it would naturally. And my natural regeneration isn't anything to sniff at. Once it is saturated again, I rise back into Light Meditation, a state I'm going to try to stay in as much as humanly possible for the benefits it offers.

Exploring the tanned hide, I'm interested in noticing the differences between the original hide, the hide soaked with brain-soup, and the hide now. Not being a biologist or chemist, I can't say exactly what's happened on a scientific level. However, what I can see is that it's different. The oils that soaked into the hide before have now become part of it on a different level, the fibers of the hide coated and protected by them.

I cut off a small piece of the hide for later reference and then try to grow the tanned hide to replace the piece I cut off.

It's hard, very hard. Much more difficult than simply regrowing the raw hide. But hard doesn't mean impossible. I have to try to replicate the changed fibers as well as the oils that saturate them, and generating all of that new material takes probably four times the mana that simply regrowing the hide did. And regrowing the hide was already mana heavy. But it still doesn't even come close to how difficult regrowing River's arm was. I have a feeling that particular task, even if it was one of the first I did with the Skill, will be my benchmark for a long time yet.

Still, trying to replicate the hide with Flesh-Shaping is mana intensive enough that using a single tanned hide and simply growing it to have a never-ending source of material may not be sustainable. Tanning with magic, however, seems to be a possibility.

And, of course, I am currently dealing with a Tier-two nere hide, a beast whose skin is armored enough to repel most attacks and magical enough to hide itself almost perfectly. It's possible that creating a simple buckskin equivalent with paranax hide wouldn't require nearly as much mana.

For now, though, I want to complete the tanning process and make my new material waterproof. That, of course, means smoking it.

Fortunately, I've already spent some time considering how to smoke my hide. With my magic already saturating the flesh, it doesn't take too much effort to close up the small holes I created for the bark-fiber cord to pass through.

Then, folding it in half, I expend a lot more mana to make the edges match up with each other. It takes a good half an hour, as I have to refill my mana pool several times, but that's not too bad—I spend some of my Meditation wondering whether my new Master rank in Energy Manipulation might actually allow me to consume my Energy store to refill my mana or health.

That could come in useful if I'm in a situation where one of my Bound is severely injured—or I am. It's probably worth testing, though it's unlikely to be something I practice regularly since I'm trying to gain Energy for leveling up. Well, unless I find that I *can* increase my stat points purely with Energy—and that it's cheaper to do that than level up. But still, that would mean that I would want to keep the Energy for other purposes than regenerating my resource pools.

Actually, didn't I do something like that before? Though, not with Energy, precisely. I remember all the way back to my experience in the middle of the vine-strangler forest, when I almost died from falling for the venomous creature's trap. I ran out of mana, ran out of practically *everything*. I'd drawn from River, pulled his mana from him, and then when his mana ran out, I think I accidentally pulled at his health pool too. Certainly, whatever I did hurt him.

But that's something to consider later. For now, I bind the edges of the hide together on all sides but one, creating a large open-mouthed bag. Then, after thinking about it, I form four more holes at the top and feed two lines of bark-fiber cord through the holes so they cross inside. If they catch on fire, I might need to use sinew instead, but hopefully, they'll be far enough above the flames not to run that risk.

Of course, I need a frame to suspend the hide above the fire since I don't have a handy tree here. In the end, I decide to go with a sort of teepee structure with crossbars to keep the hide in a tubular shape. I could have just wrapped the hide around the outside of the teepee, which would have worked well enough but would probably have caused lines of unsmoked hide where it was pressed up against the branches.

Since the teepee is pretty tall, I do this in the middle of the cave—it will make ventilation easier as well. And because the hide is pretty heavy, I run a ring of cord around the base of the teepee through some notches in the branches to hopefully prevent the legs from splaying outwards.

Rigging the hide tube up takes a bit of awkward effort, and I wish that River was here—I could really do with an extra pair of hands. But he's not, and I don't want to wait until he returns from the hunt, not if I can do it myself. Innate stubbornness keeps me going, and eventually, I get the thing roped up. The weight of the hide is on the point where the teepee branches cross, and the crossbars are holding the opening of the hide in a roughly circular shape. When I step away, I'm cautious about it, fearing that it will collapse as soon as I let go, but it appears I've done a better job than I thought.

With the whole contraption apparently stable, I pause, tapping my lips in thought. My memories tell me that I should attach a heavy water-drenched cloth to the bottom of the hide in a sort of "skirt" to ensure that the smoke from the fire is directed straight up into the hide bag. But what should I use?

Most of my clothes are not particularly heavy, and I'm not keen on destroying my few pairs of jeans—they're pretty good for wearing in the forest since the material is quite thick even if those that are still at all intact are rather ragged now. Maybe

I could use the paranax hide? I don't need to keep it for actual tanning—it's nothing special, so I can easily replace it with the hide of any of the creatures my Bound bring home. If I douse it in water and keep doing so, I should be able to keep it wet enough not to easily catch light. It's not like I'm intending on there being a whole load of flames, anyway.

Satisfied with that as an idea, I pull the paranax hide out of my Inventory and then go to fetch the other things I'll need.

Bastet is the one staying with me today, so I go over to where she's absorbing an Energy Heart. I hate to disturb her, but I need to get water from the stream and a load of green leaves to burn. Considering how often I seem to get attacked near there, I don't think it's a good idea for me to go alone.

"Bastet?" I call quietly. She's immediately alert and opens her eyes, a sharp gaze in them that softens slightly as she realizes there isn't any sort of problem.

Yes?

I explain what I need to get, and she pushes herself willingly to her feet. She makes a chirping sound to summon the cubs, and they bound over from where they were playing. Well, two of them do.

"Where's Trouble?" I ask Bastet, looking around. He's vanished.

Then I hear a rustle behind me and quickly turn as my knife appears in one hand. I only just manage to redirect my blow as I recognize the form leaping out at me from behind a bush, and I end up over-extending as I pierce the air above Trouble instead of the raptorcat cub himself.

"Don't *do* that," I scold him. His tufted ears are already pinned against his head in fright—clearly, he wasn't expecting me to *attack* him. Bastet makes a scolding kind of chuff, and I sense her telling Trouble that if he'd gotten hurt, it would have been his fault. Or something of the sort.

I'm feeling slightly rattled at almost accidentally impaling one of Bastet's cubs and am glad that she doesn't seem to hold it against me. On the one hand, I need to tone down my traumatized responses. On the other, it might actually keep me alive out in the forest, so perhaps not. Or not yet, at least. Well, I guess it will depend on how often the cubs decide to use me as their practice target . . .

The trip down to the riverbank doesn't take very long. I fill my empty pots with water and pile a whole load of leaves into my Inventory. We aren't attacked, which makes a nice change, so we end up being quite efficient.

I also get to see the cubs practicing their pouncing on things *other* than me. The cubs turn out to be very good hunters of small, mouse-sized lizards, beating even their lightning-fast reactions to play with them. I don't think they've ever looked more like cats than when they are torturing small lizards by not killing them but also not allowing them to disappear into the undergrowth.

I look forward to going out hunting with the whole group—it will be interesting to see how they've changed as a result of both the sparring and hunting practice.

Once we're back, I'm hit by a brainwave. Rather than saturating the whole of the paranax hide, I control my mana so that it fills only about a centimeter's width along one edge. It takes quite a lot of control to keep the mana in that single area and to fill that area to bursting, but I manage—probably my new Master rank in Energy Manipulation is helping me on that. I also sense that it's unlikely to last for long once I shift my attention, but that's okay for my purposes. Hopefully.

After dunking the hide into a pot of water I brought up from the river, I arrange it around the base of the nere hide so that the edge I've filled with mana is pressing against the bottom edge of the tube. I'm not sure whether this will work, but with a backup plan in mind if it doesn't, I try to connect the two hides together.

The materials resist being combined. The substances they are made of feel different. But they're not, surely. All flesh is essentially the same. Even between my flesh and that of the creatures here, there aren't that many differences. Probably if I looked at their chemical composition, I might find some small differences, but we all have cells that function similarly. Our cells all require the same sort of energy to function and generate that energy in the same sort of way. Why shouldn't the flesh of one animal be able to connect to the flesh of another? Especially two animals from the same world.

With that in mind, I focus my will on forcing them to make the link that *must* be possible. They resist for a little longer before conceding, and the two merge at the edge to create a single whole. Relief mixes with a sense of victory at the validation of my theory.

With the skirt formed around my hide bag, I then hook it around one of the teepee legs so that it's out of the way of where I need to create the fire. After setting up the fire as normal, I use a fan to encourage the fire to burn more quickly, wanting to have glowing embers more than flaming logs; it's not too long before I manage to achieve the kind of fire I want.

After once more dipping the paranax hide into the pot of water, I place a whole load of leaves over the top of the glowing embers, though I take care not to smother the fire completely. Carefully arranging the hide so that the paranax skin skirt is around the edges of the small fire, I make sure that all the smoke fills the nere-hide bag. Watching tendrils of smoke leak out of the holes in the top of the bag, I settle in to watch my hide—I have no desire to come back to find it all in ashes because the fire went out of control and caught on my precious crafting material.

As I settle back on my heels, I can't help my mind wondering about other applications of what I've just learned. If it's possible to join one piece of hide to another, what else could I join? Could I connect it to myself? Create living armor that moves like my skin because it's indeed connected to me? Could I offer my Bound more protection in certain areas? What about natural weaponry—could I give myself claws? Or spiked knuckles so that I'm never without a weapon?

If I attached the hide to myself as another layer of skin, I think I'd have to form blood vessels within it. The whole reason I have to tan hide is because it's essentially dead flesh and tanning stops the flesh from rotting. I wouldn't want to attach something to myself that would then putrefy. So blood vessels would be a must. Though, I might not put in nerve endings, as then I'd start feeling pain. Then again, that could cause other issues . . . but nothing that I wouldn't already have to deal with if I'm wearing it as armor. Though, armor is easier to remove . . .

It's an interesting question. And if I can connect blood vessels into hide and add it as another layer of skin, what else could I add? I've already been thinking about wings. What if I took a pair of wings from another creature and shaped them so that they suited me? Or what if I could add another pair of arms—extra limbs could definitely come in handy. Pun intended. Or a tail? A venomous stinger could offer me an edge in a fight.

But when do changes like that—if they're even possible—turn me from human to . . . something else? I did promise myself that I wouldn't become a mad scientist, and this kind of Frankensteinian modification is definitely well into the territory of mad scientists.

Besides, how would I even control all those new additions? My brain isn't wired like that, and there's no way I'm going to mess around with my neurons—I simply don't know enough about how the brain works, even with magic helping me. Having wings would be pretty useless without the nerve and brain connections to make them function.

No, big changes are probably a *bit* too far beyond my capabilities, even if I did decide that I wanted them. But perhaps a bit of skin enhancement just to protect some of my vulnerable areas wouldn't be too much? Then again, those areas are generally vulnerable because they're joints, which require flexibility to work properly. Building up too much thickness in those areas could cause other issues.

It's a question for later. For now, I have a perfect opportunity to work on expanding my understanding of fire. The three days I've spent healing my soul have both increased the urgency of me gaining Fire-Shaping and possibly given me the tools to do so. For all I know, it's the damage to my soul that has so hampered me.

To that end, I spend some time Meditating next to the fire, sitting out of the way of the little smoke that escapes my hide bag. It's interesting to compare what I see and feel this time to previous times. Here, the fire is much cooler and barely holding onto life. The connections are fewer and much shorter, but they are still there, sinking into the leaves over the glowing embers.

The determination and perseverance of fire are showcased here: true flames are absent, but the fire eats at the wet fuel, nonetheless. When it starts flagging, the energy gained from consuming the leaves not quite keeping up with the energy expenditure of burning off the liquid, I attempt to offer it a little of my own mana. I do that by sending a small ball down a connection that reaches out to touch me when I put my hand almost into the fire.

I got the idea from my last attempts to understand fire and my realization that we are, in some ways, the same. We both need fuel to burn, energy of some sort. Fire uses chemical energy, an exothermic reaction providing it with more energy to continue or grow. I depend on chemical reactions too, from food. Yet, mana has proven itself able to replace certain healing functions of the body and has indicated that it can take the place of proper hydration and quite possibly nutrition too. It seems logical that a fire might also be able to use it as a replacement for some of its own needs.

Working out how to pass the ball of mana over to the fire connection is the most complicated part of the process, but even that isn't too difficult—the point of the fire connection is to absorb, it seems, and I'm sure my new Master Skill greases the way. The fire receives it very happily, flaring up in the spot where that connection originated and then dying down a few seconds later.

Probably as another benefit of my more advanced Energy Manipulation, or perhaps Meditation—or even both—I can see more of what happens to the mana as I pass it over. The mana that leaves me and the energy that the fire consumes are different. The fire transforms my mana easily into something it is able to consume.

Perhaps that's natural—fire is all about transformation, after all. I'm seeing it happen before my eyes as it transforms the leaves into usable fuel and then ashes. It makes sense that it could do the same with the mana I feed it.

Pulling back a bit, I stare at the fire sightlessly with my physical eyes. Is this the key that I've been missing? Lay-on-Hands has been referred to on a number of occasions as "healing" magic. When I use Flesh-Shaping, does my mana change? I've never noticed.

Deciding it's worth a little investigation, I pick up the piece of hide I cut off from the rest of the nere hide that is currently being smoked. Touching the mana inside, I do notice some subtle differences to it now that I'm paying attention. Is this why I can't get out as much of my mana as I put in? Because it's being changed as I do it, and the rate of conversion back to "normal" mana isn't very good?

Either way, it seems that I've confirmed that I'm using a different type of magic when I engage in Flesh-Shaping, and I know I used healing magic with Lay-on-Hands. So that lends evidence to the idea that fire also has its own type of magic . . . and that Fire-Shaping might require me to find a way to transform my own mana into that of fire.

I spend some time feeding the fire with magic, being careful not to give it too much at a time—I don't want my experiments to accidentally make flames leap up inside my hide bag. Instead, I just start offering it a unit at a time, then try my best to reduce even that down to a fraction of one since a whole unit still proves to be a lot for a fire this subdued.

While I do that, I observe carefully with as many senses as possible to try to work out exactly what's changing about the mana to make it into fire mana instead of my normal mana.

After a while, I start noticing a certain difference. It's impossible to describe and takes a mixture of sight and feel. Nonetheless, it's enough for me to start trying to replicate it.

The rest of the world almost falls away, and I have to consciously focus on pulling myself out of the state every so often to check on my hide's progress. As my attempts to transform the mana fail again and again, I find myself getting frustrated.

Knowing that frustration isn't going to help at all, I pull myself fully out of Meditation, then stand up and stretch a bit. A few squats and push-ups help remove the lingering irritation from my system.

I then investigate the hide over the fire with both eyes and magic. A few moments later, I withdraw my hand, nodding in satisfaction. The inside of the hide seems to be fairly thoroughly coated in the tar carried on the smoke and should be waterproof enough now.

Of course, that's only half the job—I need to smoke both sides. Fortunately, reversing the bag doesn't take too much effort. I undo the knots holding the top of the tube to the teepee. Knowing that I was going to be doing this, I tied easy-release knots, so undoing them is a matter of seconds.

After pulling the cord pieces through, I reverse the bag, dip the skirt of the paranax hide into the water again—something I've done a few more times since starting this process by briefly swinging the whole tube away from the fire—then string the hide back up over the fire.

After checking that the fire is doing fine—it is—I pile on a few more leaves. I spend a few more minutes just making sure that the process is going off without a hitch, then return to my attempts to convert my mana into fire mana.

It has to be almost halfway through the smoking process of this second side by the time I make something of a breakthrough. Something clicks in my mind and I suddenly manage to transform my mana into something approximating what I saw with the fire. The only problem: it's in my internal matrix, and apparently, fire mana and my Energy channels don't go well together.

Actually, that's an understatement.

CHAPTER THIRTY-THREE

Intention

I shout in pain as what feels like an explosion goes off in my hand.

The Energy channel I was holding the mana in ruptures completely, and my finger quickly burns black. I grit my teeth against the agony and consciously use Sensation Management to dim the pain down to more manageable levels.

The fire mana—or is it explosion mana?—has vanished or been used up, leaving a mess behind it. Fortunately, thanks to Flesh-Shaping, I can heal my damaged finger, and after all my experience regrowing a good portion of my internal matrix, dealing with the rupture of my Energy channel takes only a few minutes to do.

I never thought I'd be grateful for the damage the Pure Energy did to me, but in healing myself, I have to admit that I've learned a great deal. I probably wouldn't have been able to transform my mana into fire mana without having the experiences I had. And even if I had still managed it, I would have been completely stuffed if I'd damaged my internal matrix like this without having already had the experience of rebuilding it.

As it is, I've learned a painful lesson, and even once I'm fully healed, I pause to work out what to do next. Clearly, I can't transform the mana within my channels, ergo, I need to do it outside my channels. The issue here is that, so far, the only time I've managed to control magic outside my body is when I've fed it into another body or the fire.

Maybe I need to extend a connection beyond my skin? I wonder. *Or could I use one of those connections that are already out there drawing in Energy?* It's worth a try.

I attempt to send a bead of mana down one of the channels leading out of my body. It works, but it slips through my mental fingers as it reaches the end of the channel. After trying a couple of times with the same result, despite my best efforts, I decide to attempt another approach.

While my internal matrix is ovoid and I'm unable to see exactly how it fits into my body, I've become aware that when I lay a hand on my Bound and send mana to their bodies, it's easier to do it from certain parts of my internal matrix than others. I'm increasingly convinced that my internal matrix *does* correspond to parts of my body, but it's hard to know exactly which parts when they're vastly different shapes.

Still, that helps me now. I use the section of my internal matrix that I know leads to my left hand and, in particular, the small section that I am pretty sure leads to my index finger. For some reason, mana pulses more easily through my index fingers than through any of my others. That and my palm itself.

The issue is that, as always, my internal matrix remains within my skin—I haven't yet managed to overcome that barrier except by diffusing the mana into my body first. Given what happened earlier, I'm even more hesitant to try transforming mana when it's diffused in my flesh than when it's sitting in an Energy channel. Ideally, I want to move my Energy channel out of my flesh before trying it, but, as previous experience has taught me, the loops of my mandala refuse to shift beyond my skin.

But even if I can't *move* my Energy channel, maybe I can *extend* it. After all, I have several connections that naturally extend into my environment. I'm tempted to try transforming mana in one of those, but I'm not sure where they come out—they have never been part of my Flesh-Shaping. I wouldn't want to accidentally light a flame in an unfortunate place.

Ideally, if I can extend an Energy channel from my index finger, I will have a predictable place to generate fire—and maybe other types of magic later. And it's better if it's my left hand since my right hand is most likely going to be occupied with a weapon.

When I first started working on my internal matrix, even regrowing the bits that had been damaged seemed impossible; extending the internal matrix further was a daydream. Fortunately, I've learned a lot since then, even if that was only a couple of weeks ago in real time. With my observations of how Wisdom points affect the connections leading outwards, I have a good idea of where to start.

Pulling mana from my Core, I feed it to my finger strand and then start trying to push it outwards. It's exponentially harder to do this than it was to regrow my internal matrix. If I can compare, it's the difference between a plant growing roots in a field that has already been ploughed and that same plant trying to grow in stone. When I was repairing my internal matrix, the strands "knew" where to go next; I just had to provide the energy and intention.

This time, though, I'm pushing into new areas that have never been touched before. Not only that, but I'm trying to push past what I think is my domain, or maybe it's my soul. It's just a guess, but given the relative ease with which I control magic within my skin compared to outside it, I have to imagine that it's linked to what Kalanthia demonstrated a while ago.

It takes a lot of focus and a lot of mana—I actually have to channel the mana from my Core through to the strand rather than taking a few units at a time—but eventually I succeed.

Like trying to go through a wall, the connection is blocked. Until suddenly it isn't, and it surges forwards as if I've finally punctured the plaster. The quick progress rapidly grinds to a halt almost as soon as it starts, as if behind this wall, there's another even harder one. But I've gotten through my skin, and that's what's most important to me right now.

I release both intention and mana with a sigh of relief, reaching up to rub at my temples. A burgeoning headache blooms, but a quick pass with Flesh-Shaping to reduce the slight inflammation in my brain sees it ebb rapidly.

Excited to try to use my new strand with my new conversion process, I soon send a bead of mana to the end of my finger and then beyond. Wary of another explosion, I only send a single unit of mana to the end of the strand. I almost hold my breath as I once more convert the unit of normal mana into what I hope is fire mana.

Before my eyes, a tongue of flame appears at the tip of my finger, and a wave of elation runs through me. The exhilaration is quickly followed by something else as my sense of victory causes my concentration to lapse.

"Ow!" I exclaim as the fire singes the top layer of my skin. Losing control of the mana unit in my surprise, I shout again as the fire quickly consumes all of it in a single burst, the flame growing to double its length and then winking out just as quickly after.

My finger is red and already starting to blister, so I quickly send my flesh magic into the area to soothe and heal. I'm a little disappointed that I don't feel the nagging sense of a notification waiting for me—have I not acquired Fire-Shaping or something similar to that yet? I check just in case I've gotten a message without the sense of it being there, but my fears are confirmed when I see the lack of notification.

As I stare sightlessly at my finger, I hear a scrabble of claws and see Bastet come running, her ears pinned back and fangs bared. When she sees I'm alone and unharmed, she slows and then pads over to me. Her lips lowering over her teeth, she sniffs at me, a faint hint of disapproval coming over the Bond.

What did you do? I smell burning meat. I'm a bit shamefaced that she can so quickly detect what I did to myself despite me having already healed the obvious injury.

"Nothing serious. I'm just trying to learn how to use fire." Then a thought suddenly occurs to me as I look at her. Didn't she just gain the ability to breathe fire from her Evolution? "Actually, could you help me with something?"

She cocks her head to one side. *Perhaps. What?*

"I'd like to watch you breathe fire, to see what you're doing differently from me," I tell her. "Is that okay?"

She casts a dubious look around the cave. *Not in here.*

"No, I meant outside."

Yes. Now?

I'm about to answer, then hesitate as my own glance around the cave reveals that I'm still in the middle of another project right now.

"Not now. But when I've finished working on my armor for the day?"

I'll be outside, she says with a wave of agreement over the Bond. Turning, she starts trotting out. *Try not to hurt yourself again,* she admonishes with a flick of her tail just as she clicks through the entrance way—unlike River and me, *she* doesn't have the slightest difficulty with the low entrance.

"Mother cat." I chuckle to myself at her maternal scolding. Honestly, it kind of feels nice. Especially since she doesn't try to stop me from doing anything, just tells me to be more careful if I hurt myself while doing it. And calls me out if it seems like it's a bad idea all-around.

I wonder what I'll see when I watch her breathing fire. Maybe I should touch her at the same time, try to see what's actually happening in her body. Actually, it would also be a good time to find out if I can replenish her mana pool from my own. After all, she's only got 150 units of it. Although I use my mana for a lot more than she does, it could be useful to know if I can send mana *to* her just as easily as I can draw it *from* her.

But before I can go and explore those ideas, I really want to finish this project. Having proper armor will make a big difference to my survivability, and I'm so close to being done. Checking the hide, I realize that I've spent so long working out how to do fire magic that the smoking process is pretty much finished—fortunately, it didn't catch light while I was distracted.

I detach the hide bag from the teepee and find it's fairly easy to locate the connection between the paranax hide and the nere's—since I wasn't trying to make the join seamless, it's only attached by a few fibers. These are easily severed, and the paranax hide drops to the floor.

The nere hide is heavy, the weight of the tar from the smoke adding to what was already a hefty burden. Still, with my new Strength attribute, it's no real challenge. It may slow me down and fatigue me a bit when I'm traveling with it on my body for long distances, but I don't mind that too much—the added protection will be worth it.

Now, two important points to cover: First, can I form it into armor just with magic? Second, can I tan a hide from scratch with magic alone?

But neither of those need to be done in here, and between a smoky cave and the sunny, fresh outdoors, I'll pick the outdoors—even if when I exit the cave, I realize that it's suddenly gotten cloudy, the sun that was present when I went in to smoke my hide now hidden.

Maybe it'll come out again later, I say to myself hopefully. It would be a pity if I lost the best part of the day while stuck inside.

For now, though, I settle down against the wall with the nere hide on my lap. Then, after shivering a bit, I realize that it's colder than I thought and go to get my jacket from my bed inside before continuing.

Topping up the hide with my mana doesn't take long and only uses a fraction of my mana pool. Sending my mind into the hide, I register the new changes. Interestingly, I can't affect the new coating of the hide at all. Is it because it's a derivative of plants rather than flesh? But I was able to affect the potions . . . Though, to be fair, that was only after the plants had already interacted with the venom.

I have an immediate suspicion that I won't be able to replicate the effects of smoking with my magic—it's more of a coating than something that's affected the nature of the flesh. Oh well, at least I was able to speed up the soaking part of the process. Maybe I'll find an alternative to smoking that uses animal parts. *Would coating the hide with animal fat work?* I wonder.

On the positive side, manipulating the flesh is still easy enough, though I do run into a snag when I try to extend the hide—the coating doesn't extend with it.

A pity, I say to myself as I try unsuccessfully to find a way to transfer the smoke coating along with the hide. *Looks like I'll only be able to work with what I've got here.*

Lesson learned: finalize the design of my hide armor *before* smoking. At least I have a lot of hide here. And while it isn't the salamander hide, it is a Tier-two beast and a pretty tough one at that. Plus, the tanning is finished. Even if I replace it with the salamander hide later, I might as well have some better protection in the meantime.

I succeed in creating very rudimentary armor with a minimum of effort. First of all, I split the bag back into a single length of almost rectangular hide. Next, I make a hole for my neck, briefly splitting and then rejoining the flesh so it's tucked snuggly against my throat. In an effort to gain a little more protection as well as to reduce chafing, when I'm making the hole for my neck, I shift the hide that's in the way upwards at an angle so it works as a sort of gorget. It only covers a few centimeters of my neck, but something is better than nothing.

After further splitting the hide in some strategic places, I end up with armor around my upper arms and wrapped around my torso and upper legs. I have to leave some slits in strategic places so that I can move easily—there's a reason why armor tends to be much thinner around joints. It does leave me a little vulnerable when I extend my arms upwards or at certain angles, but hopefully, that won't be my undoing.

At least my sides are pretty well protected; instead of cutting away the excess hide at my sides, I overlap the piece from the back with the piece from the front, offering my flanks double the protection that my breast or back has. As a bonus, it means I don't waste any of the leather I've spent hours tanning. Something coming at me from below is still going to cause me issues, though—I don't have anything between my legs. What I have done, is create a kind of skirt that flaps before and behind me with slits ending just below my hips. Hopefully, that will be enough to protect my most vulnerable inner thigh arteries from attacks from the front and back.

I jump around a bit, testing my range of movement, and make a few minor changes as I feel things shift. Suddenly having an idea, I pour mana into the front and back of my armor to thicken the breast and backplate. When I compare this to the rough breastplate and backplate I first tied around myself a few weeks ago, I marvel at how far I've come.

Not that it hasn't taken its time. I really do hope that magic will speed things up; otherwise, outfitting myself in both clothing and other armor is going to take forever. Not to mention replacing my boots—my dress shoes are getting to be practically unusable.

Well, maybe that can be my next task: making boots that cover the rest of my legs.

Actually . . . , I think to myself, hit by a sudden wave of inspiration. I hurry back into the cave and grab a couple of things I left behind next to the still-smoldering fire.

Sitting back down on the ground, I start pouring mana into the paranax hide. It's not particularly armored, but with how much I've been able to affect the nere hide, I have a feeling that I'll be able to change that.

It's not tanned either, but it has been smoked along with the nere hide, though my frequent dunks of it into water probably haven't done it any favors.

It takes a while to fully saturate the paranax hide, but my new ability to drop into Heavy Meditation and significantly increase my mana regeneration makes it possible in not too long a time.

The sun is reaching its zenith overhead when I succeed. I don't care so much about this hide, so if I mess it up, it's not the end of the world. With one hand touching the offcut of nere hide and the other touching the paranax skin, I do my best to treat the fibers within the paranax hide the same as in the nere hide.

Feeling that something's missing, I have a brainwave and take my project over to the tanning pit. I dip one corner of the paranax hide in the solution, the oils of which have risen to the top, and soon feel the difference.

The oily sheen on the top of the water is sucked into the paranax hide like it's a sponge, my magic guiding it to saturate the fibers. A process that would usually take hours of absorption and then hours of drying is accomplished in less than one.

It's not that it's effortless—emptying my mana pool still gives me a headache and makes me feel nauseous and weak—but it's a lot quicker than doing it the way I did the nere hide before.

In the end, I have a length of thin hide that isn't as supple as my armor but will probably become so with a bit of wear. With a bit more effort and imagination, I'm soon standing in two new leather boots. Interestingly, it's a *lot* easier to shape the paranax hide compared to the nere one. I don't know if that's because I did more to it magically or because it's a thinner hide to begin with. Or because it's from a weaker creature—it could be that too.

The soles are very thin, so I send magic to change that, thickening the sole so the stones beneath my feet are now barely detectable. The boots reach just above my knees and, while a bit stiff, are flexible enough that I can move in them fine. I commit a bit more magic to thickening the areas that don't need to bend, then grin as I grab a spear from my Inventory and start practicing with it.

Satisfied with my new creations, I walk towards where Bastet is playing with the cubs—well, juvenile raptorcats now, I suppose. She seems to be teaching them pouncing technique by demonstrating, then letting them leap at her from the bushes. Now I know why Trouble thought it would be a good idea to jump at me the other day.

"All right, Bastet," I start, then freeze. She does exactly the same as me, and we both turn in unison to face the forest.

Something's wrong. A sense of unease ripples through me, and I close my eyes to drop into my Core space.

The connections to my Bound who are not present are jangling with alarm. They're too far away for me to tell what's happened, but I sense that they are closing the distance between us.

"Something's happened with the hunt," I say to Bastet, my voice tight, as soon as I exit my Core space. She sends a grim sense of agreement.

CHAPTER THIRTY-FOUR

Where There's Life

The time it takes my hunting Bound to reach us seems like an eternity but is probably only around half an hour. Though my first reaction was to run towards them, in the end, I decide just to travel down to the river with Bastet and the cubs and stay there.

This is for three main reasons. One, I sense that none of my Bound are near death, or at least not to the point where minutes might count. Two, I don't know exactly what the problem is. If they're being chased by something that they've accidentally angered, it would be better for us to have a defensible location, so staying close to the den is a good idea. At the same time, if they're injured, I can heal them and then they can wash off here, and it's at least a little closer to them. And three, my sense of where they are is too vague to risk running towards them and then missing them—it's not like it's a good idea to run through the forest shouting loudly to make sure we find each other. Especially if they're injured or being chased by something that they're trying to lose.

After spending a few minutes fidgeting, then realizing from the progress my Bound are making that it will still be quite a while longer, I decide to use the time as productively as possible.

Meditation has never felt harder to enter, but thanks to my new rank in it, I'm able to calm myself down despite the situation. After topping up my mana pool, I start feeding more of it into Bastet. Whatever has happened, it should be helpful to do that. If one of my Bound is significantly injured, I can use her as a mana reserve to draw on. We do take advantage of the time we have to run a couple of brief experiments, but it seems that she can't use it as an extra resource pool to fuel her fire breath. Perhaps it's because it's my mana? At least *I* can use it if she gets injured, though.

Once we've determined that, I find there's little to focus my mind on to keep me from fretting. What could have happened? With two Tier-two kiinas, a lizard-man who's close to Tier two, a lizog, and an aerial scout, what could have taken them unawares? Is it a hunting party of lizard folk including Pathwalkers and Warriors that has somehow found us? Is it a group of beasts that has been unexpectedly difficult to combat and is refusing to give up the chase? Is it something else that has been pushed out by the vine-stranglers? Could it be something of a similar level to Kalanthia? Maybe another mother seeking to find a safer area for her offspring and finding my Bound to be tasty snacks?

What's odd, though, is that even if my sense of where and how far away from me my Bound are is pretty vague, I'm becoming increasingly sure that only three of my Bound are approaching me; the other two are not. If anything, they're getting further away. I can sense that one of them is Sirocco—the Bond between us is different enough that it's relatively easy to tell.

Only by spending some time meditating on it am I able to identify the other Bond as Fenrir. Even more strangely, he seems . . . asleep? The Bond is muted, the emotions muffled in the same way as happens when he's asleep.

My other Bound are all broadcasting different degrees of worry, fear, and urgency. At least they're all alive. Has something happened to Fenrir? If so, what? Why would he be asleep? Wouldn't it be more likely for him to be awake or dead?

When I see my Bound traveling through the trees and running towards us, I'm relieved to finally get some news; anything is better than the tortuous turning over of possible scenarios I've been doing.

Bastet and I stand from where we've been resting. We scan the trees behind my Bound; nothing seems to be chasing them. Or, if they are being chased, their pursuers aren't hot on their heels.

Are any of you injured? I send to River as soon as he comes into range of our mental communication.

Yes, but not seriously, he answers quickly, a sense of worry and urgency coming over the Bond.

As they get closer, I see the truth in his words. It seems like all of them are injured, their scales or feathers bloodied. However, it doesn't look too bad. Hades is limping a bit, and Persephone has a badly torn wing—those seem to be the worst I can see. I immediately go over to check them out.

"What happened?" I snap tensely at River. He's injured as well, blood marking his scales in multiple places.

Fenrir's been taken. His mental voice rings clearly even as he half bends over to heave in air. The kiinas are better off, but they look tired too.

"Taken? Taken by what? Or who?" I ask sharply. At least the lizard folk's way of communication isn't impeded too much by being out of breath, and our mental connection isn't impacted at all.

A great beast. Not explaining any further, River shoves a memory at me. I pause in my healing to check it out, more able to multitask now than in the past but still not able to juggle directing mana at the same time as reviewing memories from my Bound. The image is unmoving, but I draw in an abrupt breath as I see it.

I absently pass it over to Bastet, then see her tense out of the corner of my eye and hear her instinctive growl as she sees it too.

It's big, that's the first thing. The image that River has sent includes Hades, so

I can see that the creature is slightly taller than him—and it doesn't appear to be at full height. It's wider even than that and appears more like a giant spider with ten legs than anything else.

It has a multi-segmented body, but it's not like a millipede. Instead, this one appears to have a main body, perhaps a thorax, with a head on one end and a multi-segmented tail on the other. In the image, the tail is halfway through a swing towards Fenrir, who's attempting to gnaw on one of the creature's many legs. Even though this is an image of something that's already happened, I see the stinger on the end of the tail and wince.

It's furry, perhaps the first native creature I've seen here that isn't either scaly or feathered. It also has massive mandibles, and these are more like a wasp's than a spider's. It doesn't appear to have eight eyes, either, but the four on the front of its head and the two on the sides are definitely enough.

"This attacked you?" I ask, horror going through my body. With the clear strength and size of the creature, I suppose I'd best be glad all of my Bound are still alive, even if two are currently missing. "And where's Sirocco?"

I realize that I've stopped healing Hades and turn my attention back to that even as River replies.

It came out of nowhere, he confirms. *None of us knew it was there until it was on top of us. We kept it at bay for a while, but none of our weapons could get through the hard armor protecting it except for Fenrir. Oddly enough, it didn't seem to be trying to kill us, aiming more to cripple us.*

Well, that would explain why their injuries appear mostly fairly superficial. Hades's limp has been caused by some heavy impact, but the blunt damage doesn't actually take too long to sort out. Moving on to Persephone's wings, I listen as River continues his report.

It tried to strike all of us with its tail spike, but we all managed to dodge it. Until Fenrir didn't. That was the moment River had sent over the Bond. *I did my best to deflect the stinger but was too out of position to do so.* His tone is full of shame. *It knocked me away with one leg, and by the time I stood up again, it was crouching over Fenrir.*

He pauses for a moment, reluctance coming across the Bond.

"Tell me," I urge. "I need to know." River tilts his chin upwards for a moment, then visibly forces himself to continue.

We tried to attack it to get at Fenrir, but it just defended itself. When it stood up, we couldn't see our packmate. Not until we looked at its belly. River seems unable to put his thoughts into words, and instead sends another image. I pause my healing once more to look at it.

The creature looks even more like the spider I compared it to with a webbed parcel now stuck to its underside. It only takes me a brief moment to understand that Fenrir is wrapped in the web.

It did not try to attack us further, River continues after I start healing again, feeling a bit numb. *It just ran off with Fenrir attached to it, leaving a mess of sticky substance that trapped us until it was out of sight. I considered chasing it—although its trail was not obvious, Sirocco could easily find it—but thought that, since our efforts hadn't worked before, we should return here to seek your aid instead.* He pauses for a long moment. *Master, I'm sorry,* he says, sounding wrecked. *I failed you.*

"What?" I ask eloquently, confusion filling me. "How did you fail me?"

We all know that Bastet is your second and leads the hunt if you are not present, but if neither of you are there, command falls to me. Therefore, the responsibility of losing one of our members falls to me too. I accept the consequences.

I stare at the lizard-man. Seriously, what kind of society are the lizard folk? His tendency to self-blame all of the time can't be solely due to the Bond . . . can it? Because yes, he was in charge, but was this actually avoidable?

"Look, you've said already that the creature came out of nowhere, right?" I ask, waiting for his acknowledgement before continuing. "And that you did your best to protect Fenrir but were unable to in the end, right?" He admits that it's true. "Then what on earth could you have done to prevent this outcome?"

I should have called for a retreat sooner, River replies quickly, showing that he's been turning this over in his mind for a while, probably ever since it happened.

"Okay, that's true, but do you think you would have been able to escape it? That it would have let you go before it got what it came for?" Because that's the conclusion I've come to, with all the evidence I've seen. Not aiming to kill but aiming to sting. Then, as soon as it had stung a creature successfully, it stopped its actions, wrapped Fenrir up, and ran away. It seems likely to me that it was searching for live prey, for whatever reason. That's fortunate for Fenrir—for now. Though, I don't know if I *want* to know exactly why the creature wants live prey. Visions run through my mind of all sorts of possible reasons.

No, River admits after a moment. I almost forgot the question I asked him, my thoughts racing so far in another direction, but I manage to recall it after a brief instant.

"Then I don't see anything that you could have done differently that would have had another outcome. Where is Sirocco? Chasing the creature?" That's the only thing I can think that she might be doing—she hasn't broken the Bond, so she hasn't cut her losses and flown away.

Yes, River confirms. *I sent her to watch where the creature goes and what it does. She should be able to find us later and tell us what has happened.* He hesitates, eyeing me. *I . . . thought that you might wish to pursue. Is that correct?*

I pause for a moment, surprised that he even needs to ask the question. Then I remember what kind of society he comes from and understand.

"Of course we're going to pursue," I tell him with emotion. "Fenrir is still alive, and while there's life, there's hope. Now, let's get right to it."

CHAPTER THIRTY-FIVE

Will You Carry Me?

We need to get going as soon as possible, but setting off without even thinking about what we might need would be stupid.

The first thing I consider is supplies. Fortunately, with the number of slots I now have in my Inventory, I keep very little outside of it, only things that definitely won't deteriorate and that I'm unlikely to need at a moment's notice. I take advantage of being by the river to fill as many containers of water as possible. I don't have time to boil it now, so I'll either have to take a chance and drink it unboiled or build a fire later to boil it then. I do still have some water in my canteen from earlier, at least. And I should get the stew I cooked earlier from my stove.

Fortunately, I've had some time to sort out my weapons—with four flint-tipped spears between River and me, a good supply of arrows, my mace, and a backup mace, we should have everything we need. I haven't had time to make a shield, but that's just too bad.

My Bound are all well equipped with their natural weapons, and River is carrying one of the aforementioned spears. That, plus our various magical advantages, will have to be enough.

The alternative is not one that I wish to consider.

Despite the distraction, I've managed to heal Hades's limp fully. I've also quickly scanned River and Persephone. They're all injured but, as River said, not too badly. The worst damage is to Persephone's wing—if she could fly on a normal day, she wouldn't be able to at the moment. As it is, I don't consider it essential to heal the injury completely. Not right now, anyway. We need to get moving—the longer we delay, the further Fenrir gets and the more likely it is to be too late by the time we get there. I encourage my healed Bound to wash in the river. Traveling while smelling of blood isn't a good idea.

I break the connection with Persephone and dash up the hill towards the cave, waving down Bastet and River when they move to follow me. Pausing at the cave entrance, I meet Kalanthia's golden eyes. They look startled—did I wake her up with my abrupt entry?

No matter. She can go back to sleep after, if that was what she was doing.

"Fenrir's been taken by a creature. We're going to rescue him," I tell her urgently, the image of the spiderlike creature appearing in my mind's eye and making me shudder once more. I try to push it towards Kalanthia—she might appreciate the warning if this creature is hunting in the woods in this area.

At my words, a shape pressed against Kalanthia's flank perks up.

Can I come? the young nunda asks eagerly.

"No," I say at the same time as Kalanthia gives off a negative wave of intent. "It's likely to be too dangerous, and we need to move quickly. I don't have time to look after you." I feel a wave of indignation from her at my last words.

I can look after myself! Lathani objects strenuously. *I bet you're taking the little siblings with you.* It's a good point, but I don't have time to argue with her.

"That's Bastet's choice to make. *You* are still *your* mother's responsibility. She doesn't want you to come, so you're not coming. End of discussion," I tell her sharply, frowning at her. Plus, we haven't even gone into the forest since that unfortunate time. Going to fight a dangerous creature like this *really* isn't the time to test how well Lathani will listen to me in a combat situation. Kalanthia rumbles to confirm my words. "I'll see you when we get back." Hopefully, with Fenrir.

With a quick nod to Kalanthia, I duck into my alcove and pack my stew-filled pot into my Inventory. Taking a moment to glance around my alcove, I check that I'm not missing anything. A sudden thought occurs to me, and I grab three of my jackets from my bed—I suspect I'm going to need them as bedding if nothing else.

I also spot my fire starter sitting next to the hearth, and my stomach swoops a little at the thought of accidentally leaving that behind. I assumed that it was in my Inventory since that's where I normally keep it. River, however, has recently been starting some of the fires for his own potion experiments, so I've been leaving it there to be accessible to him. But if I could repeat my earlier success with fire, maybe I'd be able to light it myself anyway. Still, it's not worth banking on that.

Another, more thorough glance around reveals that I haven't overlooked anything else. Ducking out of the alcove, I head back towards my Bound.

Good hunting to you, Markus Wolfe, Kalanthia sends to me as I cross the threshold. I pause for a moment to send her a sense of grim acknowledgement, then continue.

"Let's go," I tell them after taking a moment to grab the half-eaten carcasses from their last hunt and put them in my Inventory. While eating Energy-rich meat is better for them, meat from my Inventory is better than starving.

Without a word, we turn and head down the hill. At first our progress is slow: I have to keep stopping to dive into my Core space to get our heading since I can't do it while moving. I actually get most information from Fenrir's Bond; though I have a very vague idea of where Sirocco might be, it's clearer from Fenrir—probably because my Dominate Skill is a lot higher than my Tame Skill. At least I know that Sirocco is following Fenrir, so by finding one, we'll find the other. Hopefully, the place the spider has taken the lizog will be easy enough to find. Searching for Fenrir in the approximate direction I know he's in while that beast is hunting does *not* sound like fun.

It doesn't take long for me to get frustrated with our slow progress—there has to be a better way than me stopping all the time to sink my mind into the Bond between us. Of course, the alternative to stopping is to *not* stop, but then I risk sending us in the wrong direction for a while before correcting it—especially since it seems like Fenrir is still moving. But maybe there's another option.

"Persephone, will you carry me?" I ask in frustration. When the kiina radiates confusion, I shove my thoughts at her, my emotions of fear and frustration inevitably attached too.

Very well, she replies with composure, crouching down for me.

No, Hades responds, stepping between us and glaring a little at me.

"We don't have time to—"

She is becoming increasingly egg-heavy. I will carry you.

I pause. Fair point. "I was going to heal her at the same time," I point out without the anger that was starting to kindle before his explanation.

You can heal from a distance, can you not? he asks, and it sounds like a genuine question rather than a pointed one.

"To an extent," I say a little dubiously. "But I will need physical contact to transfer the mana to her in the first place. And you will have to stay close together." Especially when healing an injury as delicate as what's happened to her wings. But looking on the bright side, this should be good practice for me for healing from a distance.

Hades crouches as Persephone did, and I climb onto his back. Once I've settled myself with my feet hooked around his wings, sitting so my weight is directly over his back feet, we take off again.

"Is this okay?" I check with Hades quietly.

It is fine, the kiina responds stoically, but I sense it's an extra strain for him—I see why he didn't want Persephone to have it in addition to her pregnancy. I resolve to get off and run with them as much as possible.

For now, though, I lose focus on my surroundings as I dip into my Core space to check that we are still reducing the distance between us and Fenrir. When I come out of my Core space, satisfied, I call Persephone over. She presses her body as close as she can to her mate without either of them tripping each other. Reaching out with a hand, I channel my mana pool into her.

"You can move a little away," I tell her after I've almost completely emptied my pool. "Not far, though." She doesn't argue and moves just far enough away that she doesn't have to pay quite so much attention to not bumping into Hades at every step.

Focusing, I direct the mana within her towards her injuries, starting with her wing.

By the time Fenrir stops moving, we've actually made some decent headway into narrowing the gap between us and him, especially when the creature carrying him started to slow down about halfway into our journey. I've fully healed all three of my Bound who were injured in the fight and have started feeding everyone present some of my mana.

We've been moving fast for a good few hours, and everyone needs a break—even me. Although I wasn't running all the time, I did take my turn to give Hades as much of a break as possible. Of course, when I was riding, I wasn't exactly idle either.

Once I healed all of their assorted injuries, I actually concentrated my efforts on boosting Hades, trying to make up for my weight causing him more strain. I used my Flesh-Shaping to soothe aching muscles, repair broken or strained cells, and give him more energy. It's not something I've done before, but with a mixture of the remaining knowledge from Lay-on-Hands, my exploration with Flesh-Shaping, and my knowledge from biology at school, I cobbled together something that seemed to work.

Even as my Bound rest a little, I tiredly move around from one to the other and do the same thing to everyone as I was doing to Hades as we ran. The three raptorcat cubs are particularly tired, lying slumped on the floor like piles of feather-fur and flesh that don't intend to move ever again. I clear out the buildup of chemicals in their body, which is acting similarly to lactic acid, and soothe and build their muscles so they're just that little bit stronger and more resilient.

I'm not sure why Bastet decided to bring the cubs with us; I guess it's to do with the pack moving together. Or maybe she doesn't want to leave them alone again. Either way, they've done an excellent job at keeping up with the rest of us. I did notice that Bastet copied my idea, though—when we paused for me to either climb back onto or off Hades's back, one of the raptorcat cubs would leap onto Bastet's back, held in place by her wings. That way, each cub only had to run two-thirds as much as the other adults. Myself excluded, of course. I did notice that I'm still the slowest of the group—when Hades carried me, we all moved faster than when I was running alongside. Even the cubs seem to be faster than me, though their stamina isn't as good. But that's where being carried at regular intervals by Bastet came in useful.

I pull out the two half-eaten carcasses that I dumped into my Inventory before we left. Everyone descends like they're half starved. Actually, considering that they were hunting before the whole debacle, they may be feeling *more* than half starved.

I'm hungry myself—apparently, using as much mana as I have been in the last few hours, not to mention the physical activity, is an excellent appetite stimulant. Not tempted by the raw meat, I pull out various bits of food I've made. A sort-of flatbread, a pylobus platter of savory soup, and the stew I made earlier, seasoned with salt and herbs. And some berry tea in my sneleon shell.

We're all still digging in hungrily when we hear a very slight noise from the bushes nearby: the rustle of a leaf being shifted just a little.

Everyone automatically reacts with caution. Food and rest are forgotten when potential danger is nearby. Even the cubs tense and push themselves to their feet, their teeth bared.

I pull out my spear, then cast Inspect Environment. It *might* enrage whatever the creature is, but I'd rather know what we're dealing with here.

The result isn't what I expected. I ignore all the red and gold of the plants around as my attention is grabbed by the new blue color outlining a shape. A *familiar* shape. And one I wasn't expecting to see here. Though, thinking about it now, I probably should have.

CHAPTER THIRTY-SIX

Forced My Hand

Stand down," I say to everyone, relaxing my own grip. I feel confusion from River and the kiinas, but Bastet seems to already know who's there. It makes sense—her sense of smell is better than any of the others present, who seem to be primarily sight hunters. "Lathani, come out," I tell her wearily.

The bushes rustle a bit more, and then the nunda cub emerges from them, the shadows clinging oddly to her as if reluctant to give her up. I don't even need her to speak to know how she's feeling: her body language tells the whole tale. Defiance on the surface with forward-tilted ears, stiff shoulders, and a lifted tail, but hints of guilt clear, nonetheless, in the way she slopes forwards. It might be shame over being caught, but I'm pretty sure it's more that she knows she's not meant to be here but has come anyway.

"Why are you here?" I ask with crossed arms and a glare. "I'm sure that your mom and I were *very definite* earlier about you not coming on this trip."

I don't see why I should be excluded. I didn't even have to ride on anyone's back to keep up, she accuses defiantly, her teeth slightly bared.

"Because both your mother, the strongest being I know, and I, the person you've acknowledged as pack leader before, said so! This is *exactly* the same problem as happened last time. You just don't listen!" I half shout back at her. I sigh forcefully, then breathe in deeply, trying to calm myself. Getting angry at her, even if I'm *furious*, won't solve anything. "How did you even get here? Have you been following us?"

Yes. And you didn't even realize I was here until now. She seems to think that should mean something.

"We weren't exactly watching for pursuers," I tell her, a little exasperated. Though, honestly, it is a bit of a failing on our parts. What if whatever was following us so quietly was something waiting for the moment to strike? We were traveling pretty fast, but that doesn't mean we could have just escaped any danger; Lathani has proven that.

Well, I'm here now, so I'm coming with you, she announces, like that's the end of the matter. Bastet growls at her tone, crouching as if seconds from pouncing on her to teach her respect, and River shifts uncomfortably. Conflict between me and Lathani is always difficult for him given his past history with the cub and his loyalty to me.

I want to refute her, want to send her packing back home. She will be in danger.

More, she might *be* a danger. Last time, she caused and then leaped into a veloci-raptor fight without seeming to recognize the issues she was causing for everyone around. How much more of a liability might she be in this far more dangerous fight?

But at the same time, I can't just leave her here in the forest. Quite apart from the fact that she probably would refuse to stay unless I tied her to a tree, there are far too many dangers that an inexperienced nunda Lathani's size would struggle with. If her mother is in hot pursuit, which she may be, that would be the ideal scenario—I could pass Lathani over to Kalanthia for a judicious scolding, and they could return to the cave. But I have no idea if that is the case or not. And we don't have the time to find out.

Which means that there's safety in numbers. Lathani will have to stay with us until or unless I find indications that her mother is following.

I sigh and return my gaze to Lathani, who, wonder of wonders, has realized that she shouldn't interrupt my thought process.

"Fine, you're coming with us," I say unhappily. Her body language immediately changes, clear elation running through her at the acceptance. Confusion and sur-prise come across the Bond from my Bound at my changed mind. "Only because it would be more dangerous to do anything else now that you've forced my hand," I tell her with a hard edge, staring sternly at her. "If your mother comes, I'll happily relinquish you to her care."

She won't come, Lathani interrupts cheerily.

"Why do you say that?" I ask with a frown. *Did Kalanthia change her mind?*

Because she doesn't know where I've gone. She won't find my trail either, Lathani tells me with a completely inappropriate happy chirp.

"Fantastic." I sigh. That means there's going to be a frantic nunda mother when we return. Assuming that Lathani is right, of course—Kalanthia is powerful and may have tricks to track her cub that Lathani's not aware of. "I'm taking no respon-sibility for if you get injured or killed," I grumble, though I don't mean it—invited or not, Kalanthia will most definitely take any damage to her cub out of my hide. But I'll do my best to keep Lathani safe for her own sake as well. "Let me make one thing clear, Lathani," I tell her, pinning her gaze with my own. "While on this trip, you obey me or any of my Bound without question. In this hunt, you are at the *bottom* of the pecking order. Do you understand me?"

She grumbles and looks away, her posture showing displeasure. I move closer to crouch down in front of her, then put my hand on her neck and gently but firmly push with my fingers to indicate that she should look at me again. She does, a bit unwillingly.

"Your mother talked about consequences," I say quietly but very firmly. "Maybe you're mentally prepared to be hurt. Perhaps you think you're even ready to face death. I won't say whether you are or not. But consider this: are you ready to watch others get hurt because of you? Last time your disobedience created a fight that we didn't need to be involved in. Fortunately, no one was hurt. This time we're going into a much, much more dangerous situation. Listening and working together is going to be *essential*. If you don't . . . do you want to see Bastet be injured and realize it's your fault?" She jerks, her eyes going wide. "Or die? What about River? I know you've gotten closer to him since the rocky beginning of your relationship. Are you ready to watch him be hurt because you refused to dodge when someone told you to? Or die because he moved to protect you when you disobeyed the order to retreat?"

She's broadcasting her emotions, and I feel the denial and rejection of my words. I press harder.

"What about me? You are precious to me, Lathani. If I see that you're in danger, I will try to protect you as much as I would any of my Bound. We're going to save Fenrir because of that. But could you live with yourself if you disobeyed an order and then I died while trying to protect you from the consequences of your choice?"

My words are hitting home; I see the horror in her eyes. If she could tear up, I'm sure that there would already be rivers running down her furry cheeks. As it is, her fur is dry, but I think that I'm getting through to her. Good. I don't want to scare her unduly, but the fact is that she's chosen to add complications into something that was already going to be a nightmare. I don't think *I* would be able to forgive her if she caused the death of one of my Bound because of willful disobedience. We were lucky last time, but we can't rely on luck forever.

It's one thing if we get hurt or worse in a fight; it's quite another if the injury was easily avoidable. The more I can impress the dangers into her head now, the better.

"My Bound and I have hunted together extensively"—some of us more than others, admittedly—"and trust each other's judgement. I have no doubt that if I give a command in the middle of the battle, they will follow it."

Well, if I told Hades to abandon Persephone to danger, I have some doubts about him obeying that. But since I know that the male kiina is intensely protective over his mate, I wouldn't give that order unless it was absolutely necessary. And if it was absolutely necessary and would, in fact, be the best option for protecting his mate overall, I'm sure that Hades would recognize that and follow it. But I won't say all of that to Lathani.

"We work together as a team. We do our best to support our teammates, not expose them to danger," I continue. "I don't have the same confidence in you,"

This gets a new reaction, one of indignation. She shakes off my hand and pins her ears back, glaring at me.

I wouldn't put anyone in danger!

"You already have!" I snap back at her, dropping my hand to my side and standing up to glare down at her. "Not only last time we went out in the forest, but already now! By coming here, you have added an extra element to an already complicated situation. Right now, I should be feeding mana into my Bound, preparing all of us for the fight ahead, but instead I'm having to talk to you. Your actions *already* have a price—and right now, it's not you paying it!" I breathe more heavily, my anger rising despite my attempts to control it.

Taking in and letting out a couple of deep breaths, I feel the rising tide ebb a little.

"Listen, Lathani. I love you like family." I'm amazed at how easily the words fall out of my mouth—if only I could have been as open as that with Lucy. "But if even a single action of yours in the next few hours makes me fear that your presence will put the rest of us in danger, I will tie you to Persephone's back and you'll both be out of the fight."

I mean it too. And from the wave of sudden support from Hades, I can tell that he'd be happier with that solution. Persephone's disgruntled response both to me and to her mate, on the other hand, proves that she won't be happy if we end up doing things that way. Nevertheless, I don't doubt that she would accept it, however grumpily—that's exactly the point I was trying to make to the juvenile nunda.

No! Lathani protests.

"Then promise me that you'll obey *any* order," I tell her, shaking my finger in her face. "That's the choice now. Accept that you are at the bottom of the pack hierarchy or be sidelined completely." There's a long moment when I can't read her emotions from either her body or her eyes. She's clearly taking care not to broadcast them either.

Fine, she accepts finally. It's sulky but genuine.

"You'll obey any order from any of us?" I check, not relenting.

Yes. I stare at her expectantly. *I'll obey any order. From any of the pack,* she continues, the sulkiness leaving her tone to be replaced with resignation.

"All right." I sigh, suddenly feeling even more exhausted than I was earlier. I look around at my Bound. "Looks like Lathani's coming with us," I say, probably pretty redundantly—they were there for the discussion, after all—but it feels like something I should officially acknowledge.

The others seem to take that as the cue to reach out to Lathani in acceptance, ranging from the standoffish greeting of the two kiinas to the enthusiastic headbutting of the raptorcat cubs. Bastet actually moves over and bites Lathani's ear before rubbing against her. Not that hard, but enough to make Lathani yowl slightly—evidently, the raptorcat hasn't quite forgiven the nunda for her disobedience.

River's own emotions are a little complicated; he's probably not comfortable going into danger with the young nunda again.

Are you sure about this? he sends to me. The message has the feel of being a private one—I've started getting to grips with how messages directly sent between two on the "web" feel different from general broadcasts.

No, I send back to him alone. *But I don't see any other option. If she's a liability, I'll carry out my threat of tying her to Persephone's back and sidelining both of them, but I'd rather not lose a capable fighter if I can avoid it.*

He accepts that with a silent sense of dissatisfaction. I don't blame him, but it's too late to take her back to the cave—we've already lost more time than I hoped this rest stop would take. Fortunately, my Bound kept eating while I was dealing with Lathani. I didn't, obviously, but should be able to at least eat my flatbread while we move.

"Come on, everyone. We need to go," I say grimly.

CHAPTER THIRTY-SEVEN

Problem of Communication

The trees are thinning; we're heading up one of the mountains' sides. It's not the same mountain as the one Kalanthia's cave is on, nor is it near the site of my arrival. Instead, it's one a bit further down the range.

It would be nice if that was an indication that we were likely to be in less danger than if we were deep into the forest, but the fact that I know there are at least two very powerful beings living in areas of low Energy density is less reassuring. Kalanthia has chosen to live in a lower-density area for the sake of Lathani, and the squid thing lives in the salt lake under the mountain, perhaps because it can't go anywhere else.

So, in reality, we may end up facing anything. At the very least, we're likely to face that monstrous spiderlike creature.

I sense Sirocco arriving before I actually see her; the sun is setting, and a mist is embracing the upper slopes of the mountains. Since we're now on the upper slope of this mountain, swirling mist obscures our long-distance vision. It's not very thick—at the moment. I suspect that might change.

Rain may even be in our near future. I become suddenly glad that I've taken a few minutes every day to oil my weapons with fat and that my hide armor has been fully tanned. Hopefully, everything will come out fine.

We pause as I communicate Sirocco's imminent arrival. A dark shape wings its way through the mist from an unexpected direction and then comes to land on my shoulder. With my thick nere-hide armor, I don't feel her impact nearly as much as I'm used to.

"What's been happening?" I ask, my muscles tensing. I sense that Fenrir's still alive and that he's awake now but feeling very groggy.

Sirocco sends a series of images to me, which I quickly pass on to my Bound.

"Right, so now we all know what the situation is—" I'm interrupted by the nunda juvenile.

I don't! I'm not as good as Mother at hearing thoughts, and those images were too quick for me to see, she complains. I close my eyes for a moment and sigh. Sirocco sends a sense of surprised question.

No, I didn't want her to come, I answer the bird privately. *She followed us.*

Sirocco responds with disapproval and concern.

I know, I tell her, trying to send reassurance along the Bond. *She promised to be good.*

When Sirocco sends a sense of doubt along the Bond, I just sigh again but don't respond. It's not like I have any major reassurance for her. And with this added problem of communication . . . I should have thought about it before.

"How much of our internal communication can you understand?" I ask Lathani. She cocks her head sideways.

What is on the surface or has strong emotion attached. But when messages are sent too quickly, or are very complex, or are things like these images, I don't get it, she answers with a hint of shame. *Mother says I will be able to do that after my Evolution.*

"Much good that does us now." I sigh. "This is another reason why you shouldn't have come," I say in frustration. "Having a Bond and a means of communicating quickly and silently is a major benefit to our fights." After all, having to do everything verbally means potentially attracting attention at the wrong moment or taking too long to communicate a message—sending an abrupt feeling of danger and a sense of the direction it's coming from is quicker than shouting "Look out over there!" for one thing.

Then why don't you offer me a Bond? Lathani suggests.

"No!" I yelp quietly at the idea. "Your mother would *kill* me."

She wouldn't, Lathani argues.

"Yes, she absolutely would! Maybe you don't remember, but she almost bit my head off when she *thought* I was trying to Tame you by feeding you cooked meat right at the beginning of things." The young nunda tilts her head the other way.

No, I don't remember that, she admits. *But could you not offer me a temporary Bond—one just for now? If it's gone before we return, then Mother will never know.*

I'm about to say no immediately, then hesitate. Actually . . . maybe that's not such a bad idea. I could use Tame on her, offer a Bond that only lasts a day or something. Surely that wouldn't leave any marks on her soul? Or if it did, very minimal ones? I'm not convinced that Kalanthia wouldn't notice, but if the Bond was already dissolved, would she be so angry about it? Especially if the reason for the Bond being in place was to protect Lathani from suffering the ultimate consequence for her bad choices? And this might be a way around my concern about Lathani becoming a loose cannon in the middle of the fight.

What do you think? I send down the Bond to my present Bound.

The kiinas, as expected, are not too bothered.

If it will reduce risk to my mate, it is a good idea, is Hades's opinion. Persephone is just as practical, but in a different way.

Communication within the pack is important. This will improve communication.

Sirocco sends agreement, throwing her vote in for Bonding with Lathani if I insist on letting her be a part of the battle at all.

I agree, is Bastet's thought too. *If Lathani is going to join the fight, then she should be a full part of it.*

Are you not letting the cubs join? I ask.

She sends a sense of negation. *No. They know to find a good spot to hide and to pay attention to our movements in case we decide to retreat.*

And will they obey? I ask a little sardonically, casting a glance at the expectant juvenile nunda sitting within our circle.

They are not yet at this difficult age. They will obey, Bastet reassures me. Not *yet* at this difficult age, she says. Great—so we have this to look forward to from the cubs as well . . .

But that is future-Markus's problem, so I forcibly move my thoughts on.

And you, River? I ask my only silent Bound.

The Great Predator is not one I would dare anger, he warns. *But,* he continues with reluctance, *I suspect that she would be even more angered if her cub were to die.*

Yeah, that's my thought too. I sigh mentally. All right, looks like everyone is in agreement about inviting Lathani to—temporarily—join our little posse.

"I'm going to offer you a Tame Bond," I tell Lathani. "It will just be for the next few hours, okay? If this ends up taking longer than the night, we'll have to renew it. Any questions?" I pause for a moment.

What will happen? she asks, suddenly sounding a little uncertain. I frown in confusion.

"What do you mean?"

Will it . . . Will the Bond hurt? Or do we have to battle or something? Mother warned me about battles, but I didn't understand what she meant. Interesting—Kalanthia seems to know a surprising amount about Taming. I briefly wonder how.

"No," I reassure Lathani. "Not for this type of Bond. This one is more of a negotiation: I put in requirements and promises, and then you respond to either accept them or put in a counterproposal of requirements and promises. When we both accept, the Bond snaps into place. No pain, no battles."

Then, I can change things?

"You can," I answer slowly, "but I will be putting in the requirement that you follow instructions from any of my other Bound—you've already agreed to it, so I don't see any problem with formalizing it. If you change that, you won't be taking part in the fight. You'll be sticking with the cubs on the sidelines of the battle." Actually, maybe that's not such a bad idea. If I could frame it as Lathani protecting the cubs, she might even agree. Unless she realizes that's my reasoning, which isn't beyond the realm of possibility—she's increasingly intelligent.

Perhaps Lathani realizes that I'm seriously considering sidelining her again because she hastily confirms that it won't be a problem for her to agree to following orders. I then check if she has any more questions. She doesn't, so I initiate the Bond.

Into my side of the "trade window," I put the time limit—only until the dawn—and my own requirement that she follow the clear orders of anyone within the network of Bonds without question. I do put in the proviso that if following the order would put her at immediate risk of harm, she can choose not to. At least this way we all have a bit more insurance against her willfulness; yelling at her after the fact for disobeying at the wrong moment is one thing, but the actual reality of it could have tragic consequences.

In return for my requirements, I promise that I will never intentionally order her into a position where she is guaranteed to get hurt without her full knowledge and consent. I promise that I will protect her as much as I am able and that I will not order her to be sidelined as long as she has not proven to be a danger to either herself or others.

Lathani hesitates for a moment, then accepts the Bond without adding in anything extra. I don't know if it's because she didn't think that I would accept what she would like to add or didn't feel like a short-term Bond like this needed any further additions. Either way, I feel the Bond snap into place between us.

It's interesting because I sense that the Bond is as different from Sirocco's Bond as it is from my Dominate Bonds. It's actually somewhere in between. Where I sense that the control of my Dominate Bonds is entirely in my hands and that Sirocco's Bond is split equally with each of us able to control our own ends, I sense that Lathani's leans more towards the former than the latter.

I don't know if it's because she didn't put any of her own requirements in before accepting or because freedom wasn't such an important thing for Lathani as Sirocco. Maybe it's because of the requirement for obedience within the agreement for the Bond itself, something that is absent from Sirocco's. Either way, I sense that in this case, *neither* of us can break the Bond within the time limit. I also sense that I can control Lathani with it in the same way as with any of my Dominated Bound, as long as I don't contravene what I promised when creating it.

It's a relief in one way but a concern in another: is this more likely to leave marks on Lathani's soul? And if it does, are they likely to look like a Dominate Bond that was then broken? Well, it's done. If Kalanthia's going to get angry with me for the Bond, there's nothing I can do about that right now.

I sense that there's a notification waiting for me—no doubt Taming Lathani has triggered a rank-up to Tame. I quickly open it, and sure enough, that's exactly what it is.

Congratulations!
You have advanced a Class Skill past Beginner. Tame is now Novice 1. Due to your use of this Skill, two new effects have been discovered.

Effect 1
You have offered this Skill as a connection between equals, allowing the potential for it to become something closer than the original contract allowed for. Hereafter, the original terms of the contract can be modified without explicit agreement from both parties as long as both parties subconsciously agree to the change.

Effect 2
You have taken inspiration from Dominate for the terms of a contract. Henceforth, as a modification of Effect 1, a Tame Bond can become a Companion Bond, following the same procedure as with a Dominate Bond.

It's nothing particularly groundbreaking, though I do note that Sirocco apparently *couldn't* have been offered a Companion Bond before this. Hopefully, the first effect won't cause problems with Lathani in the middle of the fight. Then again, I doubt I'm likely to subconsciously agree to her becoming a loose cannon again, so perhaps not.

Closing the message, I resolve to look at it in more detail later. For now, we have a lizog to rescue.

CHAPTER THIRTY-EIGHT

Worn Thin

Now that we have a Bond, I quickly send the images from Sirocco over to Lathani. The bird followed as the spider monstrosity went running through the forest. It ran in almost a straight line in this direction, only moving around a couple of areas, which I mark on my map with an exclamation mark—if this creature was avoiding them, we probably want to be wary of them as well.

Breaking through the trees made it both easier and harder for Sirocco to follow. Easier in that it was simpler to fly through the open air of the mountainside rather than needing to dodge all the trees; harder because her stamina pool is still rather small for the amount of flying she needed to do.

Eventually, the spider headed into a cave mouth, something wider than it is tall—the spider had to lower itself a bit to enter. Sirocco flew close but didn't dare go in. She heard movement and a number of different animal noises; some she recognized, some she didn't. It seems like there's a whole menagerie of creatures in there. However, whether they are hostile or victims as well will remain to be seen. Though, that said, the two states are not exactly mutually exclusive.

Time for me to try to find out more information. We have an insider; hopefully, I'll be able to connect to him as I did once before. While I'm itching to run inside and save him, I know that any information I can get will be helpful and might be the difference between succeeding in our mission and failing. The spider hasn't killed Fenrir yet, even though it's arrived back in its den. It must have some other reason for bringing him back. We have time.

At least, that's what I tell myself.

Settling down to the ground against Bastet, I close my eyes and drop into my Core space. A cursory glance at Tame reveals the new complexity to it; though, since it didn't change significantly, the new additions are limited to a few more woven threads added to its intricacy.

However, my aim isn't Tame but the Skill that sits right next to it. By this point, I'm a lot more familiar with my Core space than the first time I accessed it, and I've realized that the pathway I followed before into Fenrir's mind actually originates in the depths of Dominate.

Threads spool out of the Skill, winding and weaving with the rest of the golden tapestry, easily mistaken for just another thread of the whole. As I move ever outward, they are some of the strings that trail off into nothingness. Except I've come to recognize that they don't disappear—I am just unable to see their whole length.

However, when it comes to my Bound, I'm able to *feel* it.

Mentally touching each of the five threads that stem from my Dominate Skill, one of which stems from the golden weave of Companion Bond that wraps around Dominate rather than the center of Dominate itself, I dismiss the ones that lead to River and the kiinas. Once I find the one for Fenrir, however, I start running my mind along it, doggedly following it out of my Core space.

Here is the difficult moment. I did it by accident all that time ago, but intentionally doing it doesn't seem to be as simple. I'm limited by my Core space, unable to move past it and through the Bond into Fenrir's mind.

Frustration builds. This is important! I don't want to be taking my Bound into the fight completely blind. Especially when I *know* that this is possible.

Realizing that the frustration is probably actively impeding my continued efforts, I take a moment to pull on Meditation. I'm not in it properly, only Light Meditation at most, but I use its calming and pacifying techniques to bring a bit more clarity to my mind.

Perhaps I'm overthinking this? Maybe because I'm expecting it to be difficult, it is? When I did it before, I had no idea what I was doing. I just . . . did it. It's possible I need to do the same now. Easier said than done.

I draw heavily on Meditation to keep my mind smooth and placid as I slide down the Bond once more. No fear, no worry, no anger disrupts the peacefulness of my mental presence. I do my best not to even pay attention to exactly how far along the Bond I've gone. I just . . . move.

And then, suddenly, I realize that I'm not in my own mind anymore.

It's not the same sensation as before. Last time when I entered Fenrir, I became part of his thoughts and almost lost my own sense of self as I was drowned in his mind. This time that doesn't happen.

Maybe it's because I'm using Meditation to calm my own mental presence—it may have the side effect of keeping my mind distinct as well. Or perhaps it's because I'm expecting it to happen, so I don't get immediately submerged in Fenrir's personality. It could also simply be that I'm more practiced with all this nonphysical business.

Either way, I find that what I've gained in clarity of my own mind, I've lost in Fenrir's. Before, it was like I *was* Fenrir, receiving the information from his senses like I was him, thinking like I was him, reacting like I was him.

Now, I'm a bystander. I sense his emotions but cannot see out of his eyes. It's more like what we had during our Battle of Wills, actually. A thought for later, perhaps . . . But for now, I need to get the information I came for.

Fenrir? I ask. We're still a little too far from the cave for our normal mental communication to work. It's pretty short-range, and I didn't want to get close enough to the cave that we might end up provoking the spider creature prematurely.

The lizog is fearful, hungry, in pain, and a little angry. But mostly fearful. It's not terror—it feels like he's been through terror and it's worn thin, only to leave a deep dread behind. He doesn't seem to think that there is any hope. Does he not realize that we would come to rescue him?

His emotions are so strong that he doesn't respond to my mental voice—I sense that it's unable to penetrate his fear-filled mind.

Fenrir, can you hear me? I ask with a little more force. Still nothing.

Reaching out with my mental presence, something I do automatically while intentionally trying not to question how it works, I stroke his mind as I would his body. *Fenrir, we're here. We've come to rescue you.*

I repeat similar platitudes while also trying to send a sense of calm and peace at him. I can only liken it to a fearful animal or child who's curled up with their hands over their ears and their eyes screwed shut, hoping that if they ignore the world, the world will ignore them too. As I keep going with my calming strategies, though, the tight curl unwinds a little, hands pull away from ears, and eyes open.

When he realizes that I'm there, Fenrir doesn't respond in words but in sensations. If we were physically present together, I think I would have been bowled over by the enthusiasm with which his mental presence knocks into mine.

Relief, joy, longing . . . All of that hits with almost enough force to push my mind out of his body entirely. Since that is the last thing I want to happen right now, I try to send more calming vibes to him.

Yes, we're here to rescue you, I confirm, *but we need information from you first. Just to check, you can hear me now, right?* The wave of confirmation from Fenrir is enough to verify that. *Okay, can you show me exactly what you've seen since you entered the cave?*

The lizog shoves a memory at me, and I go silent as I focus on experiencing it.

I swing below the body of a powerful predator. I feel woozy and weak, having only just woken from an unexpected sleep. I try to shift, but my body is not responding to me. I am trapped within bindings, pinned almost completely against the belly of my captor.

I start getting control back over my limbs, but they remain weak; the best I can do is try to scrabble against the sticky ropes binding me. I even try to chew them, but my powerful jaws aren't sufficient to free me; the bindings flex and resist the crushing power and sharpness of my teeth.

I can see little, trapped under the creature's belly as I am, but I recognize when we have entered a darker place by the way the floor and light level change. I see little around me even after my eyes have quickly adapted to the dimmer light. There are empty hollows around us and many areas covered with the white material that still holds me to my captor's body.

Then we stop. I feel movement along my sides, and the white bindings, which had resisted everything I could try, tear easily away. I fall to the ground, my slow and weak limbs unable to break my descent. Landing heavily, I feel pain, but nothing serious.

I wish to leap to my feet and attack my captor, but my body still refuses to follow my desires. Instead, my feet scrabble uselessly against the stone floor below me. I growl, the sound of frustration just as useless in deterring my captor. I want my pack!

The powerful predator above me shifts, and I suddenly feel intense pain pierce my flank. Even when the creature shifts again, the pain does not vanish and instead continues to throb.

Then a leg comes and shoves me sideways. I roll into a side cave, an area a bit bigger than I am but not by a lot. Still unable to do more than scratch at the ground and bite the air, I watch as my captor starts layering on the bindings. I'm left in almost complete darkness; only the faint glow allowed through the white material covering the entrance to my cave permits me to see anything.

In time I get the strength in my limbs back, but it does me no good. The material blocking the entrance to the cave is as impenetrable as always, and the small space allows me little opportunity to build up a charge.

I am equally unable to do anything about the pain in my flank, which continues to ache and burn. The creature has left more of its binding over my flank, and I am unable to shift it off. I've even caused damage to myself in my attempts to chew it away, but short of gnawing a hole through my own flesh, I am unlikely to succeed in removing it. That doesn't stop me trying, though.

I pull myself out of the memory with an audible gasp. Apparently, viewing things from my Bound's point of view while in their minds means pretty much *reliving* the memory. Good for information purposes, yes, but it takes a moment for my mind to resettle as *Markus* rather than some Markus–Fenrir hybrid.

I need to discuss this with the others.

Thanks, Fenrir, I tell the lizog, trying to give him a mental pat while sending approval at him. Even hungry, tired, and in pain, he perks up at that. *I'm going to go for now, but we'll get you out as soon as we can, okay?*

The sense of faith and joy with which he meets that is enough to bring a tear to my eye—if I could cry in this kind of mental space, that is.

How to leave is another question, but in the end, I find it is just as simple as arriving. Thinking too hard about it only puts obstacles in my way. What turns out to work is just relaxing and willing myself to be back in my body. And then . . . I am.

Opening my eyes, I turn to my anxious-looking Bound.

"Okay, so this is what Fenrir saw . . ."

When I'm finished, there's silence as they digest what I've told them.

I recognize the description of this creature, River says suddenly. *Though, I thought it only to be legend.*

I look over at him in interest.

"Tell me," I invite.

The spider monster is a figure of fear. Brood-mothers tell misbehaving hatchlings that if they do not do their chores or are lazy when gathering resources, they will be taken by it. Taken back to its lair, where they will be implanted with its eggs and meet an end as meat for its spawn. I . . . didn't think it was real.

He sounds horrified. I don't blame him—I'm pretty uncomfortable with this whole thing myself. I mean, that a creature might implant others with their eggs is understandable—lots of insects do it on Earth. That a much larger insect, even if it's not actually an insect at all, might do the same to much larger prey is equally logical.

And it does explain why the creature might have kidnapped Fenrir in the first place: it wants fresh meat for its offspring, not dead. But that does mean we're on a bit of a timeline—the eggs must be due to hatch soon.

Why do I think that? Because it's trapped its prey in a small space with no food or water. If we chose not to rescue Fenrir, he would die of dehydration within a few days. In that time, he would also consume some of his own body to keep going through a starved state. That would in turn mean less food for the offspring.

So no, I don't think it will take very long for the hatchling to emerge. Perhaps it has already. Which means that our urgency for getting Fenrir out, and the egg or hatchling removed, is high.

But how?

CHAPTER THIRTY-NINE

The Battleground

The sun is heading towards the horizon by the time we're ready, but we still have a good hour before sunset. Hopefully, that will be enough—I don't really want to fight this creature in the dark, even if all of us have pretty good eyesight in low-light conditions. But it's been worth spending a bit more time to make sure we're all going to be fighting in good condition. Approaching a fight like this while tired, half out of mana, or at all injured is stupid.

The steadily decreasing light level is one of the reasons that, after we're all set up, my first move is to drop into Fade, then move towards the cave entrance. I have my bow in one hand and a bunch of arrows covered in one of River's poisons in a hastily made quiver on my back. The quiver, actually, is just a thin layer of hide that I grew to make a long pouch diagonally across my backplate. It took a bit of trial and error, but now I can easily access my arrows.

That is only the most recent change I've made to my hide armor; in the run here, as well as after we stopped, I made small edits to it in places where it was rubbing. My new boots needed particular attention to make sure that they didn't rub my feet raw. One of the many benefits of Flesh-Shaping: never having to deal with new-shoe pain again.

Concentrate, I tell myself, rubbing my damp hands against my armor. I'm nervous but confident in my companions. Most of them, anyway.

Nocking an arrow to the string of my bow, I use my improved night vision to determine where the creature is in the dimly lit cave.

Not wanting to risk accidentally piercing one of the web-covered caves for fear of hitting Fenrir, I aim for a dark patch that is glinting a little bit in the small amount of light still entering the cave. I loose my arrow and am gratified when I hear the dull thud of impact with flesh, followed by a high-pitched shriek of pain.

A moment later, the creature comes barreling out from the dark cavern, its ten legs skittering quickly and easily despite its crouched position. I take the chance to shoot two more arrows to join the one currently hanging out of one of the creature's bulbous black eyes.

They both hit, though one bounces off the hard chitin, causing no damage. The other misses the eye I was aiming for but sinks into the web spinner's toothy maw, causing another pain-filled shriek.

The creature is starting to be too close for comfort, so I drop Fade, leap onto

Hades's back, and quickly flee with the kiina towards Bastet. As we run, I do something I wanted to do right at the beginning but decided not to for fear that it might lose us the element of surprise—cast Inspect Fauna.

Danaris

Tier 2 beast (Evolved)

Special abilities: Web spinning, Unknown

Health: 4560u

Mana: 10u

Minimum Willpower recommended to Dominate without other impacting factors: 63

Known for the females' tendency to take live prey to fill "larders" for themselves and their offspring, this beast is cunning, quick, and has formidable armor to protect itself. Its ability to spin different types of threads from protein is a weapon it can deploy to entangle even the strongest foe. Caution is advised when approaching this creature.

My mind races as I consider the new information and send it out to each of my Bound. Such high health! Because of its size, or because it traded mana for health? Both, perhaps. Either way, it's higher than I expected and justifies why my whole hunting group was unable to make headway. Hopefully, our new composition will make a difference.

I can take Dominate off the table except as a last-ditch distraction attempt, though—my fifty-three points in Willpower are ten less than I would need to reasonably stand a chance. Even if we managed to whittle the creature's health down or tie it up sufficiently to impact its Willpower, we would still be unlikely to close the gap sufficiently. Clearly, this creature is significantly more powerful than my kiinas. Maybe it's further in its Evolution?

I do take special note of its web spinning being mentioned as a weapon. I didn't see that happening in the fight with my Bound before, but maybe it didn't consider it necessary. Or maybe it wished to save its webbing for when it captured one of my Bound. That's possible—being a protein, there is surely a limited amount of the material, and replenishing its stocks must take time and probably food. Still, I have no desire for any of us to be entangled. And there's also that "unknown" to keep an eye on.

Such is the speed of my thoughts that we're only just approaching Bastet as I finish my analysis. After dashing past her, Hades skids to a halt and turns around.

The danaris barrels towards us, its eyes fixed on me with anger and killing intent. It pays little attention to the raptorcat in its path. A mistake.

Timed to the split second, Hades claps his wings forwards and sends an air-blade towards the spider's head. Simultaneously, Bastet breathes in deeply and then releases her fire breath.

The flames catch hold of the air-blade and set it alight. The air-blade, now a *fire*-blade, crashes into the danaris's head.

Apparently, whatever the spiky hairs covering the danaris are made out of is a material that's particularly vulnerable to fire. The creature shrieks once more, this time actually making several of us wince as the sound reaches painful decibels.

Its two front legs come up to scrub at the ball of flames its head has become. I can't help hoping that the fire might cook the thing's brain and end the fight there. Unfortunately, we're not that lucky.

Though the hairs seem to be particularly flammable, the rest of the chitin appears to be much more resistant. The fire dies down all too quickly.

I find myself wishing dearly that I could affect it from a distance; following my discoveries from earlier today, I realize that I can sense the fire with more than just my physical senses, but despite my best efforts, I am unable to do anything to it. If I could, I would give it mana to burn hotter and for longer, but there is no connection between me and it to use.

Still, it's not that bad: these are just our opening moves. If we managed to slay the creature with them, great, but we weren't expecting to. Especially not now knowing just how big its health pool is.

While the creature is still distracted by the remnants of fire, Lathani leaps out from where she was hiding behind a rock. She is tasked with taking any possible opportunity to give it an injury, however small, as long as it won't put her in danger.

That's one reason we wanted to draw the creature out of its lair: being able to decide and control the battleground.

As predicted, her attempt to dig into its body with her claws and teeth is a failure, the chitin resisting her natural weaponry perfectly. Still, she had to try it. We do learn something valuable, though: the hairs on the creature's body are more comparable to spines, which break and get stuck in flesh.

That didn't come up much in the last fight either—the kiinas mostly used air-blades and their teeth, Fenrir used his teeth, and River used his spear. None of them tried to use claws, which means that they didn't accidentally come into contact with the short spines, like Lathani.

Pain shoots down the Bond from her, and I quickly focus on the mana I fed into her earlier, which is still floating around her body. I mentally urge Hades to get closer, and it only takes me a few moments to push the nasty spines out of Lathani's paws, along with the contaminants they introduced, and then close up the holes as a stop-gap solution since I don't have time to heal her fully.

By the time I tune back in to the fight, the danaris has been distracted by Persephone and Sirocco. The former is sending small air-blades at the spider creature, one after another. With her mana pool of a hundred units and each small air-blade only taking five or so units, she has a few in the tank, but not that many.

Sirocco, on the other hand, is doing what she does best: swooping for the weak points. One eye is already damaged by my arrow, and she's trying to blind its five others. Even though its head is now free of the flames, and cleared of its spines, the creature is rather distracted by the two sets of attacks.

But that's not likely to last too long.

My mind works over the situation busily. We made our plans for the opening moves without knowing too much about the creature's strengths or weaknesses. Although we still don't know too much about the latter, we have more knowledge about the former.

It's quick, it's strong, and it has one weapon that we haven't seen in action as well as one we have—its stinger. At the same time, it is covered by a defensive layer that will quickly exhaust the stores of mana in my Bound if I have to be pushing spikes out of them every time they make an attack that requires contact with the enemy.

A defensive layer that is vulnerable to fire, even if the rest of it isn't.

Can you do another fire attack now? I ask Bastet hurriedly, using our Bond to communicate across the distance between us.

I can, but I will be exhausted of both mana and stamina, she warns.

That's fine, I tell her. *River can carry you out of the fight if you can't move yourself.* I cast a look over to the lizard-man, who has so far been watching the fight with a tight expression. I know he's itching to get in, but it's too dangerous for close fighting right now. From the ground, anyway.

He sends agreement down the Bond, and I hurriedly turn my attention back to Bastet.

Okay, on three, I tell her. *Hades, Persephone, try to catch the fire with air-blades too.*

I am almost exhausted of mana, Persephone informs me, tiredness in her mental voice.

That's fine, I reassure her. *Keep enough back that you can move, but otherwise, send a last big one along with Bastet's fire, then pull back.* I sense Hades's uneasiness at how unprotected his mate will be and his relief that she will be out of the fight for a bit. *Join River and Bastet—you should be safer together,* I say to reassure both of them.

Hopefully, if my plan goes as I'm intending it, the danaris will be too busy dealing with the next attacks to try to get revenge.

One, two, three! I count, and the attacks all launch simultaneously.

Two powerful air-blades fly towards the danaris again, each touching the fire breath that emerges once more from Bastet's maw.

The danaris tries to dodge the fire-blades, clearly understanding that they cause pain and damage, but with the short range, it doesn't succeed. One crashes into its abdomen; the other glances across several legs, setting small fires on each of them.

The fires won't last long—already they greedily consume the flammable spines within easy reach. But hopefully, they will last long enough for me to prepare our next attack.

Even as part of my attention is on the results of my Bound's attacks, the rest of me is focused on doing what I've done twice before now: transforming some units of mana into fire mana. I'm using the same channel I used when I produced a plume of fire from my index finger.

The stress of the situation is a hindrance, making it ten times more difficult to focus sufficiently to achieve the result I want. Meditation is a lifesaver here—drawing on its calming qualities means that I succeed in transforming the few units of mana I send down to my finger.

Focusing on directing it outwards so that it doesn't once more chargrill my own flesh, I connect a line of mana from my Core to the tip of my index finger. It's the first time I've tried to do that, so I'm flying by the seat of my pants a bit here, but inspiration came while watching Bastet's fire breaths. If I can do this . . .

After pulling a torch out of my Inventory, I light it and keep clutching it tightly in my right hand—it's a backup in case this doesn't work. Ending the plume of fire from my index finger is far easier than creating it, though I have to be careful not to accidentally suck the last bit back into my internal matrix—that probably wouldn't end well.

I urge Hades into the fight, part of me disappointed that riding in while looking like a human flamethrower is probably not the best of ideas.

Hades runs in closer to the danaris, his whole focus on getting me to my destination as quickly and safely as possible. The spider creature is still distracted by the fire-blades he and Persephone sent with Bastet's help, so we're able to get in close before it realizes we're there. I reach towards the closest leg with my torch, but it shifts away from me before I can brush it with the fire.

Closer, I urge Hades, and he complies.

A leg almost collides with us, and I twist around to slam my torch head against it. The flames eagerly take hold and light up the spines covering the chitin with ease. Even as I pull away, I'm interested to sense that there's a connection linking me with both the torch's head and the flames now spreading on the danaris's limb. Maybe it's because I created it from my mana, but I can actually give it instructions. I send the flames to chew eagerly up its leg, feeding on anything it can reach.

The danaris shrieks again as it feels the heat of fire scorching its leg. It turns its full attention to us. That's good in one way: it gives Bastet and Persephone a chance to recover. Sirocco too—I'm vaguely aware of her message that her stamina is getting low. It also gives River the opportunity to come in and attempt to stab at the gaps between the creature's chitin. Maybe the piercing impact of his spear will have more effect than the other attacks so far.

However, that comes at the cost of us now having to avoid legs that are as long as Hades is tall when he's standing fully upright, and a stinger-laden tail, which flashes down whenever we are in range.

I want to move away, get some distance between us and this thing, but I can't. Not if I want to maintain my connection with the fire—there isn't enough for the fire to consume on the danaris's body if I want it to survive, so I need to continue sending it mana. Unfortunately, that means I have to be close by.

Directing the fire and maintaining the connection between us takes most of my focus now, very little able to be spared for dodging. It's fortunate, therefore, that I have such a capable mount and partner in this fight. Hades and I communicate seamlessly, the kiina already used to working with a partner and perfectly intelligent enough to understand what we're doing here. Our mental connection makes it even easier.

We don't even need to put thoughts into words. I send him a sense of when we're getting to the edges of my control, and he moves back in closer; he sends a sense of danger and where the threat is coming from, and I shift my body to avoid it.

I honestly wouldn't be able to do this without him. But I don't have the brain-power to be able to think more than vaguely about that.

With my mana helping to fuel the growth, it's easy to direct the fire to spread from where it latched onto the danaris's leg. Traveling upwards and downwards, it wipes the whole limb free of those nasty spines. It acts like a cleansing hand, the spines crumbling to ashes in its wake. It would be good if it could do more than that, but the chitin is annoyingly resistant. Even worse, the danaris seems to have realized that the fire is hot and annoying, rather than actively damaging, and has decided to ignore it in favor of dealing with us first.

It might regret that decision before we're through, though.

My heart suddenly rises into my mouth as the danaris whirls around almost too quickly to follow and slams its leg solidly into River. The force and direction of the blow takes us all unawares—with how much it was focusing on Hades and me, to have it suddenly attack River is a shock.

I lose focus completely on what's around me and send that part of my attention down the Bond to River to check his state. He's injured but not too badly. At least, not as badly as might happen from a solid leg of chitin slamming into a body at high speed.

His scales have spread some of the force of the blow, cracking a few of them. The skin itself has only torn in a couple of places, but that minor surface damage belies the real injury: deep tissue damage, bruised organs, and cracked ribs.

Feeling like I have two dogs pulling on their leashes in different directions, I mentally strain myself to keep the fire fed, even if I'm not able to direct it much. At the same time, I redirect as much of my focus as I can into healing River's body.

Closer, I tell Hades again, this time sending a sense of where I need to be in rela-tion to River. Within moments, the connection I have with my lizard-kin Bound stabilizes and improves. I grab at the mana already floating around in his body and direct it to the most serious injuries. The rest will have to be done later, but I don't want him running around with internal bleeding if we can avoid it.

It takes more time than I'd like, but a lot less than if I hadn't already gotten Flesh-Shaping to Journeyman. By the time I've fixed the worst of the damage, I've depleted more than half of the mana I managed to feed into him.

Still, I'm glad that I had the time to empty my mana pool into my Bound a few times while traveling here—it would have otherwise been impossible to manage

SHAPING 293

healing as well as keeping the fire going, however little mana that's actually taking per second. As it is, it's a real struggle to manipulate both streams of mana coming from two different sources at the same time.

Frankly, I doubt I'd even manage if my Energy Manipulation Skill hadn't so recently ranked up to Master, even if multitasking with multiple streams of mana wasn't something that explicitly improved in its description.

Resurfacing to awareness, I duck at the last moment as its stinger passes through the space where my head was a split second ago. I wouldn't have actually been hit by it even if I hadn't moved, though—Hades has also taken evasive maneuvers and jinked to the side with a flap of his wings.

He sends me a wordless feeling of becoming fatigued, and I sense that the last few minutes have been hard on him. As I see what's going on, I realize why.

The danaris is enraged, and its speed has picked up to a pace previously unseen. It's clearly taking all of Hades's agility to dodge the constant attacks. With half of our group currently lying low and recovering, we are the sole focus of its attention. River is only just getting back on his feet from the last blow, and Lathani is nowhere to be seen.

She hasn't vanished, though—I sense where she is even if I can't see her. But given the last unsuccessful attack, I don't blame her for waiting until a better moment appears. As it is, we appear to have had little impact on the creature so far—it's still moving perfectly well, and though one eye is weeping a blackish ichor, the other five are perfectly able to see.

However, the spines are now pretty much gone, which opens the creature's legs and body up to the teeth and claws of my group. The fire is still there, though it's starting to gutter now that its fuel has vanished. Without fuel, I sense that the draw on my mana is becoming more hefty than it is really worth. However, before I let it die, I want to at least give it a final hurrah.

Before I do that, though, I check in quickly with all my Bound. Bastet and Persephone are still pretty low on mana, but they've recovered enough not to be hit by the exhaustion and nausea that accompany an empty mana pool. Sirocco is apparently still a bit low on stamina, but among my Bound, she's the quickest to recover it, so that shouldn't be the case for long.

River is still pained by his remaining injuries, but he sends me a quick feeling of grim readiness. He will do his best to do what I ask of him. He's also taken one of his own healing potions—a non-envenomed one—so that should help his healing a little. I tell him to use as many as he needs.

As for Hades, I pull at the mana within him and do my best to heal the effects of muscle overuse, even if I can't yet replenish his stamina directly. If the faint sense of gratitude is anything to judge by, it does something at least.

Just hold on a little longer, I tell him, sending my own sense of gratitude down the Bond even as we jerk from one side to the other to avoid a double blow of legs as they crash down.

The rest of you, attack when it's distracted, I tell them all. *Hades, create some distance when they do.*

Feeling nothing but grim assent, I focus on the fire. Feeding it mana piecemeal, I direct it to crawl up the body of the danaris towards its head.

The spider creature ignores the fire, having learned that it poses little threat to its defenses—at least, it's posed little threat up until now.

As I feel my Bound poised to move and Hades dodging below me, my own legs locked around the base of his wings to keep myself in place, I suddenly pour mana into the fire.

Time for it to go out with a bang.

CHAPTER FORTY

Unpredictable

Around the danaris's head, the flames become brighter by an order of magnitude, going from their previous relatively cool orange and red to yellow and almost white. I push mana into them, then cut it off when I'm down to only two hundred units.

With the severing of my mana, the connection I have to the fire goes too. But that's okay—I still have the torch flickering on the ground where I dropped it while I was distracted. And even if I can't get to that one, I have other torches in my Inventory and the ability to light them. If we need them, of course.

Surely it can't have coped with a fire that hot, no matter how good its chitin is, I think hopefully to myself. *If nothing else, won't its brain, or whatever it has that passes for one, have boiled inside its head?*

The danaris is immobilized as the fire starts to die, and my Bound take full advantage of that.

Hades beats a hasty retreat, his head hanging low and his chest heaving, even while the others move in. Bastet and Lathani snap at the thing's legs, trying their best to crack the chitin—at least the fire's destruction of the spines has made it safer for them. River joins in, striking at the joints of the danaris's limbs. His impact is almost immediately felt—within a few moments, his flint-tipped spear manages to pierce a thin bit of chitin. Liquid jets out of the hole, and that leg goes limp.

Persephone darts in and out, her toothed maw not finding much purchase on the defensive layer even now. Sirocco is the only one of my Bound who doesn't fly in, but I understand: with the fire still wreathing the creature's head, there isn't anything she can really target right now. I feel her frustration and try to send soothing feelings down the link. Ultimately, she's not the strongest combatant, but she makes up for it with her scouting abilities and being able to get a literal bird's-eye view.

Since I would also try to aim for the danaris's eyes with my arrows, I decide that it's not worth probably losing my arrows pointlessly. Instead, I decide to join my Bound in striking at the danaris's legs. I pull out my mace and leap down from Hades's back to run in. The stone head of my mace crashes into the chitin with an audible thunk, but my weapon rebounds off the armor without leaving more than a small mark, while stinging my hands badly. I frown and strike again, aiming for the knee joint or ankle joint or whatever is the closest, but it's still above my head, which limits the amount of power I can bring to bear.

Still, the added damage of Blunt Weaponry helps, and this time I hear a bit of a crunch. Another blow later and I, too, see a jet of liquid escaping as a second leg goes limp. Heartened, I set to striking the next leg.

Only a few moments later, the fire wreathing the danaris's head and keeping it immobilized dies completely. In its wake, it reveals a sight that both gladdens and frustrates me. There is damage, but not nearly as much as I'd have liked. The danaris's eyes are gone, only holes left where the burned and evaporated orbs used to be. Its mandibles have been eaten away too—the substance they were made of was obviously not quite as fire-resistant as the rest of its body. That's all good.

The issue is that the material making up the structure of the head isn't nearly as damaged as I would expect it to be after a fire as hot as this one was. There are scorch marks visible against the dark gray of the material itself but little more than that. And from the way the danaris is now moving, it most certainly hasn't done sufficient damage to its internal organs to kill the creature.

As the fight progresses, though, the spider's movements make it clear that there has probably been more damage than is immediately obvious. Where before it was moving fluidly, each of its limbs moving perfectly in relation to the others, now it is moving jerkily, far more uncoordinated.

That doesn't remove its danger. Indeed, in some ways, it might actually increase it, as its movements are a lot less predictable than before. From what I saw of the battle from Hades's back, the main issue so far has been that it's fast; the blow that hit River is one of the few that was truly not foreseeable.

Now, though, it might suddenly drop a couple of feet on top of me or one of my Bound, or its tail might flash in to stab at the air suddenly even without a clear target. One of its legs might flick out at a strange angle or curl inwards unexpectedly to strike at one of my Bound snapping at the underside of its abdomen.

Few, if any, of these movements appear to be intentional; if anything, they look more like the kind of abrupt twitches that might characterize someone having a fit.

Perhaps the fire has done some damage to its brain, I think to myself as I back away. I bite my lip as I stare with narrowed eyes at the scene.

Even worse than the unpredictable movements of its legs and stinger, though, is the fact that the webbing weapon the description warned about has started to come into play. In the same abrupt and unpredictable way as all of its other movements, sticky white webbing is being shot every which way. Sometimes, it even entangles its own legs in the material, but since its chitin seems to be as resistant to that as anything else, it doesn't impede itself too much.

The result is that the surface below the spider is becoming increasingly treacherous, with my Bound having to have eyes in the backs of their heads to make sure they're not about to be stuck to the ground at the worst possible moment.

I only know that the webbing is sticky because Lathani accidentally steps in a patch and then almost takes a blow from the stinger because she can't jump out of its way. It's only because Persephone collides bodily with the segmented tail and pushes it off course that it slams into the ground rather than the nunda.

I manage to get her free a moment later by essentially forcing her paw to shed the outer layer of her skin and fur—and the webbing with it. She's much more careful after that to avoid the gleaming patches of white dotting the rocky ground below their feet.

Back away, everyone, I order, and they quickly obey. Even once they've gone, the danaris still jerks around, proving that this is more of a seizure than a directed attack. My Bound eye the danaris warily as they take the moment to have a breather, but they're clearly ready to jump back into the action as soon as I give the word. *Don't go back in until it's stopped seizing as much,* I tell them.

Despite the danaris not actually actively fighting back against my Bound, it's still a difficult opponent. It's not only because of its unpredictability or the way it's turning the battleground into a minefield. The main reason is the same as always: its incredible defensive exoskeleton. Fenrir, ironically, would probably do a better job than any of my other Bound thanks to his powerful bite pressure.

But although the lair is probably left unguarded right at this moment, I'm not inclined to go inside to find him right now: we don't know what might be waiting for us in the cave, and all of us are needed here. Well, Sirocco not so much, but she doesn't do well with caves as a general rule, nor does she have particularly good vision in the dark.

No, there has to be another way. Ideas flicker through my mind but are summarily dismissed. A trap with rocks or tree trunks falling onto the spider—too long to set up. I don't know if the issues the creature is experiencing are temporary or permanent, but I don't want to wager on it being the latter.

I catalogue each of the weapons I'm carrying but dismiss all of them. The two that have proven to have a decent effect are River's spear and my mace. My bow might be good if I had the accuracy to hit its joints, but as it is, I'm far more likely to miss than hit it, despite my increased Dexterity. Using my mace, however, requires me to be close to its flailing legs, so it's definitely not the ideal plan. I'm slower and much squishier than River, for example, and he already came off worse from making contact with one of those powerful limbs.

No, although I'm not as loaded with mana as I would like, I think that magic is my only real option here. And at least I have a way of quickly replenishing my pool.

I explain my idea to Hades and feel his consent. Pulling almost all of the mana in his body back into mine, I refill my mana pool to overflowing. Then I leap onto his back again, taking a different position from before. Crouching with my feet on the joints of his wings rather than hooking my knees there, I'm rather precariously balanced. He keeps his head up, and I use his neck to help me stay in place. He trots into the action, choosing to come up from behind the danaris, and heads towards its flailing and twitching tail. This reminds me of nothing more than a dying wasp's sting, the way the abdomen pulses and its stinger emerges convulsively. However, it's also the area where we're least likely to encounter a leg flying through the air and threatening to take our heads off.

There, Hades pauses. I pour all my power into my legs and push myself up explosively. Jumping into the air, I grit my teeth as I focus on where I want to go. A directed air-blade from Hades helps me move just a bit further. He softens the usual cutting edge of the blade, but it's enough to carry me to land on top of the creature, right between the tail section and the round body section all the legs are attached to.

I hit the danaris's back with a thump that it can surely feel. If it can, though, it shows no sign. I stay tense for a good few seconds as I wait for the tail to flip up like a scorpion's and stab me or for a leg to twist to slam me off its back.

Neither of those happens. Maybe it's because it doesn't know I'm here. Maybe it does, but it can't control its limbs enough to rid itself of my presence. Or maybe its joints don't even work like that.

Either way, it looks like I might be able to have an effect here.

I place my hand on the spider creature's back and focus on sending my mind into its body.

Unlike with my Bound, I meet with strong resistance as soon as I push my mind through my skin. I grit my teeth as I set my Willpower against the resistance. We struggle for what feels like an eternity but is probably only a few minutes.

Refusing to let myself entertain the idea that I might be outmatched, that I might lose this battle, I keep pushing. An inch, a centimeter, a millimeter . . . Ultimately, it doesn't matter how much progress I make, as long as I keep moving forwards.

And then the resistance gives way, like my opponent has decided to give up this battle in order to win the war. Because what I now sense is that I have a certain amount of freedom to roam, that I can scan its body the way I can other bodies. But I also sense that if I try to *do* anything to the body, the resistance that faced me before will be back, and more intense besides.

Still, being able to see inside the danaris's body is a step towards being able to do *some*thing. The battle took over half my mana—that includes the overflow that seeped into my mana pool slowly as I emptied it—and a good bit of my mental energy. I take the break with just as much concealed relief as the danaris itself.

The creature's body, at first glance, is completely alien. I struggle to identify any of it. Then, as I spend a little more time going over what I can see and sense, I realize that most of the organs are actually relatively familiar, just different shapes and with slightly different functions. *I thought spiders had to drink the liquified remains of their prey?* I find myself saying mentally as I see the horror of a toothed throat lying behind its mandibles.

Then again, as much as it's like an Earth spider, it really isn't comparable. I see the organs that obviously produce the silk, the venom glands that lead to the tail spike. I see weird-shaped lungs and an elongated stomach and intestine. *Ouch, that looks like it hurt.* I almost wince as I see its stomach and the digestive pockets that surround its brain—they appear to have taken the bulk of the fire damage, as they're ruptured in multiple places.

I'm pretty sure I can see brain damage too, which explains the odd convulsive movements of the creature. However, it's not all good news: as the resistance showed me, the danaris is very much alive and kicking, and the damage is already noticeably healing. We need to stop it before it recovers its health.

Pulling almost all the way out of the body, my mind works busily over what to do next.

Trying to give it an aneurysm is out of the realm of possibility. I instinctively know that the more integral an organ is to the functionality of a creature, the more it will be defended. That eliminates its lungs too; though, I do send a quick message to all of my Bound about where their openings can be found—if River or someone can block them, that might do the job for me.

Frankly, any attempts to change *anything* are likely to be met with high resistance. *But what if the thing I'm changing isn't actually a part of the danaris at all?*

CHAPTER FORTY-ONE

MAD

Staying on the back of the spiderlike danaris is difficult; even if its apparently inadvertent convulsions aren't aimed at shaking me off, they might have the same effect if I'm not careful.

Gripping the insectile monster's thin waist between its abdomen and thorax with my legs, I pull my knife from my belt and another item from my Inventory. Closing my eyes, I send my mind into the item in my hand—a gland full of venom.

It's the gland River managed to get from the creature that lured me deeper into the forest of vine-stranglers after we killed the salamander. Given its effects on me, it's a pretty powerful poison. Hopefully, it will have just as much effect on this danaris.

Of course, I'm not just going to stab the massive spider with a knife coated in this venom; I'm going to try to do more than that. For that reason, I pour my remaining mana into the small organ. Fortunately, it turns out to be just about enough—I'm panting and nauseous by the time I sense that the organ and venom inside are saturated, but it's done.

I open my eyes again and notice with some trepidation that the movements are starting to be a little less jerky and more fluid again. The danaris is healing. I need to get a move on, especially since my Bound have obviously noted the same things as me and have started attacking again.

Using my knife, I stab between two plates of chitin, doing my best to open up a hole, however small. A cry comes from below, and River sends me an urgent image of the danaris coating Bastet's feet in the sticky web, pinning her down.

Defend her! I send back to him with emphasis. *Or get her out if you can. Hopefully, this won't take much longer.*

My full focus switches to manipulating the venom into the hole I've made. As I feed it into the spider creature's system, I fight against the creature's will and follow the venom into the danaris's body.

I win again not because my will outmatches that of the danaris, but because the venom isn't something recognized by the creature's system. Though my ability to sense the beast's body is limited, my mind and magic can travel relatively easily within the venom. Travel . . . and multiply.

As my mana returns bit by bit, I dedicate it to increasing the amount of venom that is affecting the danaris's systems. I'm increasing and enhancing as much as I can, but since I haven't spent time studying the venom, my understanding of how it works is limited. However, since I've saturated both it and its organ with my magic, I do have *some* understanding, and it's this that I use to enhance and hasten its effects.

The massive spider creature under me falters. I feel its legs fail for a moment. For good reason: the venom has managed to eat its way into the thin tubes of fluid under the creature's exoskeleton that act as hydraulics and operate its limbs. Backup systems seem to kick in, and I've only managed to get into a small portion of the hydraulic tubes, so it rights itself quickly. But I feel elated at the sense of progress.

Heartened, I pour as much mana as I can into the venom, draining myself dry again and again. At the same time, I sense that the danaris is focusing as much of its attention as it can on trying to clear the poison out of its systems.

From a message I receive from one of my Bound—I'm concentrating too hard to even tell who—I realize that both of us have gone completely stock-still. Apparently, the spider creature has decided that I'm a threat worth paying its full attention to.

We struggle against each other, a new type of Battle of Wills. The situation teeters on a knife's edge—the danaris's capacity to regenerate is powerful. Perhaps that's the unknown special ability mentioned in its description. I damage one part of its body, and it swoops in with its regeneration to heal, or at least plaster over, the injury.

I'm running out of resources. My mana regeneration just isn't fast enough to keep up with the rapid pace, and I find myself giving ground. If this keeps up, it will push my venom out of its body before I manage to destroy any vital organs. I redouble my efforts, pulling all the venom I can in to attack the brain—no brain, no consciousness, game over.

It seems to understand the danger it's in and redoubles its own efforts to heal the damage I inflict almost as soon as I've caused it. I need more mana.

I send out a desperate wordless message to my Bound and get an answer.

A small weight landing on my shoulder offers me the opportunity to pull some more mana into my empty reserves. Sirocco doesn't hold a huge amount of it, and I can't even pull all of what she can hold out of her, but it's enough to replenish my pool sufficiently.

At the same time, I sense my Bound moving below me, but it would take too much focus away from my internal efforts to work out what they're doing. Instead, with my mana pool almost full again, I pour the resource into the venom.

The danaris is unable to deal with my suddenly empowered efforts, and the venom multiplies beyond its capacity to purge. I start getting more of a foothold as the danaris is unable to heal all of the damage I'm now able to inflict. Still, I focus on the alien brain of the creature, eating away at it with an enhanced version of the poison that almost killed me.

The spider creature rallies and tries desperately to force me out through sheer willpower. It fails. I bury my presence within the venom, where it can't put any pressure on me. The venom eats and eats . . . and then it's done. I've cut the connections between the brain and the body.

Somehow acting on autopilot, as if it has a backup routine or some other way of controlling its body, it seems to take an attitude of mutual destruction. The legs that were frozen suddenly leap into life, flailing at my Bound. I sense their surprise and pain as River is once more hit by a leg, Persephone too.

Only half my attention is now on the venom as I search for a way of halting the danaris's attack or discovering whatever organ it's using to think. With the rest of my focus, I sense Hades's immediate protective fury as he leaps into the fray, his wings spreading to cover his fallen mate.

And then the danaris stills. It's not dead. I still feel signals shooting around its body, even as I frantically try to disrupt them.

Get out of there! I yell mentally, my vague view of its system informing me of what it's about to do.

In a final MAD attempt, the danaris rears up on its back four legs and actually manages to tip me off completely. But that wasn't the main aim of its action. Instead, it aims its tail end at my Bound and sends out an immense amount of white web, probably emptying its web-making organs completely. It coats all of my Bound who were underneath it, which is basically all of them except for Sirocco. And Fenrir, of course.

Then it pauses again. A moment later, its stinger projects a spray of greenish droplets through the air, and the liquid lands on the web and immediately soaks into it. A moment later, I have to scramble to avoid the creature as it crumples to the ground. Dead, or close enough to count.

But I can't check—my Bound are in trouble. I scramble to my feet and stagger towards them; the effects of the mental and magical battle are taking their toll on my body. I can't focus on that, though. My Bound need me.

That final spray was clearly poisonous, and they're already suffering. I don't know if it's the same venom that acted as a sedative for Fenrir, or if the danaris had multiple venoms to inject, but either way, I don't want them being exposed to it for any longer than absolutely necessary.

I still have a bit of mana left, but not a lot. Though the most effective method would probably be to feed mana into the webbing to saturate it and gain complete control over it, I don't have enough in the tank for that, and I definitely don't have the time to Meditate in between attempts.

No, I'm going to have to do this another way.

Choosing to leave my companions who are visibly struggling for the moment, I go for one who is worryingly still: Bastet. She's next to River, who is clearly trying to cut his way out of the webbing with his spear, though not making much headway. So, my own idea of using my knife to cut through is probably out. I'll try anyway.

I have to walk over the webbing myself, but fortunately, it doesn't seem to be particularly sticky: this one was clearly meant more for confinement through quantity than for adhesive properties. Even better, my hide boots keep me removed from the poison itself, so I get to Bastet—the one who has the lowest health at the moment—without being affected.

Crouching down, I try to cut the web with my knife. No good. It's tough to cut through for one thing, and as soon as I do, there seems to be some sort of sticky substance inside, which very quickly coats my knife blade and blunts it. I tuck my knife away, praying that I'll find a way of getting the sticky substance off later.

My next attempt involves touching the webbing near my raptorcat companion. I focus mana into my finger, then push it into the web but try to limit its spread. Instead of saturating the whole network, I only want to saturate the immediate area at my fingertip. Then, once it's saturated, I break it apart.

It's slow at first but speeds up with practice—good thing, too, as I'm very much aware of the slowly weakening movements of even my most active Bound. They're all alive—I know that—but I still don't know if the poison is only a sedative or something more threatening than that.

And then Bastet's free. I grab her and lift her out of the area, then lay her down gently. I immediately connect with the small pool of mana left inside her, then use the same strategy as I did earlier with Lathani to free her from ongoing contact with the poison: I flake off everything that's currently touching it. That does mean she loses a good portion of her feathers, but those are replaceable.

Even that brief contact with the poison reveals something I was fearing: the venom is not designed purely as a sedative. That's certainly part of its effects, but the end goal is a lot more . . . permanent. I need to get them all out and clear of it as soon as possible. Not easy considering how low on mana I already am. I'll have to hope that I'm able to get most of them out with the mana that's within their own bodies, otherwise I don't know how I'm going to do this.

For now, I shove two of River's potions down Bastet's throat—that will have to keep her going for now. I simply can't spend the time or mana to get her fully healed.

Returning to the webbed area, I go for River next. He's not the worst off, but he should be able to help me keep the others going until I can properly clear the poison out of them. Hopefully, he has significantly more potions than I do.

CHAPTER FORTY-TWO

Emotions Aren't Logical

It doesn't take too long to get a system going. River, as I hoped, is able to help me with the others. He isn't as badly off as Bastet or Lathani, probably because he curled himself into a ball when the first lot of webbing landed and used his spear to catch some of the strands.

That gave him a good position to fight against the constriction of the webbing after the second attack landed and less exposure to the venom itself. Plus, it seems like his scales were a pretty good defense against the deadly substance, the only access to his flesh being offered by places where his natural armor was already pierced.

He's certainly much better off than either Lathani or Bastet, whose skins seem to have relatively easily absorbed the venom. The fact that Lathani is still Tier one is probably a good reason for why her health is declining even quicker under the web trap than Bastet's. Honestly, her good-sized health pool is probably the only reason she is any better off than Bastet at all—at 810 health units when full, her pool is better than Bastet's was at Tier one.

I therefore head towards Lathani straight after retrieving River, and the lizard-man joins me to help break through the strands holding her to the ground. I can only hope that the kiinas' scales protect them as much—or better—than River's did. I would hate to lose any of my Bound, but if I let Lathani die, the rest of us won't outlive her for long due to Kalanthia's vengeful retribution.

In a choice between Lathani and any of my other Bound, I'm forced to choose Lathani—and I don't think I'll ever forgive her for putting me in that position if one of them dies. I recognize the hypocrisy, but emotions aren't logical.

As soon as Lathani is free, I pass her over to River to shove health potions down her throat. Meanwhile, I hurry over to work on the kiinas. At least Sirocco didn't get caught.

Persephone isn't doing too badly, though her health is declining more and more quickly. She's currently sitting at just over two hundred health points; Hades is still at more than half health. Probably the main reason for Persephone's lower health is the blow that hit her soon before the grand finale of the fight.

I work as quickly as I can to get them free, finding that Hades, as expected, shielded Persephone from most of the attack. His position crouched over her with his wings spread means that there's actually little poison coating the female kiina's scales, though there's a lot coating those of Hades. Like River, the small cuts he picked up in the fight are the access points for the venom.

I could probably pick the kiina up with my increased strength, but it would be a strain. I don't have to, though—like River, Hades and Persephone are both capable of walking out of the mess, though Persephone is in more than a little pain.

With all my Bound finally free, I tiredly set to dealing with the actual injuries.

Lathani is my first target. With only fifty health points remaining now, and the health potions that River keeps feeding her barely keeping up with the continued damage from the poison circulating around her system, she's the most clearly in need of healing.

I do take a moment to do a quick scan of Persephone's body, though—since she's pregnant, I'm aware that there could be dire consequences for the eggs growing inside her. From the way Hades's concern shows in his shifting movements and his emotions leak into our Bond, he's aware of the same.

Fortunately, it appears that Persephone has some degree of internal control and is managing to keep the poison away from the eggs. That's at the expense of it more negatively affecting her own body than it normally would, but it's nothing I won't be able to help heal. When I have the time and mana.

"You're doing well," I say to Persephone soothingly. "Just keep at it, and I'll be with you as soon as I can, okay?" I lift my hand and stroke the side of her neck. It's instinctive, but the kiina presses into my palm, closing her eyes and panting weakly. I turn my head to see Hades giving me an unreadable look, even the Bond not giving much of a clue. "What?" I ask impatiently, then decide to ignore it when he just turns his head away. I don't have time for this.

Going to my knees next to Lathani, I pull at the pitiful amount of mana still left in her. After healing her earlier, and more recently using the mana to flake off webbing twice, there's not much for me to work with. Fortunately, River has some more stored within him, so I pull at that to be able to work with more than just fumes.

I flush out the poison from Lathani's body, working methodically to shift it bit by bit. Perhaps saturating the venom itself and then manipulating it directly would be a good idea, but that would take more mana than I have to spare. As it is, even just working with Lathani's body to force all the poison out of a slit I cut in one of her veins takes almost everything I have. I use the last of my mana on healing damage that could potentially cause her lungs to fail.

As it turns out, the venom attacks the central nervous system. It probably *is* the same venom as was used on Fenrir but in a much higher dose, since sleeping pills tend to do the same thing. However, just as too high of a dose of sleeping pills can have serious effects, I imagine that too much of this poison can too.

"I need to Meditate," I say wearily after quickly checking on Bastet. Her system seems to be more robust than Lathani's—because she's into her second tier? Either way, the healing potions that River keeps pouring down her throat are helping her natural healing to almost keep up with the damage the poison is doing.

She's still unconscious, though, and I hope that that's just because the venom is designed to first send its targets off to sleep and then kill them, rather than because some serious damage has been done that I haven't yet been able to detect.

I only have three more healing concoctions, River warns me. I nod.

"Okay. Space them out as much as possible, please. But I need to Meditate." Not only do I need the mana regeneration, but I also need the clarity of mind and a break. The battle has been hard on all of us, physically and mentally.

As I drop into the third level of Meditation, trusting in my Bound to protect me, I realize that the frenetic situation means I didn't think of doing something that would have helped: using at least Light Meditation to bolster my mana regeneration while working on healing my Bound.

I don't think it would have worked in my battle with the danaris. That required just too much focus and mental activity for me to do any level of Meditation—not at this point, anyway. But healing my Bound? I should be able to combine that with the lightest level of Meditation. And *that* means I should be able to do more at a time.

Once I sense that my mana pool is full again, I shift to Light Meditation and open my eyes. My mind feels refreshed, and a headache I didn't even realize I had is gone. I still feel strained, like I've overexercised a muscle that's not used to being used to that extent, but it's better than before.

It's amazing what a little meditation can do. Or Meditation, at least.

"Right," I say to no one in particular. "Let's do this."

CHAPTER FORTY-THREE

Enemies Into Friends

B y the time all of my Bound are healed and awake, night has fallen and I'm completely exhausted. Not so much physically as mentally. I've used my magic more today than ever before, I think. Yes, I technically might have used more mana in total when I was practicing saturating different carcasses and hides, but that was in a completely non-stressful situation. This, where it's the wellbeing of my Bound in question, is a different story.

But finally, everyone is fine, including Persephone and her babies, which has allowed Hades to finally settle down. While I was healing her, I had a feeling that making the wrong move and hurting any of the beings I was working on would lead to him doing his best to kill me. I mean, I don't think he'd have succeeded, but it would have been uncomfortable for all of us if he'd tried.

The danaris, fortunately, is definitely dead. I was half worried that even with the connections between its brain and its body completely destroyed, it might find a way to repair them sufficiently to keep living. Or worse, that it might have some backup organ that might allow it to survive. But no, it's gone.

Unfortunately, none of us feel like eating it. As a beast that I'm sure had to be near the top of Tier two, its flesh must be full of Energy. But as it is, even Sirocco turns her beak up at it. I suppose that with the venom I controlled still flooding its system, its meat might be spoiled anyway, but apparently, no one wants to take the risk of being poisoned by its sedative once more.

Instead, I pull a couple of carcasses out of my Inventory. Although Sirocco and the kiinas are reluctant to accept the Energy-less meat, they're obviously hungry enough from the battle to eat it anyway. For myself, I pull out a nice pot of thick stew containing meat, potato, and a couple of the plants I've found. Seasoned with salt and that basil-mint leaf, it's satisfying both to the mouth and the stomach.

As I eat, I eye the danaris carcass again. Poisonous or not, I do want to harvest a few bits from it before we go. A good bit of that chitin for one thing, and its venom for another. But for now, there's something more important to do: rescue Fenrir from where he's waiting patiently for us to come. Seeing that my raptorcat companion seems to be satisfied for now, I speak to her.

"Bastet, can you go and scout the cave, please?"

Can I go too? asks Lathani. She's been rather subdued since the battle. I'm not sure exactly why, and I didn't want to invade her privacy too much by diving into the Bond between us—unlike Sirocco, I sense that I could do that with her. Perhaps it's because she's finally experienced what a true fight is. Yes, she was present for the fight with the salamander, but she wasn't really a part of that one.

"Sure," I say after a moment's thought. "But," I continue, a serious expression on my face and a stern tone in my voice, "do you know now why you shouldn't have been in that fight at all? Why coming with us against both my and your mother's instructions was *dangerous*?" Perhaps she'll recognize it now, when she hasn't before.

But I didn't die, Lathani points out with a hint of her usual attitude, apparently not completely subdued.

"You didn't, but do you realize just how close you *were*?" I wait for a moment, but she just looks away from me. "You got down to forty-one health points, Lathani. *Forty-one!* Out of *eight hundred and ten!* That's only *five* percent of your health left!"

Lathani makes a grumbling sound, and I just know that I haven't gotten through to her yet.

But I survived. I just . . . I just wanted to be part of the group. It seemed like it might be . . . fun.

I want to shout at her—what about this was *fun*?—but refrain. That's not what she needs. "And was it fun?"

I mean . . . She hesitates. *It was nice to work as a team but . . . no. It wasn't fun.*

I nod slowly. "That's because survival isn't fun," I say quietly. "We're here to save Fenrir, not because we want the . . . glory of the fight." I eye her—she doesn't look convinced. Perhaps I need another tack. "Have you thought about what would have happened if you'd died here? What would have happened to the rest of us?"

That startles her a little. Clearly, the question has never occurred to her. As well it might not—the young think they are immortal. And perhaps it says something about just how much the time in this world has matured me that I no longer think that *I* am.

I wasn't going to die, she says finally. *And if I did, then . . . I don't know. You'd have taken my body back to Mother?* She seems far too blasé for the situation.

"And you think that your mother would just accept that?" I chuckle humorlessly. "She'd have *killed* us, Lathani. Heck, she might still kill me for Binding you at all, but we've covered that one already. But if you died? Under my watch?" I shake my head. "I should have kept you away from the battle entirely," I murmur more to myself than anyone else. I should have known better. Rather that Lathani be angry at me for keeping her safe than dead.

Yes, I know she somehow managed to survive all that, but frankly, that's more to do with luck than anything else. I should have benched her, tied her to the back of Persephone, kept them both safe. But then we might not have won this—though neither Lathani nor Persephone were exactly key elements of the fight, they both contributed to our final victory.

I sigh mentally. Hindsight is apparently twenty-twenty, but even that's not enough to tell me if I made the right decision here.

She wouldn't, Lathani interjects weakly, startling me out of my thoughts. It takes me a moment to remember exactly what she's responding to. I give her a long look until she shifts to avoid my eyes. She doesn't believe her words herself, even. *Fine. She wouldn't have . . . taken it well.*

Finally, I sense the right kind of emotions coming from her side of the Bond, the rebelliousness absent.

"Precisely. Your actions don't only have consequences for you. Remember that." It's something I have to keep in mind more too. "But Lathani," I add, not wanting to leave it on that note. The nunda juvenile looks up at me with wariness, as if expecting another reprimand. "Well done on that fight otherwise. Bastet and River told me that they almost didn't need to order you at all—you worked well as a supportive team member. That's exactly what you should have done."

Surprised pleasure floods down the link from her side, and I reckon that she'd be blushing if she could. She turns back to Bastet and pads off towards the cavern without another word, but I know she's happy with the praise.

While I wait for the two feline-types to return, I rest and muse over the fight. About Lathani in particular.

Honestly, apart from not wanting her there in the first place, and the scare at the end, I'm pleased with how she operated in that battle. River and Bastet between them have filled me in on what happened while I wasn't able to watch. Though none of them managed to do as much as render a limb ineffective, apart from the one River disabled at the start, they kept working at it. At best, they hoped to find a weak spot; at worst, they would provide a distraction to help me. That was their thinking, anyway, and I agree with it.

Lathani followed their lead perfectly, using her agility to land blows and bites on the spider creature's legs. Though none of them had much impact, her physical weight often shifted the leg off-course, sometimes making the creature over balance by a little. Of course, it had ten legs, and at least seven were working, so there was no chance of making the creature fall over by affecting a single leg, but her efforts still had an impact on the battle, however small. Especially after the fire fried some of the danaris's ability to control its limbs.

She also moved in of her own accord to help defend Persephone when the kiina was slammed off her feet by a blow to her mid-back. Actually, the kiina was lucky not to be paralyzed by that attack—the bones of her spine were damaged, but her spinal cord wasn't affected. That's fortunate because even if I think there's a high chance I *could* mend a spinal cord, there's no way I want to *have* to.

Overall, she showed a lot more judgement than she did in the battle with the velociraptors. She actually worked as part of the team rather than as the loose cannon I was concerned about. She still has a tendency to continue with the same strategy whether it works or not, but she displayed a lot more willingness to listen to her elders—even when uncoerced by the Bond—than previously and now has a better ability to react to the situation at hand. Of course, she *does* have the Bond in place. I wonder what impact that had.

Oh well, the Bond will be gone in a few hours, and then we'll be able to see on our next hunting trip together. Assuming that Kalanthia doesn't kill me for Binding her cub, of course.

But that's something for later, even if it is rather worrying me *now*.

I sense more than see Bastet and Lathani coming closer, their natural stealth abilities combined with the darkness making them hard to distinguish.

"What did you find?" I ask the pair as they materialize out of the gloom and into the puddle of torchlight.

No more enemies free, Bastet answers my question promptly. Lathani is still looking a little subdued. Maybe Bastet had a word with her too while they were out of hearing range. *Many creatures behind white walls.*

Well, that matches what I got from Fenrir's own memories; the fact that all the creatures are behind what I guess are webbed walls makes it easier. Even if we aren't here to hurt any of the other animals, if they blocked our way to rescuing Fenrir, we would have to.

"Is it safe enough to bring the cubs along?" I ask her. She pauses for a moment in thought, then lets out a chirruping sound.

A moment later, a patter of light feet heralds more shapes entering the torchlight, previously invisible in the shadows. I guess that's my answer, then.

"You were safe?" I ask Stormcloud when she comes to rub against me in greeting. She chirps at me, which I interpret to mean "yes," then goes to join Trouble and Ninja in tearing eagerly at what's left of the carcasses.

They watched the battle from a tree, Bastet informs me. I suppose that's as good a seat as any. It's probably the least likely to be vulnerable to attack—unless a snake or bird came along to eat them, of course. Actually, it's just as well they weren't anywhere near the danaris and its sedative-soaked web. With their undoubtedly small health pools, they'd have probably succumbed to it before I could get them out.

Anyway, that was why they were out of the battle completely. Though, as I take a good look at them, I realize that they probably will be joining us in battles against normal opponents soon enough. That means creatures that are Tier one, not a creature like the danaris, for obvious reasons. My little raptorcub nephew and nieces—or should I consider them cousins? Aunt Bastet?—are growing up fast.

But speaking of growing up fast, the sooner we can get the spawn of that danaris out of Fenrir, the better. As soon as everyone in the group appears to have eaten their fill and replenished the energy they used in the battle, I decide it's time we make a move.

"All right, then," I say to everyone as I pack the carcasses back into my Inventory. "Let's go get Fenrir out." At least my mana has had a chance to replenish a bit. It would have worked faster with a deeper level of Meditation, but I wanted to spend that moment with my Bound, just eating with them and relaxing in the knowledge that, despite appearances at times, we actually managed to win the battle without casualties.

I sense that I have some notifications waiting for me, but I'm more anxious to get Fenrir out than to check them. Whatever it is can probably wait for now. I do focus briefly on shifting my Energy absorption to my debt just in case I've somehow earned enough Energy to level up again. That's the only thing that's likely to be time sensitive. I could probably have checked them earlier, but I didn't think of it—I'm tired, and the night isn't over yet.

Grabbing my torch, we head towards the darker spot in the already dark terrain. Neither of the moons has risen yet, so we're experiencing the world as dark as it gets. I even drop into Fade, just to benefit from better vision in the dark, but I pull out again when I realize that the torch works against me in that state. It's too dark for me to extinguish the torch and rely solely on Fade, so I guess I'll have to just be careful when moving.

As we enter the cave cautiously, the flickering light of the torch illuminates a surprising number of webbed prison cells. The cave itself is quite bare with none of the half-eaten webbed bundles that I might have expected to be hanging down from the ceiling. Though, on second thought, the danaris didn't really seem to be the type of creature that would be able to climb a wall and hang on the ceiling like the house spiders I'm familiar with from Earth.

There is a small pile of something odorous that I don't want to investigate on one side of the cave, but other than that, it's just a beehive of walled-off cells.

As I try to sense which one Fenrir is trapped within, I wonder idly how this cavern was created. It certainly doesn't look natural, but unless the danaris had Earth-Shaping or something similar, I don't know how it could have made this place. And I don't think it had Earth-Shaping—it certainly didn't show any indication that it did; wouldn't it have done so before it died if it could?

So what, did it dig this place out itself? But a good portion of the holes seem to have been made in the stone of the mountainside. It was strong but surely not *that* strong. Its legs would wear away before the mountain did, I would think.

Maybe it was some other creature that was either chased out by the danaris or had already abandoned the cave for whatever reason. At least, I hope they don't use this cave anymore—for all I know, the danaris was in a constant war with some termite-like species that can chew through stone but not through web, and some of these webbed-off cells aren't cells at all but tunnels.

Well, I'm only really here for Fenrir anyway. If I can find him, that is—the Bond tells me that he's nearby but not exactly where he is. I don't want to just start opening up these cells willy-nilly. Not only might I potentially give entrance to the original occupants, but who knows what other creatures the danaris amassed to be part of its larder?

Then I feel like hitting myself in the forehead. I have a *far* easier way of finding out information about the world around me. *Inspect Environment.*

The pulse goes out of me in an expanding ring. For a few moments, I can see all the creatures hidden behind the webbing as the red glow outlines them, just like the pylobuses were visible even hidden underneath foliage.

My eyebrows rise in surprise at just how *many* creatures are here. At least fourteen, but it fades before I can count them all. But not, however, before I take note of the single creature that is outlined not in red but in blue.

Moving over to the door of the cell, I once more employ the same method I used to cut my Bound out of the venom-laced webbing. Within a few moments, the covering is falling away, and an ecstatic lizog almost bowls me over as he leaps at me, making hissing noises to express his happiness at seeing us again.

"All right, all right," I say through my laughter, the similarity to a typical Earth dog, happy when its master comes home, once more impossible not to think about. "We're here. Now can you let me up?" After all, sixty kilograms—or more—of solid muscle sitting on my chest is not the easiest thing to shift in the awkward position he has me in.

Sending a hint of apology across the Bond along with his gratitude, Fenrir leaps off me and goes to greet the rest of the pack. I push myself to my feet again, brushing off the dust that has coated my new armor. Seeing the patch of white webbing that I cut away to release Fenrir, I pick it up and finger it thoughtfully.

It's not sticky, that's the first thing I notice. Actually, it's surprisingly soft. It's also pretty strong and thickly woven. Wrapping it around the exposed skin of my hand, I nod unconsciously. It's quite warm. As a test, I send a bit more mana into it. The energy is absorbed relatively easily—the material clearly counts just as much as "flesh" as the venom did earlier.

A smile creeps over my face. I think I've solved my undergarment situation. Heck, if I do this, I'll have armored undies, given how strong the material is. It'll also help with my issue of getting cold in the approaching winter. Honestly, I think this is the best find I've made so far this week.

Once Fenrir has finished expressing his happiness and gratitude to all the members of our pack—even the raptorcat cubs, despite them not actually doing anything but *being* there—I call him over.

"Let's get that thing out of you," I tell him, pointing at an area in front of me as I settle down to the ground. I sense Bastet, River, and Hades communicating between each other about who should go on guard and where. Sirocco stayed outside anyway, not enjoying being confined indoors. Persephone and Lathani both settle near me, Persephone watching the other cells with watchful caution, Lathani watching me and Fenrir with curiosity.

What are you going to do? she asks.

"He's got something from the danaris implanted in his flank," I tell her, not sugarcoating it. "An egg, or multiple, is my guess. We need to get it out before it hatches and starts eating him from the inside out." The nunda cub recoils in disgust.

It did that? Disgusting. Then she looks around at the number of cells and the creatures trapped behind them. *Are they . . . ?*

"Yes."

All of them?

"Probably." I shrug. "Now, let me concentrate, please?" I request pointedly. She goes quiet immediately and turns her attention back to me.

I close my eyes and sink into Light Meditation to help with my mana regeneration, then press my mind into Fenrir's body. I'd rather dedicate as much focus to this as I can—I don't want to accidentally miss any of the parasites if there are multiple.

The visibly bulging area in Fenrir's flank is still just as painful as when I entered his mind earlier, perhaps more. The wound has actually started getting infected. It's unsurprising—the slice the danaris made in his flesh probably introduced bacteria. In addition, it's clearly not a part of his body, and he's been unconsciously trying to reject it, inadvertently worsening the situation.

But it's okay. It's nothing I can't heal with enough time and mana. He's alive—the parasites haven't yet eaten anything important.

As it is, there *are* multiple, but only three. Well, there *were* three. One has already hatched and cannibalistically consumed one of the others. It's interesting that it hasn't yet started trying to eat at Fenrir's body, preferring instead to consume its own egg case and the egg case and body of its sibling. The other egg contains a shifting mass, but it hasn't yet hatched.

The baby danarises are ugly things about the length of my index finger and more similar to fat larvae than their spider parent was. Though, I can see an element of similarity: the larva that has hatched shows a slight definition in its body shape that is reminiscent of its parent's three-part body. It also has ten small legs, but they are completely dwarfed in comparison to its bulbous abdomen. That it can move at all seems a miracle, but it clearly can.

It has no resistance to my magic as I sweep through its body. At least, I sense that it attempts to, but its resistance is the equivalent of a person trying to hold back the sea with a bucket—useless. The one that hasn't hatched yet is even less aware and doesn't so much as attempt to resist.

I sense that I could liquefy their internal organs with even less effort than it would take me to heal a papercut. But would that be the right approach here? After all, I have no desire to leave an enemy at my back, but what if I could turn those enemies into friends? Or not *friends* but *Bound*.

Using Dominate on them will be easy as anything—at the moment, the creatures are complete babies with no resistance. I would probably have even been able to Dominate them when I first arrived in this world—if I had managed to get past their parent, that is. Maybe I should feel bad, but having so recently fought the creature they obviously become completely nullifies that inclination. I don't know how fast they grow, but I'm not willing to keep them around without a Bond in place.

However, I should probably offer them some food—and not my lizog, who they will no doubt turn to eating once they've fully finished consuming the eggs from which they hatched. And their unfortunate sibling too.

Getting them out is simple enough. As I flake away the skin the protective webbing is attached to, the nasty incubation area in Fenrir's side is easily revealed. As I look at exactly what's been hidden beneath, I have to admit to feeling pretty sick and wondering whether I really do want to leave *any* of these larvae alive. After all, having fewer creatures that propagate in this way has to be a good thing.

Then again, as long as the larvae are fed and protected, surely they don't have to eat meat that is still on a living creature. Well, I guess I'll find out.

Based on the relatively small entrance wound and the way Fenrir's skin is bulging around the larvae, I have to guess that the danaris had some sort of ovipositor to insert its eggs into the flesh of its victim. I suppose it makes a sick sort of sense—if the eggs only just fit in, they will be harder to get out and will be more protected than they would be with a massive open wound.

Not that that makes much difference for me.

Gently pouring mana into the area, I expand the size of the wound, then start healing the damaged area so that the larva and the egg are forced to and then through the hole they entered. They fall on the ground with a wet sort of thud and the larva immediately scrabbles at the ground, showing signs of distress. I'm not surprised, but I'm not particularly sympathetic either. Yes, it's a relatively defenseless baby . . . but that's *my* lizog it was going to eat.

After taking a moment to pull another small carcass out of my Inventory, I create a little area around it with sticks also pulled from my Inventory. Placing the larva and the unhatched egg in it—at opposite sides of the area just in case the moving larva wants to continue its cannibalism—I cover the area with my shirt. The reason I do that is that I suspect the environment might be a bit breezy for them—they're used to the protected environment of Fenrir's body, after all.

That done, I turn my attention back to healing my sluggishly bleeding Bound even as I send a brief thought to my other Bound to keep an eye that the creatures don't escape. Continuing with the healing, I make sure to take extra care in pushing out any further foreign bodies, whether bacterial or material, and letting them drain with the blood.

It doesn't take too long before Fenrir is healed and as good as new, not even a scar showing any indication of what happened. It's taken a lot of mana, of course, but staying in Light Meditation has definitely helped me regain what I used more quickly.

Fenrir is delighted to finally be free of the nagging pain in his side, and he leaps at me again to express his joy. I can't resist stroking him and making a fuss of him too—at times I was worried that I might lose him forever.

Now that the most important task is done, I need to think about other matters, like what to do in the immediate future.

It's dark for one thing. Though heading back through the forest is possible and may not even be too dangerous considering the group we have, it's certainly riskier than traveling in the light. The dark would hamper Sirocco and me in particular, who don't have very good night vision.

Even though the others have reasonable or good night vision, none of them are primarily nocturnal creatures, so it would still impact them. That would mean that we'd have to slow down so as not to trip over roots and break ankles or legs.

Honestly, it makes more sense to stay here until dawn and then travel back in the light, but I put the question to my Bound. The response is unanimous: stay here.

Well, that makes the decision easy, I think with a little humor. I suppose it's not too surprising that they'd agree on that: it was a tiring journey here and then an exhausting fight with the danaris. Not to mention that several of them were hunting before Fenrir was kidnapped. They want their sleep, and so do I, if I'm honest.

The next question, of course, is where to stay. Remaining inside the cavern should be the easy answer since here we'd be protected from the elements and less likely to suffer from a surprise attack. The problem there is that it's not exactly quiet in here. And it stinks.

The other webbed-off caves each have their own occupants, beings that are scared, in pain, and unhappy with their current accommodations. Trapped, with no occasion to leave for a toilet break, they've no doubt defecated and urinated in their areas—from terror and agony, if not need. It certainly smells like they have, and the evidence in Fenrir's erstwhile cell supports this theory.

I could probably ignore the stench to sleep—I'm tired enough. Though, I'm not sure that I could so easily block out the sounds of so many creatures' suffering—or whether I even should try. There is another factor to consider too. Although it's probably fairly unlikely, there's also the possibility that one or more could break out in the middle of the night. In such a case, they'd be unlikely to recognize us as the ones who killed their captor; instead, they're far more likely to just straight out attack us.

Of course, there's a simple solution to most of these issues, though not an easy one: release the creatures within and deal with the larvae. I should probably do it anyway—I have no desire for more danarises to be running around the forest, kidnapping other creatures, and propagating further. At the very least, I need to kill the larvae inhabiting these other bodies and then redirect the victims so that they don't see us as easy prey and attack.

Another possibility occurs to me: I could just kill everything currently in this cave except for my Bound and the couple of larvae I wish to keep. It's probably the easiest solution and offers the bonus of Energy for myself and whoever of my Bound help me kill them.

After a moment of thought, I shake my head and dismiss that possibility. Well, I relegate it to Plan B status. I have another idea. It's riskier and will take much more of me than Plan B, but it also has much more potential payoff. Plus, it's more humane and would give me less guilt to add to what I'm already carrying.

My inspiration comes from remembering how I saved Sirocco from the thornbush in the vine-strangler forest. Because of that, she wanted a Bond with me, and she's since proven to be an invaluable member of the team. Who's to say the same might not be true of these other creatures? Though, I won't force it on them if they're not interested.

Longingly, I imagine curling up with Bastet and River on something soft cobbled together from items in my Inventory. Or even some of that soft webbing . . . *No, I can sleep later*, I tell myself firmly. *This is an opportunity I'd be a fool to miss. And sleeping while they're suffering . . . That's just cruel.*

However, that means letting creatures out individually, healing them, feeding them, offering them a drink, and then offering them the chance to leave. Only if they choose to stay can I then offer them a Bond. I might exhaust myself with healing only to find that none of them choose to stay to take the Bond. Or only a few.

That's the risk I have to take, I decide. I'd feel bad just condemning all the creatures to death, anyway—they are as much victims of the danaris as Fenrir was. And releasing them with gaping holes in their sides and probably foreign bodies from the hatchlings as well is basically just giving them a more distant death sentence.

"All right, this is what I want us to do." I start to outline the plan that I've pulled together. It's not particularly complicated: the main thing is that I figure not everyone needs to be awake the whole time. I need help just in case one of them turns violent when I'm not in a state to defend myself, or if it turns out that one of the creatures is unexpectedly strong. But I don't think I need everyone hovering at all times. Heck, it might even work against me—if the creature is convinced that it's about to be eaten, it's unlikely to take my healing well and might even turn violent in self-defense. We therefore work out who should be awake and when. For the first attempt, we decide that everyone will remain awake, but only Bastet and River will be near me.

Deciding to take a logical approach, I start near the entrance of the cave and pick the first webbed cell to the left. First, I try to use Inspect Fauna—logically, that would seem the best option. But it fails, perhaps because I can't actually see the creature. After a moment of thought, I use Inspect Environment again. It's not as good as Inspect Fauna, but at least it gives me a sense of what's inside and whether it's dangerous to me or not.

The creature seems to be curled up in a lump, which makes it hard to see details, but the relatively faint red color to it indicates that it's probably not too much of a threat. Heartened, I move closer. As I try to send soothing thoughts to the inhabitant, I use my mana-coated finger to slice halfway around the webbed disk.

"It's okay. I'm trying to help you," I say soothingly, not expecting the creature within to understand my words but hoping that the tone will communicate my meaning somehow. Pinching a little of the material between my index finger and thumb, I pull it back slowly.

I'm wary in case the creature shoots out some sort of attack, making sure that no part of me is directly in front of the now-open section of the cell. No clawed limb, or biting mouth, or venomous stinger emerges. I take that as a good sign.

Once more coating my finger with mana and tracing it along the web, I dissolve

the threads holding the "door" shut. Bit by bit, I pull the material back while murmuring soothing words until the creature inside is revealed.

It's one of the reptilian deerlike creatures I've seen before. It's terrified, pressing
itself against the back of the cell, which isn't even big enough for it to stand. The
entrance is even smaller—the danaris must have just shoved it straight in without
much care. In fact, from what I see of the dried blood around the entrance to the
cell, it probably has more injuries than just the expected one.

"It's okay. Come forward. I just want to help you," I say encouragingly. If ever it
would be a good time for Animal Empathy to kick in and help me communicate, it
would be now. While I'm wary about potentially enraging it, I need to know more
details about it.

Stio

Tier 1 beast
Special abilities: None
Health: 250u
Mana: 100u
Minimum Willpower recommended to Dominate without other impacting fac-
tors: 15

Fleet of foot and agile, this herbivore usually travels in groups of between five
and twenty individuals. Prey to anything that can catch them, few succeed in getting to any stage higher than Tier one.

I draw back a little from the entrance to the cell and encourage Bastet and River to
do the same. They do, though they seem uneasy about it. I understand their caution
and even check with them that they don't have any specific reason to be worried.
They don't—they just would prefer to be closer to the potentially violent beast.
Not that I'm too worried about this one. Herbivore and prey beast both imply that
there's not too much for me to fear.

After confirming that this creature, a stio, is herbivorous, I pull out a few plants
that I've been storing in my Inventory for my own consumption. After placing
them in the entrance to the cell, I also pull out one of my pots of water and a pylobus shell. I fill the shell and place it next to the plants.

Patience is the next requirement, something I don't usually have much of.
Fortunately for me, the deer is clearly thirsty, as it doesn't take long for it to stick its
head out of the hole and dip its pointed muzzle into the water.

Shifting closer carefully, I keep murmuring soothing words, resorting to the
kind of nonsense people often use with animals as I move. The deer is obviously
aware and wary of my approach, but apart from a few flinches here and there, it
clearly considers the water more important than keeping away from me.

When that bowl is empty, it skitters away, but when I refill it, it approaches again. This time it's willing to tolerate me staying by the entrance to the small cave. Frankly, I don't know if Animal Empathy is helping me, if creatures in this world are generally less wary, or if this deer is *really* desperate for water, as I was expecting it to take much longer than this.

After it's had more than half the bowl again, it diverts to attacking the plants lying in the entrance, clearly starving. I gaze at the creature. Helping this one is complicated by it being almost trapped by the shape and size of the entrance to its cell: I will have to hurt it more to get it out, which will probably completely undo the progress I've just made.

While I'm a bit doubtful about whether this creature will be a good fit for our group, I think I'm going to need a Bond to get the stio out at all. I could just leave it to die, of course, but condemning it to die of dehydration just because I don't think it will be useful to me is more than I can justify to myself. So, offering a Tame Bond it is. I suppose I could always cut the Bond later if it proves to be useless to us.

It said that the minimum Willpower stat required to Dominate the stio was fifteen points; I wonder whether that has any impact on Tame? Well, perhaps I'll find out.

Catching the deer's gaze, I invoke my Skill.

"Tame."

CHAPTER FORTY-FOUR

Beyond What I'd Thought
Reasonably Possible

By the time dawn's light is peeking over the horizon, I've gone past the point of exhausted and into being almost delirious from tiredness. My brain feels wrung out, and an ache permeates the whole of my body. Even my Core is throbbing, the constant emptying and refilling having put it under strain. Unfortunately, I don't think I've earned a new Masochist achievement for my pains. Instead, I sense that I need to take it a bit easier on the casting magic front for the next few days or risk rupturing something. I suspect that it would be either my Core or Energy channels that would be damaged, and I know that I could repair them even if they were, but I'd rather not have to deal with it in the first place.

Fortunately, I'm done, or at least, that's what I realize after I reach for the next webbed hole only to find myself grasping into the thin air of the cell entrance. I've done the whole tour of the cave, returning back practically to where I started.

My brain is numb enough to barely be able to register this fact, and I allow River to guide me to sit next to a little fire he set in the middle of the cavern. I'm surrounded by shapes, some familiar, some less so. I feel a sharp pain somewhere inside and a brief sense of loss. It takes my overtired brain far too long to realize that it's the sensation of Lathani's Bond snapping.

I have enough awareness to be relieved about that: however much it helped with the fight, however right it felt to have her properly as one of us, it's really not worth enraging Kalanthia with an active Bond when we return. Enraging her more than she probably already will be, anyway.

Sleep, Master, River tells me firmly, a rumble in his throat. *You have done everything necessary. You need to rest.*

I don't have enough energy to argue with him and drop into a dreamless sleep before I even lie down.

When I wake, it's obviously been a number of hours. Not enough for me to be fully rested, but my mind actually feels like it might be able to work. I'm also ravenous, so I immediately pull out a bowl of thick stew as soon as I sit up.

I drink it hungrily by using a rough spoon I managed, at some point, to find some time to carve—it's really no more than a slightly indented piece of wood—and am single-minded in my focus until it's all gone. My thirst still continuing to annoy me, I next pull out my canteen and finish the water left in it.

With all the animals drinking from my big pot, I'm going to have to do some work to restock my supplies of safe drinking water. Or just take the risk that whatever parasites or diseases I pick up from drinking contaminated water directly from the river I'll be able to deal with by using Flesh-Shaping. I still need to refill my containers, whichever choice I go with in the end.

My thirst and hunger levels satisfied for now, another basic need becomes uncomfortably obvious. I sidle out of the cave and find a spot to the side of it to do my business. After covering the smelliest parts with some earth I dig up with a stick, I return back to the cave.

Pausing at the entrance, I have to take a moment to just absorb the sight. By the end of the night, I was so exhausted that even with my higher Intelligence stats, I'm unable to bring up any clear image of what the cavern looked like.

Now, though, is a different story.

My efforts were successful beyond what I'd thought reasonably possible. Every single webbed cell is now open—all fourteen of them—and a good two thirds of the occupants have remained. If the sight of prey beast sitting warily beside predator wasn't sufficient, the number of connections I now feel from my Core space is more than enough proof. In the course of a single night, my group of Bound has more than doubled.

Of course, it's not as simple as that. Although I'll need to spend more time analyzing each of the new Bonds independently, I know that they are not all designed for the long term. Some, in fact, I sense will run out in the near future; I decide to put analyzing those to the top of my list.

I would love to say that I remember each and every one of the beasts as the unique individuals that they are . . . but I don't. Frankly, after the fourth, the rest started to blur as my exhaustion took over. Hopefully, my sleep-deprived self didn't promise anything I shouldn't have.

I also have the nagging sense of notifications informing me of some, probably significant, changes to my status sheet. Just as I'm about to open it, I'm interrupted by Bastet.

What are we doing now, Pack Leader?

That's a very good question. A very good question indeed . . .

Kalanthia may be worried about Lathani, but honestly, I'm not feeling all that keen to hotfoot our way back there knowing her reaction is likely to be poor. Even if, in a sense, it's at least partially her own fault for not keeping sufficient watch on Lathani, despite knowing we were going after something that had managed to kidnap a lizog.

However, I do need to get back to the cave in the near future—there are still a number of preparations I need to make before we engage with the quest. And despite grumbling about Kalanthia's lack of surveillance of her cub, I know that

SHAPING   321

she'll be worried and I don't want to force it to extend longer. But there are several good reasons not to go right now.

I look up at the sky, estimating the time, then check my map to remind myself of where we are in comparison to home. It took us a good few hours to get here, and that was with all of us running flat out and me riding Hades most of the time. Not all of my new Bound are likely to be capable of either that speed or distance. Especially not with how poor a state most of them are still in.

With as much time as I've spent asleep, the sun is already past its zenith. Much as I dislike the idea of staying in that smelly cave longer than we need to, it might actually be the best option for us. We can then set out at dawn tomorrow and spend as much time during the day traveling as is necessary.

It gives everyone a day to rest and recover and offers me some time to get to know my new Bound. I'd like to become familiar both with them and their Bonds and to figure out how to integrate those who are going to be sticking around into our life. Hopefully, Kalanthia won't mind us descending with such a large group of extra bodies. Well, if I survive seeing her again, anyway.

"We'll stay here for the day and night," I answer Bastet, the cave going silent as I speak, all eyes within it fixing themselves on me. I feel a hint of unease at having so much focused attention on my person, but I power through it with the same kind of mask I used to use in the occasional big meeting at work where I was obliged to speak. "I want to get to know all of you a little, and delaying until tomorrow will allow our slower and weaker members to make the journey back home within the day. As it is, I suspect we'd be risking traveling through the dark if we left now."

What do you wish us to do, then? Bastet asks next, the rest seeming happy for her to speak for them.

I hesitate. There are lots of things that *need* doing—collecting food and water are just the top of the list—but until I know what everyone is *able* to do, I can't correctly delegate. And until I know what exactly is in each of the Bond agreements, I'm not willing to send off my most competent Bound, as I can't be certain that my safety will be guaranteed. If they were all Dominate Bonds, I would be, but as they're Tame Bonds, it might be another story.

"For now, just rest and relax." Hopefully, that will give me the time I need to review the Bonds. Then I wrinkle my nose as I look at the various piles of excrement both inside and outside the cells. "Actually, if any of you can find a way of reducing the smell and making this cave a little more comfortable, that would be good. But we won't be staying here for long. Also," I continue as a thought occurs, "I'd like all the pieces of white webbing put in a pile, please. But don't touch the web outside—it's soaked with venom, and I don't want to have to heal any of you." More to the point, I don't want to tempt fate and risk something bad happening to my Core through overuse. "I'll let you know when there are other things to do."

Master, River interjects hesitantly. *Many are still hungry and thirsty. The aid you offered helped, but they have been without for too long. You may recall that some were nearly dead when you opened their cages.*

That's unfortunately true. I think back to my vague memories of last night's marathon. Three of my new Bound were so weak that I thought them too far gone when I removed the web covering their cells. I tried anyway, and their flesh sucked in mana like a hungry sponge, the energy helping to make up for some of the damage that starvation and, more importantly, dehydration had caused. Invariably, these chose to take the Bond.

In fact, there were only four where the Bond was not successful. I recall that one of them was Tier two and had probably only recently been caught. Although it accepted the food and water, it rejected the healing as much as it could and beat a retreat as quickly as possible. I'm thankful that it was clearly not predatory, probably the only reason the danaris managed to catch it, and it didn't seem interested in a fight. I was only barely able to send a wave of Flesh-Shaping into the larvae in its wounds to kill them before the beast vanished. Hopefully, it won't get sepsis, but if it does, then that's on it.

Two of the others came out fighting, and of those we were only able to calm down one enough to heal it. Even then, it only allowed me to remove the danaris larvae within its wound and to close the hole in its side before it took off. The other one my Bound didn't manage to pin down, and it escaped with the larvae in its wound. I can only hope that if the larvae survive, they get eaten by something bigger.

As for the final captive, that was our only death, unfortunate as it is to lose anyone at all. It was unreasonable and too powerful to pin. I think that the pain and perhaps knowing what was going on had driven it mad. I don't blame it, but at the same time, it was getting too risky for my Bound—I wasn't willing to lose one of my companions for the sake of a creature that was unable to see when we were trying to help it.

But that still leaves me with ten new Bound, one of which was a massive surprise—I'm itching to speak to him. But River has a point.

"All right. Let's all go down to the closest water source. Sirocco, can you find that, please?"

The bird sends me a wave of acceptance, then wings her way out of the cave—apparently, she overcame her dislike of being inside it at some point during the last few hours.

"We'll move together at the pace of the slowest member," I tell everyone with a little sigh. Looks like I won't be able to check my notifications for a while. *Unless . . .* , I wonder, eyeing Hades. *Was his willingness to carry me before contingent on it being the most efficient means of transport or battle?*

Only one way to find out.

CHAPTER FORTY-FIVE

Management

As it turns out, Hades isn't too bothered by the idea of carrying me. Perhaps I have more hang-ups about it because of associating that sort of thing with horses and vehicles. He seems to be approaching it from the logical perspective of questioning whether it's important in some way and will improve the security of the group in general. Since prioritizing finding food and water over staying here to look at my notifications is arguably to help the group, he is willing to carry me.

Before hopping on his back, I go around the cave and grab all the sections of web that were previously covering the cells. I tuck half of them into my Inventory and hook the other half onto my belt—I want to see if there's a difference between them having been in my Inventory or not.

I also take a moment to look at the collection of ugly larvae that I've amassed through the night. With two or three in each creature, I managed to collect a total of twenty-seven squirming creatures.

My original "cage" was nowhere near big enough; at some point during the night, one of my Bound—probably River—expanded it so that it's now an extended ovoid and using the stone of the cave as one of its walls. The others are blocked off with sticks and chunks of wood. Did he ask me to give them to him? Perhaps—the latter half of last night is enough of a blur that he could have danced naked in front of me and I probably wouldn't remember.

Well, he's always technically naked . . . Skinless, then, perhaps.

Anyway, it's probably just as well that he changed the shape. As I noticed when I saw Fenrir's wound, the larvae are more than a little voracious and preferentially cannibalistic: the carcass I put in originally is almost untouched, as the larvae first killed and consumed their brethren over eating other meat. Or maybe it's because the carcass is lacking in Energy. Just in case that's the reason, I carefully direct a bit of my mana into the meat. Then I hesitate.

I'm about to leave to allow my Bound to eat and drink—what should I do with all these larvae right now?

"River," I say quietly, and my Bound quickly appears beside me. "How secure would you say this enclosure is?" He eyes it, then looks back at me.

None of them succeeded in escaping during the night, the lizard-man informs me. *They do not appear able to climb unless they have something to brace themselves against, falling back every time they try. The only time any of them even came close to escaping was when I was re-forming the cage—I left a small gap, which one managed to squeeze through.*

I was right—it *was* River who expanded the cage. But good to know.

"So, you think they will be safe enough if we leave them here for now?"

As long as nothing investigates the cave while we are gone, he agrees. Then he eyes me again. *Though, I am unsure how many will remain if we leave them until dusk: they seem particularly keen on eating each other's flesh,* he comments with a little distaste. I suppose that as cold as the lizard folk's society seems, they don't actually encourage cannibalism.

"True, but that might be a good thing," I say, putting words to the practical voice of reason inside me. River frowns.

How, Master? Do you not wish to Bond many of them?

"I'd rather have quality over quantity," I tell him. "If only one remains when we return, then it is the best of them all at surviving. And that means it might be more powerful later than a group of mediocre danarises would be."

But what if it dies later?

I understand where River's coming from—given his own species' rather lax approach when it comes to rearing young, he's used to a very high mortality rate. There, quantity is definitely the most important factor.

"I hope it won't and I will do everything necessary to make sure it doesn't." I shrug. "Between being able to get meat for it and heal it if it's injured or sick, there should be a good chance of it surviving." At least, I hope I can deal with sickness, but I figure that Flesh-Shaping should be able to, as long as I know enough about what I'm doing.

In the end River sends over the sense of a shrug and says, *As you wish, Master.*

After covering the cage with a couple of shirts, I take a moment just to check there are no holes the larvae could squeeze through, then reinforce a couple of places that look like they might shift if a larva tried to climb. Then, casting another glance around the cave, I head towards the entrance and hop on Hades's back.

"All right, everyone. Let's go," I say, and our large cavalcade starts moving towards the forest line.

I open my message panel, and the first message in the list almost makes me fall off Hades when I try to leap in the air with delight. Hades isn't appreciative of my rambunctiousness, but he settles when I send him a sense of apology down the Bond.

Congratulations!
You have earned a Skill: Fire-Shaping

Fire-Shaping
By studying fire, you have become capable of transforming your mana into fire

mana and have proved yourself capable of controlling and shaping this magic according to your will. Henceforth, you will now be more easily able to summon fire at a thought and shape it. However, as you have also learned, fire has its own will, and further practice will be required to fully master it.

I finally got it! I cry mentally. After all that time trying to get it, I've *finally* earned Fire-Shaping.

Wondering why it suddenly happened now of all times, I read over the description again. This time around, I notice that it mentions both that I can summon fire at a thought *and* shape it. Perhaps that's my explanation.

After all, it was only just before we set off to rescue Fenrir that I worked out how to transform my mana into fire mana, burning my finger the first time I did it. I didn't have the opportunity to experiment with it as I was intending before the hunt went wrong. Then I was too focused on other things. It's only in this most recent battle that I started actually using it.

So I guess it makes sense that Fire-Shaping would only have happened now. But now that I *have* earned it, I have much more hope that I will be able to learn other shaping Skills. After all, this particular notification has given me something that is, hopefully, a good clue into what I need to do to demonstrate sufficient knowledge to the System for it to ease the rest of my efforts.

First, I need to transform my magic into a different form. That's clearly stated in the description of Fire-Shaping, and I know it's true of Flesh-Shaping too. Lay-on-Hands mentioned healing magic, and I've noticed the difference between my normal mana and what I use when healing my Bound. I didn't have to work out how to transform mana into "flesh-shaping" mana in the same way, but Lay-on-Hands must have been a bit of a shortcut—healing magic must be similar enough to make the jump easily. Perhaps if I'd been given Fireball as a Skill, I might have more quickly been able to leap to Fire-Shaping by observing and exploring it.

Second, I need to actually shape something with my new form of magic. Once again, for Fire-Shaping, it says that in the description. And for Flesh-Shaping, that's exactly what I did when I caused an aneurysm in the salamander's brain, despite the original intentions of the Lay-on-Hands Skill.

So for Earth-Shaping, I reckon that I'll need to first discover how earth mana is different from my mana, then work out how to shape it. Simple, right?

Probably not, but at least now I have somewhere more hopeful to start.

Resolving to test out this new Skill at a better time and in a better place than sitting on my Bound's back, I open the next message. This one is more expected and informs me that Animal Empathy has significantly increased in level. Frankly, considering the amount of communication I had with so many different animals last night, I'd be more surprised if it *didn't* rank up.

Congratulations!
You have advanced a Skill past Novice. Animal Empathy is now Initiate 1. As well as becoming more able to interpret the communication cues of animals you observe, you have become able to mimic some of the cues to convey a message. Note that not all physical communications will be possible to mimic, but the addition of mana into this Skill can help to compensate for some of your body's limitations. You can attempt to mimic non-physical communications with mana. Success in mimicking communication cues is directly related to your familiarity with the subject of your attempts and your capabilities with mana.

Yep, that Skill definitely got a real workout last night. It's potentially useful, though, especially with trying to convince non-telepathic beings to consider a Tame Bond. Or to not eat us.

Hopefully, familiarity with similar creatures will carry over to helping my attempts to communicate with a new being—and not mean that I accidentally insult it in the way that's so easy to do with foreign languages. I'm not entirely sure what it means by "your capabilities with mana," but I can only imagine that it relates to my control or my mana pool, so it probably links with my Intelligence stat. Or Wisdom. Or both.

Moving on, I see another rank-up message.

Congratulations!
You have advanced a Class Skill past Beginner. Inspect Fauna is now Novice 1. Due to your use of this Skill, two new effects have been discovered.

Effect 1
Gain more information about how much Willpower is required to Dominate a being in its current state. More information may be offered that gives insight into what might convince the being to take the Bond. Chances of extra information being offered increase with each level of this Skill past Novice.

Effect 2
You now have the option to send out a more subtle probe for information about a subject visible to you. This probe will stop acting as soon as it detects that the creature is likely to become aware of its presence. This will therefore potentially return less information than the usual use but has a much lower chance of alerting the target.

Now, this one is interesting—more information about the Willpower required to Dominate a creature in its current state? Is that linked to whether the creature is scared or trapped or something? And if so, is that because of the number of Bonds I made last night with creatures in poor condition, probably with pretty low Willpower? Thinking about that makes me glad I didn't choose to use Dominate—I'd be feeling a bit guilty now if I had. As it is, though, I'm just interested to see what it actually tells me in the moment.

Knowing what the creature might want to be offered is useful too—it could have increased my success rate with Bonds last night even further or meant that I knew not to even try with the ones that tore up Hades and River. I can imagine this being useful with the lizard folk and, frankly, any time I consider Bonding a creature. I wonder if it will say whether Tame or Dominate is the best choice or if that decision is still left up to me.

The second effect is also pretty interesting. The chance to send out a subtle probe that has a low probability of alerting the target? Useful! Especially once we descend into the valley and potentially encounter creatures that it may be dangerous to draw the attention of.

Of course, I do note the fact that it says "lower chance" and not "no chance." It doesn't say which stats affect the probability of the probe being detected, but I suspect that it's probably more to do with a comparison between my stats and those of my target. If my target outclasses me too much in stats, probably in either Wisdom or Willpower—or both—then the chance of being detected is likely to be much higher. But either way, it's a good new effect.

Incidentally, having now had three Class Skills rank up, I'm starting to wonder whether having two new effects is standard or more reflective of the diverse uses I've been putting my Skills to.

The final message is a bit of a surprise: Tame has ranked up again!

Then again, perhaps I shouldn't be too astonished—I did just Tame about ten different creatures in a single night. If two Bonds alone got me to Novice, maybe I should instead be shocked that ten new Bonds didn't shoot me all the way to the peak of Journeyman.

Congratulations!
You have advanced a Class Skill past Novice. Tame is now Initiate 1. Due to your use of this Skill, two new effects have been discovered.

Effect 1
Quantity is its own version of quality. However, to gain the full benefit of this, delegation is key. You can now nominate Managers for teams of up to five additional individuals. The Managers will have a more limited version of your control over the Bonds. Note that no control will be accessible by your Managers that has not already been ceded to you. Due to your diverse types of Bond and the fact that the division between Tame Bonds and Dominate Bonds is not always clear, Managers can be either Tamed or Dominated beings, and their control is not limited to only others of the same Bond type.

> Effect 2
> You have made the choice of diversity over homogeneity. You have more than
> fifteen Bound and no more than two of the same type. As a result, you have a
> choice to make.
> - Group special abilities: Once per day, per Bound, each of your Bound can
>   use an ability from any other of your Bound.
> - Individual enhancement: Once per day, per Bound, you can borrow an abil-
>   ity from any of your Bound.
> Which ability would you like to choose?
> Group special abilities / Individual enhancement

This is new. This is the first time I've had to make a decision on a rank-up
message. And it's a hard one. From what I gather, the first option would allow
each of my Bound, once per day, to copy a special ability from another of my
Bound. I have to guess that the kiinas' air-blades and Bastet's fire breath would
be the main candidates here, though it's possible some of my other new Bound
have special abilities too.

That could be pretty powerful. Imagine all of my Bound sending an air-blade
at the same time and overwhelming an enemy. Or half sending an air-blade and the
other half setting fire to them with fire breath. That's definitely a way of turning
quantity into quality as the first effect talked about.

On the other hand, giving *myself* the ability to borrow abilities would be pretty
awesome. Right now, it's more limited than the group option: I would only be
able to borrow an air-blade twice and fire breath once, and whatever my other new
Bound have as well. But this could turn me into a *really* badass beast—once per day.

I briefly bask in dreams of pouring out attacks like some sort of magical gun
turret in the future, when I potentially have access to attacks of every element and
not just one. But after a moment, I shake my head and push it away.

It might be cool, but I mustn't make my decision based on cool factor. No,
there's a more important element to take into consideration—resources.

Both the kiinas' air-blades and Bastet's fire breath use mana. The air-blades are
relatively economical in mana use—they only seem to take ten units or so. The fire
breath, on the other hand, is rather heavy in its mana consumption, as it generally
takes seventy or more units of mana at a time.

I need to check out the stats for all my new Tamed Bound, but of my core
group, only Bastet, River, and the two kiinas have the mana pool to even pull off
a single fire breath. However, they could each pull off an air-blade. So, unless borrowing the ability is "free," which I seriously doubt, then clearly there are other
considerations than just the once-per-day limitation here.

At the same time, although my mana pool is significantly better than any of
those of my Bound, what if, in the future, several more develop abilities more along
the lines of Bastet's mana-consuming one than the kiinas' relatively economical

one? In that situation, even I wouldn't be able to get the complete benefit of having access to the full pool of my Bound's abilities.

There's also another factor to take into account: replicability. With sufficient study, could I succeed in replicating the attacks of my Bound all on my own? I've so recently gained Fire-Shaping and haven't really fully gotten to grips with it yet. When I do, what if I could learn to do a type of fire breath by myself? Or even not have to rely on it being a breath attack—what if I could make jets of fire come out of my palms like a flamethrower? Could I learn to create a wind attack of my own?

Honestly, given what I've learned to do so far, I suspect that I'm far more likely to learn to create an attack that is at least similar to what my Bound are capable of than that all my Bound will be able to do the same.

Plus, another thought. What if by essentially having access to mana abilities before reaching Tier two, my Bound are therefore more likely to develop mana abilities? It's an exciting thought. Though, it does bring up another question: what if abilities can only be shared within the Tier?

I frown at the text hanging in front of my eyes. It is stubbornly silent, not giving any indication whether my sudden fear might be true or not. *Well, it doesn't say that there's a limitation like that,* I think to myself. *It talks about once per day, per Bound—surely if Tier was a limitation, it would list that too. Should I take the risk?*

Because, honestly, I think I'm leaning more towards group empowerment than personal empowerment. If I'm trapped or out of mana or need to keep my mana for all the other magical things I'm able to do, then I've essentially wasted this choice.

Just like the first effect mentioned, delegation is important. As the most recent battle and subsequent night proved, I have enough uses for my mana at the moment. Unless I double or triple my mana pool, I'm unlikely to have much spare mana floating around in times of crisis—certainly not enough to become a magical gun turret.

So, just as the first effect is linked to improving the group, I think the second effect should be too. And I've been so caught up in trying to make my choice for the second effect, I haven't even properly considered the first.

The ability to raise some of my Bound to the position of manager both excites and frustrates me. I was wondering how the hell I was going to be able to properly direct so many Bound, but this is an easy solution. But it *is* frustrating that even in a world that never knew humans before me, I can't get away from corporate hierarchy. At least this time I'm at the top! Though, it is interesting that I can essentially grant a certain amount of power over the Bonds to my managers. I already know that Bastet and River will be my first candidates, but I will have to spend some time considering who the others will be and who I'm going to assign to them.

Suddenly, I become glad for all my experience in HR. I wouldn't have any clue where to start otherwise. But as it is, I know to draw up a job description of what I'm looking for, create profiles of all the candidates—both for manager roles and for their teams—then put them together to create teams focused on different strengths.

Strangely excited to get started, I choose "Group special abilities" and confirm "yes" when it asks whether I'm sure, then close the window.

We're traveling through the forest. When I check my map briefly, I see that we're heading away from the cave and into an area that has no detail on my map. By observing the cavalcade for a bit, I realize that we're following a combination of Sirocco's scouting and Fenrir's nose. Hades is traveling beside Persephone, right in the middle of the group—the safest position, I guess. Probably a good idea with me focusing so much on my notifications.

Seeing that we're still traveling, I decide to quickly look at my status screen. There have been enough changes to it that I want to actually see them.

Name: Markus Wolfe		Race: Human	Class: Tamer
Level: 13	Energy to next level: 68%	Energy absorption rate: 32u/hr	Energy towards debt: 85% (250)
Intelligence	36+1 (+5%)	Mana: 496/555 (15u/IP)	
Wisdom	42+2 (+5%)	Mana regeneration rate: 1100u/hr	
Willpower	43+10 (+25%)	Health regeneration rate: 53u/hr	
Constitution	22	Health: 330/330 (15u/CP)	
Strength	20	Stamina: 120/120	
Dexterity	20	Stamina regeneration rate: 200u/hr	
Class Skills:		Non-Class Skills:	
Dominate – Initiate 2		Flesh-Shaping – Journeyman 8	
*Companion Bond		Stealth – Novice 3	
Tame – Initiate 1		Animal Empathy – Initiate 2	
Fade – Initiate 3		Meditation – Journeyman 5	
Inspect Fauna – Novice 1		Energy Manipulation – Master 1	
Inspect Flora – Beginner 9		Sensation Management – Beginner 7	
Inspect Environment – Beginner 9		Spearmanship – Beginner 6	
		Archery – Beginner 5	
		Blunt Weaponry – Beginner 3	
		Knife-Work – Beginner 5	
		Fire-Shaping – Beginner 3	

In addition to the rank-ups, Flesh-Shaping went up *four* levels, which is particularly impressive considering it's already in Journeyman and I've definitely felt other Skills slow down their progress at that point. I can only guess that it was because I was healing so many differently shaped creatures—and sometimes having to heal far more quickly than usual when my targets were doing their best to escape. Healing non-Bound was also a big challenge, even though their unhealthy states made it easier than I experienced with Lathani when she was being difficult. Of course, the work I did with the venom also probably helped—that was definitely a different use of Flesh-Shaping from my normal healing.

Several of my Skills went up a little. Fade went up a level, as did Inspect Environment, Archery, and Blunt Weaponry. Knife-Work went up two. I guess that's probably linked to my use of a poisoned blade, but it could also be because of how I cut the larvae out first with my knife to reduce the amount of mana I needed to expend. I also got a nice chunk of Energy, either from the danaris or from Taming so many creatures.

Honestly, I'm still not entirely sure if I do get Energy from that. I seem to get some with Dominate, but with Tame? I haven't noticed, but I've generally been more focused on other things each time. With Sirocco, it was the vine-strangler forest. With Lathani, it was saving Fenrir. With all these others, it was more about getting through the whole lot so we could sleep in safety and peace.

Perhaps one day I'll be able to definitively answer the question, but it's not today.

Seeing as we're still traveling, I pull one of the bits of spiderweb off my belt. Once more fingering it, I try to identify its texture. Somewhere between wool and silk, I decide in the end. It's warm, far warmer than silk, but it's not nearly as scratchy as wool. This will be *perfect* for clothes.

After pulling one of the pieces from my Inventory, I close my eyes and compare them. Surprisingly, there's not much difference. Both accept my mana and take about half my mana pool for a piece I'd estimate at about half a meter squared, more or less. The one that was in my Inventory takes a little bit more mana, perhaps 350 units where the other takes a little less than 300, but it's not a big difference. Certainly not if I compare to what saturating carcasses is like.

Does that mean the danaris didn't feed much Energy into this when it was creating the woven material? Or is it because it's a product rather than an implicit part, so it's less saturated anyway? Or perhaps it's because it's been sitting around for days—maybe it did have more Energy but lost it over time? Though, in that case I would expect there to be significant differences between the pieces that I haven't put in my Inventory, and there don't seem to be.

Once the pieces are saturated with mana, I test my control over them. To my glee, I discover that I can basically do the same thing with this material as with hide: I can change the shape easily. If it remains the same volume, it takes precious little mana to change, but I can also expand it with extra investment of mana.

I test some weapons on the material too, as much as I can while riding on Hades. While I doubt it will have much effect on blunt damage since it has no rigidity to it, which is part of its attraction, I discover that it does have some potential as armor. My flint arrowheads battle to pierce it, although they would probably have more luck when traveling at speed, and my wooden spear fares even worse. I can manage to cut it with my knife, but I have to put some effort into doing so.

Clearly this material isn't as strong as Earth spiderweb would be scaled up, but it's *far* better than I could achieve with plant fiber and much more flexible than equally armored hide would ever be. And if it has the same effect as silk does on projectiles, this is definitely a good find.

Tucking the patches of web into my Inventory, I resolve to create some clothes for myself at the first possible opportunity.

Now, on to more important matters: the job description for a manager.

Opening my notes panel, I start the process that is still all too familiar to me, despite my time in this survival forest. It seems like you can take the human out of Human Resources, but you can't take the resources out of the human—even if we did try, much to my shame now looking back on it.

At least this time I won't be squeezed from both sides, feeling the directors breathe down my neck via my manager as they push to offer as little as possible at the same time as the candidate is pushing to get as much as possible, knowing that I'm going to have to find a compromise that risks satisfying neither party and that this could cause the candidate to go elsewhere or my manager to override me and offer something that is probably a slap in the face to the person I've been in contact with, which they'll probably blame on *me* . . .

No, this time *I'm* the director, and the balancing act is going to be different, though perhaps just as delicate in its own way.

By the time we reach the river, all the erstwhile prisoners drinking thirstily at the clear water, I think I've jotted down a few important points. But those can wait until the immediate tasks are done.

I hop off Hades's back and thank him for carrying me. I give him a little stroke down the neck, and he leans into the touch for a moment before rearing back and giving me another suspicious look, just like he did when I did the same to Persephone. Am I doing the kiina equivalent of flirting or something?

"I'm just trying to express my appreciation," I tell him. "If you don't like it, say so, and I'll stop." He seems to consider the question warily for a moment.

Just appreciation? Nothing else?

"Just appreciation," I assure him. "Perhaps friendship."

And for my mate? he demands.

"The same." I'm pretty sure I was right with my suspicions—this *is* some form of kiina courtship.

Then I will allow it as compensation for my aid, he tells me loftily, pressing his neck to my shoulder insistently. I contain my laughter as I lift my hand to stroke at his smoothly scaled neck—as long as I stroke downwards, anyway. Ah well, even if it *is* a form of flirting, he seems to like it well enough.

After a few moments of just enjoying a little bit of peace, I move away.

"River, will you come with me?" I ask. The lizard-man immediately moves away from the new Bound he's been standing next to and walks quickly over to me.

Where are we going, Master? he asks curiously.

"Just a little upriver so I can collect some uncontaminated water."

He tips up his chin briefly in response, and we walk away together in companionable silence.

While we don't go far, I do make sure the sight lines are a little obscured between us and the main group. For good reason—I don't want our conversation to be detectable by the others. One other in particular.

"One of your village?" I ask as soon as I think we're far enough away. I dip my water containers into the stream and, deciding to just risk it, drink thirstily straight from one of the pots. The clear, hopefully uncontaminated water tastes delicious, better than my boiled and cooled versions for sure.

Yes, River responds a little cautiously to my question. *One of the other Unevolved.*

"How was he taken?" I ask. "We're pretty far from your village, aren't we?" I pull my map up to check. Sure enough, although we've headed vaguely in the direction of River's village, we're much higher up the mountainside than it is. It's like a triangle: the distance between Kalanthia's cave and the village is the hypotenuse, and where we are is the point of the third angle. Not a right angle, but not much bigger than one.

Catches-leaves has never been known for his navigation skills. He used to even get lost in our village when he was a hatchling. He is a year younger than I am, and frankly, the fact that he survived to adulthood has always been a bit of a mystery. To my knowledge, he's disappeared three times, only to eventually make it back to the village rail-thin and on his last legs. But always with enough to grant him access to the communal carcasses. River pauses, looking and feeling contemplative. *I sometimes wondered whether he should have been called Last-chance-lucky instead of Catches-leaves. It certainly would be more apt.*

"So, you don't think it's an indication that the Pathwalkers have sent out a hunting party for us?" I check with him. That, actually, was the first thing I became concerned about when I had the time to think about the implications of a lizard-kin being caught by the same creature that also came close enough to Kalanthia's territory to catch Fenrir. While it could be explained by the danaris ranging widely, this area is almost as far from the lizard folk's village as we were near Kalanthia's cave. The chances are that this other Unevolved was closer to the danaris's hunting range when he was caught.

River hesitates.

Catches-leaves would never be chosen to be part of such a hunting party, he answers.

"But . . . ?" I prompt, hearing it unspoken in his voice.

But I suspect that there likely is one, nonetheless, he continues reluctantly. *They would have had to search for our tracks after going around the Forest of Death, and I doubt that Shaman would have been part of the hunting group, so the ones that were following us probably returned to the village before sending out another party. But I wouldn't be surprised if they're in the area.*

"Won't they know that we're with Kalanthia?" I ask, a little surprised.

Not necessarily, he answers. *Just because we took Lathani does not mean that we are in league with the Great Predator, who they may believe to be dead. It will no doubt have occurred to them, but they will be reluctant to trespass on the Great Predator's territory without proof of her death. Too many were killed in the first expedition; the village can't afford to lose the same number, let alone even more. No, I think they will try to find and then follow our tracks, hoping that we are not connected to the Great Predator and that they will be able to pursue the village's justice without invoking her wrath.*

Eyeing the number of creatures around me now, I grin a little sardonically at River.

"They think we're an easy target, huh?" I ask with more than a hint of irony. He seems almost apologetic on behalf of his village.

They do not have all the information.

"No kidding," I mutter in response as I return to filling my containers. Then, glancing back up at River, I ask another question. "Does Catches-leaves not know?"

River does his equivalent of a shrug. *He is not the most observant. Nor is he involved in any sort of decision-making, being at the bottom of the hierarchy. I asked, but he couldn't seem to say for sure whether there were more or fewer Warriors around. Shaman was there before he was captured, though—as was Herbalist. They are rather . . . unmissable. Even by Catches-leaves.*

"So, we'd better assume that they are hunting us." I sigh. Hopefully, Kalanthia will be keeping more of an eye out this time. I seriously don't want to return to find that she's been brought near death again. Or worse—killed. Even if that would let me off the hook when it comes to Lathani.

Master, I have a suggestion, River says, breaking into my thoughts. I send a wave of expectation through the Bond, prompting him to continue. *I think you should Dominate Catches-leaves.*

All right, that wasn't what I was expecting.

"Why?" I ask, surprised.

He's feeling very anxious.

"About the Bond?"

River sends a sense that it's linked to but not exactly that. *He's always followed the rules of the Pathwalkers. Even when he was starving in the wilderness. He was always terrified that he wouldn't have a home to come back to, that he would be banished from the village if he ate something.*

"Even if there was no way of them knowing?" I can't help but ask, taken aback by just how strict the rules of the lizard folk seemed to be.

If he disappeared for a week and came back looking as well as when he left, they would know he'd eaten something, River points out. Okay, fair.

"He's eaten something now, though, right?" I check—though my memories really aren't clear, I'm pretty sure that he was one of the emaciated ones.

He did last night—he was too starved to resist. That's why he's anxious. But he's refusing to eat now, and he really needs the sustenance.

I blink as I try to make the right connections to understand what River's getting at without saying it directly and how that relates to him suggesting that I Dominate a creature who's already taken a Tame Bond.

"So," I start slowly, "you think I should Dominate him so I can force him to eat? I don't want to do that," I tell River firmly. Shouldn't that be Catches-leaves's choice?

Yes, but not entirely. Catches-leaves isn't convinced that we have the strength to offer him what he's used to with the village. That we don't have the protection or the healing. He doesn't realize how much better *it is with you.*

While it's nice to hear River's enthusiasm, I'm still not convinced that this is the best option.

"Can't we just *show* him what it's like?"

Master, please, River pleads. *Catches-leaves will* die *if he doesn't eat soon. And he won't eat until he realizes that you are a stronger, kinder leader than the council of Pathwalkers and that being banished is worth it. He's offered to serve you temporarily in gratitude for releasing him, but he would be much better off if he served you alone, like I do.*

That's part of what's worrying me: I still don't know River's true feelings on the subject. What if his argument is being motivated by his own sense of Bond-induced loyalty to me?

"I don't see why I need to *force* it," I tell River firmly. "Surely he will eat when he gets hungry enough? Like he did when we released him from the danaris's clutches." The lizard-man seems unexpectedly frustrated by my continued reticence. "River, why are you being so emphatic about this?"

He paces for a little in silence, then stops and turns to me.

I do not know what others of your kind are like, but from what I have seen, you operate differently from us. For us, strength is paramount. The village is led by the strongest Pathwalker and its defenses are directed by the strongest Warrior. They are both far stronger than the Unevolved, who in turn are stronger than the hatchlings. It is thus that the hierarchy is determined.

"How does that relate to the topic at hand, though?" I protest. River sends me a look that brings me up short—I've never seen him look quite so reproving. I let him speak.

Catches-leaves does not know your strength. We killed the danaris, but that was not you, that was us. He needs to know that you are powerful enough to command his permanent service, not just his temporary service, offered out of gratitude. Only then will he adapt to being able to eat as we do. Without that, he will serve quietly at the periphery before disappearing back to the village—except, by that point, he will be easy prey. I fear he will not make it back. I . . . I don't want to lose another one of my kin.

I digest the information in silence. I think I understand, as much as I dislike the idea. And it kind of makes sense: at the very least, he needs to know that I'm stronger than he is. He would probably feel better knowing that if it comes down to a clash between me and the Pathwalkers—which it probably will—I would come out victorious. He needs that to give him a sense of security.

This is going to be a repeated theme with the lizard folk, isn't it? Their society is based on strength, so of course any new leader needs to prove that they have the strength to overcome the old. Maybe this is what River's been trying to tell me all along.

Though, I do wonder exactly what's driving River right now. Is it just because Catches-leaves is another lizard-kin, or is this some sort of psychological tactic to make himself feel better? Is being Bonded to me justified if I can convince others of his kind to do so? Perhaps I'm reading too much into this. Ultimately, if Catches-leaves isn't going to eat during the whole of his time in the Tame Bond, *something* needs to be done. Whatever his reasons, River is clearly trying to save Catches-leaves' life, though he's advocating an odd way of doing it. Odd to me, at least.

"Okay, thanks for the information," I say, standing up. All my water containers are now filled, and I've got the answers I need, even if they aren't exactly what I want.

Returning to the group, I pull a number of carcasses out of my Inventory. I'm running pretty low—we'll need to do some serious hunting soon—but this should be enough for now, even with as many mouths to feed as there are.

"All right, everyone, listen up," I say, once more quailing a little inside as every single eye comes to rest on me. Except for the one who has eyes pointing both forwards and backwards, that is. "If you prefer to eat meat, come and help yourself to the carcasses here. No arguing—share and share alike, please. Any arguing or attempts to attack another Bound will mean that you are required to step to the side and won't be able to eat until everyone else has finished," I warn.

Even if the Bond I have with them doesn't allow me to directly order them to step aside, there's always good old-fashioned physical force. Though, I hope it doesn't come to that.

"If you prefer to eat plants or insects, feel free to forage around the area. Please don't go far, though, and make sure to send an alert down the Bond and run back here if you detect any danger." They are all still looking at me. "Okay, then. Go ahead?" I finish, more questioningly than I intended.

Still, it seems to have had the right effect: about eleven creatures, including Lathani and the cubs, move towards the carcasses I've set at small distances apart. Another three shift towards different areas. Two start grazing the bushes and the plants poking out of the leaf-litter floor covering. One starts rooting through the leaves themselves, finding grubs to eat. That one is rather curious: he looks like a scaly orangutan with four arms and a long tail. That he's as comfortable in the trees as he is on the ground is made clear a moment later when he swings up into the branches above.

One is conspicuous as he stays apart from all the others, not starting in on a carcass or hunting for food in the undergrowth, and pointedly looks away from those who are eating. I guess that makes my next move obvious.

Starting with Catches-leaves it is.

CHAPTER FORTY-SIX

Hierarchy

The new lizard-man is standing next to a tree, pointedly not looking at the mix of creatures clustered around the carcasses, his nostrils flaring as they catch the scent of the food. His hide is tight on his bones and his tail is far thinner than River's—perhaps they keep fat stores there and Catches-leaves' are running low. Those surrounding the bodies are already devouring the available meat—a flock of locusts, only carnivorous ones.

"We're *really* going to have to go hunting," I murmur to myself as I watch. Although I have the vague idea that not all the Bonds I have are permanent, or even of particularly long duration, feeding them for as long as they *are* Bound to me is going to be a challenge. Then again, more mouths hopefully mean more bodies to actually do the hunting in the first place.

Putting that issue to the back of my mind, I walk over to Catches-leaves. Speaking of short Bonds, his definitely is: he only offered me seven days but offered to obey me in everything within those days, as long as it does not put him up against his village.

Not remembering exactly what my Inspect Fauna told me about him, I cast it again from a few paces away.

Samuran: Catches-leaves
Tier 1 beast (Unevolved)
Special abilities: Stealth
Health: 720u
Mana:110u
Minimum Willpower recommended to Dominate without other impacting factors: 25 (10)
Bound (Tame – 7 days) of Markus Luke Wolfe. Most commonly used weapon is a club, though this beast is capable of using claws and teeth when required. Social beast with strong capacity to form bonds.

Samuran, eh? That's different from what River's information said. Is it because of the different Bond? Because I used Dominate with River, did that somehow allow me to change his species to the name I was using? Except Sirocco's just says "bird," and she has a Tame Bond too. Perhaps it's because I used Inspect Fauna on

Catches-leaves before I offered him a Bond. I didn't pay much attention to what the Skill told me, but maybe it kept a record somehow. It's a different name from what Kalanthia uses, which sort of answers that question too.

It's interesting that Catches-leaves already has some sort of special ability—Stealth. So, it is possible to have abilities at Tier one? Maybe it's only in special cases. Anyway, I guess we have some of the answer as to how he's survived this long: he's a sneaky little bastard, apparently.

He also has lower health but higher mana than River. The Willpower required to Dominate is the same, though, and easily manageable. If I go down that route, anyway. Is the ten in brackets a reflection of his current state? I guess it must be—I suppose it makes sense considering we're already Bonded and he's literally starving.

Otherwise, the description at the end is much the same, though, apparently, Catches-leaves is more prone to using a club than a spear. I suppose it makes sense: he seems to be much lower on the hierarchy ladder than River, so I guess a Pathwalker wouldn't make a weapon for him to use. A club is much more easily found in nature, even if he could make his own spear if he chose.

However, those are thoughts for later, if at all, given how short the Bond is. Closing the message, I start moving closer to Catches-leaves again. He startles as I crack a twig near him. He flinches into a crouch, and his mouth opens slightly to bare his teeth.

"It's okay," I say to him, noting his gaze as it snaps towards me. I frown as I look at his eyes. Is it just me or are they unfocused? "I'm not going to hurt you."

Catches-leaves pushes himself back up to stand, his body language still wary, his spikes roiling with orange and red. I wait for him to say something, but he remains silent.

"All right, then," I say softly to myself, then clear my throat awkwardly. "River . . . Runs-with-the-river, that is, said that you're not willing to eat."

Not permitted, he replies. The mental communication is far more closed-off than River's has ever been. That's probably because after touching souls in the Battle of Wills, holding emotion back seems a little pointless; Catches-leaves and I haven't done that.

"It *is* permitted," I argue, wondering how he will respond. "That's why the carcasses are out there."

Not permitted. I have no tokens. The Pathwalkers would be angry. This time a little emotion slips through Catches-leaves's tight control. I'm briefly hit by a moment of bone-deep hunger and desperation to eat. It seems like River's assessment of the situation has been spot-on so far.

"But we currently have a Bond," I point out. "And I say it's fine." Catches-leaves looks away.

Not a Pathwalker, he replies after a moment. *Only here for a short time.*

"Only because you wanted it that way," I remind him. If I had to guess based on River's words just now, the short duration is because he doesn't think he can last much longer than that without food. Frankly, I agree with River's doubt about whether he can even last that long, but I guess he knows his own limits better than I do. His words about me not being a Pathwalker are also concerning—if he needs me to be one to feel able to eat, I'm not sure how well I'll get through to him. I really don't want to just Dominate him for the sake of it, but if it will save his life . . .

"Look, I'm willing to offer a longer-term Bond—a permanent one. Then you could eat as much as you like." I gesture at River. "Does he look half starved to you?"

Another bit of emotion slips through the blockage: an instant of longing. Then it's shut away like it never existed. Catches-leaves slumps and turns back to me.

The Pathwalkers hunt you. You are prey. Runs-with-the-River is already doomed; I do not wish to be included. I agreed to a temporary Bond only in gratitude for freeing me. For what little my service might be worth. I'm not sure I'm meant to hear the last—it's quiet, and even the changing color of his spikes is subtle.

"The Pathwalkers will be the ones who regret facing me at the end of this," I tell him, meaning every word of it. The more I've learned about the way they run things, the more I want to interfere. Even if I didn't have to deal with the samuran village to keep them safe from Kalanthia, I'd probably end up doing so anyway. He doesn't look convinced, though.

He glances at me again, and once more I frown. I'm sure of it—his eyes aren't focusing on me.

I . . . have seen no proof that you have the might to face even one of our Pathwalkers, he tells me earnestly, if nervously, but I'm only half listening.

"Catches-leaves, how far can you see?" I ask abruptly. The lizard-man hesitates.

My . . . I can see, Catches-leaves replies but with so much defensiveness that I become almost convinced of what I already suspected. Moving slowly, I bring my hand up to almost cover his eyes. He shifts restlessly, but doesn't object or back away.

"I'm going to move my hand away. Tell me when it starts getting blurry or you can't see it anymore."

As you wish, he consents reluctantly, and I start moving my hand away. I'm barely past the end of his snout when he interrupts me. *It is blurry.*

"Okay, well done," I tell him. "Now I'm going to keep moving. Tell me when you cannot identify what the object is at all." I keep moving slowly but steadily further away.

I cannot identify it anymore, Catches-leaves says reluctantly when I'm only three paces away from him. He sounds miserable. I'm not surprised. No doubt this is what he would consider to be his greatest weakness. If the Pathwalkers knew about it, would they turn him out automatically? Or would they allow him to continue living in the village as long as he continued providing?

Though, how he's able to hunt—or survive—in the forest when he would probably be considered legally blind without corrective lenses, I don't know. Maybe that's how he got an ability while still Unevolved: he had to learn it to survive. I'm abruptly filled with admiration—I know how daunting it feels to consider life with only one eye, and that was with good vision in that eye. To live for over *two years* in this dangerous environment with such limited sight is something else.

Unfortunately, I'm no eye doctor capable of prescribing lenses, and even if I was, I have no way of creating them. However, thinking about my own eyes brings up another possibility. I turn and beckon my other lizard-kin Bound.

"River, come over here, would you?" The lizard-man comes easily at my call, stopping just short of me, and eyes Catches-leaves quizzically.

Master, I thought you were going to use Dominate on him? he asks, and I sense that it's a private communication between us.

I never said I would. I wanted to get more of an idea of the situation.

River's tail shifts restlessly, clearly not pleased. But that's not why I called him over.

"Catches-leaves has very weak eyesight," I say bluntly. The samuran in question stiffens as I reveal his weakness so easily, even as River stills. "I'd like to compare your eyes and see if I can fix his." For a moment, it's almost like the world holds its breath. Then it turns out that it's not the world, it's just Catches-leaves doing that.

You think you could help me? he asks hesitantly, letting out an explosive breath. It's almost like he fears that even voicing—well, his version of it—the possibility might mean that it doesn't work.

"It's possible," I tell him, "though not guaranteed." I don't want to raise his hopes too much: I don't even know what the issue is. But . . . I'm actually pretty confident. I healed my own eye in my first days in this world. Since then, my Skill has undergone a massive change and is now capable of regenerating organs, repairing and *creating* flesh, and mimicking other areas of flesh. Heck, I already healed an eye when Fenrir's was damaged in sparring and regenerated River's arm when the Skill was still practically new to me. I wouldn't be confident in doing this without the template of River's healthy eyes, but with it?

Of course, it's possible that it isn't an issue with the eyes at all; I'm not sure I'm so confident about healing brain damage, so there is a chance it won't work. But I won't know that until I've had a look.

"Are you willing to let me try," I ask him, "knowing that there's no guarantee it will improve anything?" Catches-leaves breathes in and then out shakily.

Even the possibility that it might work is . . . more than I've had ever since Herbalist said it was incurable. Please. Go ahead.

"All right." I consider the situation for a moment. "Let's sit down," I suggest, then match action to words and sit cross-legged on the ground. It's not the most comfortable place, but I reckon that I'm going to need my full concentration for this. Sitting down means that I don't have to pay attention to staying balanced on my feet. Plus, I should be able to use at least Light Meditation to keep my mana regeneration up, if not Medium Meditation, since I won't be moving.

The two samurans haven't moved and just shift uneasily. I look up at them, raising my eyebrows quizzically.

"What's the issue?"

It's hard for us to stand again, Master, River reminds me after a moment of hesitation. *We are vulnerable here.*

"That's a good point," I reply slowly. "But the sooner we can help Catches-leaves—if we can at all—the better. And I honestly think you should sit down," I say directly to the lizard-man in question. "It's likely to be painful since I don't really want to mess around with your nerves. It may also be disorienting if it works. River, you can just crouch if you prefer. I need to be able to touch you, and preferably on your head, but you don't need to sit."

River nods and quickly shifts into a crouch, bowing his head so I can reach it. After a moment more of hesitation, Catches-leaves sinks to the ground, shifting awkwardly into a sitting kneel. Good enough.

He's twitchy but doesn't flinch away when I touch the space between his eyes. Instead, he leans closer so I don't have to stretch to remain in contact with both samurans. Closing my eyes, I pull on Medium Meditation to help calm my mind and increase my mana regeneration. Then, I sink my mind into my Bound.

I've made good progress with my Flesh-Shaping recently, so sinking my mind into both samurans at the same time is difficult but not impossible. With my hands on their heads, I don't have to travel far to compare their eye structures. Relief fills me when I realize that, indeed, there are significant differences between the two of them. Although there are also differences between their brains, they are only slight and surely not enough to account for the vast gulf between their abilities to see.

Catches-leaves's eyeballs are the wrong shape, and the lens inside seems to be completely malformed. Frankly, it's a bit surprising that he can see at all. I make a mental note to compare River and Catches-leaves's hearing and sense of smell—from what I've gathered from River, their kind are usually almost as sight reliant as humans are. River's sense of smell and hearing are better than mine, but not significantly. But maybe Catches-leaves has adapted to his lack of sight.

Well, hopefully, he won't have to endure it any longer.

I hear the pained breaths and clicks that Catches-leaves lets out as I start reforming his eyeballs, using River's own as a template. It's surprisingly simple. I almost act like a 3D printer: I scan River's right eyeball, then reshape the flesh of Catches-leaves's right eyeball to match.

It's not an exact copy, though, as I do have to change the size a little: Catches-leaves's skull is just a touch smaller than River's. Because he's younger? Or just because he's smaller naturally? I also have to make sure I reflect that change when I re-form the connection between the eye and the optic nerve leading to the brain.

That part in particular uses up a whole chunk of mental and magical energy. I know just how important it is that it's correctly connected. My Energy channels start aching again when I'm just over halfway done—it probably isn't the best idea to do this fresh off my sleepless night healing so many different creatures, but I'm afraid of leaving Catches-leaves the way he is for much longer. At least I've had something of a break in between the sessions—my Core isn't aching as much as it was earlier.

When I think the first eye is done, I check again and then once more, just to make sure I haven't made any mistakes. Then, pulling out of my trance with a sigh of relief, I let my hands drop and open my eyes.

You're done? Catches-leaves asks. Even his mental voice is trembling, like he can't bear to know the answer, can't bear to find out that his hope has been dashed.

"I've done your right eye," I tell him. He still keeps his eyes shut.

You're not going to . . . ? He sounds so *disappointed*—it practically breaks my heart.

"If this has worked, I will," I tell him quickly. "But I don't want to do both eyes and then find out that I've accidentally made it worse." I feel Catches-leaves's trepidation at the thought, a bolt of fear slipping through the link. "So, open your right eye, and let me know whether it's any better."

Catches-leaves hesitates, but then slowly cracks open his right eye.

CHAPTER FORTY-SEVEN

Honored Pathwalker

For a moment, my newest samuran Bound looks absolutely stricken, and all I get from the Bond is a sense of intense emotion. Fearing the worst, I'm trying to summon up the courage to ask him exactly what has happened, but I am arrested when he instead starts grunting and clicking.

It's so beautiful, he breathes, his mental voice sounding utterly awed.

"You can see?" I ask hesitantly but hopefully.

More than I ever believed was possible, Catches-leaves confirms. He closes one eye, the one I haven't yet touched, and then looks around. *Is this what you see? All the time?* He sounds so disbelieving that my heart goes out to him. And I don't even know what he's seeing exactly.

"What can you see? And how clear is it?" He doesn't answer for a moment, seemingly still taking everything in.

I can . . . I can see the trees. And . . . Runs-with-the-river, I can see you! You're a lot scrawnier than I thought you were, he says. I can't hide the smile that suddenly takes over my expression at River's affront. Catches-leaves, apparently oblivious to the flickering orange in the other lizard-man's spikes, continues. Actually, I wonder how well someone so shortsighted would do with a communication system that is at least half visually based. Perhaps that's part of the reason for River's low opinion of Catches-leaves.

I listen carefully to his continued descriptions, satisfied with everything he can see. Although I don't know exactly how good River's eyesight is, from his thoughtful nodding, it seems like Catches-leaves compares pretty well. Maybe one day I'll be able to actually improve someone's eyesight beyond the normal baseline—maybe even my own. But I'll have to have a better understanding of *how* to do that first.

"Well, it seems like it's been a success," I comment after Catches-leaves's monologue tapers off. "Would you like me to do your other eye now?"

I don't even need a verbal response: the immediate eagerness that flows across the Bond answers my question.

Having done it once already, the second eye is relatively simple to fix. I have to reverse some of what I did on the other eye so my magic won't be inclined to just make a direct copy, but between working with the template from River's left eye and Catches-leaves's fixed eye, I'm pretty sure it should be good enough now.

When he opens his eyes again, this time eagerly, he is suffused with a joy so deep that I never thought it was possible for *anyone* to feel that much. Not expounding about what he can see this time, he instead twists to face me fully.

Lifting his chin as high as it will go, he speaks, even his grunts and clicks sounding joyous, vibrant blues and a deep purple curling through his spikes.

You have given me sight! For the first time in my life, I can see everything. *I can never repay you for this, Honored Pathwalker, but ask of me what you will. I'm yours. Now and forever.*

As he speaks, I'm surprised to feel the Bond between us break like an elastic band. There's a sharp but short backlash, which makes me frown, but I don't have time to react more than that before I feel another Bond snap back into place. It's significantly deeper than before and far more permanent.

I recognize the feeling immediately: it's a Companion Bond.

My jaw slackens and surprise robs me of speech briefly.

"What . . . ? How . . . ?" I ask with the little brain power that remains to me. Did he just . . . initiate a Companion Bond? Is that possible? Apparently so.

I am convinced of your power, Honored Pathwalker, greater than any of the other Pathwalkers. Not one of them could offer me my sight, but you have done so and without even requiring anything of me first. For the first time, he hesitates. *I know you already have a capable assistant in Runs-with-the-river, but if you would accept my service and offer me your guidance, I would also be honored to call you master.*

My eyes are still wide, and I feel like there's been a bit of an overload of information. Fortunately, these days I'm better at dealing with too many revelations given at once.

"Let's just slow down a moment," I suggest. "So you're willing to Bond with me for longer because you're confident that we—that *I*—can protect you?" I ask slowly.

I hope that is the case, Catches-leaves admits, lowering his chin to look me in the eye. *However, you have given me the means to better protect* myself *and have proven yourself capable of what I had considered impossible before this. Your skill in magic proves that you should be counted as one of the Pathwalkers, for all that you were not born of our village. Why, then, should I not believe what you said about being capable of winning against the Pathwalkers?*

Well, I suppose that answers my question as well as indicates exactly why he's had a change of heart. I hope with him that he's right about me being able to win against the Pathwalkers. However, I appreciate his faith, especially since it doesn't appear to be blind. Is it too early to joke about such things?

"Next question, then. How did you just do that?"

Do what, Honored Pathwalker?

"Break the Bond and then recreate it." His confusion doesn't seem to have lifted.

I don't know. I just . . . did it? he responds tentatively. *Was I wrong, Honored Pathwalker?*

"No." I sigh. "No, I'm happy that you trust me this much. It's just that I don't understand how it happened." Particularly because I thought that the Bond between me and my Companion had to already be deep. How could my Bond with a lizard-man I met less than a day ago be significant enough to qualify?

Not to mention that I thought *I* was supposed to be the one to offer it, not just have it snap into place without my say-so. Who's the Binder here, anyway?

The samuran does his equivalent of a shrug with a flick of his tail.

I felt—feel—immense gratitude for your aid. I owe you my life twice over since I do not know how much further I could have gone with the way things were, but I was too afraid to change them. Too afraid of having nowhere to call home, no protection against the dangers that surrounded me, unseen. You have not only given me my sight but also another option.

"Then you'll eat now?" I ask, a little wryly. *If I'd known all that was required to make you eat was to completely recreate your eyes and replace our Bond with a Companion one, I would have started with that,* I joke to myself wryly.

He lifts his chin briefly and is, when taking everything into account, predictable. *If you will permit me to.*

"Yes, I permit you to eat." I sigh again, a little exasperated. "In fact, it's a standing order that you can eat the meat of any carcass and whenever, as long as it's not one I've specifically told you not to consume. Okay?"

I understand, Honored Pathwalker. And, Catches-leaves hesitates before continuing, *what should I call you?*

"I prefer my name. Markus," I tell him immediately.

As you wish, Catches-leaves responds, and my eyes narrow in confusion at the slightly disappointed tone. *May I be excused to eat . . . Honored Markus?* he asks before I can challenge him on it.

"Oh. Sure. Go ahead." I watch as he lifts his chin briefly and then turns to walk towards the closest carcass, his steps a little hesitant but excited. When he gets to the already half-devoured body, his hunger is clear in just how quickly he rips into the meat.

"Well, that went better than expected," I remark to River, pushing myself to my feet. "But is it just me or did he seem *disappointed* at the end there?" When no response comes, I look at my Bound. He's focused on Catches-leaves, and I'm a little startled by his expression, little that there is on his actual face.

Touching the Bond, I realize that I'm not mistaken: River is *jealous.* Of what? Or who? Catches-leaves? Why would he be jealous of the other samuran? And what is that other emotion I feel? Betrayal?

"River?" I ask quietly. "What's wrong?"

The lizard-man seems to shake himself free of his funk, the faint orange that was coloring his spikes dying down to be replaced with a neutral green.

Wrong, Master? Nothing.

But I *know* that he's lying. Or at least, he's not telling me why the Bond still feels like a lake whose surface is still but that churns with strong, conflicting currents underneath. I hesitate but remember that the last time I tried to just ignore this sort of thing, I had to have a talk with him over it anyway.

"River," I warn, my voice hardening. "Don't lie to me." Then I allow my voice to soften. "If you don't want to talk about it, then say so. But don't tell me nothing's wrong when it's clear that something is."

River looks at me for a long moment, his expression unreadable, the Bond roiling with conflicting emotions.

I . . . Do you wish to replace me?

My eyes go wide in surprise. "What on earth would make you think that?"

Catches-leaves is . . . younger. He joined you completely willingly, without requiring you to do anything in return. He hasn't harmed those you care for. And now his sight is at least as good as mine. He would make a better assistant for you. The last is said in his equivalent of a whisper, his colors muted and his vocalizations barely audible.

"What makes you . . . ? Why would I . . . ?" I stop, closing my eyes, and hold up a hand to pause anything River might say while I try to sort this out.

I'm almost completely sure that this is some sort of cultural misunderstanding because I really don't see why there would be a problem otherwise. So perhaps that's where I should start—with straightening that out.

"All right, can you explain what 'assistant' means to you, please?" I think I already have an idea from previous discussions but would like it clarified here.

It is a position of particular importance in the village, River answers promptly, *as it requires aiding a Pathwalker directly and, by default, grants being able to learn from them. I was the assistant for Herbalist: that's why, despite only being three years old, I was relatively highly ranked in the village and was allowed to access the communal carcasses whenever I wanted. Except the Pathwalkers' or Warriors' ones, of course. I was chosen because I was fast and strong and good at finding herbs in the forest.* He says the last with a sort of well-worn pride—not one that makes him arrogant, but one that he's drawn upon many times as a motivation to keep going.

I know that kind of thing. There were times in my life where I had to do the same. When my pride seemed all that I had left to me.

"So it's a coveted position," I summarize.

Yes. And each Pathwalker usually only has one *assistant.*

I nod slowly. "And you would call the Pathwalker you assist 'master,' I guess," I continue, putting several pieces together.

That's right.

"So, because you call me master, Catches-leaves has assumed that you are my assistant?" My eyes widen as realization dawns. "So his request to call me master was actually a potential bit of betrayal for you." After all, Catches-leaves offered to become my assistant while knowing that River already occupied the position. And, if all had been the same as in the village, that would have meant knocking River several notches down the hierarchy to install himself as a more influential figure.

Of course, that's not how things work with our pack, but Catches-leaves doesn't know that, and I don't like what it says about his character that *that* was the first thing he tried to do.

I . . . It's possible that he was offering to be an additional *assistant to you, Master. It does happen occasionally. Catches-leaves has always been the lowest in the hierarchy because of multiple reasons, which I now realize were probably due to his inability to see. It is not surprising that he might take any opportunity to raise his status now that he is not forcibly kept at the bottom.*

River might *say* those things, but I sense a certain amount of satisfaction with my clear outrage at Catches-leaves possibly trying to take his position.

"I hope you realize how important you are to me," I say in an abrupt non sequitur. Because, honestly, regardless of whether I should be angry at Catches-leaves or not, I don't want River doubting how much I appreciate his presence. "You've worked hard for our group, have been there for me time and time again, and have helped and supported everyone else, both with hunting and herbalism. You and Bastet are my right and left hands.

"Catches-leaves may be able to offer a lot—only time will tell—but even if he suddenly becomes my star warrior, or can find more useful plants than you, or develops a way of farting rainbows, it won't matter. Not to us. He might become a friend, but I'm not going to forget someone who already *is* my friend." It's probably not terribly eloquent, but I hope the earnestness with which I say the words is enough to convince him. "And if it bothers you that he has sight that is as good as yours, well, I'll just have to figure out how to improve your vision so it's even *better*," I say with a grin.

River looks at me properly for the first time in the whole conversation.

So . . . you're not replacing me?

"Not now, not ever," I assure him. Then I hesitate, wondering if I should say what is on the tip of my tongue. After a brief moment of thought, I decide to go for it—if I don't say it now, it might never be said. "One day I will be able to give you the choice to leave if you want, with no strings attached, neither implicit nor explicit. But I will never force you to go."

His expression is softer than it's been all day, and he's about to reply when we both hear a sound. It's a shriek of pain. A *familiar* shriek of pain.

After briefly glancing at Bastet, who's just jumped to her feet, all three of us run towards the scene of trouble.

CHAPTER FORTY-EIGHT

Scene of Trouble

*S*cene of trouble and scene of Trouble, I grumble to myself as we run. What has that damn raptorcat got himself into *this* time?

Can you scout ahead? I ask Sirocco and receive a grim acknowledgement from her. *Stay with the group,* I send to Persephone next. *But be ready to come if we call,* I add to my communication with Hades. For the rest of them, I send out a blanket order to continue eating but to be ready to run back to the cave if necessary.

I'll be glad when I've figured out how to do that delegation thing; frankly, trying to manage this number of Bound mentally is just too much.

By the time I've managed to do all that, we're approaching where the shriek came from. There, we meet an unwelcome sight. Trouble *and* Lathani have managed to disrupt a small family group of those mini triceratopses. Trouble is limping, and Lathani is lying worryingly still against a tree.

"Take care of the beasts," I snap at River and Bastet while mentally signaling Fenrir to come—we're going to need the extra support. After a brief moment of hesitation, I also call for Catches-leaves. He's as thin as a rake, but he's survived until now in even worse condition. Perhaps he can help.

While doing that, I run as quickly as I can to Lathani's side.

She's breathing—thank whoever might be listening! But it looks labored, and painful whimpers are coming out with every panting exhale. Immediately, I lay my hand on her shoulder and send my mana into her.

Not being my Bound anymore makes it more of a struggle than before. Much more. This is far worse than when I tried to heal the mere scratches from the velociraptors—perhaps it's because these wounds are significantly more serious.

"Lathani, you need to let me in," I plead with her. "I'm trying to help you!"

She doesn't react. Has she even heard me? I push against her resistance and make headway, but it's like trying to walk up a river. Her Willpower must be lower than mine, but her body is unconsciously recognizing my presence as a threat. That's the downside of Flesh-Shaping over Lay-on-Hands: there's no automatic recognition of my intentions as beneficial, even when they are. And with her unconscious . . .

She's hurt badly—I can tell that with my eyes—and nothing I discover with my magic disagrees with that impression. If I don't manage to make some headway soon, I'm going to lose her.

If she doesn't react in the next couple of minutes, I'm going to have to Dominate her,

I realize with a sinking sense of doom. Damned if I do, damned if I don't. I doubt Kalanthia will take the death of her cub while I sat by any better than us coming back with the traces of a Dominate Bond on her soul. But that's the only way I can think of to do it.

Unless . . .

It's a risk, but it should work. If it doesn't . . . No, it should. I arrange myself so that I'm lying next to Lathani and in contact with her at several points, just in case.

Keep us safe, I order River and Bastet. *I won't be able to defend us.* Then, prying open Lathani's closed eyelids, I invoke my Class Skill.

After entering the soul space for the Battle of Wills, I don't step forwards at all, though I do note the surprising amount of pressure that immediately hits me. I could push against it but only with difficulty. But that's not my intention.

"Lathani!" I shout at the figure lying still opposite me. "Lathani!"

I hear you. Stop shouting, she responds grouchily. Relief goes through me. I don't want to move any closer than I absolutely have to, not wanting to chance my luck any further.

"We have no time to spare. You *need* to let me heal you," I tell her forcibly. "If you don't, you're going to die. Do you hear me?"

. . . I do, she says, her voice faint. I hope that's because of shock rather than her being so close to death that she can't even properly speak in this space.

"And will you let my magic into your body without resistance? Because we don't have *time.*"

I will, she responds, her voice thankfully stronger.

Hoping that's enough, I turn and run in the opposite direction from her.

Thank you . . . Pack Leader, I hear, just before the world fractures around me. Hit by the consequences of "failing" a Battle of Wills, I'm completely paralyzed. My heart in my mouth, I try to send mana into Lathani's body.

To my huge relief, it works. I was banking on that: the last time I failed a Battle of Wills, I was unable to move, but I continued to be able to communicate with my Bound. I hoped that might mean my ability to control mana continued even with the paralysis.

It seems like my gamble has paid off, as my mana flows into Lathani's body almost as easily as it did when she was under a Tame Bond. I quickly discover the most important areas to work on—her punctured lung and half-crushed heart—and pour mana into them.

Fortunately, my previous scan and healing of her body means that my Skill knows exactly what to fix and how to do it, and I can concentrate most of my mental energy on sending mana into her as quickly as possible. Trusting my Bound, I go into Medium Meditation to increase my mana regeneration as much as possible.

Her ribcage is fractured in several places, her spine damaged. There are puncture wounds in her chest and a fracture in her skull. I can imagine what might have happened: taken by surprise, she was unable to dodge as a mini triceratops gored her in the chest, lifted her off her feet, and sent her flying to slam into the tree. It's unsurprising that she was so badly hurt.

By the time she's healed enough to safely stand—meaning that the spine damage, fractured ribs, punctured lung, and bruised heart are more than half healed—the noises of the battle behind have ended and my paralysis has long since worn off.

I take a short break, just to find out what's going on. Lathani is stable, but some of my other Bound might not be, even if I don't have any sense of them being in danger of immediate death. I keep a level of Light Meditation, though, as I need to regenerate my mana as quickly as I can.

"How's it going?" I ask, moving slowly towards my group of Bound. They are standing around the four mini triceratopses, looking tired but not too badly hurt. River is limping—one of the creatures seems to have gotten him in the leg. Catches-leaves is looking tired but unhurt, a bloody chunk of wood hanging from his claws.

Bastet has a number of bleeding gashes over her body, but they seem mostly shallow. Fenrir looks as though he was run over by a truck, but he's tanky enough that he would probably get through even that without too much damage. Sirocco looks unhurt.

The triceratopses are looking much worse. One has part of its skull caved in—given how thick their skulls seem to be, Catches-leaves must be significantly stronger than he looks. Two others lost their eyes and bled out from either their throats or an artery behind the front legs. As for the last, it's actually still alive, but completely lame: Fenrir's work is plain to see in the crushed bone that now makes up two of its legs.

I don't see any evidence of Bastet's fire breath—perhaps she feels it would have been too dangerous here in the forest with Lathani and me lying completely helpless to the side of the action.

We thought you might like to Bind this one, Master, River suggests as he gestures tiredly towards the still-alive triceratops. Well, alive for now: it won't be alive for long if I don't heal it, with as much blood as it's leaking.

"Good thought," I tell him with a tired grin of my own—healing Lathani hasn't exactly been *easy.* "Where's Trouble?" I ask, realizing I can't see the troublesome cub.

With shame suffusing his body language, the juvenile raptorcat slinks out from behind one of the carcasses. He's obviously injured but not heavily so. Considering that this whole mess is his and Lathani's fault, he can deal with it until everyone else has been healed. I pin him with a look.

"Why the hell did you go running off by yourself?" I demand. He shifts a little bit, and I understand something to do with "hunting." "Well, you did a fantastic job at that, didn't you?" I snap at him angrily. He cowers a little at my clear anger. With a huff, I decide that I'm not in the right state of mind to even chastise him. Though, I should probably leave that to Bastet, anyway—she'll do a far better job than I would.

Instead, I turn to the most heavily injured of my Bound. Sending mana into

Fenrir, I heal the deep bruises and hairline fractures in several of his bones. Rather than having actually been run over by one of them, I have to guess that he latched onto the triceratops's leg and then just stayed attached, no matter how much he was battered or slammed into the ground. He really is a pit bull.

My mana running low, I approach the triceratops. River has a good point: this creature would probably be a lot more useful to us than several of the other ones back with the kiinas. Especially if I could use Flesh-Shaping to enhance its already hefty defensive abilities.

Should I try to use Tame on it? I wonder for a moment. Then shake my head. Ultimately, it was an antagonist to my group, though I'm not sure of the complete story behind how and why Lathani and Trouble ended up facing four of these creatures while "hunting." If I didn't have the ability to heal, it would be doomed to die in the near future—either because of another predator or from starvation. Offering it a Bond could even be seen as a mercy on my part. It's not the same as the creatures in the cave who hadn't offered any harm to my family. Apart from the danaris and its larvae, anyway.

Casting Inspect Fauna, I focus on wanting more information about whether this creature would be open to a Bond, and if so, what would help convince it. I might as well go into the situation with as much information as possible. I don't bother trying to keep the probe subtle, though.

Cyran
Tier 1 beast (Unevolved)
Special abilities: None
Health: 1560u
Mana: 20u
Minimum Willpower recommended to Dominate without other impacting factors: 30 (15)
Open to a Bond: No
Impacting factor: Protection
This herbivore is not to be underestimated. Possessing a particularly stubborn and determined nature, this creature lives life by going through obstacles. It cares little whether they are vegetal or animal in nature. Few Tier-1 predators hunt these creatures, and none when they are protecting young, as they are particularly aggressive at this time.

Protection, huh, I think to myself, noting how, apparently, the chance of Inspect Fauna revealing a way of convincing the creature to Bond has triggered. If this was a parent protecting its young, then the fact that we've just killed them all may significantly impact my ability to talk it round, however easy it appears for me to be able to force the issue. Alternatively, it may be indicating that I should *offer* protection to convince it . . .

Ultimately, is there any harm in trying? At worst, I'm paralyzed for ten seconds while surrounded by my Bound. I could even use that time to regenerate mana quickly, ready to get healing when I recover.

Mentally shrugging, I decide to give it a go. Approaching the cyran, I stare into its pain and rage-filled orbs.

"Dominate."

CHAPTER FORTY-NINE

Screwed

I open my eyes thoughtfully as the Battle of Wills fractures around me and gaze at my new Bound for a moment. As it turns out, this one wasn't the big mama of the group and was instead one of her daughters. As a result, it was a bit less of an ordeal to convince her that we could become her new family than I thought it might be.

My mana having regenerated a bit—apparently, being in a Battle of Wills automatically counts as being in some form of Meditation—I immediately start to work on her legs. It takes me a couple of mana loads to heal them, but as I found with Catches-leaves, after having done one, the other turns out to be easier.

Once her legs are mostly healed, she pushes to her feet and eyes the rest of my Bound warily.

"You're one of us now," I remind her. "None of us will attack you or hurt you intentionally. Except in sparring," I add after a moment. "And then only to help you grow stronger."

Sighing a little tiredly—emptying and filling my mana pool several times in a row always makes me feel exhausted—I eye the rest of my Bound.

"Let's head back to the rest of the group," I say. "If you can all move well enough?" I get a series of assents from everyone around. Except for Lathani, who's still out cold. But that's okay—I just head over to pick her up. Since I've already dealt with her spinal injury and the puncture to her lung, it shouldn't cause her any further damage.

We make our way back to where Hades and Persephone are standing protective guard on the rest of my Bound.

You must have been successful since you have returned and did not call for us, Persephone analyzes neutrally as we come into view. Then she raises her head in surprise as she sees the hulking behemoth accompanying us. *A new companion?* she asks next.

Yes and yes, I send back to her with a sigh. *To add to the menagerie,* I tell myself privately. Goodness knows what Kalanthia's going to think when I come back with almost three times the number of Bound I set out with. Though, she might be more concerned with ripping me a new one over Taming Lathani earlier—hopefully, only figuratively. At least I didn't end up needing to Dominate the nunda cub.

"Everyone can relax a bit," I say. "Problem solved." The creatures around me react in a variety of ways. Some actually relax, going back to drinking, eating, or

resting. Others don't seem quite so reassured and continue gazing around themselves nervously. Honestly, I don't care too much. I need to fully heal everyone
who was injured, then bring those carcasses back here for my meat eaters to enjoy.
Sooner rather than later.

Actually . . . maybe I don't have to wait until everyone is healed.

"Hades, Persephone, can you take a group of helpers back to the battleground
and bring the three carcasses from there back here, please?" A moment after, I feel
the nagging sense of a notification. With a hunch of what it might be linked to, I
quickly pull it open.

You have designated your Bound "Hades" and "Persephone" as Managers. Would
you like them to co-lead a team or each lead a team separately?

Co-lead / Lead separately

A smile pulls at the corners of my mouth. Well, at least *that's* easy to trigger.
After hesitating for a moment, I decide on the second option. While I reckon they
could co-lead a team fine, I remember that there was a limit on the number of
beings that could be part of each team. I don't know if the limit is the same if it's
co-led, but at least this way I know I'm doubling up the potential numbers.

Would you like this team to be temporary (ending at the end of the assigned task)
or permanent (requiring intentional dissolution)?

Temporary / Permanent

That one's easy; I pick "temporary." Although I reckon that River, Bastet, Hades,
and Persephone should each have a permanent team at some point, now is not the
time to decide who should be part of those.

With my choice, the boxes disappear, and a couple of numbers appear in the
corner of my vision near my health, stamina, and mana bars. Focusing on them
allows me to look at them properly. I see "Had" and "Per" written with a fractional value of zero out of five below them. Within a few minutes, those numbers
have changed to four out of five for each team. With a quick glance at me for my
approval, the two kiinas are off, their teams trailing behind them.

Unsurprisingly, most of the creatures are meat eaters, but there are also two
herbivores and one omnivore present. Or I assume that, at least, based on what
they've been eating so far. I'm not surprised Persephone chose them—they're the
biggest of my Bound apart from the triceratops, and their strength will no doubt
be useful in the task.

With that delegated, I turn to healing my Bound.

Getting to Lathani last, I'm surprised that she's not woken up yet. I send a scan through her body, hoping with a sinking heart that I didn't miss something vital. Sitting back after inspecting her body closely, I find myself puzzled at her ongoing unconsciousness. As far as I can tell with my magic, she's fully healed—yet she's still asleep.

"Any thoughts?" I ask Bastet, who's come to investigate. She nudges Lathani and sniffs at her for a bit.

She will wake when she's ready, pronounces the raptorcat.

"But what if there's something wrong?"

There is nothing wrong. Her Energy channels are in great flux.

"She's working on her Energy channels now?" I exclaim. Is this really the time and place for that?

Bastet hesitates for a moment. *It is not necessarily something she has chosen to do. Energy channels are often malleable after a realization that has shaken one's view of the world. She has not yet Evolved; it is most likely happening by itself and keeping her asleep until it has finished.*

"But if we hadn't won the battle, she could have *died*. Why would her unconscious self have let her get into such a vulnerable position?"

Clearly, even her unconscious self trusts you to keep her safe.

While a part of me is undeniably flattered by that, the rest of me can't believe just how irresponsible unconscious-Lathani is being—and I really don't understand why Bastet is so blithe about it. Not when we both know the stakes if Lathani is killed before we get back to Kalanthia. I know that I've been guilty of spacing out and becoming distracted at the wrong time, but at least I know to wait until I'm somewhere safe to do something like working on my Energy channels! And I can't even blame her for it, since she hasn't actually chosen to do this.

Going off hunting with Trouble, on the other hand, I can *entirely* blame her for. Or whatever it was she thought she was doing. I thought that she'd matured past that sort of loose cannon behavior. Or was it only the effects of the Bond?

I huff, trying to get rid of my frustration and, yes, worry before it causes me to lash out at someone undeserving.

"Can you keep an eye on her, then?" I ask Bastet. "Let me know when she wakes up."

Of course, she agrees, settling down next to the nunda juvenile. I glance around and see Trouble sitting sulkily next to River.

"He's in time-out?" I ask Bastet, my eyebrows raised.

He is to spend some time thinking about exactly what he did and how he should have better approached it, Bastet answers. To me, that sounds pretty much like a time-out. Well, it's probably good for him to do that. Perhaps we should require the same of Lathani when she wakes up.

"Did he tell you why he was out there with Lathani?"

Bastet sends me a feeling of uncertainty. *He was unclear. They were hunting; that's all he would tell me.* Which is as much as I'd gathered from him before.

"I see," I murmur, glancing between the two of them. If they're going to team up on a regular basis, I'm going to be completely gray long before my time. Or they're going to be dead. Hopefully, after all this, Kalanthia's going to be more on the ball with Lathani. Frankly, I'm still surprised that she didn't come after us, even if Lathani said she'd given her mother the slip. Where is all the maternal anger and protectiveness that she's exhibited on many other occasions? Why couldn't she use her magic to work out where Lathani went?

Well, we have to deal with the hand we've been given. And right now, I have something else I need to do: get to know my new Bound.

By the time Bastet lets me know that the nunda juvenile is showing signs of waking, I've managed to finally make some good progress with each of my Bound. While I haven't managed to name them all yet, I now know exactly which ones have which type of Bond, sorting them into three general categories.

Out of my ten new Tamed Bound, I've already "lost" one: Catches-leaves, who had a temporary Bond, now has a Companion Bond. Then there are three others who have a similar kind of Bond—a temporary one, which ranges between fifteen days and three months. All three of them are predators and completely different sizes. The one that looks a bit like a spinosaurus is the biggest. When fully upright, he's just a little shorter than I am, and his spinal ridge is impressive, if a little smaller than I remember pictures of spinosauruses depicting. The next is slightly bigger than Bastet herself and has a wicked bone spike on his tail. He's completely scaled and has several bone protrusions elsewhere on his body, making him a thorny prospect to attack. That didn't seemed to deter the danaris, though. Finally, the last is also the smallest, a little bigger than a saltwater otter and with vicious-looking claws and teeth.

Three more have an indeterminate Bond, but each has their own specific requirements. The grub-eating orangutan-resembling henerm requires me to find at least two females of his kind to join him within the next few months. A second wolfish-looking creature already has a pack and will only continue with her Bond if I can prove to the others that they ought to join us too. The final one is a herbivore and has simply required that I offer her sufficient food for herself and any young she has and expressed a preference for having more of her kind. This, in fact, is the deerlike stio, which was the first creature I released.

The final four Bonds have the sense of this being a sort of trial period, as if they want to see whether being part of our team is better than going it alone or trying to find others of their kind. In this group are three carnivores and a herbivore, based on their food of choices during our rest break. One is very small, much like a pine marten but scaly. She seems very shy, hiding away in the shadows as much as possible. A second is also small—only up to my knee—but completely opposite in personality as far as I can see. He looks a little like a baryonyx and has vicious-looking fangs. Inspect indicates that they're venomous too, which should make him a good addition to a fight—now that he's on our side. The third carnivore is a wolvezard, much like the beast that almost killed me when I first arrived in this world. Apparently, it's called a mea—according to Inspect Fauna, anyway. As for the herbivore, she is the one with eyes that can point forwards and backwards at the same time, like a chameleon. She doesn't look like one otherwise—more like a parasaurolophus, but her back legs are more like a kangaroo's.

In some way, the sheer range of sizes and shapes is a good thing since it should mean I can find various uses for the different Bound. Their numbers, however, are slightly daunting, though I'm likely to lose three of them as their Bonds come to an end. I'm busy trying to work out who might be a good fit to put together in more permanent teams when Bastet interrupts me with news about Lathani. I quickly hurry over to the rousing nunda cub.

"Lathani," I breathe in relief before putting on my professional face. "How are you feeling?"

Better, Pack Leader, she says with none of her usual attitude in her voice. While part of me appreciates that, the rest of me would much rather she'd decided to be like that *before* running off and almost getting herself killed. Again!

"Then can you please explain to me why the *hell* you thought running off with *Trouble* of all companions was a good idea?" I demand, having to work very hard to prevent my voice from rising above an acceptable level. I compromise by making it harder and sterner instead.

Lathani looks away, her body language as slumped as Trouble's was when I first confronted him.

I . . . I wanted to be useful.

"Useful?" I hiss. "Exactly how is going off and enraging a group of cyran *useful?*" She looks even more abashed.

We didn't mean to! We thought there was only one of them. And that it would offer lots of meat for you. I heard you say that you needed to hunt. I thought that I could do it—I'd been doing so well with Mother when I went out hunting with her. I thought I could do it on my own. Then little-sibling spotted me going into the bushes and followed me. I tried to send him back, but he told me he'd tell Elder if I didn't let him come, so . . .

"So you did," I conclude with a heavy sigh. With that exhale, a whole load of my frustration and anger are released, leaving me simply tired. The excuse of so many children and teenagers: I didn't *mean* to.

My thoughts can't help but go back to that immensely painful time when my own choices led to the death of my mother. And while, looking back on it years later, I know it wasn't my fault that the driver who hit us was drunk, it *was* my fault we were out on the road at all. My lies and my cowardice that landed us in the wrong place at the wrong time. Like Lathani, I didn't mean to.

"You need to stop doing this, Lathani," I tell her earnestly, a note in my voice that's almost begging. "Do you realize just how close you came to death this time? Again! And it's the second fight that you shouldn't have been in within the last two days alone. This time it was because you snuck away without even *telling* any of us; last time it was because you disobeyed me *and* your mother."

I know I bear some responsibility for that: it was my decision to Bond her and then permit her into the fight with the danaris. But at the same time, I was forced into making a decision by the fact that she followed us in the first place and the knowledge that if I didn't Bond her, she would have probably tried to join us at the wrong moment. However, there *were* other options than the one I chose, so I accept some responsibility for that.

This particular situation, though . . . No, I don't accept any of the blame here. Yes, I said that we needed to hunt, but I'm not Henry II, whose followers interpreted his own frustration as a desire to kill the Archbishop of Canterbury at the time. Lathani might be my responsibility in as much as she's a youngster under my care, but she's *not* one of my Bound. Not since her Tame Bond snapped with the dawn.

I know, Lathani says, drawing me out of my furious thoughts. I have to mentally dial back to work out what she's responding to.

"Do you, though?" I ask, my anger resurging. "Your lung was *punctured*, Lathani. Your heart was *bruised*. Your *spine* was damaged enough that you would have been paralyzed if I hadn't been there! Even without any more intervention from the cyrans, you'd have died within a few minutes. With them present, you would probably have been crushed after they'd dealt with Trouble." My hands are waving in the air with my passion, the fear bubbling within me and turning to rage.

I know, Lathani says again, this time with a depth of understanding that makes me pause. *When we were in that odd space, I felt my life dripping away from me. I felt my soul for the first time. And then after, I felt life fill me again as you poured your own strength into me. For the first time, I understood.*

Her fervor makes me pause.

"Understood what?" I ask a little uncertainly. She hesitates.

I cannot explain it. But in that moment, I understood something important, something that changed my path in life. I understood why it is so important that we work as a team. And I understood . . . what we could become together.

I eye her, my words blocked in my throat. I want to keep railing at her—I've built up a head of steam that yearns to explode. But at the same time, she seems so earnest, so sincere . . . I just can't.

"All right," I say finally, my anger all bubbled away. "Just . . . You can't keep doing this, okay? Making choices that impact the others around you as much as, if not more than, you yourself." Yes, I know—practice what you preach and all that, but I'm working on it.

I understand. And I'm sorry, Pack Leader. I eye her for a moment. An apology certainly isn't amiss, but there's something wrong, something I'm picking up in her body language or emotional projection.

"Lathani, why does that sound more like you're apologizing for something that hasn't happened yet rather than for something that has?"

Because I am, she says, sounding almost regretful over it.

"Lathani?" I ask, half a question, half a warning.

Pack Leader, you have protected and guided me, opening doors to my future that would have stayed closed if not for your actions. We are stronger together than apart. You have risked your own life to protect mine, and so I give it to you. We are Bound, now and until death.

"Lathani!" I exclaim, even as part of me can't help wondering why this sounds like a marriage vow. "What are you—" And then I cut myself off as I feel it snap into place.

My eyes widen in horror, and I can't help a sudden realization from going through me.

Thanks to what Lathani has just done, I am now completely and utterly *screwed.*

INTERLUDE THE THIRD (1506)

It is dusk on the same day of Lord Nicholas's visit to the Oracle. He still bears some marks from the dust of the road, though the enchantments in his clothes have ensured that there are few of them. The runes anchoring the magic are hidden cleverly within the embroidery on his doublet and vest, an expensive but convenient enchantment that no noble with two golds to rub together would be seen without.

"Do you wish me to attend to you, my lord?" asks Sarran. The manservant hides his fatigue well, but Nicholas knows him well enough to see the tightness at the corners of his eyes and the slight limp to his steps. Abruptly, he feels slightly guilty for dragging the man out with him, especially when he knows Sarran is unaccustomed to riding. Of course, it was his right to do so as his lord, but as his friend, Nicholas knows that Sarran has other tasks, which spending the majority of his day out with his lord means he is unable to accomplish. And that he would most likely prefer to be able to sit without pain.

"No, I will be fine," Nicholas answers. "Have the evening off. If I need something, I will call another to bring it." Sarran bows in response, a mixture between relief and disappointment flashing across his face, almost too fast to register.

"Would you like me to draw you a bath first, my lord?" he murmurs quietly, his expression once more blank. Nicholas hesitates.

"I would appreciate that," he admits. A ghost of a smile flashes across Sarran's face.

"Then I shall do so." With another bow, he turns and gingerly walks away.

"And go see our healer, for the gods' sakes," Nicholas calls after him. Sarran pauses and turns back.

"I'm fine."

"You're walking like you're a geriatric old commoner." This time the expression on Sarran's face is plain: insult.

"I'm *not.*"

"You are," corrects Nicholas. "And I'm the lord, so obviously I'm right," he teases. Sarran crosses his arms over his chest.

"I'm *fine,*" he answers firmly, his gaze almost daring Nicholas to gainsay him again. The lord can't stop the smile from breaking out on his face. No one in his household but Sarran achieves the perfect balance of competence, perfect manners, and fire.

"Just go and see Jerry, you stubborn mule," he orders his manservant lightly. "I'd do it myself, but it's never been one of my strong suits."

"I know. I've heard the stories," Sarran replies sardonically. He eyes Nicholas, then sighs. "You're not going to let this go, are you, my lord?"

"No. Consider it an apology for forcing you to sit on a horse for half the day."

It doesn't take long before the manservant sighs again. "Then I'll thank you for your consideration."

Nicholas's smile widens—anyone else would think Sarran was just being polite. He, however, can hear the "which wouldn't have been necessary if you'd had the consideration in the first place" that underlies it.

"Of course. You take such good care of me, how can I do anything different?" asks Nicholas innocently, seeing his barb hit home in the slight frown that momentarily creases Sarran's brow. "Go on, then," Nicholas prompts, waving his hand at Sarran to shoo him away. The manservant bows again—picture perfect, as if to spite Nicholas—then turns on his heel and strides off, obviously making more effort to conceal his limp.

When he turns the corner, Nicholas goes back to what he was doing before Sarran interrupted. To be honest, sending the manservant away wasn't just for Sarran's sake: what Nicholas is about to access is only for the lord's eyes or those of his chosen heir.

He strides down the corridor until he reaches the right part of the wall. The enchantment is concealed and requires a drop of blood from the lord's line to be flicked onto the wall to even reveal where the keyhole lies. And the keyhole is no normal one: instead of a key, it requires him to place his hand on a certain area. He feels the usual tug, the magic verifying that the one seeking entry holds the correct Class *and* that their magic is authorized.

Only once both of those have been verified does the door appear and crack open. Pushing at the stone, Nicholas opens it enough to enter, then closes it behind him.

Magical lights are automatically triggered, illuminating the room with steady and smokeless brilliance. The lights are kept fairly low so as not to accidentally blind anyone when they reflect off the items held within.

Cores fill the shelves on both sides of the room, and the wall directly in front of him is filled with books. One side holds Cores for consumption, for times when there are few worthy beasts to hunt. Most Classers without the backing of a noble House, or even some of the Lesser Houses, would salivate just at this—for many, it would offer the chance of gaining many levels and even extending their lives just a bit more. But the worth of those Cores pales in comparison to the worth of those on the other side.

These are the worked Cores, the ones that hold untold amounts of knowledge. And not only knowledge but Skills. Skills that Nicholas's family has worked for generations to add to the repository of their house. Each of the lords has contributed his or her own personal Skill, with a few notable exceptions.

Nicholas's eyes are inexorably drawn to six gaps. One in the small group of Class stones. One from the bigger collection of healing Skill stones. And the other four are scattered among the assortment of knowledge stones. Of all of them, the one from the group of Class stones is the hardest to replace. No other family has exactly the same Class as his family—their hallmark, their heritage. But at least he didn't give the candidate any of his family's special Skills. They are too precious to waste; this Markus Wolfe will need to prove that he is worthy of them.

"A precipice, the Oracle said," Nicholas muses quietly to the still air of the treasure trove. "Yet if he traverses it, he will be more powerful than I had imagined. But will even that be enough to achieve what must be achieved? He only has a year, after all. Or will I see the destruction of my family in my own lifetime?"

Reaching out, he runs his fingers over the stones, watching as they spark subtly in reaction to the presence of a Classer.

"Light god Warrior, he who brings victory in the fight. If the candidate should arrive and be ready to wage war, I shall bring you an offering of gold and weapons. Neutral god Hunter, he who is patient and determined in the kill. If the candidate should arrive and be able to hunt my enemies, I shall hunt and dedicate the kill of a powerful beast in your honor. Neutral god Binder, patron of my house, she who weaves the only unbreakable bonds. If the candidate should be both powerful and willing to aid us, I shall"—he swallows—"break the Bond between myself and my favorite horse, Tempest, and dedicate the breaking to you."

He feels the attention of the gods descend on him. First, he feels the attention of Warrior, the god's presence like that of a battle, his voice the sound of roaring and screaming fighters.

"Your candidate is beyond my reach. I cannot aid him there."

As quickly as the god's presence arrived, it departs, only to be replaced by the still, patient, attentive presence of Hunter.

"My brother speaks true. The candidate is beyond my reach. I cannot encourage him in the hunt until he enters my domain." This god's voice is the sound of an arrow in flight and then the dying scream of the creature struck. He departs as quickly as his brother.

Nicholas deflates. He should have expected it, but it was still disappointing. Yet he had only heard from two of the three gods he appealed to.

"My follower," Binder says, her voice snaking into his mind with the clinking of chains, the rustle of the pages of a contract. Her presence is the heaviness of obligation, the weight of burden. And yet, conversely, it is also the lightness of a burden shared and the warmth of ties of emotion that bind as thoroughly as any steel link or ink-drawn contract. **"As with my siblings, I cannot affect him in that other world. However, for the sake of your and your family's devotion to me alone, I will ensure that when he arrives, he shall be Bound by any promise he makes to your House. For this, I do not ask any sacrifice."**

"Thank you, Binder," Nicholas answers hoarsely. "You are too generous." Her presence vanishes a moment later, leaving behind a pounding headache. The attention of the gods is never something to seek without cause—even if they don't decide that your plea is unworthy of them, or even actively insulting, their presence is difficult to bear for any but their dedicated priests.

Now he can only hope that the Oracle is right in her predictions—and that whatever choice lies ahead of the candidate, he chooses rightly.

End-of-Book Stats

Name: Markus Wolfe		Race: Human	Class: Tamer
Level: 13	Energy to next level: 72%	Energy absorption rate: 32u/hr	Energy towards debt: 85% (250)
Intelligence	36+1 (+5%)	Mana: 496/555 (15u/IP)	
Wisdom	42+2 (+5%)	Mana regeneration rate: 1100u/hr	
Willpower	43+10 (+25%)	Health regeneration rate: 53u/hr	
Constitution	22	Health: 330/330 (15u/CP)	
Strength	20	Stamina: 120/120	
Dexterity	20	Stamina regeneration rate: 200u/hr	
Class Skills:		Non-Class Skills:	
Dominate – Initiate 2		Flesh-Shaping – Journeyman 8	
*Companion Bond		Stealth – Novice 3	
Tame – Initiate 1		Animal Empathy – Initiate 2	
Fade – Initiate 3		Meditation – Journeyman 5	
Inspect Fauna – Novice 1		Energy Manipulation – Master 1	
Inspect Flora – Beginner 9		Sensation Management – Beginner 7	
Inspect Environment – Beginner 9		Spearmanship – Beginner 6	
		Archery – Beginner 5	
		Blunt Weaponry – Beginner 3	
		Knife-Work – Beginner 5	
		Fire-Shaping – Beginner 3	

Bound Information

Named Bound:
Bound – Companion – "Bastet"
Health units: 1300/1300
Mana units: 150/150
Stamina units: 460/460
Progress to Tier 3: 2%
Lifespan remaining: ~37y 1m

Bound – Dominate – "River," Runs-with-the-river
Health units: 830/830
Mana units: 70/70
Stamina units: 300/300
Progress to Tier 2: 71%
Lifespan remaining: ~34y

Bound – Tame – "Sirocco"
Health units: 120/120
Mana units: 75/75
Stamina units: 190/190
Progress to Tier 2: 59%
Lifespan remaining: ~16y

Bound – Dominate – "Fenrir"
Health units: 1020/1020
Mana units: 20/20
Stamina units: 380/380
Progress to Tier 2: 51%
Lifespan remaining: ~25y

Bound – Dominate – "Persephone"
Health units: 920/920
Mana units: 100/100

Stamina units: 600/600
Progress to Tier 3: 20%
Lifespan remaining: ~32y

Bound – Dominate – "Hades"
Health units: 880/880
Mana units: 110/110
Stamina units: 550/550
Progress to Tier 3: 21%
Lifespan remaining: ~31y

Bound – Companion – Catches-leaves
Health units: 720/720
Mana units: 110/110
Stamina units: 290/290
Progress to Tier 2: 23%
Lifespan remaining: ~37y

Bound – Companion – Lathani
Health units: 810/810
Mana units: 190/190
Stamina units: 430/430
Progress to Tier 2: 11% (52%)
Lifespan remaining: ~268y

Other Bound:
Temporary Tame Bond – Predator
Like a spinosaurus but with a smaller spinal sail.

Temporary Tame Bond – Predator
A little bigger than Bastet with a bone spike on his tail.

Temporary Tame Bond – Predator
A little bigger than a saltwater otter with vicious claws and teeth.

Indeterminate Tame Bond with special requirements – Omnivore
Find at least two females to join him.
Like an orangutan with a long tail (henerm).

Indeterminate Tame Bond with special requirements – Predator
Prove to the others of her pack that they should join too.

A wolfish-looking creature.

Indeterminate Tame Bond with special requirements – Herbivore
Offer sufficient food for her and any young she has.
Deerlike creature (stio).

Trial-period Tame Bond – Carnivore
Small, much like a scaly pine marten, and shy.

Trial-period Tame Bond – Carnivore
Around knee height, and like a baryonyx with vicious, venomous fangs.

Trial-period Tame Bond – Carnivore
A mixture between wolverine and lizard (mea).

Trial-period Tame Bond – Herbivore
Looks like a parasaurolophus with kangaroo legs and eyes that point in two directions at once.

Author's Note

Thank you for reading *Shaping*. It's people like you who keep me writing! I'd really appreciate it if you could leave a review on your way out—reviews help other readers to find books they enjoy, so if you've enjoyed reading about the raptorcats, Kalanthia, River, and Markus, please share the love.

If you'd like to be notified of when my books launch or other versions of my books come out, please sign up to my newsletter on my website: www.winterswritingcorner.com Everyone who signs up will also receive three side stories from the Taming Destiny universe as a thank you!

More side stories and advance chapters are available on my Patreon page: https://www.patreon.com/user?u=90740676

I'd like to thank my Royal Road readers and Patrons for helping to point out the inconsistencies and mistakes the first time around, as well as the encouragement they gave to keep writing. I'd also like to thank Podium for their hard work in helping with the rest of the transformation into a professional manuscript and for creating the audiobook (available on Audible) and print version (perhaps available in a store near you!).

If you want to find more great books to read, this group has lots of recommendations: https://www.facebook.com/groups/LitRPGsociety

Thanks again for reading. I hope you enjoyed this book, and I look forward to seeing you in the next one! With most of his preparations made, Markus needs to turn his attention to fulfilling his word to River and dealing with the samuran village and the vine-strangler forest that threatens it . . .

About the Author

S. L. Winter is a writer, mother, and avid reader living in France. She first encountered LitRPG while searching for new fantasy stories to read. Although not a dedicated gamer herself, Winter was immediately hooked by the idea of fantasy worlds inspired by game rules. Three years and hundreds of devoured books later, here she is—writing her own!

RESPAWN YOUR CURIOSITY

follow us on our socials

 podiumentertainment.com

 @podiumentertainment

 /podiumentertainment

 @podium_ent

 @podiumentertainment

Podium

www.ingramcontent.com/pod-product-compliance
Lightning Source LLC
Chambersburg PA
CBHW030507120726
47904CB00005B/1372

* 9 781039 482432 *